Helen Dunmore was an award-winning novelist, children's author and poet. She published twelve novels including *Zennor in Darkness*, which won the McKitterick Prize; *Burning Bright*; *A Spell of Winter*, which won the inaugural Orange Prize in 1996; *Talking to the Dead*; *Your Blue-Eyed Boy*; *With Your Crooked Heart*; *The Siege*, which was shortlisted for the 2001 Whitbread Novel of the Year Award and the Orange Prize for Fiction 2002; *Mourning Ruby*; and *House of Orphans*. She was posthumously awarded the Costa 2017 prize for her poetry collection *Inside the Wave*.

PENGUIN BOOKS

UK | USA | Canada | Ireland | Australia
India | New Zealand | South Africa

Penguin Books is part of the Penguin Random House group
whose addresses can be found at global.penguinrandomh

Penguin
Random House
UK

First published by Viking 1993
Published in Penguin Books 1994
Reissued in this edition 2021

001

Typeset by Jouve (UK), Milton Keynes
Printed and bound in Italy by Grafica Veneta S.p

The authorized representative in the EEA is Penguin Random
Morrison Chambers, 32 Nassau Street, Dublin D02

A CIP catalogue record for this book is available from the E

ISBN: 978-0-241-98855-8

www.greenpenguin.co.uk

MIX
Paper from
responsible sources
FSC® C018179
www.fsc.org

Penguin Random House is comm
sustainable future for our busine
and our planet. This book is mad
Stewardship Council® certified p

HELEN DUNM

ZENNOR IN DAR

PENGUIN BOOKS

One

One faint shriek. Then another. Three girls fling themselves over the top of the last dune and skid down warm flanks of sand. Marram grass slashes their ankles and sand kicks up behind Clare and Peggy, into Hannah's eyes. She's the heaviest and the last. Dazzled, laughing, out of breath, prickling with sweat under their dress-shields, they flounder through the knee-deep shifting white sand, and then down and down in a heap on the hard, flat beach. Clare and Hannah collapse together, their mouths full of each other's hair. Their ankle boots are heavy with sand. Their hair has come down, and their straw hats flop against their shoulder-blades. They clasp each other. They smell of sweat and sunburned hair, and there's a faint smell of violet perfume from Hannah, who has lavished the last precious drops of Wood Violet on her wrists and under her ears. She doesn't know where she will get another bottle, but today she has something to celebrate. There is her half-day's holiday from the shop, there is this perfection of early summer, and, above all, kept until last for fear of the ill-luck which always trudges in the wake of complete happiness:

'Johnnie's coming home!' she sings out, throwing herself on her back and kicking up her legs into the blue dizzy tunnel of sun above them. Peggy and Clare smile into the sky, but they say nothing. They have talked the subject out on the long walk over from St Ives. John William is coming home. Only Hannah sometimes still calls him Johnnie. Clare has known the news since early morning, when Nan sent Kitchie flying up with a message to say that John William was coming home because he was going to be made an officer.

'It means he's got to go to a camp,' said Kitchie, gulping tea and bread and margarine in the Coyne kitchen, 'a training camp for officers. He'll be in England for three months – could be more. And by then the war might be over, Nan says.'

Beady Peggy knows, because she'd happened to call in at the draper's when she was taking little Georgie for a walk that morning, and there was Hannah slashing radiantly at puce ribbon for Hetty Date, cutting off a piece a good twelve inches longer than the two yards Hetty paid for. I ought to get a length of cream ribbon for my panama, calculated Peggy, hoisting stout Georgie on to the counter stool.

'Why couldn't John William have sent a telegram, anyway?' she asks now, prettily critical as always. They all know that John William's letter was posted in London, and that he hadn't made it clear exactly when he had been sent back from France, or how much leave there would be before he had to report at the camp. But they'll know all this soon, once he is home.

'I'd a thought he'd come straight home,' says Peggy brightly, slipping a glance from Hannah to Clare. The cousins close up immediately, just as she knew they would, like a couple of sea-anemones when you poke them. Those Treveals. So close you can't get a knife in between them. All the same, Peggy likes to try.

'Don't be stupid, Peggy,' says Clare. 'He wouldn't send a telegram. Think what it might do to Aunt Sarah.'

It's true that Sarah Treveal's a poor thing, unsteady in her nerves, but who can blame her when telegrams have only one meaning these days. The sight of a post office boy coming up the street is enough to stop anybody's heart. When Mrs Hore had the telegram about William she chanced to have fetched out a kitchen chair to sit in the sun on her step, and so she was forced to watch the telegraph boy on his bicycle as he rode down the street, whistling in the sun, and then slowed down and stopped his whistling when he saw her, out of respect for what he guessed he had in his hand. He got off his bike and wheeled it towards her, and he held out the envelope in his left hand. A boy of fourteen. What did he know about the weight of what was in that weightless bit of paper? He handed the telegram to Mrs Hore, and then he seemed to be waiting for something, so she went in to fetch a penny for him. She did this before opening the envelope. There was no need to make haste. She knew what was in it, she told Nan, because her eyes had burned in her head as she watched the bicycle come down the street, just as if she'd been foolish enough to stare into the sun.

'I could read *him*, the way he looked at me,' she said. 'I needn't a had the telegram at all.'

It's a rare hot Saturday in May, and the girls are out in it, free for the afternoon. Hannah is free until she has to go back to sprinkle the shop-boards with water and sweep the dust. Peggy is not required until six o'clock, because little Georgie's parents are taking charge of him themselves for once, and he is going to visit his grandmother. *Not required* like a piece of luggage which is indispensable but can go in the guard's van for the time being, thinks Clare. And Clare has done her week's baking, and made her father turn out of his study while she cleaned it. Her bread came out of the oven hard and grey, but even Francis Coyne is unlikely to be fastidious about it. No one can do better now, not with this flour. It is all they can get, and Clare knows they are lucky to have it. In the cities women queue for hours, and besiege the bakers' shops as soon as they open. But she won't think of that now. It is Saturday afternoon, and she is lying in the sun, which fixes on her dark dress like a burning-glass, soaking away the tiredness in her thigh muscles. Out of the wind, it is almost too hot. She hoists herself up on her elbows, and the wind tugs at her again. The coast and country stream with light. Sea and grass pucker like cat's fur under the warm May wind.

The girls' hair flaps across their eyes. They struggle to catch up the ends and pin them tight, but it's no good. Oh, well, what does it matter.

'Keep still, Peggy, till I pin it up.'

Flushed, giggling, they start to put themselves to rights.

But not Clare.

'God above, Clarey, what are you doing?'

Clare's fingers flicker down the hooked side-fastening of her dress. She's done it. She hauls up a double handful of the dark blue cotton stuff and pulls it over her head. Her close-fitting bodice sticks, and she wriggles herself free of it. The last of her hairpins comes out and her plait swings loose, then begins to unrope itself, strand over strand. In her plain white chemise and petticoat she bends to unlace her boots, then kicks them off. Hannah and Peggy watch her. A slow smile curls at the corners of Hannah's mouth.

'You're never going in!' she breathes.

Clare strips off her stockings. Now petticoat, chemise, stays . . .

The warm wind blows across her body. She shivers with delight, raises her arms.

'Oh, it's lovely!'

Hannah glances at Peggy. They both look round.

'There's no one to see us,' says Clare.

And it's true. Behind them the Towans are bare and dazzling. The wide beach curls away towards the estuary. Larks scream as if they have thrown themselves up into the sky and stuck there. Over the sea there are gulls slanting across the bay with scarcely a wing-beat, tilting, balancing themselves on currents of air. The tide is nearly full now, and the small waves are tipped with foam by the wind.

'What about the coast-watchers?' says Peggy.

'There's no one around,' says Clare. 'Oh, come on. You did last year.' Before you went to work for the Smythes and learned to run like a hen and stick your finger out when you drink tea, she thinks.

She stands there, making her arms swim through the air. She is white and glistening in the stream of light reflected off the sea. In her dark blue dress she looks as shallow-breasted and narrow-hipped as a young girl, but naked she is bigger. White, firm, curved, imperfect. She is older.

'Oh, go on, then,' says Hannah, beginning to undress. Clare twists her hair up to keep it out of the salt and tramples her dress out from under her feet. Hannah folds her skirt and bodice. Her big dark-tipped breasts swing free as she pulls off her petticoat. Peggy takes off her neat pearl-grey skirt and striped blouse. Then she hesitates, eels her way out of her petticoat, but will not take off anything more. No sense in trying to persuade her. Peggy is sweetly smiling and delicate and biddable; Peggy is also as stubborn as . . .

'Stubborn as a cat,' Clare said once. 'She'll purr and wind herself round you until you think you can do what you like with her, but have you ever seen her do anything she didn't want?'

Now they are ready. Suddenly they're ageless, girls from anywhere, from any time. They catch hands and run towards the water. Hannah and Clare run straight and easy, seaside girls who are used to broad, flat sands, and to roads over the moors with the wind against them. Peggy has learned a more ladylike way of throwing out her legs from the knee. She runs ineffectually: perhaps she is expecting someone to help her? Peggy is the slightest and smallest of the three. Her body bows, sheltering itself.

The girls stop by the water's edge. Peggy raises the hand which isn't holding Clare's, and shades her eyes.

'Fishing-boat coming in,' she pants.

But it's so far away that they don't need to bother about it. No one will see them at that distance. It's just a black speck among the bob and glitter of the waves. Peggy's always had better eyesight than anyone else.

The water grips their ankles like an icy bracelet. They spring back, then slowly, cautiously, in again, then back as a bigger wave licks up their calves.

'Mother of God!' says Clare, hopping on one leg.

'There's only one way to do it,' says Hannah. Once again she's the guardian of their childhood, the one who always knew how cold the water was, how far out they should swim, how long it was before they had to go home. The one who packed their jam sandwiches and bottle of tea into wet cold sand under the rocks so that it would be cool at dinner-time, while Clare and John William ran off heedlessly, straight into the sea . . .

'One . . . two . . . three . . .' chants Hannah, forcing them all deeper into the water, but Clare and Peggy wriggle out of her grip.

'It's all very well for you,' complains Clare, eyeing Hannah's thighs and buttocks. 'You're subcutaneous.'

6

But Hannah isn't listening. Eyes shut, blind with purpose, she feels her way into deeper water. The water surges up her, splashing her thighs, pubic hair, belly. She dips her hands in the water and rubs them over her shoulders.

Then she's in and swimming. Paddling like a dog, she swings round to the shore, shouting, 'First in! First in!'

'Come on, Peg, or we'll never hear the last of this,' says Clare. The next wave rolls water up her thighs, and she gasps and shrinks away from it, standing ridiculously on tiptoe.

'Aaah! Aaah!'

Hannah wallows, laughing at Clare. She raises an arm to splash her cousin all over her tender stomach and breasts with a thousand prickling icy needles –

'No! Don't! I'm coming in.'

Clare presses her lips tight and charges, galumphing into the waves. Waves slap, water shimmies on her eyelashes. She's in. She turns like a fish, so cold that at first she can't even breathe, then she gives out a long gasp and a scream to Peggy who is still hovering in the shallows.

'I'm in! I'm in!'

It's too cold to swim. Hannah and Clare roll and bathe in waist-deep water, just where the waves break. Clare's hair straggles down her body. They call and threaten and scorn, but they can't get Peggy in. She is paddling dreamily along the edge of the water, stirring the sand into clouds. Her head is down.

'I'm getting out,' Hannah chatters. 'You'd better. You ought to mind your chest.'

'In a minute,' Clare replies.

Second in, she must be second out. And she wants the sea to herself for a minute, the noise and swell of it, her bare flesh rocking in salt water.

But it's too cold. So cold you could die of it. Slowly, legs dragging, she hauls herself out. The sea is thick and resistant. The wind doesn't feel warm any more. Hannah is lolloping along the beach, getting dry. They have no towels. Aching with cold, Clare begins to walk up the beach. Behind her the sea sighs like a disappointment.

Hannah has chocolate in her pocket. She can save a handful of sweets all week, so as to cram all her pleasures into the one afternoon that's her own. She doesn't have to go to the shop on Sundays, but she might as well. Sunday is chapel, teaching Sunday school, cooking for the family because Aunt Sarah needs to lie down after the walk back from chapel. Aunt Sarah has a female complaint which she will confide to any other female who can endure the mosquito whinge of her voice and the meaty, intimate smell of her breath. Clare shudders. Every Sunday Hannah bastes the meat, and her faint scent of violet is drowned in fumes of gravy and fat.

But even on this perfect day something is missing. Hannah has not had her letter from Sam. There is no new, limp envelope in her pocket, so new that it hasn't yet moulded itself to Hannah's curves. And it's the end of the week, so she should have had a letter by now, or at least a postcard. Perhaps he's on the move again, to another of those places he's not allowed to name. She knows other girls who'd worked out a code with their best boy before he was sent out to France, but she and Sam hadn't bothered. Sam was not much of a one for writing, and Hannah doubted privately whether he would have remembered any code had they managed to invent one. Besides, it had begun to seem as if Sam would never be sent out. He was in barracks so long, and then he caught chicken-pox and had it badly, when the rest of his draft went out. He was so bad that he was put in the isolation ward of the military hospital, and the letter she had from him there was baked brown from its fumigation. But just when they were getting used to the precarious safety of Sam being nowhere in particular, neither a soldier in training nor a soldier at the front, he was sent out with the next draft.

He's never been a good letter-writer. She shouldn't worry so much. Only a thin few lines each time, hoping this finds you as it leaves me, and always the same love at the bottom. His letters are never clean. She holds them up to her mouth and nose and breathes in the musty, terrifying smell of them. But they mean safety, another week of confidence that she's going to get him back again, brown and strange and maybe with that blind-drunk look in his eyes she's seen in other men on the train back from Bodmin Barracks, on leave. But there'll be nothing wrong with him which she can't cure, she is sure of that. No matter what, she only needs to get him back again. She shivers, thinking of the smell of him. His hands. The way he leans back and groans as if she is hurting him. She rubs her legs briskly with her petticoat and shivers again.

The chocolate is soft and warm. Peggy won't take any. She hasn't got cold, like the others, she says. And chocolate is precious. Clare lets her small piece melt under her tongue and spread out across her palate. Her body starts to tingle. She snuggles into a warm hollow of sand and shuts her eyes. She can hear the sand hissing, moving past her ears where her weight has disturbed it. When she was a child, Father warned her not to dig here in case she set the sand moving. There'd been a boy buried one July afternoon, when Clare was five. A visitor's child. They scrabbled to get at him, but it was no good. His mouth and his eyes and his ears were full of sand. His face was blue and bulging by the time they got to him, though her father did not tell her that. It was Uncle John, big and doom-laden in Nan's kitchen. And the state of the poor boy . . .

He'd shat hisself all over, said John William secretly, when the children were kneeling by the kitchen fire in the near-dark.

She thinks now of the boy's desperate fight against the sand which feels so soft and loose and playful until it's on top of you. Maybe it began as a game. He was pretending to be buried, then suddenly the sand was too high and beginning to squeeze in on him, and he called out, though at first he thought it was part of the game and in a moment the sand would give way and turn back into that easy soft stuff he could make into castles and dams. But the sand hissed at him again and then he could not turn his head for the weight of it and he was screaming until it filled his mouth and nose and he breathed it in, dragging it down into his lungs, dry and parching, and then the sand covered his eyes. Still no one could get at him.

She breathes shallowly. The fabric of her chemise is like a clasp.

'I won't think of it. Let me not think of it any more.' So she used to pray when she was little, scrunched up at the side of the bed, bargaining for a good night as the cold seeped into her from the oilcloth. 'And let me have no bad dreams or nightmares or think of bad things in the night.' It was not the way to say her prayers, she knew that as she knelt there, chilled and guilty. She had said her proper night prayers with Father and then slid back out of bed for this illicit begging-session.

Peggy hugs her knees, looking along the coast, duty plucking at her.

'I'll have to be getting back,' she said. 'I've only got till six.'

'Can't they ever give you a proper day off?' asks Hannah. 'You didn't get home at all last Sunday, did you?'

'Oh, well, Georgie needs me,' says Peggy, vaguely, proudly. 'He won't go off to sleep without I sing to him. And he likes me to give him his supper. He won't eat an egg for his mother. She don't like it!' Peggy giggles suddenly and subversively, then the mask of responsibility drops over her face again.

'Sounds like a spoiled brat,' murmurs Clare. She tries out, briefly, this alternative life. Governess for a delicate child whose parents have come down to Cornwall for the sake of his health. They are after good air and a cheap governess, and they have got both. They call Peggy a governess, but really she is sick-nurse and nurse-maid and cook for him too. Peggy does it all. Even empties the slop-bucket, I wouldn't wonder. What would it be like, to form your life round the shape other people want? She opens her eyes a little and looks at Peggy's back and the wisps of hair at the nape of her neck. Peggy's hair is thin, but she makes the best of it, fluffing it into fair curls at her temples, piling it over a little cushion of false hair.

'Oh, well,' says Peggy complacently. 'Georgie's used to me. They get like that. I don't mind.'

Clare rolls over and pillows her face on her arm. She rubs her cheek along the silky underside of her left forearm, and smells her skin. She remembers how she and Hannah and John William would lie on the warmest patch of sand they could find, after bathing, close as they could 'to get warm' in a muddle of bare skin and tangled legs. John William's salt-stiff black hair would scrub into her face. Hannah smelled of cloveballs. John William smelled of almonds and salt when he was clean from the sea.

'What do I smell of?' Clare asked once, and John William twisted round and buried his face between her bare white chest and her arm. But he did not smell her skin. He put his mouth on the inner, whitest part of her arm and sucked. There was a sharp, pleasurable, drawing sensation on Clare's skin, then John William raised his head and saw the mark he'd made. His suck had brought up a perfect circle of reddish-purple pinpricks.

'Now look what you done to Clarey!' said Hannah.

But when Clare looked at it closely, she liked the pattern of it. Who'd have thought that just John William's mouth could do this? Like Nan's pincushion with the pins all set in it. And John William smiled proudly.

'You could a made her bleed,' said Hannah.

Could he? All three looked at each other.

'Could he really, Hannah?'

'Course I could. It's cos you're so white, see, Clarey.'

Yes, she was the whitest and frailest of them all. And she had a real dead mother, while they had only whinging Aunt Sarah. And Nan always told them they had to look after Clarey. Clare looked at John William and laughed, showing her white teeth.

'Don't roll about like that in your chemise,' says Peggy sharply. 'What if somebody comes? You ought to get yourself dressed decent.'

'This 'ud be dull compared to what they could have seen five minutes ago,' says Clare. But all the same she reaches for dress and stockings, shakes out sand, does them up. Her hair is drying. Wet, it looks almost black; dry, it is dark red. Her features are almost extinguished by the blaze of light on them. Hannah's broad, strong-planed face survives. Peggy is pretty, as always.

Clare stands and looks out to sea. There's a good view of the lighthouse from here. Water curls whitely, breaking round it. But you can't see the lighthouse-keeper's little garden from here, where the earth is seeded with salt each winter, then sweetened again with blood-and-bone and a coating of agar each spring. Now there's a boat coming round the point. Not a fishing-boat. A patrol. Lucky they'd got dressed. The patrol-boat sweeps right in here sometimes, nearly to the shore. Now, it keeps on coming black and squat through the sea. She wonders why they're round here today? They've been further down all week, off Zennor Head. Nosing blunt-headed under the cliffs, looking for something. Looking for fuel-dumps, someone told Grandad. She wonders what a U-boat looks like when it rises above the water. It must be very like a basking shark, she thinks. She has seen basking sharks from the cliffs, lying offshore in warm weather, seeming to do nothing and said to wish no harm, though they can turn a boat over if they are frightened. But the U-boat strikes, then it comes up black-shouldered and streaming with water and lies there watching to be sure of its kill, while men thresh in the oily water, and nobody comes. Next day the waves are full of tins and oil and smashed wood.

'Come on, let's go. It's getting late.'

The sun is much lower now. The shadow of the dunes covers them as they start to toil up through the sand.

Two

Low drystone walls fill the vegetable garden with sheltering heat. A thin white-fleshed man in soft grey trousers bends over his spade, puts one foot on the lug, pauses. A trace of coconut blows past him from the gorse, then the spice of wallflowers. Gorse blazes in a long tongue of pure yellow all down the hill above the cottages. Beyond his garden wall the land slopes, glistening, down to the farm and the sea beyond. It is a landscape of irregular small fields shaped by Celtic farmers two thousand years ago. Lichened granite boulders are lodged deep into the hedges. They stand upright in the fields, a crop of stone. Lanes run tunnel-like between the furze down to the farms. Here, by the cottage, the lane dips and dampens and is lined with foxglove and hart's tongue fern and slow drops of oozing water. It is so quiet here. He has heard no human noises at all since he walked up from Lower Tregerthen, the Hockings' farm at the bottom of the lane. The men are working several fields away this afternoon, carting dung for mangels, and the wind blows their voices away from him. He shades his eyes and looks right out towards the sea. It is bare, glittering like a plate. He will walk there later, he thinks. Then a sudden uproar of lowing makes him turn. The cows three fields away to the right are staging their daily stampede, striking the hard ground with their hoofs and jostling each other. Three of them break away and canter to the field gate, lashing their tails. He laughs. He likes these small wild Zennor cows which imagine they are buffaloes in their tiny wind-swept fields. These are not the milky, huge-rumped Midland creatures he's used to, with their slow tails switching as they eat their way across a meadow. Here, the grass is sweet but the herd must scramble for it.

He hears the steady flagging of the breeze in the petticoats he hung out on the line that morning. They are hung deftly, so that they keep their shape and won't flap against the briars. They are white, soft, full petticoats, with good lace on the bodice and hem. The lace comes from his wife's first trousseau, prepared for her first marriage, and she has kept it through divorce and remarriage.

The soil is poor but healthy. William Henry has brought up five loads of dung from the farm. Lawrence has spread the dung and cleared stones and weeds. He is growing vegetables to eke out his tiny income. He earns his living by his writing, and it has shrunk close to nothing since his novel was seized by the police in November 1915 and prosecuted for obscenity. The book is shameful, say reviewers and prosecution. It is a thing *which creeps and crawls*. It dishonours the lofty sacrifices of our soldiers. All the publisher's copies have been destroyed, and the book is banned. He does not know when he will be able to publish another novel. But with a remote cottage rented at five pounds a year, and cheap rural living, he hopes that he and his wife may get through the war. He has turned his back on London, on reviewers who puff themselves up with rage and trumpet that his book *has no right to exist*, and on influential friends whose support is lukewarm and who have trimmed their sails to the winds of censorship and war. He grows vegetables because he has no money to buy them, but also because it delights him to see bright sparks of life coming out of the earth.

The soil is clean. Fragile carrot tops poke out of the earth, the broad beans are shooting, and soon his potatoes will be sprawling over the potato hill. He plans to make their household self-sufficient in fresh food. He notes that the cabbage plants are drooping: it's been a dry, brilliant month, hot for May. Here spring comes early and there are few frosts, but wild nights and salt-soaked winds kill off just as many plants. The heat on his neck is Mediterranean, glowing, scented. The sea is dark, with a broad purplish stain where the channel deepens. It would remind him of Italy, except that the land here is darker and wilder.

He will not look backwards, at the sprawl of England and the dark blotch of London, seething with rumour and propaganda. He'll work the land here. And he'll go over and help on the farm at Lower Tregerthen because he loves the life of that farm as he loved the life of The Haggs years ago. He loves to peel pickling onions and talk in the kitchen as the hens run by the open door. He loves William Henry's dark, warm smile as he pulls off his boots and sits on the settle by the fire, turning over the pages of Lawrence's *Geography of the World* with respectful fingers. When the hay harvest comes he'll help again. Let the other farmers murmur about *free labour at Lower Tregerthen* when they come into Zennor churchtown on a Sunday morning. They know everything that goes on, and now they are bitter with losing their own sons to the war. This bold, sculpted landscape is a watching landscape. A human being is a dab of movement in it, visible miles off in the fields. Absolutely spied-upon. Your neighbour may be listening, stone-still in the lane below your cottage, and you will never see him. But he will hear every word you say as you sit talking to your wife near an open window. He will listen to Frieda's German voice reading aloud letters from her German mother. He will hear them singing strange-vowelled Hebridean songs from the new collection a friend has sent them. He will spy on their rages and their reconciliations.

Neighbours listen, and murmur, and the murmuring spreads as quickly as flowers of gorse opening to the touch of the sun. The farmers around Zennor pass on the news. Newspaper columns tell them that it is their patriotic duty to watch, to inform, to spy for spies. There has never been such spy-fever as there is in England this summer, brewing like the unseasonal heat of May. The farmers' wives sit in their traps after church on Sundays, ready to be driven home to their dinners, and among talk of heifer calves and the price of eggs they whisper about the foreigners. The German woman. The man who speaks against the war. The farmers and farmworkers drive over the moors to market in Penzance, or down to St Ives for the Saturday market, and the talk goes with them, half jeering, half judging. Talk licks its way from one mouth to another. These two may think themselves remote, aloof, left to birdsong and the pecking of the typewriter. But they are not. Most inflammatory of all, they act as if they are alone and have to account to no one. They act as if this countryside is really the bare, shouldering granite wilderness it appears to be. This brazen couple ignores the crossed, tight webs, the drystone walls, the small signals of kinship, the spider-fine apprehensions of those who've lived there for ever once they feel a fly strumming somewhere on their web.

He may have fooled the Hockings, but he don't fool us.

Food shortages are reaching crisis-point as U-boats down the incoming merchant ships. At last the government has been galvanized into action, and voluntary rationing is being introduced. At last land is being ploughed up to grow desperately needed food. In London and Manchester and Birmingham allotments sprout. Half a million of them have been dug within the past year. Sooty, industrial air keeps off blight and rust as effectively as Atlantic winds. In Nottinghamshire miners dig up waste ground, and keep rabbits in their backyards. He knows them so well, those miners sitting on their heels against a wall, raising their faces to the weak sun, wrung out after their long shift underground. Widows scratch earth without proper tools and with only dim childhood memories of Gran's cottage garden to guide them. The rationing system does not work and the only margarine they can get tastes like axle-grease as it congeals around their children's teeth. Bread is short. The rich eat tins of imported larks, while rumours fly that the Germans are melting down corpses for oil. At home, within government offices, there are better-kept secrets. The country is lurching towards the point where there will be only two weeks' supply of food left. Lords and ministers look eastwards to Russia, where revolution is breaking like a wave on the heels of hunger and war. The menu at the Ritz still offers five courses larded with cream. And those who can afford it must eat up all the caviare, because the poor would never swallow those clotted, salty, unfamiliar globules. To eat caviare is to perform a service to one's country.

The man leans on the lug of his spade, then eases it in. There's not much space left, but he can get a catch-crop of salad stuff just here, out of the wind. Radishes, some spring onions, a bit of lettuce. The King has just issued a proclamation urging his people to eat less bread: 'We, being persuaded that the abstention from all unnecessary consumption of grain . . .'

There are stray marigold plants which have self-seeded from the summer before. He bends down, works the soil loose around the stems of the plants, and lifts them out. Under the wall there's sandy soil where thrift and valerian grow. He fetches a trowel, makes space for the marigolds and dibs them in. The sharp scent of their leaves comes off on his fingers: he sniffs them. The petticoats belly out over his head, then flatten and hang limp in a sudden drop of the wind. The sun sucks out smells of turned earth, bruised onion, marigold. Larks shrill high up, so constant that he no longer attends to them. He runs his hand over the wall, liking the fit of one stone into another. But just here the wall is loose: it has been hastily repaired, hand-to-mouth. He applies a little more pressure and the top rows of stone rock gently. Perhaps he could take down the top three rows of stone and rebuild them? There will be time. It is a slow, patient job, the kind he likes. He kneels to look more closely at the base of the wall. There is a clump of white foxgloves, not yet in flower. He remembers them flowering in the long June dusks last summer, like lights. Now they show their stubby buds again. He has seen the year round in this cottage. He did not think to do so, but it is comforting in the shipwreck of the war to watch the seasons come round again here.

There is a cry from the window. She has woken up. She leans out over the sill, her broad forearms pressed against the stone. She is magnificent, frowsty with sleep, looking to him like the pulse and colour of health itself. But she is not quite well today, she says, and she went up to bed after their lunch, to sleep or perhaps to watch the light move round the white walls and to think of her children. If she thinks of them while she is with him, he always knows. There is a particular look on her, not so much sad as intensely recollecting something in which he has no part. He darkens with rage. 'Aren't I enough for you?' he asks her.

Or he is tender, mending her shawl for her, telling her what they are going to have for dinner, bringing in a handful of the first lettuce, seducing her back to the present.

'Aren't I enough for you?'

Now she leans out, feeling the sun on her arms, and waves to him. She sees row after row of little vegetables pricking the earth, more than they can possibly eat, she thinks. But it is good for him. It eases the lines of strain on his face. And that terrible look he has sometimes, after reading one more letter from a friend chiding him for his stupid obstinacy in opposing this war as he does. Does he think he is an Old Testament prophet, crying woe unto the people? He certainly behaves like one. And one must be frank, people won't stand for much more of that sort of thing. He reads through such letters and throws them on the table in disgust. Then she sees his 'white look' burning on his face. He will burn himself to nothing. So let him go to his vegetable garden, and to the farm, even if it leaves her on her own, listening to the constant sift of the wind over the roof.

She runs her hands back through her thick, rather coarse golden hair. She is putting on flesh again, even though there is almost nothing to eat. She is hungry for good things. She daren't think of cakes, of pastries and cream, of whipped hot chocolate and *torte* after skating. He has put in some wallflowers under their window, and the heated scent of them rises to her, so that she leans out to catch more of it, to draw it up to her. Soft pansy-brown clumps of them, spiked with seed pods, with bees working away at them. He thinks *he* is the only one who notices such things, but she loves them too.

He goes back to his work, hoeing between rows of onion-sets. She sighs. She'll get dressed and make tea for them both. There will be letters, perhaps, from their *real* friends. Perhaps there will be one from Katherine. No one else writes such letters as she does. But they have to be careful now. They must not write what they think any more. Lorenzo is almost sure that letters are being opened and read. They are beginning to blunt some words and to sharpen others with hidden meanings. But no one is going to frighten Frieda out of writing to her mother in Germany. And she *will* read the *Berliner Tageblatt*, where she finds the names of men she grew up with among the lists of the dead. And their younger brothers too, who were children when she knew them. Or perhaps she will read of the exploits of her cousin whom they call the Red Baron, Manfred von Richthofen, who shot down five British planes in one day last month. But how can anyone be so stupid as to suspect her? How can anyone be so petty? After all she is a British subject. How can they call her a Hunwife? Indeed she has shown her preferences by marrying not one but two Englishmen. She has children here, even if they are not the children of the man she is married to.

'No. I must not think of the children.' It is dangerous to think of the children. It is like Lorenzo thinking of the war. *The children ran from her.* They ran from her when their governess said, 'Run, children! Run!' They saw their mother and they ran. She had come to meet them from school, and there they were with the governess. She heard their high, sweet voices, but she could not hear what they were saying. Barbara had a blue hat on, a new one which she had never seen. Then Frieda was stumbling towards her children with her arms open to seize them and hold them and breathe in the warm smell of their hair and their skin. But the governess had been told not to let the children see their mother, the wicked woman who had run away and left her husband and her children. She called out: 'Run, children! Run!' And the children ran. They did not know who I was, Frieda tells herself. They were frightened and they did not recognize me.

The light changes again as a fresh ripple of wind crosses the landscape. For a moment it looks like heaven. While it looks like this, nothing bad can happen. Let them fret and bluster with their boundaries and rules and prohibitions. Let them tamper with our mail and carry on with their surveillance which is so clumsy, so ponderous that it is comic. Surely it can never come to anything? We must continue to live as usual, to show that we have nothing to hide, that we are not afraid. These oafs of military police – they are just something one has to live with. Something decent people pretend to ignore.

Here, they are hundreds of miles from London's tumour of officialdom. Here, it is nearly all sea. Little dots of people on rock, a huddle of grey farm buildings wherever the land folds in to make shelter for them, then miles and miles of sea, stretching sheer to America.

'Aaah, how beautiful!' she says, opening her white, powerful arms. She will make tea for them both, and then they will go for a walk. She turns her back on the window and starts to pull on her stockings. Her husband bends too, rasping his hoe through the bindweed he can never quite eradicate. Each fragment is capable of rooting itself, and forming a fresh stranglehold on his young plants. It is rank green bindweed with its coarse white flowers, not the little, scented mauve-striped convolvulus which grows along the cliff-path.

Another boat noses into sight, heading for the cliff-base. It looks like nothing from here, but it is full of living sharp-eyed men, doing their job. Only doing their duty. What a world this war has made, where everyone is doing his duty, or what he conceives to be his duty. There is a rumour of a German fuel-dump near here, tucked into one of the hollow, sea-echoing chambers along the coast, ready to feed the submarines. You could never search this whole coast. And the U-boats are prowling along this coastline, sinking ship after ship after ship on the Western Approaches, leaving the British authorities helpless and raging with the pent-up secret of their helplessness. U-boats prowl, bread queues breed, allotmenteers dig up the railway embankments. If there is no food, will there be revolution here too? What if the soldiers at the Front get letters from their dear ones at home saying: *We are hungry. We are starving. You must help us.*

She dresses, he digs. Neither sees the patrol-boat swing right in, balancing itself on the swell. It is taking advantage of the calm weather to come close under the cliffs, searching for evidence. Is there a patch of oil, or a place where someone might set a signal-light? The boat rocks while its crew look and listen. Their eyes rake the rocks. Nothing. *But there must be something.* It is four o'clock. The men out in the fields straighten as they see the girl reach the gate with a cloth-covered basket and a jug of cold tea. She will hand it over the gate to them, because she does not want the dung on her skirts. Meanwhile the postman toils seven miles uphill from St Ives, with the *Berliner Tageblatt* in his saddlebag.

Three

Six o'clock and the house is silent, as Clare opens the porch and stands still just inside the front door. Westerly light drips through stained glass on to her hair, through the languid figure of a craggy-jawed Pre-Raphaelite beauty. Her long green robes make green blobs on the black and white tiled floor. Clare runs a finger round the outline of a big, bare foot which peeks out of the draperies. She used to reach up and huff her breath on the toes to see them cloud. She used to think the figures were angels, not second-hand Lizzie Siddals.

'Is that you, my darling?'

It is her father's fond, light, abstracted voice.

'Have you been out, Clare?'

She goes down the hall to her father's room, which smells musty after the sunshine. The room is small and full of furniture: a brown, slender-legged bureau desk, two fat brown leather armchairs, a table, a dark crimson Turkey rug. The window is open to let out the smell of his cigar. He only smokes in this one room, out of consideration for her. A narrow-skulled Burmese cat turns and glares at her from the armchair opposite Francis Coyne.

'Sheba,' he croons reprovingly.

Maps are sprawled out, open, on the floor, the chair arm, the rosewood dining-table at which they never dine. Clare's own sketchbooks are piled up on a corner of the table.

Francis Coyne is mapping the distribution of travelling plants in an area seven miles around St Ives. He is more interested in travelling species than in the close-rooted kind which has always been at home here, clinging to its habitat. Seeding by bird-droppings, accidental migrations in sailors' knapsacks, carefully harvested pods and cuttings which survive, freakishly, half-way around the planet: these interest him. When Clare was a child, the only fairy stories he told her were the stories of plants: their places of birth and their uprootings, their adventures, adaptations and survivals. At six and seven and eight she had listened, fascinated; now she's nearly twenty, and she has become impatient. Or perhaps she had never been patient, or even interested at all. She had drunk up attention, and even if it came to her filtered through a strange dialect of pedicels, racemes and bracts, she was capable of burrowing past the information to the cadences of her father's voice, his smell, his light hands that never clasped her as tightly as she wanted. Now Francis Coyne is supposed to be writing a book, and Clare is supposed to be helping him. He is a self-taught botanist, an amateur, as he will admit to anyone who asks him. No expert. But it is his enthusiasm, gentlemanly and kept well within bonds.

'Don't pretend,' says Clare. 'You know I've been out. And it's six o'clock. We went right up to Hayle and came back on the railway.'

His eyes gleam briefly, acknowledging that yes, he isn't as absent-minded as all that. He has noticed her absence, but he preferred to go on fossicking among books and maps rather than realize the time and light the kitchen stove and think about what there was to eat. It was only what she'd known and expected.

'You make tea while I wash,' says Clare. 'I'm all salt – look.'

She holds out her arm, and he peers. It's true, there is a delicate rime of salt on her skin.

'Been paddling?' he asks.

'Swimming.'

'You must not take cold, Clare.'

He says it because he feels he should, but they both know that Clare chooses for herself.

'Have you anything to show me?'

'I didn't take my sketchbook.'

Clare is the one who can draw. Her pencil sketches are delightful, her father thinks, firm, yet delicate, beautifully shaded. He has taught her which details she must include for botanical drawings. But she has not taken her sketchbook.

'I'll light the stove,' he says with conscious generosity.

'No, don't do it yet. I'll boil the kettle over the kitchen fire. I asked Hannah, but Uncle Arthur hasn't any kerosene. There won't be any until the middle of next week; Wednesday, Hannah thinks.'

'Can we manage until then, with what we have?'

She shrugs. He doesn't really want to know, so why does he ask? She will have to manage.

'I shall finish this, then, while you get ready.'

And he relapses, book in his hand. She peers. It is some privately printed slender volume of poems. She hasn't seen it before. Surely he can't have been spending money on books again? Well, she will say nothing now. The cat, pleased that Clare has gone, knocks lightly against Francis Coyne's dangling hand. The hand curls and caresses the cat's long spine, which pours away under his touch.

The whole golden evening arches over the bay as Clare goes upstairs. Her calf muscles ache from scrambling the dunes:

she'd like to have a bath, but there isn't enough fuel to heat the water. She pauses at the tiny landing window and looks out. They're high up here, in one of the rows of new villas built twenty years ago, already well weathered by winters of storms. The houses have stone-cladded fronts and stained-glass panels in their porches, and little gardens which are no more than backyards. But the rooms are light and airy. Her father thinks the house hideous. He has lived there since the builder signed off in the plaster of the front sitting-room, and he and Clare's mother were left to tiptoe around the raw newness of the house, planning its decoration.

Clare was two then, kept up in lodgings in London until the house was habitable. When she first came, she was frightened by the noise and the size of the sea. It was winter, and she thought their house would tumble down the hill and into the dark grey fighting waves. Her father would have preferred one of the whitewashed cottages down in the town, among narrow lanes and sudden astonishing views. But her mother wouldn't think of it. Dirty, insanitary places, full of noise and drunkenness when the boats came in after a successful catch. She loathed her husband's taste for the naïve and local. Dimly she felt that it insulted her by putting her firmly and gently within the category of the picturesque. She loathed the way he refused to know right from wrong. He could well afford to have such fancies, being what he was, coming from where he did; but she could not. She had left this town half trained as a maid by the minister's wife, made bold by a frightened ambitiousness which she revealed to nobody. She would touch fine things, smell perfumes and silks, put out bon-bons in silver filigree dishes on walnut dressing-tables. She was to be polished. The scouring away of her had worked. She was not what she had been, and yet she wasn't quite what she had been moving towards. She worked her way up to lady's maid in a secluded terrace with its own railed gardens in Kensington, not far from Brompton Oratory. Her hands were perfect, broad, with cool, tapering fingers. She had a touch that would soothe anyone, and a gift for dressing hair so lightly and easily that her lady scarcely felt the pins going in. Just her lady to dress. No daughters. Engagements to luncheon, callers, concerts. A muddle of Kensington ladies fluttering from house to house for tea and soft, murmurous, complaining conversations.

A celibacy of servitude, almost classless, had begun to shroud Susannah Treveal. She came across Francis Coyne in the course of it, and had scarcely thought of him as a man, let alone as a man with a possible sexual interest in herself. After all, he came to tea with his mother. She had dressed his mother's hair one afternoon, when Mrs Coyne had been struck down by migraine and had had to lie down upstairs in one of the cool bedrooms with wistaria tapping against the windows.

She was soon enlightened by the other staff. These Coynes were not as grand as you might think. They had the name, but Coyne Park was not what it sounded. All the land had been sold long ago to meet recusancy fines, and now there was just the place itself, with the Home Farm and a few cottages in the village of Coyne. Oh, the name might sound fine, but you wouldn't catch Ethel or Ivy working there, away down in Somerset with nowhere to go but between blank green fields. And the Coynes always had too many sons. Francis was the third, and he was no more likely to inherit than a parakeet in a cage. The eldest son was married already with a long family in the nursery. Francis's mother survived on this relation and that. He'd have a small income and he'd have to look like a gentleman on it. Wouldn't you think he'd have the gumption to go into the army? And he couldn't go into the Church. Pity, that. It was a useful place for younger sons.

'Why not? Why can't he?' asked Susannah, seeing Francis suddenly in a pulpit, long hands laced as he looked over and down at the congregation.

'They're Romans. Didn't you know? *She's* always bobbing into the Oratory.'

'Oh!' squeaked Susannah, who had been named for the mother of all the Wesleys. This was worse than his lack of money.

Yet she felt for him. There was something about him. His long, finicking fingers: the general uselessness of him. He was a luxury item. He could make her laugh. He was light, he took nothing at its full value, she thought, not even the marriage which made her sweat and tremble at night beforehand. She said nothing to them at home. She kept dumb as a hare. Her wooden little letters didn't cease, for fear they'd suspect. For nearly two months she traipsed to the presbytery of Holy Cross every Wednesday night, with Francis, to receive instruction. She couldn't help it: the first time she set foot over the threshold she crossed her fingers behind her back, fearful that her sinning body would burst into spontaneous fire. She assented to every proposition put forward by the priest, who was kindly and tired and impatient of Francis's love of argument. Before she knew it she had *turned*. They would be able to have a nuptial mass, though they had no one to ask – Francis's family were horrified by the marriage, her own knew nothing of it, and Susannah had no friends but her fellow-servants. Francis had friends, young men who laughed too much, in her opinion. She imagined that these friends would come to an end, after their wedding.

She could avoid telling her family of her courtship but not of her marriage. It would not have been beyond her father to mount an assault upon London, in the pride of his foreignness and his honesty, should he suspect from her change of address that she had taken wrong ways. So the letter was written, and she closed off her mind to the rage and torment she could feel far down in that bony, jutting finger of land. They did not come to find her or fetch her. She wrote again when Clare was born, and received a present of a shawl from her mother, who had four huge virtuous sons and preferred girls. Susannah began her campaign to come home, away from Francis's friends and the traffic and books and rare, terrifying visits to the Café Royale and the eddy of people who either believed in a god she could not believe in or in no god at all. Sometimes she suspected Francis of belonging to both these camps at once.

Besides, she'd become delicate since giving birth to Clare. She did not put on weight. She coughed, and her breath smelled. They would be better down in Cornwall, where living was cheap, the air was pure, and Francis could write his books, since this was what he wanted to do.

And they could get a fine new house with no damp in it, no insanitary passages, no bad drains, high up above the bay, triumphantly above the piggling streets where she'd lived as a child. He objected that there was no convent school for Clare, but surely he could teach her himself – with all he knew, what better arrangement could there be?

Two years after they moved, she was dead of phthisis. A hard and ugly way to die, but he had stuck to her right through it, paying for doctors, injections, special diets, Jaeger wool. He held bowls for her and changed her sheets after she woke at three o'clock, wet with a night-sweat. By the time she died she was almost convinced that he must have really loved her, and had not married her simply in order to carry out some mazy fantasy of his own or to get his mother off his back for ever.

She wouldn't let the child come in her room. 'Don't let Clarey come near me. Send her downalong to Mum's.'

The lady's maid speech was nearly gone now: used up, like her breath. Clare went down to the insanitary cottages, and played by the harbour with her cousins and second cousins, and ran out to see the boats come in with the other children, getting in the way, getting yelled at, jeering at the blue lobsters which crawled over one another in their pots, insect-like, claws tied for the London market.

At home, the shut door. Father going in and out, smelling funny, and a doctor with legs like scissors as he got out of his trap. Covered bowls and buckets. And all night, whenever she woke, she could hear gargling and coughing from the thing that was there, behind her mother's door.

They all went to see her buried, a foreign and appalling experience for Susannah Treveal's family. Francis had insisted that her requiem be said in the little chapel at Coyne. She was his wife, and she would lie among the wives of the Coynes. Besides, there was no Catholic church in St Ives yet, though the site for it in Street-an-Pol was bought in the year of Susannah's death, and the Catholic community was growing fast. So there sat the row of Treveals, Nan and Grandad, Uncles Arthur and John and William and Stanley, their wives, their children. Not one of them had ever set foot in a Catholic church, nor had they thought ever to do so. They sat there upright and disbelieving as the coffin containing their child, their sister, was asperged and muttered over, and the censer was swung around it. It was a strange gathering of Methodists and Coynes and Francis's atheist friends from London.

And look at him now, alone with black-drenched four-year-old Clare, at the chapel door. He did not quite look as a widower should, but Nan allowed for the pinch and tuck God had put into his lips, which made him look as if he were smiling slightly. All the Treveals had seen with their own eyes how he had looked after Susannah. And now he had this child to rear. Susannah's brother Stan's wife had no children, although they'd been wed for twelve years. It was a female trouble she had. She would take the child gladly and leave Francis free for his work. Clare would be in the same street as Nan and Grandad, and just a step away from her cousins, clattering off to school with them. It would get her out of that sickly house up the hill, full in the face of the gales. So the Treveals reasoned among themselves, and the idea grew and shimmered as it passed like a blown bubble from one family branch to the next. However, there seemed to be no right time to tell Francis of it. After the funeral he stayed at Coyne with the child for a week or so, while the Treveals went back home. They came to meet him at the station when he returned to St Ives, but he preferred to walk straight home with Clare. 'She must get used to the house without her mother in it,' he said to Nan.

Francis Coyne set off uphill with the child, both of them walking soberly, but not downcast, not easy objects of pity. Then Francis bent suddenly and scooped Clare up on to his shoulders and balanced her there, a smudge of black dress and red hair bobbing against the pale tearing early winter sky. He had hold of her boots, and she gripped him firmly around his neck, spoiling his collar. Both of them leaned forward as the hill steepened, then they went out of sight together.

Clare lived half up the hill and half down the hill. She eased and flitted between the cottages and the villa, speaking two dialects, learning two pasts, instructed in two faiths. Grandad could not bear the idea of Clare 'bobbing and ducking', first in the mission up the hill, and then in the newly built church of the Sacred Heart and St Ia. So he refused to think of it, and absolutely ignored that part of her life. First Communion, Confirmation; Nan might question and remark, but Grandad never would. Instead, he told Clare of Wesley ranging the spine of Cornwall, preaching at quarries which were flooded with people as if with water. She learned the Wesleyan hymns and the legends of John Wesley's childhood. The rectory at Epworth, the savage parishioners who tried to burn the Wesley children alive, and five-year-old John plucked out of the flames by his rescuers. '"A brand plucked from the burning." Pray that'll be true of Clare Coyne.'

Clare's education did not begin or end at fixed points. Reading was easy. She would have liked to go to school, but there were delays, bothers that were never specified. Soon there was no need for her father to explain to her why she could not: she understood. There was enough money for her French and arithmetic lessons with dull Miss Purse, and the rest her father taught her. And there were so many people around her who could teach her particular, desirable things. Her cousins taught her to swim and whistle, fish and torment crabs, handle a boat and lie. Aunt Mag taught her plain sewing. Clare liked the tick of her needle through cotton. Nan and Aunt Mag made everything: drawers and petticoats, shirts for the boys, summer frocks for Clarey and Hannah. Clare saw a sampler and longed to sew one herself, so that Nan and Grandad could put it upon the wall in its fine frame. Nan and Aunt Mag made up clothes for the draper's shop Aunt Sarah and Uncle Arthur kept, where Hannah went to work as soon as she was old enough. They worked in the front-room in good light and bad. Nan did not hold with samplers.

'Waste a time, Clarey, when you could be doing something useful. Here, thread this needle for me. Your eyes are better'n mine.'

If only Nan didn't get those sharp, shooting pains in her fingers after a day's sewing. Sometimes she could hardly hold her cup still. 'But come next season Uncle Arthur's getting yer old Nan a Singer. Think of it, Clarey.' The Singer came, black and gold, with its treadle a criss-cross weave, then a blur as Nan caught the rhythm and fed cloth across the sewing plate. Clare watched Nan's pedalling feet, so perfect in their black boots which were all out of shape at the sides because of her bunions.

'Mark that, Clarey. That un there's the tension spring. Never touch him.' If Clare touched it, the Singer would spring apart and die, and Nan and Aunt Mag would have to go back to sewing every stitch by hand, and it would be Clare's fault.

Nan taught her to cook. By the time she was ten, Clare could cook the dinner for her father and herself. Mutton stew with dumplings, spring cabbage, boiled pudding. Sarah, Arthur's wife, no longer had to go up and downhill with the Coyne dinners. Francis had paid her a consideration, but Arthur didn't like her to be so tied to another man's household. Not with the shop to run as well.

Francis thought Clare was still a child, but to the Treveals a child of ten was a worker. Her boy cousins earned money packing fish. They laid slim mackerel head to tail in salt and ice in the spring; in the summer it was hake, cod, ling, skate, halibut, and a market for all of it. In the late autumn the kipper girls came, and they teased and played rough with the boys between hours of labour. The boys were not allowed to touch the lobsters yet, for fear they'd damage a claw and spoil the price in the London market. Boys were wild and wanted watching. Their hands were raw with brine, nicked, fiery. They stank of fish, and they were proud of it. Their elbows glittered with scales. Then John William got a job after school and weekends as a grocer's errand boy. It gave him the use of the shop bicycle, and he liked it better than fish, he said, as he pushed his cycle uphill and freewheeled down, and kicked away house-dogs with his stout boots, and got given pennies. He knew all the secret drives of the big houses, with their curvy lining of blue hydrangeas and their camellias on the terraces. Hannah would go into the shop. Already she had learned the ways of it. She was quick, and deft, and she did not break things or spoil them, or make marks on cloth. By the time she was twelve she could handle the Singer better than Nan herself. She even dared to touch the tension spring, because she knew what it was for.

John William, Hannah, Harry. Kitchie, William and Mabel's only child. And Albert, Jo and George, Uncle John's boys, up on the farm and working almost since birth. They hoed potatoes, cleared furze off the crofts, leased stones, stood round while the pig was killed. The farm was small, but the land was fair to middling; with a man and three strong sons on it, it might amount to something. The farm came from their mother, who had been a Lee before she fell in love with John Treveal. She was the lucky only child of elderly parents who had nearly worked the lives out of themselves, keeping back a wilderness of gorse from their land.

The cousins grew older and worked harder, while Clare drew. Her music lessons were suspended. Her accomplishments hung in mid-air. There was tension plucking in the atmosphere, louder than piano strings: investments dipped, and her father's small income shrivelled a little smaller. Anyway, she'd hated the noise she made. Under her fingers the piano shot out notes like a machine, not a musical instrument. She'd learned enough to play songs and please Nan and Grandad with them: one good year Grandad bought a cottage piano, and he took pains to have it tuned for Clare. Her style of playing worked for Grandad's hymns. Once, when Grandad was out of the house, Hannah said, 'Clare, play one of your hymns.'

> Hail QU-EEN of HEV'N,
> thee oh-oh-cean STAR

crashed out Clare, then stopped suddenly, homesick for something that often didn't even feel like home.

'Is that all there is to it?' mocked Hannah.

Clare drew flowers, not because she liked to, but because her father couldn't draw and needed illustrations for his book. She preferred to draw faces. It didn't matter: she enjoyed accuracy of structure and colouring, and she was working. She was illustrating a book for her father. The shading of a corolla counted as work, just as much as lugging baskets full of stoned raisins, kitchen cheese and tapioca up the drive of Little Talland House.

'Clarey's keeping house for her father. And she's doing the pictures for his book, aren't you Clarey? Show us that one you showed Grandad. Beautiful.' Where Nan praised, no one else would disparage.

Clare is nearly twenty. She cooks quickly and off-handedly but well. She keeps the house clean, though she doesn't scrub the floors. Hat comes in to do that every Friday morning, and brings up with her the fish the Coynes will eat for their Friday dinner. But Clare does everything else. She ties up her hair in a white bandeau, puts on a long grey wrapper and polishes, scours, lifts, disinfects, bangs clean. If she could do it without being seen, she'd whiten the doorstep and clean the windows too, and save the money they pay Hat. Francis carries in the coals, because a young woman should not lift coal, for fear of doing something to her insides. He splits kindling in the back garden. For a botanist he is a poor gardener, but Clare grows nasturtiums and mignonette, candytuft, bushes of lavender and rosemary around their small parched lawn. Clare rolls up her father's Turkey carpet and takes it out to beat it over the clothes-line. Her figure bends and plies. She will leave the carpet out in the sun for the sea-air to sweeten it as it blows over the peninsula. She's working. None of the Treveals can criticize her for idleness.

The remains of the Coyne meal sprawl on the table. Plates smeared with ham fat and butter but no leftovers. Last week Uncle John sent them a pound of butter wrapped in muslin. They say the soldiers are sending back butter from France, but the Post Office is going to stop it, now the weather's getting warmer and oily butter is seeping out of its packaging. Clare stirs her tea. Her father's eyes flicker down the newspaper.

'They've moved Sam, we think. Hannah hasn't had a letter,' says Clare.

'Ah. You've seen Hannah today?'

'Yes, I told you, Father.'

'Does he say where? No, I suppose not.'

He looks down at the paper. Lists of dead, figures as high as cricketing scores. There won't be much village cricket, this year, up at Coyne. He thinks of Coyne. Mama rolling bandages and praying for the dead; Benedict and Marie-Thérèse praying as each year the war goes on and one more son becomes old

enough to enlist. They have been lucky so far. Young Francis is
C2 on account of his eyesight. Stephen is in a staff job. Lucky
so far. May 1917. If the war goes on for five more months, it
will get Gerard. Gerard is in perfect health, unfortunately.
Besides, they are passing young men now who would never
have got through their medical boards a year ago. So many men
have been lost, and must be replaced.

'No,' says Clare, 'she hasn't had a letter this week.'

'Did you read the letter from John William?'

'Yes, Nan showed me. But it only said what Kitchie told us.'

'Ah, it's excellent news. Excellent. All the same, Sam might
have sent Hannah a postcard.'

He hears his own voice, ridiculous, as if the boy is on a
seaside holiday, failing to write home that he is having a good
time.

'John William will be home soon.'

'We'll have to have him up here for dinner.'

But he doesn't continue. Clare will know what he means. He
is your cousin. They are going to make him an officer. Even if
he is a Treveal. They are hungry for officers now too, since half
the product of the public schools has been scythed down already.

Francis half rises. The room is chilly now. They ought to
have a fire, but Clare has stopped laying fires ready in the grate,
to be lit in the evenings. He's been sitting too long. He feels
cold. Better not to look at the lists. It doesn't do any good. He
thinks back to Coyne, and rabbiting in the woods. There's so
much blood, just from one dead thing. And the smell of it is
cloying, like water from a spring full of iron. When a creature is
freshly killed and its blood spurts out, it makes steam on a
winter morning. Reeking. Does Clare know that? What does his
daughter think of when she reads the lists:

Missing,
Missing, believed killed in action.
Killed in action.

Perhaps she doesn't read them. Those girls, what do they talk about when they're alone?

One day last September he was walking round the rocks at low tide. He turned and saw into a cove, steep, dry-sanded, trapping the sun's late warmth. There was a girl on her back, eyes shut, mouth slack, unrecognizable. But he knew the young man straddling her, working away at her. Then he knew the stylish blue and white stripe of the girl's skirt. Goods at a discount. Hannah. He turned away to stop himself looking at her white legs, straining apart on the sand, wider and wider, to draw the man deep into her body. She knew what she was about.

Now he watches Clare's hands as she stacks the china, scoops fragments of waste food on to one plate, pours dregs of tea into the slop-bowl. Her hands are calm and capable. He thinks of all that her hands have learned. She can do so many things which he has never learned to do. She can cook, sew, wash, play the piano. How can he know what she talks about when he's not there? Futile even to want to know. But he does. He imagines the girls leaning together, confiding. He pulls back sharply from the thought, flinching at his own prurience. Again he thinks of the lists. Of Hannah's spread legs. Of Sam with the sun on his back. Now Clare feels his look on her. She glances at him and half smiles, but does not stop what she is doing.

Four

Day after day it doesn't rain. Mid-May, blazing hot, with blackthorn fully out and bluebells bowed over, hanging their sappy stems in the heat. The air smells tauntingly of honey and salt.

> When the gorse is out of blossom
> Kissing is then out of fashion . . .

Clare can't get the rhyme out of her head. Her head has turned into a drum echoing it. And on this perfect afternoon she can't endure to be in the house, which is fusty for all her spring-cleaning, and dark, and dusty-windowed. She hurries downhill past the cemetery gleaming white and grey in the sun, each gravestone lapped with new grass. She skirts Porthmeor Beach, and on to the coast-path. The word *kiss* clings to her like a web she has walked through.

Dry kisses. The smell of her father's hair when she lets her lips rest on his fine-grained forehead. When she bends down over his chair arm to kiss him he looks up at her with unrecognizing, dark-pupilled eyes. He is always surprised by her touch, as if for a minute he doesn't know quite who she is. Kisses. Fierce kisses for Nan when she was little. Grappling Nan's black skirts to her, snuffing Nan's apron, scrubbing her head against Nan's waist. Grandad was never much of a one for kisses, but he liked to have Clare on his knee when he smoked his pipe, and he would let her fill it with tobacco for him. Her fingers were neat at tamping down the shag. She loved Grandad's tobacco pouch too, and he would let her unroll it and breathe in the dark, rich smell which was so much more fragrant than the smell of his burning pipe. But then she had to roll it up tight and not touch it again, for fear of the expensive tobacco drying out and losing flavour.

Kissing Hannah, when they pretended to be married under the mock-orange bush in Clare's back garden, then spitting and raging at Hannah who wouldn't take her turn as bridegroom, and who pummelled their crown of blossom to brown slime rather than let Clare have it. Hannah's raking nails left red stripes in Clare's white forearms, and Clare could not retaliate because she had bitten her own nails down to the quick. No one else had skin as white as Clare's. It went with her hair, they said, and she must mind herself and not get freckled or nobody would want to marry her. But even then it would be all right, because Nan could cure freckles with lemon juice.

Kisses. One hot afternoon when she was twelve and opened the door to the grocer's boy, John William. He walked past her, slapped their order down on the kitchen-table. First time they'd sent him up here. He'd always got out of it before, given the order to one of the other boys, taken a longer round and a heavier load rather than deliver rice and yellow split peas and suet to the Coyne house. The Coyne grocery order was not impressive, and he hated the thought of being sent to serve Clare.

There stood John William, thirteen already. This was the unfair time of the year when John William would seem to be a whole year older than she was, though the difference was only seven months. His face was impassive. His tan hid everything. And there was Clare, caught out in the middle of her washing, with her hands red and chapped from washing-soda. She hid them in her wrapper and said, 'Let me make you a cup of tea, John William.' If she'd had warning she'd have gone up and rubbed cold cream into her hands. She would have combed her hair too, for it was straggly and sticking to her forehead with the steam from the copper.

'I got to get on,' he said. He was beginning to be awkward with her, not only when he was with the other boys, but even when they were alone. He had grown so much this past year. He was well past her father's shoulder, and now he wore his black, soft hair in a side-parting and smoothed it down like a man. The bones of his face were strong. People thought he was older than he was; fifteen, or sixteen even. The shape of his cheek-bones was like Hannah's, but Hannah's face was softer, and fuller and her skin was not so dark. Their bones underneath would be the same, thought Clare. They would have the same skeletons. She was not sure if she liked her own difference from them, or if she was sorry for it.

'I've made some lemonade. It's keeping cool in the larder. Shall I fetch it?'

'All right.'

She went through the scullery and undid the larder door, where flies buzzed at the fine-mesh wire. Her lemonade stood covered on the slab. She poured a glass for him, and took a couple of squashed-fly biscuits out of the tin and put them on a plate. It seemed right now to treat him like a grown-up visitor. He always used to like squashed-fly biscuits. He was still standing by the kitchen-table when she came out. She pulled out one of the deal chairs for him but he would not sit down. He drank off his lemonade in long, smooth draughts. He was always neat as a cat in his eating and drinking. 'That's good,' he said.

He was thirteen, had just left school and was working full time at the grocer's for now. Errand boy but serving behind counter too, slicing cheese and sifting dry goods from sack to blue paper bags. She had seen him cutting cheese with wire, perfectly, but he did not look as if he was in his right place there.

'Better be going,' he said. 'I've got night-school. Got to get over there by seven.'

That night-school. It had rocked the small row of cottages where Uncle Arthur and Uncle Stan lived within a few doors of one another. Nan's was just round the corner, where the alley steepened: you could tell Nan's with your eyes shut because of the pot of sweet marjoram she kept by the doorstep. Everyone rubbed their fingers on the leaves before they came into the house. Uncle William's was further down the hill, with Aunt Mabel's just-perceptible mist of sluttishness on windows and curtains and doorstep. All of them had been fetched up to Uncle Arthur's to reason with John William, who had declared his intention of going to night-school to study. And nothing useful like book-keeping or arithmetic either. He was planning to study physics, chemistry and biology, if you please. He was going to take exams. He had been writing secretly, behind their backs, to places in London, about exams and qualifications. He had been uncovering those things which were mysteries to Aunt Sarah and Uncle Arthur. He was not going to follow Uncle Arthur into the drapery, though there would be a place made for him, and a small wage which would be all he could need, living at home. The whole family must gather.

'Let's hear if you're brazen enough to tell your Grandad to

his face how you're going to throw away everything we've worked for.'

He was. Mute and stubborn, playing his hand after years of keeping his cards hidden. He had watched them for a long while, weighing what it was worth, this life they led. He had been the brightest and the quickest of them all at school, doing sums for all the Treveal cousins, writing an impassioned essay on Mary Queen of Scots which earned him a bronze medal, a shilling, and the permanent mistrust of his parents. The other boys would have bullied him for his cleverness if he had not had a reputation as a wild, unpredictable fighter, calm for months, then suddenly lashing out and fighting until the other boy writhed and screamed out, and still he kept on until three or four of the other boys had to pull him off. He never rolled and wrestled behind the school wall as the other boys did. He went with Uncle Stan to bare-knuckle fights, held in secret with a look-out posted, in quiet hollows on the moors. He saw how one fighter danced and struck, blurring in the dazed vision of the other, then came in to strike again, splitting the skin under a man's eye, sending him blind with his own blood. He would fight like that. He concentrated, sitting tense and still, not noticing Uncle Stan and the other men crouched in their circle, making noises like dogs held back and dragging their leashes as the square of uncut corn grows smaller and smaller and the rabbits double back and forth inside it with stretched panicking eyes, and the men wait for the moment to let slip the dogs.

He would stay in the grocer's. He would earn money enough to give Aunt Sarah his keep. He would go to night-school. He would obtain qualifications. Weren't there all the others to go into the farm and the shop? Weren't they glad enough to go where they were told? Look at them. He counted on his fingers:

his brother Harry, Hannah, Uncle John's Albert, Jo and George, Uncle William's Kitchie.

Harry and Kitchie stood just inside the door in stockinged feet. Hannah had run down to the quay and fetched them up just as they were, raw from fooling about on the quay with the other lads. They had their boots in their hands. They looked and listened while the storm raged. Father crashed his chair back from the hearth. Grandad and Uncle Stan and Uncle William stood round him, holding him back. Mother shivered in the kitchen, secretly thrilled at the prospect of a discount on her groceries. Harry and Kitchie exchanged glances, wiped their hands on the backs of their trousers, and went back down to the quay. Best off out of it. And there'd be no shifting John William.

Clare had missed it all, at her music lesson, plonking out 'Für Elise'. The juice of it was related to her that evening by Hannah, but the great scene which would be embroidered and framed in family history over the years had an empty space where Clare ought to have been.

'Are you taking any exams this year, John William?' she asked timidly.

'I don't know enough for that yet,' he answered. 'But I shall.'

'Does Uncle Arthur know? Doesn't it cost a lot to take them? Father said it would.'

'I shall get it. I'll tell you something, Clarey. I've got money none of em know about.'

'Have you? *How* have you? Where did you get it?'

'I get a shilling a week more in my wages than they know of. I said to old Trevithick I'd do his books for him, when I saw all his figuring was wrong. I save it for fees. And Dr Kernack gave me a guinea. And I get given money – Christmas boxes. I don't tell em.'

Clare glowed, relaxing. This is how it used to be, with John

William telling her secret things he tells only her and Hannah.

'But why did Dr Kernack give you a guinea?'

John William hesitated. 'Keep a secret, now, Clarey? Don't tell a soul, not even Nan?'

'Swear to God.'

'Cos he knows what they don't know – what I'm doing it for. I want to be a doctor, Clarey. Course it's hard. I got to do better'n any of em in the exams. And I *can* do. Cos they're lazy, see. They don't want things enough – not like you got to want em. They don't know about really wanting. I can beat em all. Don't you believe it, Clarey?'

She looked at him. She believed it. John William had set himself like an arrow on this one thing, leaving no space for anything else, and leaving no space for it to fail to happen either. She had never thought in that way herself, about wanting things. She had only thought that you had what you had, and that was all. Now she realized that she was far behind him, and that it was no longer just because of the few months between them. But there was danger in wanting anything that much, and showing that you wanted it.

If he doesn't get it, it'll finish him, thought Clare, and she believed him.

'Only you'll have to talk like me, if you want to be a doctor,' she teased him, paying him back for the hundred times they'd all jeered at her for talking like a lady. She thought he would laugh at her again, but this time he didn't. He was thinking. His forehead tensed as he took in this one more thing he would have to consider. One more part of his plan.

'You can help me with that, Clarey,' he stated. His narrow eyes gleamed with amusement. 'I can listen to you while I'm scrattin over my books.'

'Just think. You might end up rich!' she half laughed.

He looked at her and saw her believing in him. There was Clare, not doubting that he could do it. His sore, lonely self-confidence yielded to her for a moment. He ducked his head, embarrassed to let her see how it moved him.

Was he cross? Had she said too much? She hovered, twisting her hands inside the coarse grey cloth of her wrapper.

'I'll be off, then, Clarey,' he said, and in a suddenly awkward flurry he was beside her and had leaned to kiss her warm white cheek. For a second he was so close she saw something she'd never noticed before: that the iris of his eye was rayed with black streaks and then there was a thin ring of black between the iris and white. He smelled of toffee and fresh air.

Clare remembered Nan's voice. How old had they been? Six or seven. John William hadn't wanted to kiss her when she was going away to Coyne with her father. 'Give your cousin a kiss, John William. Go on, nicely now. She won't bite you, will you, Clarey?' Everyone had laughed, and John William had stood frowning in his boots, hands behind his back, not kissing Clare.

Kisses. Just today, at dinner-time, Hannah panting at their front door, her face flaring dusky red under its usual clear brown,

'I've run all the way from our Nan's. We've had another letter. John William's coming home. Coming on the London train. Will you go with us to meet him?'

'What's taken him so long?' snaps out before she can stop herself. 'Oh, I'm sorry, Hannah! You know I'm glad really. But it's days since we had that last letter. What has he been doing?'

'I expect there were things he had to see after. Uniform and such,' says Hannah vaguely. 'Never mind that. He'll be on his way already. Quick, Clare! I've got to get back to the shop. I've had no dinner and I'm late as it is and we've a new customer coming to choose curtain stuff.'

Clare feels the heat of Hannah, standing so close, her pulse throbbing in her neck after her run uphill.

'Hannah – was there anything else – any news from Sam?'

Hannah frowns. Reluctantly she says, 'Yes. I had a letter yesterday.'

'Why didn't you say? You could have told me!'

'Wasn't anything to tell.'

Her face has shut. She turns to go, then turns back. 'Clarey. Uncle Francis gets the newspaper, doesn't he?' She fumbles for the words she wants. 'Course they can't put what's really happening into the newspaper, now can they?'

Clare thinks of the newspaper reports. Movements. Advances. Salients. The same names of ridges and fields and woods, repeated over and over again. And the lists, day after day after day.

FALLEN OFFICERS. ROLL OF HONOUR: LOSSES IN THE RANKS. *Missing Believed Killed, Seriously Wounded, Missing, Missing Believed Wounded, Prisoner in Enemy Hands, Died of Wounds...* Every shade of loss has its own category. But Hannah knows that. Column after column of names, spreading out from under the classified advertisements. And then a dispatch on another page about heavy enemy casualties, and a significant advance. Clare doesn't read the dispatches any more. They are just words which mean nothing. Father talks over the war news in the porch after Mass and it sounds like the same war news he was talking about two years ago. Except that it was new then.

'The dispatches don't tell you much,' she says, looking at Hannah carefully and choosing her words. 'You know how it is. You have to guess what they really mean. They can't put everything. What did Sam say in his letter?'

Hannah stands there, looking back at Clare. Calm, shrewd Hannah waits for something Clare can't give her. The air's gone quiet: that means the schoolchildren have gone in from their dinner play-time. Hannah bites her lip, waiting.

'Only I've never had a letter like that from Sam,' she says suddenly.

'What's he say?'

'He sounds all wrong. Not like him. I don't know.'

Kisses. Hannah and Sam, locked, melting, in the shadow of the harbour wall when Clare walks by to Nan's in the dusk. Hannah's back arched, Sam's lips on hers, his hands round her buttocks. And more than that. Clare shared Hannah's week of dread last autumn, after Sam went back to France and Hannah's *visitor* failed to arrive. Patches of crimson flaring on Hannah's cheek-bones as she slid past Clare in Nan's kitchen, hissing the good news, the relief of Mafeking.

'He sounded all wrong, Clare. And the letter – well, the letter didn't come from over there.'

'What do you mean?'

Hannah looks quickly up and down the road.

'Don't say a word.'

'I shan't.'

'It was posted in London.'

Clare is silent for a moment, slow-headed in the sunshine. Then she opens her mouth, bubbling with questions, but Hannah's turned with a switch of skirts and run off waving one hand, too far already to be called back. Already wishing she hadn't said so much. She wishes she hadn't told me, and Hannah's always told me everything.

Thank God to be away from it, away from fear and newspapers, away from letters which come too late and messages which nobody understands. Now there is not another human being in sight. Soon, John William will be here. Tomorrow morning he'll jump down at St Ives Station. He'll walk along with me and Hannah, and we'll talk. We'll be one on each of his arms. Everything will be clear again.

Clare is too hot in her plain white blouse and long dark skirt. She loosens her belt by a notch, and rolls up the sleeves of her blouse to the elbow. She has been tramping the cliff-path for over an hour. The dry turf echoes under her boots. She's turned her skirt over at the waistband to stop it from dragging in sheep and rabbit droppings. Anyway, skirts are shorter now. They have risen five inches since the beginning of the war, but not in St Ives. Even Hannah, who reads the fashion papers from London and can make up her own paper patterns, has only turned up her hems cautiously, for fear of Grandad. There are flappers in London, and all sorts of ungodly goings-on in London parks, according to Grandad. The Wesleyan Conference last year was forced to hear of some shameful goings-on in cinemas. But Hannah has other reasons for refraining from slashing off the bottoms of her skirts. You can't chop at your clothes and expect them to look right. You have to alter the whole proportion of the skirt. The girls pore over last month's *Tatler*, passed on to the drapery by the Veryan young ladies. They scan a cloudy, radiant picture of Lady Diana Manners making her début at Blenheim. Hannah looks minutely at her face and clothes.

'Butter wouldn't melt,' she remarks, as she snaps over the page.

Clare clambers up the worn, sandy middle of the path. The sun is so strong it oozes through the straw pattern of her hat brim. She'll just get up to the boulders, she thinks, then she'll stop and rest.

But she doesn't. She tugs her blouse out of her waistband and trudges on. She doesn't look at the cliff-edge on her right side, high and sheer now, deeply cleft with gorse and bramble tangling over the drop, above dark turquoise and purple water. She changes her canvas sketching-bag to her left shoulder and watches her boots as if they were someone else's, tramping on and on up the hot path, pebbles skidding away under them, puffs of sand and dust rising. Her ears are full of her own labouring breath and the pumping of her blood. She knows she's walking too fast. If she'd any sense she'd slow down to the easy swing which takes her ten miles without tiring her, the way her father taught her to walk on these cliff-tops and hills when she was five years old. But she can't slow herself down. The throb of the sun and the throb of her heart are the same thing. Hannah's face shifts and melts into John William's. Hannah's back arches, John William closes the kitchen door and leaves Clare alone with the flies buzzing in the larder.

Clare thinks of Lady Diana Manners, wide-eyed, flaunting herself. Parties and balls. Débuts, coming-outs. That is the language of her father's past, even though he doesn't speak it any more. She remembers Hannah flicking over the page, her face expressionless in its absolute withholding of respect.

Faces. What's mine like? Sweaty and hot. This hat is too tight. I'll have a dent in my forehead. Hannah's face. Could I draw it again? Might try, if she'd sit to me. I could tell her I'd do a sketch for Sam as well. John William's coming home tomorrow. His face.

Lists of names in long columns down *The Times* and the *Morning Post*, as long as columns of marching men. As many names as there are grains of sand in the sea.

She stops. The sea sighs. The long, sloping Atlantic swell

moves in at a diagonal to the cliffs. Today might be windless, but yesterday there was a strong south-westerly blowing up the dust in the streets of St Ives. The narrow land here is just a snag in the sea's passage. It's always trying to find a way through, thinks Clare, picturing the maze of passages under the cliff, and the sea fingering its way through from cave to cave, through membranes of rock. She knows of swimmers caught by the current, rolling in here puffed up and sodden white, bumping against the roofs of caves, splitting their swollen skins on projections of rock. It happens. Sometimes the sea wins. A boat wallows and breaks up in sight of the town. There are hymns on the edge of the sea, and a memorial stone. Nan ducks clothes in a vat of stinking, steaming black dye. Even white petticoats must be dyed black for decency. Dinners are brought in covered pails for the widow. The cost of the orphans' boots is shared among eight families. Nan lets her neighbour weep long enough, then tells her she must brace herself, have a cup of tea, think of her children.

There's a gap in the gorse here, and a patch of smooth, nibbled turf. A clump of thrift bobbles right of the lip of the cliff. Clare throws off her sketching-bag and lies face-down a few feet from the edge. She wriggles forward. Beneath her the sea booms into an undercliff cave, then sucks out. Close turf makes little pricks against her cheek. She hears the drowsy sound of a bee in clover. Clare's heart slows. She's dizzy with walking so fast. She lies under her hat in a small golden haze, hearing the sea drain from its chambers, then come in again. She can feel it right through the rock. She listens. The water shocks, withdraws, shocks, withdraws ... Too hot here. Drowsy herself, she rolls over –

'You're very near the edge,' a voice remarks.

Clare shoves her hat back and scrambles up on her knees. This sudden change of posture turns her dizzy. She has to look down and clutch the turf while the world heaves under her.

The man who has spoken from the path comes over to her swiftly. She feels his shadow cross her.

'Move back a little from the edge. You're very close, did you not know?'

A foreign voice, not from round here.

'I don't mind heights,' gasps Clare.

'Oh,' says the voice. 'So you thought you'd swank by going to sleep on top of the cliff?'

That's better. The swirl of black grains in front of her eyes settles into turf, minutely studded with pimpernel and speedwell. She curls her legs round carefully and sits up, smoothing her skirt over her knees. The man drops down beside her. She turns and looks at him.

Five

She sees lively, bright blue eyes looking straight at her. They
are piercing but homely too, because they remind her of Nan.
They are not the same colour as Nan's eyes, but they have her
warmth and quickness. Not many people ever look directly into
another person's eyes. They are frightened of what they may
find there. There are so many shuttered, timid eyes.

But his beard is astonishing. It juts from his face, wiry and
bright red, and then the sunlight catches it and it's all the
colours she'd never have thought human hair could be: threads
of orange and purple like slim flames lapping at coals. And yet
the hair on his head is so mild, smooth and mousy, lying flat
across his head and parted at one side. It doesn't lie very well. It
doesn't look elegant, like her father's parted hair.

'Where were you walking to?'

No, he's not from here. A foreigner. His 'you' is nearly a
soft, tender 'yer', but he's not Cornish. Nor London. Where
then? It's not an accent she's heard before. And yet his manner,
his whole bearing, is like a gentleman's. At least, it's like that
of a man who does what he chooses, and she supposes that
means he must be a gentleman. Uncle Stanley walks as if he
cares what the world thinks of him, for all his bulk and assertive-
ness. There is something quite different about this man. A sense
of freedom.

'I wasn't going anywhere,' she says. 'Just walking.'

'You should go on as far as the Carracks. There's rabbits sitting up, and a raven looking at 'em, wishing they were little juicy ones.'

'I know that part well. I've often walked there,' she says coolly, piqued again that this stranger should instruct her in her own landscape. How can he claim to know it as she does, when she has been walking these cliffs and moors and beaches since she was old enough to keep pace without whining at her father's heels?

'Are you staying near by?'

There. That'll show him she considers him merely a visitor. This is her own country. But he looks as if he believes the whole world belongs to him. He kneels on the close-cropped turf, perfectly at his ease. There are hollows under his flat cheekbones, but his eyes are brilliant. If he leaned forward just a few inches, their faces would touch. She ought to be nervous, but she couldn't possibly be frightened of this man.

'We're living up at Higher Tregerthen, near Eagle's Nest. D'you know it?'

She does. Only just at this moment she can't quite think exactly where it is . . . She screws her face up, thinking.

'Is that a part of the Hockings' farm? Lower Tregerthen?'

'It is, it's by there, just above the farm. But the cottage doesn't belong with the farm. We rent it from Captain Short, down in St Ives. I daresay you know him, too.' A little sardonic sideways look.

Oh. Yes. Now I know who you are. Or I think I do. You're the man they have all been talking about.

'Did you ever hear the like of it! Captain Short's got Germans staying up at Higher Tregerthen. They've taken his cottage. A great big German woman, by all accounts, shouting out at him in German just as if there wasn't a war on. They fight like two devils, not man and wife. And she wears red stockings, you never saw the like of them. And she's got this little bit of a husband with a big red beard. Queer-looking pair, aren't they, Mabel?'

'He looks like she found him in a Lucky Dip, that's what I say.'

Aunt Mabel and Aunt Mag exchange the smirks of women who have found themselves solid substantial husbands.

'All the same though, there are things not right up there. They say they've put different coloured curtains up. *In the same window.*'

'Why, whatever would they want to do that for?'

'*In the window looking over the sea.*'

'You mean –'

'Well, it could be, couldn't it?'

'Signals.'

'Out to sea.'

'Signalling out to sea.'

'The colours mean something. It's a code.'

'I heard –'

'U-boats. Signalling to those U-boats.'

Onlooking Stanley cuts in with authority: 'Three ships we lost in Febr'y between Land's End and St Ives, to those damned U-boats.'

'Stanley!' Nan's voice. 'We'll have no more of that language if you please, with the girls here.'

Stanley growling inside his chest. Wink from Aunt Mag.

'Lot of old nonsense anyway,' says Nan. 'Don't they say he works up at Hockings? Must be all right, then.'

'Free labour.'

56

'That's what they're like, you see, spies. It's in their nature. They get in with people. They get round them. If they weren't cunning-like, they couldn't *be* spies could they?'

'It's the Unseen Hand, that's what they call it. The Unseen Hand working for the Germans. Wasn't it in your paper, Stan?'

Stan says heavily, 'They make a mockery of us, her coming here in her red stockings, singing her German songs. Captain Short should never've let the place to em. And him in the Merchant Marine.'

Nan says nothing more. She whisks her scissors under a piece of navy-blue twill, measures, nicks in the first cut.

Hannah rolls her eyes at Clare.

'For God's sake, let's get out of here,' her face suggests silently. 'This'll go on all night.'

And out they go into the wet warm evening. The wind's blowing salt and ladders of rain pulse down the main street. Hannah links arms with Clare, and they run splashing.

It's just a lot of nonsense. But there's something ugly in it all the same, when the aunts and uncles get together, faces crowded and puffed up with that queer sort of excitement which made Uncle Stanley's eyes glisten and Aunt Mag's eyes like little bright buttons nipping glances from one face to the next, not missing a crumb of it. Clare had recoiled, as if it were something that would smear her if she got too close. They are predatory and a bit frightening, even though they are her own flesh and blood. Yes, they were like gulls circling, ready to plunge. And she'd felt as if she should join in too, cawing over the spoils, to show them that she was one of the family, never an outsider on whom they could turn and rip to pieces. But now she remembers how Nan hadn't joined in. She'd let them talk themselves out, watching with that little ironic reserved way she had.

Yes, Clare knows who he is now. But what can she say to him? She can hardly tell him that his name is all over St Ives, and that his wife's stockings are providing something for Uncle Stanley to pull his whiskers and pronounce over.

'Is it really true that your wife wears red stockings?'

'Say some German words so I can hear what they sound like.'

'Don't you know they're all talking about you?'

She can't say any of it, so she'll have to leave him innocent of the gossip which perhaps he ought to know. Anyway, he doesn't look as if he knows or cares what people think of him. And in blue daylight talk of spies and warnings seems to melt away and become ridiculous. He sits on the turf, relaxed in the sunshine. He's got all the time in the world to enjoy it and her company. His fingers feel blindly and gently at a red clover head. The bee that was feeding there has stumbled on to its next flower. He ruffles the tiny lipped segments of clover, then nods at her sketching-bag.

'You paint, then?' he asks.

'These are pencil drawings. And I do water-colours.'

'What do you draw?'

'Flowers, mostly.'

'Do you? May I see?'

In her turn she nods. He is not a person you want to refuse, when he looks at you with such warm, compelling eyes, and seems so interested. She sits still, hugging her skirt round her knees as he unbuckles the canvas straps and fetches out her sketchbook. She hands him the big, public botanical sketchbook, not her own private book. He flips the pages, quick and intent. She waits, her heart beating palpably, perhaps from the heat and the walk, perhaps because it seems to matter what this man thinks of her work.

'You can draw,' he admits, as if puzzled by something. 'This, look, this is fine.' He points to the corner of one page. It's a white foxglove she saw in a lane-bank. No good to Father, but she liked the shape of the bells lighting into flower, one after the next, up the steep stem. Yes, she agreed. It wasn't a bad drawing. She'd have liked to paint the foxglove. The nubs of closed buds were lovely to draw. She'd like to paint them, now that she understood their structure through the drawing.

'Then why don't you? You *should* paint. See, that little drawing is worth the rest of the book. Why do you draw *these* things?' And he points at drawing after drawing, careful, shaded, exact, attentive to the detail of nodes and stipules.

'I draw them for Father. They're for a book he's writing, a botany book, so they have to be accurate.' It sounds lame, even to herself. It sounds like a child talking, a child who has never got beyond wanting to please her father. Is she still a little girl coming in from her lessons to show her father a piece of work which she knows will be praised for its neatness?

'Yes, of course they have to be accurate!' he exclaims. 'But have you ever really looked at what you are drawing? You've looked at the outside, the part everyone can see. You haven't seen what it is *really*. See that bud there. Now how can you make me believe it's got anything inside it? It's empty – just a husk. You haven't drawn it as if it's got any life inside it. I don't mean you should be sloppy. But look!' He points at the small clump of sea-pinks stirring in the sea-breeze at the edge of the cliff.

'How can you look at that without wanting to draw it as if it's alive? See how long it is! Think how the roots must grip down deep into the turf, to keep it here through the gales. And it has a little frail flower bobbing right on the edge of the cliff. See how the stem gives way to the breeze. I should think it'ud lay itself down flat before the gales; but it would spring up again, as soon as the sun shone. Don't you admire it? Isn't there something courageous about it? Look how fine it is, all the time stirring with the wind so it shan't get knocked to pieces.'

Clare smiles. When she was little she used to pull heads of sea-pinks apart. The stems were so tough they bit into the tender palms of her hands. She knows what he means.

'See, now it lies right down, to protect itself. It's tough, really, not tender. Could you draw that?'

She shrugs. She feels a devil in her, to teach him something when he thinks he has everything to teach her. 'I could draw *you*,' she says.

He laughs, turning to her with delight, his eyes narrowing. His blunt stubby face is nothing special but for those eyes. Can she really draw them?

'I can, if you want me to.'

'I do.'

'Then move back a little. Like that. No – stop. That's enough. Now if you look down there, at that thorn-bush, and then keep your head just as it is. Good.'

He sits perfectly still while she takes her second, smaller sketchbook out of her bag, and an HB pencil.

'Shan't you need a rubber?' he teases. 'I hear all the girls at the Slade have bits of bread to rub out their mistakes.'

'Do you know any girls at the Slade?'

'I do, some of 'em.'

'Do you? What are they like?'

'Oh, you've a long way to go if you want to be a Slade girl. You'll have to get your hair bobbed and get rid of your Christian name. The girls call each other by their surnames there. And they live in diggings – should you like that?'

'Mmm.'

She's not really listening. She'd like to know all about it, but not now.

'It's all right,' she mumbles. 'Go on talking. It's better to draw you when you're talking.'

He falls silent.

She wants to get the whole pose. The lines of face and neck flow so naturally into the body. Light, thin limbs in green corduroy trousers. Head very upright and alert, a bit bird-like. But she mustn't overdo it and turn the drawing into a caricature. The corduroy is worn and soft, so that it shows the shapes of the limbs. The face has no good bones in it, and the hair grows oddly, flat and springy at once. You could so easily make the face common, even mongrelish. Yet it is so quick and alive. Even mischievous. In spite of all its faults of colouring and structure, it's attractive.

She draws on. It's coming. But it isn't quite right. She hasn't been drawing enough lately, and her line is not as fluent as it should be. Also, she knows he is right. She is out of the habit of looking, really looking closely. Perhaps because there are things she doesn't want to see. Shuttered eyes again, only this time shuttered so that they cannot look within. She is so many people; our Clarey, my Clare, cousin Clarey, Clare Coyne, the Treveals' Clare, poor dead Susannah's daughter. But inside she is none of them. Once she stood at her window and said her own name, over and over, 'Clare, Clare, Clare, Clare', until it meant nothing.

She's lost the bold, accurate line her drawing has at its best. Has she lost it through finicking at flower drawings? She frowns, tears her first sketch off the block, scrumples it, starts again. She would need to paint him, and not in water-colour either.

He ought to be painted in oils, to get the colour of him: the brilliant beard and eyes, the sunburn over his pallor. Behind him the sea, aqua and dark purple, wrinkling a little in the breeze. But she has no oils, and she doesn't understand the technique. There are so many things you can't get from books. The materials are too expensive for her, and Father would not think she needed them anyway. They would be of no use for colouring flower drawings. He likes her work to be meticulous rather than flowing and alive, as she would like to be. And like everyone she knows he is too easily impressed by her work. She knows that whatever talent she has is a curled up, deeply rooted thing. It has scarcely begun to unfold. She is not hard enough on herself, and no one is hard enough on her. There are so many things she doesn't know: technical things she tries to discover laboriously, from books. She flounders as she feels her way forward, and she wants criticism, not easy praise. But her father persists in believing that her botanical drawings represent the admirable sum of what she can achieve. This man doesn't, though. He is prepared to criticize and challenge her.

She sighs. 'It's not really finished, but I'll only spoil it if I go on.'

He stands up, his long thin legs stretching above her head where she still sits. He comes round to her side and kneels, looking at the drawing over her shoulder. He is so close that she can feel his breath on her neck. She shivers slightly and hopes that he hasn't noticed, but he is intent on the drawing. She lets the book lie open, and wonders what he'll make of it. She feels curiously unworried. It's as good as she can do.

He studies the drawing, picks up the book to look more closely. 'Will you give it to me?' he asks abruptly.

'If you like,' says Clare. Gently, she eases the page with the drawing on it away from the sketchbook's binding. 'You'll have to carry it as it is,' she says. 'I've nothing to wrap it in.'

But he's still looking down at her sketchbook. 'May I look through it?' he asks.

'No,' she says. 'This is just a private sketchbook. Drawings I do for myself.'

'I *should* like to see one or two,' he responds, almost wheedling, almost wistful. But she glances up and catches the comic look of determination on his face. Just because she won't let him! It makes him want the more. Clare smiles.

'There's one of my cousin Hannah you can see,' she says, and opens the book and riffles through to find the sketch of Hannah sewing at the Singer. It hadn't been easy to get Hannah to pose like that, frowning, concentrated, with all the strong moulding of her face exposed. It was the best she'd ever done of Hannah. No one had liked it, though. They thought it did not do Hannah justice.

He looks up at her and smiles delightedly, as if he has suddenly recognized her as a friend. Her mouth curls into an answering smile.

'It's very good,' he says. 'Did your cousin Hannah like it?'

'She didn't. If she had, I'd have given it to her.'

'You don't make her pretty, but you make me want to know her. What does she do, your cousin? Is she a schoolteacher?'

'No, she works in my uncle's drapery. And she does dressmaking. She's very good at it. She wants to do more, but my uncle needs her in the shop.'

He looks closely at Hannah's face. 'She reminds me of a girl I used to know. Not that they're alike – but there's a look of her.'

Clare closes her book. She feels he has stared at Hannah long enough.

'I *should* like to know her,' he repeats, with the same wistful persistence.

'I don't suppose you shall,' says Clare briskly.

'Will you sign my portrait for me? You know it adds to the value when it's signed by the artist.'

He's laughing at her, but she doesn't mind. 'Then I will,' she says. 'And when I'm famous you can sell it and make your fortune.'

'So I can.'

She takes the drawing back, about to sign it, then pauses. 'I ought to write your name too.'

'You should. Put *D. H. Lawrence*, by . . .?'

'*Clare Coyne*. But I can't put D.H. It won't look right. I need your full name.'

'It's David Herbert.'

She writes carefully, *David Herbert Lawrence, by Clare Coyne, May 1917.*

'There. But what do they call you? David or Herbert?'

'My wife calls me Lorenzo. My friends call me David, or Lawrence. My sisters call me Bert. My enemies call me – '

He breaks off, his face laughing but half savage. Clare hardly notices: she's too much intrigued by the name his wife calls him.

'Does she? Why does she? I mean – she's German, isn't she, not Italian?'

A mistake, she knows at once. A bad mistake. His face closes over.

'Yes, my wife is German. Her name is Frieda. That means *peace*. Do you understand German?'

'No.'

'This foul talk,' he says. 'I suppose the town is stewing with it.'

'Not as much as that,' she says quickly, stung by the contempt in his voice when he speaks of the town. It was as if he'd seen Aunt Mag's babbling eyes himself, and heard Uncle Stan turning over the dirty business of the Lawrences in his big, raw fists.

'Because my wife is a German. Because she is a von Richthofen. And we want to live alone, to ourselves.'

She recognizes the pride in his voice when he says his wife's family name. She's familiar enough with that pride herself. Her father talking of the Coynes, affecting to laugh at what they stand for, gently mocking their enclosed, inturned world of Coyne Park and Coyne village, yet something in him always unhappy until strangers know of Coyne, and where he comes from. But surely there is nothing to be proud of in a German name? The name is familiar too. It has a newspaper ring to it. Where has she come across it?

'I'm sorry,' she says, 'I didn't mean . . .'

He has half turned from her, looking out over the sea. Behind him, looking north, the dark deeply folded land, the edge of the world itself, wrinkled and looking westward to America. He would like to go there. Southwards the land narrows, creaming with surf even in calm weather. There is so much more sea than land, and so much more sky than sea. The sky's perfect blue thins to lavender at the horizon. The sea breathes calmly, its back to the land, lapping, fulfilled.

It is wonderful to have your back to the land, to the whole of England: to have your back to the darkness of it, its frenzy of bureaucratic bloodshed, its cries in the night. It is heaven to have your back to the long gun-resounding coast of France, echoing against the white face of England. To have your back to this madness which finds a reason for everything: a madness of telegrams, medical examinations and popular songs; a madness of girls making shells and ferocious sentimentality. That blackness is behind him now, and he will not turn round to be trapped by it. It is a slow stain of nightmare, seeping into human minds and hearts. He refuses to let it contaminate his heart. He will keep his eyes turned to the West, towards the light and the place where the sun is going.

He falls silent. How much has he said? The girl beside him is frightened-looking, her lips parted.

'You're a writer, aren't you?' she asks.

'Yes. I am.' The words are brief, but he does not sound angry any more.

'Could you tell me . . . could you tell me what sort of thing you write?'

'What sort? Ah, now there's a question. It's lucky you asked me and not the men who review my books.'

Yes, the anger has really gone, just as if the sun has poured out from behind a cloud. What a face he has! She would like to draw it again, as it is now. She says boldly, 'You know what I mean. Faces or botanical drawings?'

He puts his head back and laughs, and his red beard glistens. 'Faces! Faces every time. And the likenesses are too good, so folk hate 'em, just as your family hates your portraits. How they hate them! They'd like to burn them all up, and me with them. Oh, you'll meet the book-burners yet, Clare Coyne, and the picture-burners, if you go on drawing. Some of them do it so nicely – it breaks their heart to set a match to you, but for your own sake they've got to do it, don't you understand? And all the time they're looking at you like a dog does when it wants to bite your leg but it daren't. Then there are the others who don't pretend.'

He is still laughing, but she shivers.

'It sounds horrible,' she says. 'Why have they got to be like that?'

'Don't you pretend you don't know, Clare Coyne. There's nothing you couldn't see if you wanted to.' He taps the sketchbook as if it contains his evidence. His eyes brighten, daring her.

'I must go,' she says, glancing up at the sun. 'I have to cook the dinner and the rabbit's not skinned yet.'

'Rabbit!' he exclaims. 'You'll make a rabbit stew, I suppose?'

'I will. It's a tender young'un, it won't take much cooking. It'll eat soft as butter.' Unconsciously her voice drops into the tones of her cousin Kitchie, who'd brought the rabbit that morning, banging limp and warm against his britches.

'Do you keep house for your father?'

'I have done since I was ten,' she answers.

'Coyne. That's not a Cornish name, I think?'

'It's my father's name. He's from London – Somerset, really. But my mother was Cornish.'

'Was she? You don't look it. The Cornish are soft, dark people – aren't they? Like your cousin Hannah.'

Soft, dark, stubborn Hannah.

'Yes, Hannah's pure Cornish,' she agrees. 'She's never been north of Bodmin.'

'And you have?'

'I've been to London. Twice. And to Coyne, to see my Uncle Benedict and my Aunt Marie-Thérèse.'

He scans her. Dark red hair. White skin. 'You might be Irish. Or Scots? Are you Scots?'

'My great-grandmother was Irish. I'm like her, Father says.'

He frowns. What is it now? Doesn't he like the Irish? And yet he fires up at a word against the Germans.

'So you're a lady, Miss Clare Coyne,' he says. 'A lady who skins rabbits. I must tell Frieda. She'll like that. I wish I could get Frieda to skin a rabbit, but no, she's such a swell she can't even put on her own stockings.'

An image flits into Clare's mind. She sees Lawrence kneeling, rolling Frieda's red stockings up her legs past her knees. Frieda's legs will be white and strong, more womanly than Clare's own. But there's a blank disc where Frieda's face should be.

'You'll come and visit us?' he asks suddenly. 'Come to tea. Come next Tuesday. Frieda will like it. She ought to know more women – she knows no women here.'

'Is that sufficient recommendation – the fact that I'm a woman?'

'And the drawing,' he reminds her. 'Don't forget, I've got that. So you'll come?'

She hesitates, then, 'I could call in for butter at Lower Tregerthen too,' she agrees.

He nods, and looks back over the moor. 'I've never seen anything so beautiful as the gorse this year,' he says.

She watches him walk away. He is a queer figure with his thin legs and corduroys. He is quite different from anyone else she has ever met. She has met so few people who live out in the world. Father is always saying that she meets no one, as if he regrets it. But does he mean people like Lawrence? She smiles. Next time she will get him to tell her about the girls at the Slade. And his books. She would like to know much more about his books. She shades her eyes, and looks after him. He is holding the rolled-up drawing carefully, as if he values it. He walks away fast and lightly, raises his hand to wave, then disappears into a fold of the land.

Six

Thursday

Hannah is angry with me because I did not go with them to meet John William. They did not expect Father to be there at the station. They know he will call later this evening, with a present of cigars for John William. Nan and Aunt Sarah and Aunt Mag have boiled a ham and made gooseberry tarts and cheesecakes. I did not help them. I had my baking to do here. Now Nan will be putting aside pastry crust and ham scraps for Uncle John's pigs while Aunt Mag and Hannah wash the dishes. Aunt Sarah won't be in the kitchen. They'll have shooed her out into the front-room, so that she can sit in the wing chair by the fire and watch John William. It won't matter to Aunt Sarah what he does, or whether he talks to her or not. As long as she can sit there and watch him being alive. She knows how easily it might have been us crowded into the front parlour to receive visits of condolence, with the smell of black dye bubbling from the kitchen. How thin it is now, and how easy to cross, that line between being dead and being alive. Grandad doesn't understand it like Aunt Sarah does. He's sure that the Lord will look after John William. Every night he says the Psalm of Protection for him: 'A thousand shall fall by thy side, and ten thousand at thy right hand; but it shall not come nigh thee . . .' I love the words, but how can they charm bullets and shells? How many people are praying them? Thousands, I should think. All hoping that others will fall on the left side, and the right side, and their own will be safe. But I do light candles for him. I would give him a badge of the Sacred Heart if I thought he would wear it.

Grandad will sit at the other side of the fireplace, drinking in every word of John William's, so he can go down to the quay and smoke and retell it 'fresher than the newspaper and more truth in it'.

Kitchie will interrupt with questions. Albert and Jo and George will lounge in one by one, darkening the room, waiting for John William to come out with them. Everyone knows they'll take a drink, but as long as nothing's said, nothing's questioned.

Hannah and I stroked the cloth of his uniform when it was new and stiff, when we said goodbye and I kissed him but he wasn't looking at me. He was looking over my head at Uncle Arthur and Aunt Sarah and the boys and all the family milling on the station platform. I could not read the look on his face. Then Nan slid another packet of sandwiches into his kitbag, and I stepped back. He smiled at me then, and winked, and made us a secret world for a second, like we've always had. I wonder what his uniform is like now. He will have to have a new one if he's going to be an officer. The old one will smell like Sam's letters, muddy and frightening. When someone is killed, they send his uniform home with mud and blood still on it.

Nan will let John William smoke in the house tonight instead of making him go out on to the street. The front-room will smell of smoke and food and elderflower cordial. In two years' time they'll call Kitchie up, and we'll never get exemption for Kitchie, even though he's the only one Aunt Mabel managed to rear.

She stops and frowns at what she's just written. It sounds coarse, like a farm diary. She raises her pen to score it through, then sighs and leaves it as it is. It's true. Draw faces, not flowers, Mr Lawrence said. A blob of ink falls on the page and spreads.

John William is very brown, they say. Hannah was shy of him when he

stepped down off the train. He was like a stranger, so dark and broad.
He's weathered like Albert and Jo and George now, only it's not from
farm-work, and he's grown a 'tache. He's handsome now, Hannah says. I
hope she didn't notice how surprised I was. Didn't she think he was
handsome before? His face has changed too, Hannah says, but she couldn't
tell me how.

'You ought to have come and met him for yourself, Clarey. He asked
where you were.'

Did he? Or is that just Hannah saying it, knowing I want her to say
it?

'I'll go tomorrow,' I said. 'I didn't want to crowd him, that first
hour. There are so many of us.'

'How could there be too many of us?' asks Hannah. 'You're family,
aren't you?'

I couldn't say to Hannah that I wanted to be the only one. I wanted
the train to stop, and the steam and smoke to billow round us as John
William stepped off the train and folded me tight in his arms, tight, so
tight I couldn't feel anything but him, so close I couldn't see anything but
him.

My cousin is back from the war. There. Do I feel something? I
should. I could walk down the hill in five minutes and look through
Nan's geraniums in the windows and see him. I could lift the latch and
Nan would fetch me a plate of cold ham and call through, 'Here's your
cousin come, John William! It's Clarey!'

Here he is, close enough to touch, eating gooseberry tart.

No. He isn't really ours any more. He won't be ours as long as
the war lasts. He doesn't belong to us now, he belongs to the war. Even
when the men are wounded they aren't allowed to come home, not if the
war still thinks it can use them. Even if they are dead they can't come
home. The war takes care of it all. We never see the dead men coming
back, and it's so hard to believe in what you never see. Mrs Hore told

me she still expects to see her William coming down the street. She thinks she hears his step in the entry. He had his own way of whistling under his breath as he fiddled with the latch-string. If only she could have seen him in his coffin, she says, she would be able to stop listening for him.

Can they make enough coffins for them all? How many coffins, and who makes them? The chaplain wrote and told Mrs Hore that William had his rosary beads twisted around his rifle butt when they found him. Father O'Malley encouraged all the men to do that, so they would have their rosaries with them, whatever happened. They would have two essential things by them, their rifles and their rosaries. William was killed instantly, Father O'Malley wrote. Mrs Hore said it was good of him to write and tell her that. It set her mind at rest. She knew William hadn't suffered. But I wonder. Sam says they always write it. Shot through the head, or shot through the heart. Then Sam said something I can't forget: 'We pick up what we can find, enough to make a decent burial.'

William Hore made his First Communion with me, but he wasn't very holy.

Who made me? Why did God make me?

I should not be writing this. I should keep it shuttered. I'll have that dream again.

I won't go down to Nan's with Father. I can see John William tomorrow, after he's had a night's sleep. It'll be quieter then, and I'll see him alone.

Clare blots the page, shuts up the book, then leans forward with her elbows on her little desk. The desk is set in the bay window of her bedroom, looking out over the sea and the long flank of the cemetery. The sea is dark, wrinkled by a cool evening breeze. It is bald and empty. The war again. But long before the war, things had changed. She's heard Grandad talk of the drift-boats coming into St Ives from the herring fishery on the Irish coast. The *Agenora* fell in with a shoal of pilchards on her way back, and brought in twenty thousand, so he heard tell, for even Grandad wasn't born then. There are no catches like that these days. The seas have run dry.

Grandad told her it was more than fish they brought back from Ireland. They'd go ashore there to buy and sell, and this time they brought back some old clothes from a woman who was selling them cheap. But she didn't tell the fishermen why she wanted to sell them. Her son had died of cholera, and the clothes were full of disease. So our boats came back not knowing what they brought with them and spread cholera to the people of Newlyn, so that a man in perfect health could eat his breakfast, say goodbye to his wife, go out to his work, and be dead by nightfall.

'This is the blue cholera I'm speaking of,' said Grandad.

And the people were so fearful that they ran away, leaving the sick on the ground to die alone. A man would leave his wife, and a wife would leave her husband. The whole country was bent down with bad news like a field of wheat under the wind.

'They would publish lists of the dead on the walls, and there were midnight funerals with hearses going through the streets at midnight to keep the disease from spreading.'

'Why was it called blue cholera?' asked Clare.

'For a good reason. It turned a man blue, see, before he died. It was the way the disease worked in a man's body, and it was a terrible thing to watch.'

'You wouldn't leave me and Nan, would you, Grandad, even if we turned blue? You wouldn't run off from us?'

'Ask God to spare us that trial, Clarey.'

That was just like Grandad. He clung too close to the truth to give her easy assurances.

'Ask God to spare us from trials and temptations, Clarey.'

Grandad did not like the Irish. But she had to like them, for she was part Irish herself. How could she dislike part of herself?

But when you think of it, cholera was nothing to the war.

'A thousand shall fall by thy side, and ten thousand at thy right hand.' A thousand thousands, and yet we don't run away. Anyway, there is nowhere to run. Everything stays so calm, as if we could go on like this for ever. We don't have burials at midnight to hide the numbers of the dead, because we don't have any funerals at all. Not here. We're not supposed to pray for the war to end. We're meant to pray for victory. The boys go out to France just as they used to go off on the drift-boats, or down the tin-mines, or to work on the farms. They all go: Medlands and Pascoes, Vivians and Trethakes, Popes and Mawgans. A whole landscape of family faces crushed into thin black lines, so dense you could not read them but that your fear and curiosity made you read them. You looked out for local names. What was cholera compared to the emptiness of the sea, the quiet streets, and the clumsy-booted young men, first time away from home, entraining and vanishing through the foggy curtain of war. We don't know what's happening behind that curtain. There's a silence which all the yammering headlines can't break.

Clare thinks of the train journey she loves, from London to Penzance. Drowsing and jogging through the heavy green fields of Devon. Then the bright red sea-cliffs at Dawlish, and waves breaking nearly on to the line. As you crossed into Cornwall you seemed to go through a curtain of light. You were sealed away from darkness and soot-smells and tall crowding buildings. Even the smoke of the train seemed to blow sideways whitely and buoyantly. You were safe and nothing could snatch you back.

But since conscription the trains had been going north and east heavily laden with boys off fishing-boats and farms and shops. It's taken a long time for the war to get down to them, but it has managed it at last. The war's long fingers can winkle a boy out of a lonely cottage on Bodmin Moor just as easily as it can pluck one out of the Manchester mills. There's nowhere safe from trains and telegrams and call-up notices. There are medical examinations held at Bodmin. Classifications. There's a class for everyone, no matter what the shape of your body or its powers and aptitudes. If you have two arms and legs, the war can make something of you for its purposes. Fit for active service. Fit for light duties. Fit for non-military duties.

IS YOUR BEST BOY IN KHAKI?

As for the dead, Clare has seen none of them. There would not be enough room for them in the graveyards, and they are as near to heaven in Picardy as they could be in the long sea-resounding graveyard of St Ives. So don't mourn because there is no funeral.

I'm one of the lucky ones. I haven't lost anyone. Well, no one close.

The fingers of the war are pulling harder. They are after Harry now. They want to reclassify him, in spite of his weak arm. *Combing out*, it's called. Like combing lice out of hair. Kitchie is still too young for them. Albert and Jo and George were too quick for them. Before enlistment gave way to conscription Grandad had seen the way the wind was blowing. He and Uncle John conferred late into the evenings. George was a coast-watcher already, and now Albert and Jo volunteered. Food-producers, coast-watchers, patrollers, they had kept their exemptions so far. And how could the land be worked without them? The country must have food.

The names of Tribunal members were common coin to Grandad. He knew them all, weighed them, judged them. This one was envious; that one fair but hard. This one had a prejudice against farmers keeping their sons on the lands. That one might be bribable. Uncle John, Uncle Arthur and Uncle William listened to Grandad. Gifts of vegetables, butter, cheese, ham, were driven in from the farm. Uncle Stan, sonless, boomed and schemed on behalf of the rest of them. But how long could it go on now that all that mattered was more bodies for the Front?

Grandad curses himself now for not thinking so far ahead with Harry. Now they are saying that Harry has got sufficient use of his arm. And it is only his left arm. Harry must come up to Bodmin again for a more thorough examination. The war gets hungrier and hungrier the more we give to it, thinks Clare. It is like feeding a dog which has worms.

Downstairs Francis Coyne drinks Burgundy. The wine flushes pleasantly through his body, and he reaches out to pour himself a second glass. He has spent the afternoon in Newlyn, where he goes twice a month to fuck neat plump-bodied May Foage. Tuesday or Thursday is his day: he writes her a note beforehand. He walks from Penzance Station past the harbour wall with its slopping green water and blocks of dumped limestone exposed at high tide, and then down the beach road to Newlyn. All the time he walks he thinks of fucking, loving the word for it and the anticipation of it. Under her black skirt and white petticoat she wears no drawers on the day he visits. What he likes is to be let into her white, tight little house, to look at her for a long moment, with her hair knotted smoothly at the back of her neck and her broad white forehead and cheeks unlined, placid, giving nothing away, and her two feet firmly planted on the bit of Turkey carpet he got her second-hand as a sign of her respectability. Then he sits down in her one armchair, and she perches herself on his knee, proper and neat and upright, and his left hand circles her waist while his right feels up her plump white calves (for she has taken off her stockings too) and up her thighs, which he knows have a subtle tracery of blue veins on their insides, and up to knot themselves in her mazy pubic hair. Her head hair is as smooth and brown as a salmon-river, he thinks. And on he slips into the secret moist cleft of her body, with its folds of skin that suck and hold his finger. He loves her childless tightness and springiness. She sits there through it primly, a woman in black perched on his knee, tucking in a smile.

She has no husband. She had one once who made her Mrs Foage, but he is no more. She is nothing so definite as a widow, nothing so weak as a deserted wife, but her husband is perfectly absent. By gift or charm she has no children, nor does she show any sign that she has ever wanted them. She has other visitors, but he never sees them. She is modest in what she asks for, and modest in how she asks for it. After one brisk, business-like conversation, the subject of money has never had to be reopened. They both know where they stand. She knows how investments are, these days. And long ago she was a St Ives girl and went to school with Susannah Treveal. It gives her pleasure to draw Susannah's gentleman husband into her house. It gives him pleasure to think of the two little girls with their moist clefts still as tight as almonds, pattering to school and pattering

77

home again, not knowing that one day he would have them both.

And he has May Foage. He has her more than he ever had Susannah in her white, startled night-dresses. Sly, neat, fuckable May in her blacks. He has licked May's breasts; he has bitten her shoulders. She has rocked him, and he has heard the waves pouncing on the beach outside her cottage, as he arches over her broad, white, spread buttocks, spread open for him. How delicious she is, jouncing beneath him; how shrewd in her passivities, how nimble in her accommodations. He swirls the wine and thinks of May's cleverness. His occasional occasion of sin. He drinks the wine, and it slides along his veins, leaving them sunlit.

And here he is, home again, waiting for the tea (which he doesn't want) to be brought to him by Clare, who probably doesn't want to bring it either, since he has just heard her coming downstairs as if reluctantly, stopping on the landing, looking out, no doubt, as she does. Better not have another glass. Here she comes.

My daughter Clare. Pale face, dark dress in the doorway. Her face is mute and closed in on itself, as she puts down the tea-tray and moves off. She's incurious. She never asks me where I've been on Tuesdays or Thursdays, twice a month. I have never had to lie to Clare.

'What are you doing today, Father?'

'I'll be out most of the day, Clare. But I'll be home for dinner. I may go over to Newlyn.'

Does she smell May Foage on me? When I come home I drink wine without washing my hands of May's juices. Then I drink tea and go upstairs and pour water into the bowl in my room and soap my hands with the cheap yellow soap which is all Clare can get now.

They say the Germans are making soap out of the cadavers of fallen soldiers. They need the fat from them. *Kadaverfabriken* have sprung up secretly to process the corpses. It was preached against at Mass. I say nothing. I know the glee of an evil imagination.

My pale daughter Clare goes out of the room. She is not pretty today. Her features are shrunken, small and tight as they were when she was angry as a child, or when she was unhappy. She drops her eyelids, makes herself absent. She has her own thoughts. Thank God that we each have our own thoughts and that we can live secretly even in this small house. Clare cannot see the marks of May's hands and teeth on me. She does not hear the cries and sweet succulent noises I hear.

'Clare!' he calls, a little too loudly, his voice like a seagull's in the small brown room. 'Clare! Will you come down with me now and see your cousin?'

A small collected pause, and her voice from the kitchen, little and purposeful, 'No, Father. Hannah has lent me a new dress pattern until tomorrow. I'm going to alter my green silk. I shall see John William tomorrow.'

Her green silk. Poor child, she doesn't need to specify the colour. She has only one silk dress. He has done nothing for her. Her hands are red with housework, and they rasp when she touches silk. While he is out, she will spread her green silk on the kitchen-table, cut it, remodel it according to Hannah's pattern, sew it again. She will be well pleased with what she achieves. All last evening she was unpicking the gathers at the waistband.

It's the war, he consoles himself. It's the same for all the girls. They have never known anything else.

He ought to have been able to buy another silk dress for his daughter, to make her beautiful. But look at Hannah, she has no silk dress at all, and she manages. Yes. Her brave blue and white stripes are upended as she opens her body to Sam. The white thighs of May Foage and Hannah Treveal flex and shine. It is May, the month of May. Mary's month. He remembers Coyne and his sisters dressing their May altars, fitting more and more flowers into tiny silver vases in front of the statue of Our Lady. And he already ironic, but still liking to see them at it, liking the flush of solemnity of their cheeks, and their smooth parted lips wondering if it was beautiful enough yet, and the way they ducked and kneeled in the chapel, adorning, adoring. His thoughts widen, covering Clare, putting a new silk dress on her, grey to match the slate of her eyes, putting her in mantilla and dark gloves, folding her hands in prayer. Her hands would be smooth and white under kid gloves, her body would be hidden and quite unimaginable.

'And a pious ejaculation to go with it!' says Francis aloud, scorning himself. He picks up the box of cigars for John William. He takes up his hat and goes out, calling goodnight to Clare, glimpsing through the kitchen door his resourceful girl nipping and tucking at her old green dress in the pale May evening light.

Seven

Zennor church door creaks and opens. Outside, the unusual May heat simmers. It is noon and quiet. Dogs lie in the dust. Butterflies skim gravestones and the pointing finger of shadow on the sundial to the left of the church porch is sharply distinct. *The Glory of the World Passeth*, it says. Lawrence stops to look up at it, notes the name of the sundial-maker. Paul Quick.

He enters the cool porch, and then into the church smell of wood and stone and darkness. He knows where he is going. He walks up the aisle, turns right, kneels to touch the carving of Zennor's mermaid. She floats, round-bellied, arms raised, innocent above the curve of her tail. Her fins flick and scull. He traces the carving of breast and navel. How fine she is. He is surprised that they have not put her out of the church, or gashed her into decency with axe and chisel. They have tried to hurt her, but she lifts her hands blithely above the scars. She belongs here. She is dark and smooth as the little madonnas he's seen in Bavarian wayside shrines, and she is as faceless as they are. Her body is like a sea-wave, a crest which will never break.

The church smells of its own sunlessness, as churches do. He gets up from her side and goes out, leaving the door ajar so that sweet air can blow in and ruffle the May flowers on the altar. He'll go to the farm now and help with the furze-cutting, then tonight he'll give Stanley his French lesson. He pushes down the thought of Frieda left alone, restlessly writing, restlessly reading.

*

When the wind blows hard at night, the cottage door bursts open under its pressure, and the rain slashes in across the floor, bringing darkness and the noise of the sea. I think I hear the friends of my childhood and all the young soldiers of Marienbad who marched past our garden walls to the parade-ground. My sister Nusch and I would throw apples and pears down among the marching men, to see their perfect lines falter as the soldiers scrambled for the fruit. Now they are gone, swallowed up like all the other thousands upon thousands, and I am here on the farthest outside edge of a country which hates me. I can do nothing. I am the Hunwife. The darkness is alive and wild. A south-westerly gale bangs the waves against the base of the cliffs with a sound like gunfire. I force the door shut and look around the safe, violated room. The walls are pale pink, glowing, and the furniture we got so cheaply at Benny's Sale Rooms in St Ives is so beautiful. And yet no one wanted it. But for us it makes a home. How many more homes will we have to make? Spreading out shawls on ugly chipped chests, bargaining for furniture, hanging embroidery on the wall, finding china for sixpence to put on the dresser. Such queer, beautiful bits of china, none of them matching. The bowls with peacocks on them. I tell Lorenzo that we are gypsies, and I laugh and make a joke of it, and he believes me when I say that I don't mind it.

I think about growing up in Metz. Those white dresses we had, and our stiff-sided boots, and the hats which could never crush down my hair. There was so much of it always, springing out and curling. Like a lioness, my mother said. She called me her little lioness and she said white didn't suit me. But never mind, I would wear colours when I was grown up. Then, when we went out to walk around the garrison, my big sister Else held my hand and told me to keep close to her and walk with small steps, but I could not. Something inside me made me break out and run. If I tore the lace on my petticoat, I would throw it to the floor and kick it into the corner of the room for my maid to find and mend.

Then we were at the court of the Kaiser. We were the daughters of the Baron von Richthofen, Nusch and Else and I, and so we must talk in this way, and dress in this way, and laugh in this way. So stiff – such nonsense! – I never cared for the Kaiser. But my cousins I loved, my bold cousins with their jokes and teasing and their brilliant uniforms. They would come into a room and the air would seem to dance round them. And now when I hear of the U-boats sunk and Germans killed, I think of them all, not skating or dancing or buying flowers for us any more, but men at war, as stern and stiff as even the Kaiser would have wanted.

So I read the *Berliner Tageblatt* and scour up and down the lists of the dead, but when I have finished I hide it under a cushion or the whole day will darken for me each time I see it. I will not let the war do that to our life. So many good things come each day. I was ill – I was in such pain I could not move out of my bed. And now I am quite well again and I can walk on the cliffs, five miles, six miles, and come home and eat the pea and ham soup which Lorenzo has made. There are so many good things each day.

Only, the children. I am not fit to see my children, they say: only for half an hour in a solicitor's office with a clerk coming in to tell me when it is time for me to go. When I gave each of the children ten shillings, my husband took it from them and sent it back to me.

'You left them. You chose to leave them. You preferred to abandon your own children rather than give up *that man*. Now you must live without them.'

He would like me to die without seeing my children again. Monty and Barbara and Elsa. They have grown so much. If I held out my arms, they would not fit there as they used to do. I think of them at night, if Lorenzo is down at the farm and I'm alone. Have they gone to bed yet? Are they sleeping, or are they lying awake too, staring at the dark and imagining they see faces in it? Do they see my face? Or do they see nightmare faces and cry out for me in the dark, and I never come?

I wrap myself in the Paisley shawl Lorenzo bought and mended for me. He mended it so patiently. It was a cobweb of rents and tears, but it only cost sixpence and he saw that he could make it beautiful for me. He is late again. If he was here he would be moving around the room, quick and deft, heating some milk and chiding me for my laziness. I would play the piano, and sing, and he would sit in that chair with his head thrown back, listening to me, eyes half shut. But he is down at the farm again, laughing with William Henry and Stanley.

The Hockings are not comfortable when I come down to the farm. The talk and the laughter stop as I open the door. William Henry stands up. They do not know how to treat me, for I am a lady and a foreigner and not one of them, and yet I live in a labourer's cottage which they would not live in. Even Lorenzo looks at me across that farm kitchen as if I do not belong. So I don't stay long. I say goodnight and lift the latch and walk out into the darkness, and as I go I hear laughter and talk spurt up again, the way it always does when he is there. The yard is cool and I can smell the cattle crowding up to the field gate. I walk up to the cottage, and look down at the long slope of the fields, and the sea with the stars coming out over it.

At least there are no dark shadowy rooms leading off this one. There is only this one little pink room, with its low boarded ceiling and boxy staircase going up the wall opposite the fireplace. One warm lit room and then the window looking westward towards America. Wind and space and strangers. No Katherine next door any more. The Murrys did not like it, for it was too wild for them.

We made a home for them here. We willed them to like it, but they would not. Never shall I forget Murry squatting on the bit of rough grass outside their cottage, painting black the kitchen chairs we had bought for him, as if it were a funeral, while Katherine settled her things so that she could write. But she could not, she told me: she could not stand the way the wind blew, and the rain slashed at her ankles every time she went out. How she made me laugh! It made me feel I had never had a woman friend here in England, a real woman friend I could tell things. No one tells stories like Katherine, Lorenzo said. Before they came, he thought it was all beginning. He wrote letter after letter, talking about 'Katherine's tower'. We would be able to start the community he is always dreaming about. Well, I did not care so much about that. But I cared for Katherine: she was so fine, and small, and she made us laugh and forget the war.

It was hard for Lorenzo. Before they came here he found the cottage for them, and helped them to furnish it. He scrubbed the floors for them, and bought iron pans for their cooking. Katherine does not like to cook. She is like me, always half expecting to turn round and find a maid has slipped into the room to tell her that it is time for dinner.

Now he has shaken off his disappointment, as he does. He knows that he will never build his community here, his dream of Rananim. The Murrys could not stand it and who could blame them? This is not the place for them. Katherine talked of Bandol, and the smell of almond blossom. Here it rained all the time, and Katherine was cold, and the fires smoked and the lanes were full of farm mud. Lorenzo and I fought every day. I saw Katherine's face when we fought, when Lorenzo chased me around the table and hit me and called me a hussy and said he would make me scrub floors on my knees. I fought as hard as he did. He never got the better of me. But Katherine did not understand it; she would go away without speaking.

They would not stay. Lorenzo raged against them for weeks, but I could not. Yet it was so good to have another woman to talk to, another woman close by. Katherine was like a little mermaid herself, swimming in the cove, so slender-boned and well made in her odd, perfect clothes. Murry said it was too cold for her after Bandol, she must have the south. So they found a place at Mylor, on the south coast where it would be gentler for them, out of the storms we have here. Lorenzo says that Murry has abandoned him and betrayed the Blutsbrüder-schaft between them, so now he goes down to the farm and talks with William Henry. I do not like William Henry. He looks at me as if I am nothing, not important, just a thing belonging to my husband. But who is William Henry to look at me like that? A farmer. A peasant. Always he is dragging Lorenzo down into his fields, his farm, pretending to want to learn geography and French so that Lorenzo can explain to him and teach him as he loves to do. Then Lorenzo comes home to me and tells me I do not understand William Henry, his mind is fine and quick and he is hungry to discuss ideas. I can see that he is hungry. But for what is he hungry? There are so many people like him, who want Lorenzo and what he can give to them. They see he has a gift and they want it. But I have lived with him for five years and I know they cannot capture it.

*

86

At Zennor the wind never quite sleeps. The typescript on the table is held down by a piece of granite, but the edge of the pages still riffle and words jerk into movement like those cinematographic images children make by drawing stick figures on the corners of a notebook and flicking the pages. Lawrence works swiftly, writing by hand in margins and between the typewritten lines, making his final revision. He is writing his article on 'The Reality of Peace'. He works with intense concentration and his handwriting flows across the page. The article is nearly finished, but he senses that there is something missing: the ideas are naked, like signposts. He stops and shuts his eyes. The blind, lost faces of the men on the special conscription train rise in his mind like the faces of drowned men. He leans over the paper and writes again, faster. Then he tucks the typescript under the stone again and goes in to scrub the potatoes.

As he goes up the path he stiffens, tense. He calls out quietly but with such urgency that she comes at once: 'Frieda! Frieda!'

She appears at the door, squinting a little against the sun.

'Come here. No, not that way – come round by me. Look! Can you see her?'

Frieda pads lightly across the hummocky grass and potato hills. She looks where he points, and her tawny eyes dilate. A little slim black and yellow adder has poured herself up from a crack in the wall and is coiling on a warm stone. Her blunt head makes soft stabbing motions into the air, butting against its new summery warmth as a lamb butts the udder playfully before it seizes the nipple.

'Ah, she is beautiful!' breathes Frieda.

He watches, and frowns. 'There may be a nest of 'em in under the wall,' he says dryly. 'Should you like that?'

'I have never seen one so close. See! There is her tongue.'

'William Henry would tell me to poke out the nest. There's a plague of adders on these hills. They bite the sheep.'

'Sheep!' exclaims Frieda scornfully. 'Often I think I should like to bite a sheep myself, they are so stupid.'

The little adder flicks her tail lightly to and fro.

'She knows we're near,' says Lawrence. 'She can sense us.'

The warm wind stirs again, carrying a dark brown spice of wallflowers.

'Smell those gillivors,' he mutters. 'They always make me think of my mother's garden. She would stop still and shut her eyes to smell them.'

He is back in the small dark-soiled garden in Eastwood, treading the cinder-path to where his mother stands stock-still and oblivious of him. Her white apron blows in the spring wind, and the noise of the pit's winding-gear grates through the piping of a robin hidden in a blackberry-bush. In a minute she'll turn and see him.

'Mother!'

But he has not spoken aloud. Frieda leans against him, watching the snake as she coils again, showing her belly, her deaf body uneasy as she picks up the vibration of their voices.

'She's going.'

The snake's body elongates like water, tilts and disappears. Frieda steps over and lays her hand on the stone where the snake has been, but there's nothing but the stone's own warmth and smoothness. She looks up at Lawrence and laughs. Her face is flushed from stooping and from the excitement of the snake, and her eyes glow.

'Lorenzo, do you know who she reminded me of, that snake?'

He smiles, and shakes his head.

'Katherine. Don't you think so?'

Her mention of Katherine presses lightly on the bruise of anger he still feels towards both the Murrys after their rejection of Zennor. But Frieda is beautiful in the sunshine.

'I suppose Katherine might be an adder. Slim, and quick, and a bit wicked.'

'And her black hair, so sleek and smooth.'

'Yes. It's true that she likes to be by herself. She hates people to touch her except when she chooses.'

'Or she will bite.'

'She can certainly bite. Frieda, you know that girl I was telling you about – Clare?'

'Yes? Why?'

'You will like her. I am sure you will like her.'

His face is warm and eager, but Frieda is cautious. Will this be another of these girls who sit at Lorenzo's feet and wonder why Frieda is not safely out of the way doing the cooking?

'She needs to meet a woman like you,' he goes on. 'It will open her eyes.'

'Oh,' mocks Frieda, opening her own fierce eyes wide. 'Is that what it will do?'

Reluctantly, he grins back. She tucks her hand into his arm and pushes back the hair which is always breaking into curls on her forehead.

'I'm glad you called me to see the snake,' she says.

The wind blows at night, but by day it's calm. The weather is extraordinary: everyone remarks on it. In London, ladies note it in their diaries. Perhaps it's something to do with the war. Or perhaps it's just that people notice things more now, when they are living in a time out of time? In the parks the wounded lie out on chairs in their blue uniform with red ties. Three men hop on their crutches, swiping at a rag ball which rolls and bounces between them. They have three legs between them. The spare leg of their blue uniform trousers is pinned neatly at the top of the thigh. They look just like crickets, thinks a nursemaid as she pulls a dense creamy fold of new wool blanket up to the lips of her charge. She pats the warm hump of his bottom. He sleeps on, whole and perfect from his bunched fists to his dwindling, purple-blotched legs. She'll take him back another way, so as not to go past the men on crutches again. There is something frightening to her in their nimbleness. And there's the way they look at her as she sways past them pushing the perambulator, her white skirt creaking faintly under its tight belt, her cheeks pinkening. There's a flat, dark look in their eyes, as if they do not see her, or as if they do not like what they see. She will go round here, and back by the pond. The extra turn will be good for baby.

Eight

Clare snaps fully awake at quarter to six in her dark room. She's had to change her white lace curtains for chenille because of the war. No one must show a light to U-boats lying out in the Channel, sinking ship after ship after ship, creeping in at night to refuel at secret dumps along the miles of toothed coastline, fed by the Unseen Hand of German collaborators, a cancer working in the body militant, a nest to be smoked out by every observant man, woman and child. Or so they say. Clare hates the blotting out of her landscape of clouds and sea. The chenille is stuffy and faded, and, even though she aired the curtains in the sun for a full day before hanging them, a smell of must seeps out of them and taints the room.

She pads round her bed and swishes the curtains right back. There it is, her bowlful of sky and sea. The sun has risen behind the house, throwing long shadows down the hill in front of her. Everything is moist, fresh, dipped in new light. There are still some curls of mist over the sea, but they are clearing fast. It's going to be hot again. There's dew on her lettuces in the little kitchen garden over the lane, and her marigolds are already lolling open where the morning sun touches them. They look ripe, like fruit. Sheba picks her way immaculately through the wet grass, her tail twitching. She senses the movement of Clare in the window and looks up, then steps off again, lightly, as if she's just confirmed her opinion that Clare is not worth bothering about. At the horizon the sea is purple, but within the bay it is a dark, breathing blue. The tide's still going out. Clare clatters the sash window up and leans out. There's the milk-cart labouring its way up the hill, with Joss walking at Sally's head, talking to her so that the mare won't notice how steep a climb it is, how often she's done it, how tired she is. The white spots on his red neckerchief stand out like daisies on a lawn. Sally has her head down, shuddering, bracing herself. She's getting too old for this, but you can't get a decent horse for love or money, not with what he can afford, not with the war, Joss says each morning as he pours a long white tongue of milk into Clare's jug.

Clare will go out. She can't wait to be out of the house, away from this frowst of curtains and stale air. Down there to her right all the cottages hump, still sleeping. No, not quite all. The first smoke goes up from a stubby chimney wedged into a slate roof. Father's still asleep, in his dark red bedroom at the back of the house, closed in against the rising sun. He has had black shades fitted to his windows, because his eyes are sensitive to light. He won't get up for hours yet, and when he does he'll meander down to the kitchen in his Paisley silk dressing-gown (because it isn't one of Hat's days) and make tea for himself, whistling between his teeth, book in one hand. He doesn't sleep well, and Daylight Saving makes it even worse for him. She never sees him before eight, and it will be later today. She didn't hear him come in last night, even though she lay there, half dozing, half waiting, on edge. But before the door snicked she fell asleep, into heavy confused dreams which still hang about her now.

She stretches to shake away the dreams. The clean wooden boards under the window feel cool and smooth to her bare feet.

She's glad she got rid of her childhood oilcloth. Now she is flooded with quick relief at simply being awake in her plain white room, with the breeze stirring just a little and the summer air flooding in. She pours water into her ewer and swooshes it over face and neck. It's silky. She soaps her arms and breasts and rinses them with her flannel while her night-dress slowly slithers past her waist and buttocks and into a heap around her feet. She catches sight of herself in the glass: her pinkish nipples are stiff from the cold water. Real red-head's nipples, Hannah calls them. Her breasts are mapped with blue veins. Clare has never liked to ask if this is ugly, or not. Her shoulders please her, and her neck, and the small delicate moulding of her collar-bones. But she is not sure about her breasts, and perhaps her arms are too thin.

Today, though, her face is at its best. Her cheeks are firm, with all the contours perfectly in place, not squashed or swollen, or somehow disfigured as they are on bad mornings. She's even got a little colour. It's only from the splash of cold water, but it suits her. What a pity no one else will see it. By the time she goes downstairs, she will be back to smooth pallor. She must remember to put Vaseline on her lashes tonight, to make them grow thick. She keeps forgetting. This is Peggy's tip: it will work wonders, she says, and it's much cheaper than Lasholene. Clare leans in close to her looking-glass and stares into her own eyes. Yes, it's a very good day. Today you could call her eyes blue. Dark blue. It's because she has some colour in her cheeks. Perhaps she ought to rouge – girls do now, and no one notices. But how lovely it is this morning to be Clare Coyne. She hugs herself tightly, crossing her legs for a faint, familiar stir of pleasure. She rubs her face against the inside of her arm where her flesh is silkiest. The smell of her skin pleases her, with its trace of night-warmth under the fresh soap. It's a shame to put on clothes on a day like this. And she has nothing right for summer. Everything is worn out, after three years of war and pinched income and rising prices. If only she could cut out like Hannah. A cream flannel skirt four inches above the ankle, with a broad scarlet leather belt and a tussore-silk blouse . . . But that one outfit would cost more than Clare spends on clothes in a whole season. And scarlet would clash with her hair. She scrambles into her old navy middy blouse and navy skirt and twists her hair into a knot without plaiting it.

Nothing can weigh down her lightness this morning. This old skirt fits perfectly, showing off the narrow waist which is one of her good points, making her aware at every moment of her young, firm body. She bends to pick up her hairbrush with a flourish of suppleness. Thank God for a body which is beautifully balanced and will do everything she wants. She makes her morning offering swiftly, obliquely. Should you thank God for the size of your waist? Why not? Maybe He's glad of it too. There are enough thick waists in this world and Heaven too, surely, thinks Clare.

The beach is ridged and wet with retreating sea. A black-headed gull glides, stabs at something behind the rocks, then wheels up, crying mournfully. Clare walks down towards the softly collapsing waves. Everything gleams like pearl, like the beginning of the world. Now she has her back to the land, and there's nothing between herself and the sea. The sun is warm on her back. She has eaten and drunk nothing. She is purified and ready to receive. The little waves come to the turn, bow down, come to the turn, bow down. Their lace spreads fan-like around her scuffed boots. She wants nothing but this, to stand by the slowly falling sea and watch black glistening humps of rock appear like seals' heads, streaming with weed and water.

94

'It's Clarey, isn't it?'

It's John William. She should have known it was bound to be him. The jolt in her heart was recognition, not shock. It's like this when you've known all along someone will come. For a moment she can't speak. He comes up alongside, very close to her, and she moves half a step away. He is huge. Even on the wide beach he crowds her.

'How are you, John William?'

He smiles at her. The points of his teeth show. He's so close that she sees how his eyes are mazed with tiny red blood-vessels all around the iris.

'I'm not so clever this morning,' he says. 'We made a night of it last night, me and Albert and Jo and George.'

'What time did you get in?'

'They set off back around midnight. To be skinned alive by Aunt Annie, I daresay. I went walking.'

'You haven't been to bed?'

No, he hasn't. Those prickling red eyes, too steady and bright. His hair's matted, not combed. And he smells of beer and smoke. He never used to drink beer. It was always cider with the boys, when they could get away from Grandad.

'I don't know where I went,' says John William. He rocks on his boots, staring, pleased with himself, stiff and rigid as a dummy in that carcass of a uniform, stinking of drink. Pleased with himself he might well be, thinks Clare, crashing his way across the countryside thinking of nothing and no one but himself. Yes, he's got that look on him. A pinched yellow look round his nose. A couple of years ago that would have meant a fight, but I suppose now he's had enough of fighting.

'You should take more care,' she says sharply. 'It's a miracle you didn't fall over the cliffs.'

John William glances round the bay. 'Here's your miracle, if you want miracles,' he says.

She knew he would feel it as she does. How often have they come down here, John William barefoot, before anyone else was awake, to fish off the rocks?

'Why should *I* be here?' he asks, staring round him. 'Can you tell me that, Clarey?'

'Why should anyone?' she says. 'But you *are* here.'

Still she is not sure. Is he? He doesn't seem very present. He is as temporary as a ghost.

A ghost let in, touched, talked to. Let in once a year to eat food put out by the family. There is no sense in it. How can we still have leaves and train time-tables and welcomes? How can we expect to be glad when everyone we love is going to be dragged away from us?

'I went somewhere high up, I do remember that,' says John William.

'What, last night?'

'Yes. I can hear it now. There was a noise of sea in front of me, and something else behind me. A woman's voice, singing.'

'You'd been drinking. Or else it was a mermaid.'

'No, it didn't come from the sea,' he says. 'It came from the land behind me. I couldn't hear it quite clearly. It was a thin little voice – a foreign voice.'

'Where had you got to? You ought to know that.'

He smiles. 'I do. But I thought that if I told you, you wouldn't believe me.' Now he sounds like himself again. The bragging note has gone out of his voice.

'Where?'

'Above Pendour Cove.'

She laughs. 'However in the world did you get up there?'

'Looking for something I'd lost.'

'Were you? What was that, John William?'

'Why didn't you come down last night, Clarey? I was looking out for my little cousin, and then you never came?'

His voice blurs sentimentally. She looks at him and realizes he's still slightly drunk, even now after what must have been a fourteen-mile walk. That's why he's talking so much. Perhaps it's why he came to talk to her in the first place. That's why he went to Pendour Cove to look for the mermaid.

'You ought to get to bed, John William. You need some sleep.'

'I can't sleep,' he says. His eyes are suddenly empty of life. He sways a little. A small wave rushes around their boots, the last try of an ebbing tide.

'Waste of time to sleep anyway,' he goes on. 'I've only got forty-eight hours at home. Let's sit down by the rocks.'

The rocks are warm already. They sit facing the sea, with a pool below them where pale red anemones pulse and fray in the current of falling water. The sun falls deliciously on Clare's face. She'll freckle without her hat. Never mind. She shuts her eyes. This is just like when they were little, stealing out of Nan's with the boys, to hunt in the rock-pools at low tide when she was supposed to be going to bed.

But John William is restless beside her. He hoists himself down to the pool and kneels beside it to cup sea-water in his hands and sluice his face and the back of his neck. His hair is cut brutally short, bristling and stubby around the nape, a stubble through which she can see his scalp. All his beautiful soft black hair chopped to nothing. And all its shine is gone. It looks dead. He grins up at her.

'That's better!'

'They cut your hair too short,' she says. 'It's a shame.'

'You wouldn't say that, if you saw the lice we have out there. When you wash your clothes, you have to press all along the seams – like this – so it kills them.'

'How horrible!'

He laughs. 'It's just the way it is. Better'n getting typhoid.'

She looks down on him, hunkered by the pool, splashing himself and puffing out sea-water. He is busy and blind as a badger. The spread of his back and haunches looks scarcely human. He's undone his collar and rolled up his sleeves. His arms are brown, with fine black hair on the backs of them glistening with water, and his neck is pale where the deep line of tan stops. He's darker than she's ever seen him, but it's not the fine-grained salt and air tan he gets from working up at the farm with Albert and Jo and George on summer Sundays, helping with the hay harvest. Now his colour is mahogany, rich and somehow crude, as if it's a boot-polish he's rubbed into himself. His clear Red Indian look is blunted by the filling out of his face. His head looks small somehow, and again, animalish, quick and a bit frightening on his thick shoulders. She would not want to touch him now. His white teeth show as he calls up, 'Feels a treat!'

'Your hair will dry full of salt,' she observes.

He flicks his head and showers of drops fly off, to spatter against Clare's skirt. They make dark blotches on fading navy cloth. Then he bounds back up the rock to sit by Clare, so close she smells not only beer and smoke and salt but the smell of John William himself, unaltered underneath it all, a dry, almondy smell which is him and will always be him, a smell which even the war can't change, though it's changed everything else. He's still there. Her body gives and warms on the side where he almost touches her.

He stares out at the horizon. 'You don't get anything like this in the trenches,' he remarks.

She shifts in irritation. Why is he talking like this, with a crudity and banality which would suit Sam or one of the other lads, but is quite foreign to John William? It's as if he wants to pretend he's only got the same thoughts everyone else has. And John William's never had those, nor wanted them. He is different from the others, and she can't bear him acting the same.

'You surprise me,' she says tartly. 'I should have thought the trenches would be just like Porthmeor Beach. Not that I know anything about it, of course.'

'Good old Blighty,' he says, looking at her mockingly, appreciatively. 'I'm glad I saw you this morning, Clarey. I need your opinion.'

Her heart quickens. Something's wrong. He's going to tell her –

'Is it true what the Bishop of London's saying?'

'What on earth do you mean?'

His eyes yellow and glitter. 'The curse of lust and sin has fallen on London, according to him. Girls abandoning the decent ways they were brought up to. Is there much of that going on in St Ives?'

She slaps down her skirts and stands up. 'You're drunk. You don't know what you're saying. You'd better go home,' she says.

But he gets hold of her hem. 'Don't go, Clarey, don't rush off like that. I was only asking.'

Now he looks like himself, sharp and funny and a bit pleading. Well, he's been through a bad time. She mustn't take him up like that. He was only joking. And those articles in the paper Grandad reads are always about war-babies and sin and shame in cinemas. She sits down again. And isn't it the way he always talks, saying things other people wouldn't say?

'It's just the same here. Hellfire from Grandad if Hannah shows more than a couple of inches of leg.'

'Oh, Hannah . . .' He looks thoughtful.

'Have you seen Sam?'

He hesitates, picks up her hand which is lying in her lap, runs her fingers lightly against his palm. She's glad she filed her nails to smooth moony ovals.

'Yes. Sam's in London.'

So Hannah was right; the letter did come from London.

'But how did he get there?'

'Sick-leave.'

'But Sam's not sick. We'd have heard.'

'No,' he agrees. 'But Sam's not stupid either. Our Sam saw which way the wind was blowing. He had dysentery – well, that's nothing. Half the men have got it. But then he got blood in his stools, trust Sam for that, so they had to take him back to base camp for treatment. Course they'd a spotted he was faking it in five minutes. They're sharp enough, those army medical officers, and they know what their job is. So the next thing we know Sam is rolling around and shrieking out because he's suffering from shell-shock.'

'How do you know all this?'

'He told me himself. He's not ashamed, don't think it. He's set on living, that's all, and who am I to say he shouldn't be? He hadn't got one chance in ten, the section he was in, not with an advance due. So he gets sent back to hospital in London and the first chance he has he deserts. He made a fool of one of the VADs, I daresay.'

'But where is he now? Does Hannah know?'

'He's stopping in London. He met a girl there.'

She stares into his inscrutable face, tight on itself. He's lidded his eyes, the way he does when he doesn't want to look at someone.

'But he can't just stay there! I mean – what about Hannah? She's worried to death over him. Can't you do something?'

'No.'

'But – but he loves her. He loves Hannah. You know he does.'

John William moves his shoulders slightly. It's not a shrug, nothing as crude as that, but it's a gesture which repudiates everything she's said, and everything on which her words are founded.

'You won't say anything to Hannah,' he says quietly.

'Of course I won't,' says Clare, thinking of the letter Hannah couldn't understand, of Hannah's suspended nightmare of waiting last autumn, of the kisses she has seen and the love-making she can't imagine.

'He's going to see a new show called *Zig-Zag* tonight. Good old Sam,' remarks John William surprisingly.

'Good old Sam! I don't see what's good about it. Don't you care about Hannah at all?' snaps Clare.

'He'll come back. As much as anyone's likely to come back. You don't know what it's like out there.'

'Is it so awful?' she asks.

'You can get through it as long as you don't think about it too much. I wish I could draw like you, though, Clarey. I've seen some queer sights. Flowers in the middle of everything. You'd like the flowers: you know I thought of you a couple of weeks ago. We were in an apple orchard, not far from Arras. Where Fritz moved back a couple of months ago. All the farm people had gone, but they hadn't been able to take anything with them except what they could get on a handcart, so our officers billeted themselves in the farmhouse and we slept in the orchard. Oh, the smell of it in the night, Clarey. All those trees flowering. You've no idea. We killed a hen for breakfast.' He gives a crack of laughter. 'One of the officers wanted to shoot it. I wish you'd seen him. He got down on his belly and went stalking the hen through the long grass, as high as your waist and wet. And the old hen didn't take a blind bit of notice of him. She kept on pecking away the grain we'd thrown for her. We thought we'd fatten her up a bit first. She was a stringy dud of a creature.'

'Did he shoot her?'

'No, his batman came up and wrung her neck. She'd have been blown to shreds if the silly bugger'd shot her. No good to us like that.'

'And you all had some?'

He laughs in real amusement. 'Luckily, as it happened, she turned out too tough for the officers. So I kindly took her off their hands and made soup for the men. They quite thought it had been their own idea.'

'Officers' training camp,' she says. 'You must have been pleased.'

The same movement of the shoulders again. Another rebuff. The weakness and silliness of what she has just said echoes in her own ears.

'You could say pleased,' he says. 'It's like being born. You can feel your blood pouring through you like it's for the first time in your life. When they told me, we'd been three days in the reserve trench, waiting for orders. There's big manoeuvres on, but you never know the whole picture, only your own bit of it. I suppose I'll have to know more now. But we knew it would be bad. Everyone was on edge. Then I was sent for by our colonel. I walked up the farm lane, out of range of the guns, noticing every flower in the ditch as I walked past it. It was warm. There was a sparrow having a dustbath. Things seem to burn into your mind sometimes. I went in and saluted him, thinking what now, was there something I'd done wrong. And he looked up from his paperwork and asked me if I'd like to go in for a commission. Just like that. I was to go to headquarters to be interviewed a week later. It poured through me so I could hardly stand, and all the time I was looking at the yellow in the white of his eyes, thinking he had something wrong with his liver, or else he drank too much.

'That was the worst week. I thought I was sure to be killed, just when I'd seen my way out of it. I knew I'd be sent back to Blighty for training, and I'd been told it would be three months. The war could be over by then. All the boys were round me, telling me what a lucky bugger I was. You'd a thought they'd grudge me my luck, but they didn't. I was going right away to Blighty, and they knew there was going to be another big push coming up soon. And they knew their chances.'

He is lost to her. He is a thousand miles away, hearing the guns, seeing the ring of faces round him and knowing their chances.

'I must get back, I haven't lit the stove yet,' she says quickly. Perhaps he wants to be on his own.

'Stay a bit. It's nice here. Listen, Clarey, you mustn't worry over Hannah and Sam. Sam's all right.'

Easy, glib words again. Anybody's words. But she wants to believe them. Hannah's all right, and Sam's all right, and John

William's all right. Sam's letters stink of death and he'd rather hide with a prostitute in London than trust them here at home. But it will be all right, once the war's over.

She doesn't even try to believe it. She listens to the sea and the screaming of the gulls. They're gutting the catch round by the harbour. The gulls dive with slimy trails hanging from their beaks.

John William shifts position, frees his arm and puts it around her waist. It circles her there, warm and definite. She breathes in quickly, unevenly. He must feel her breathing. And her heart, beating so fast. She is sitting with John William's arm around her. She looks down and there is the back of his hand, curled over the light mound of her stomach, the black fine hairs on it lying flat now, the hand blunt and strong, the colour of the skin like that of another kind of creature from herself and her own paleness. The underside of her left breast just skims the top of his wrist as she breathes out. She sits as still as still. If she says nothing and doesn't move, they will stay together like this. Excitement trembles in her, and peace too. He is here, with her. No one else can touch him. For now he does not belong to the war. No matter how close he may be to the boys, they are not here. She is.

His hand begins to stroke her lightly, as he would stroke the belly of a cat. The tips of her breasts burn under warm cotton.

'There's a Red Cross concert on tonight, at the Drill Hall,' he says. 'Had you thought of going? I'd like to hear a woman singing.'

'I don't know – I hadn't considered it . . .'

No, but she's seen the poster. A Belgian woman singing in aid of the Red Cross. Opera-trained, with her piano accompanist, it said. What was her name exactly? Not Elaine, but something like it. Eliane, that was it. A preposterous bosom and a background of gunfire over a distant shore. But people are getting tired of Belgians.

'How are your Belgian atrocities?' they joke.

She can picture the concert, and the singer, her eyes wide with unshed tears against the crossed flags of Britain and Belgium. A faulty, shuddering soprano ... But it is no use criticizing. Clare had flared in passionate pity with the rest of them, three years back at the invasion of Belgium. Now it is all different. People cope by making jokes and going on blindly, heads down, without flourishes. Her father would raise his eyebrows if she said she was going to the Saturday night concert.

'A predictable type of evening, I'd have thought, Clare.'

A woman's voice. John William must hear nothing but men's voices out there, except for the VADs. Only men, day after day, living together and dying together. No wonder they talk about each other the way they do, as if the other men in the trenches are more real than all of us here. The way even Sam talked about Billy when he came back on leave after Billy was killed. Tender. You'd never imagine Sam could talk like that.

'The singing I heard last night,' goes on John William. 'That was a woman. Or a seal maybe.'

'Or a mermaid.'

'That's right. Will you come?'

'With you?'

'Yes. We could go for a walk after. Like I did last night. Tell Uncle Francis you're going with me and Hannah and he won't trouble himself.'

'Yes.' Her voice is muffled. Surely now he can hear her heart thudding through it.

Yes, we could go for a walk. Like Hannah and Sam. Just John William and me and no one else in the world. He'll talk to me . . .

His hand on her waist tightens.

'You'd better sleep this afternoon, or you won't enjoy the concert,' she says.

His face shutters against her. 'I shan't sleep.'

There is a long pause, with the sand sucking as the tide drains out through it. A bee flies past them, out of its element and dangerously low over the water. The pouncing tip of a wave nearly gets it. How long would it struggle to fly again, weighed down by its wet fur and salt-sodden wings? His arm feels less warm and she is stiff with sitting still on the rock. She must go and cook breakfast for her father. She twists to free herself and he lets her go with disconcerting promptness.

'Goodbye, then,' she says.

'I'll call for you, Clarey. Seven o'clock.'

She nods, and turns to go. He hunches forward, clasping his knees. She's going, so he'll hold on to himself, smelling his own khaki, watching his boots glitter. The others are up already, working. Essential workers they are, Jo and Albert and George, and they are there to be seen working essentially by anyone prowling or nosing up at the farm. Coast-watchers, military police, tribunal members, let em all come. The boys will be blinding their way across the yard to swill down the pig-sheds now, hung-over and breakfastless.

She doesn't want to leave John William like this, worn out and half sober. After all this is her cousin. He's neither slept nor eaten. He isn't like himself. All the intelligence which scares the others like a fire which might singe them is sleeping somewhere way down in the middle of him. Like the red core of an overnight fire, piled up with slack. Almost sleeping. And when he put his arm around her, was that really him, or was it just part of his being a soldier, part of the strangeness? Is it something which has woken up in him because of war and death, which needs to be coaxed back into cousinly sleep? Or is it just that she was there? He doesn't really need her, not Clare Coyne herself. What he needs is a girl in London, and the music-hall, and a few drinks inside him so the lights grow muzzy while an old man plays *Goodby-eee* on his violin and the audience roars its approval and John William's girl smiles at him the way she smiles at all the boys. A noble sense of renunciation swells inside Clare. She is family. Cousin Clarey. She ought to look after him.

'Nan'll make you a bacon sandwich if you come on up,' she calls to him across the sand.

But her words come to nothing. He remains sitting on the rock, looking out to sea, not wanting her.

Nine

Twenty-five to six. The confessional curtain opens behind her, and Francis Coyne walks past her, calm and everyday. He walks the length of the church, dips into the pew in front of the altar, crosses himself, bows his head.

Good, thinks Clare. He won't take long now. She feels uneasy and inhibited as long as her father is here in the church. The fruits of a bad conscience. She's deep enough in the sticky web of family as it is. The confessional queue shuffles up by one, and now she joins it. She wanted to be sure that her father would be well out of the Church by the time she made her own confession. She kneels again, sighs, pulls off her gloves. The thumb seam is splitting and she's not going to be able to mend it again. The left palm is worn too. She will have to buy new gloves. She twists her fingers together, then covers her face with her hands to blot out the milky sea-light filtering through stained glass, and the row of patient backs, bowed over in the pews. The familiar church smell comforts her as she takes a deep breath, calms herself, spins out a prayer which she can follow without panic: 'Oh Guardian Angel, sent to watch over me during my life, be with me now in sorrow for my sins. May my holy patron, Saint Clare, whose name I bear . . .'

Father's still kneeling there. He's taking a long time over his penance. I wish he'd go. What if he's decided to wait for me?

No, it's all right. She sees her father's back stirring, his head lifting. Francis Coyne crosses himself again, unfolds his long legs awkwardly, genuflects as he leaves his pew and walks out into the sunshine, putting on his hat. An obscure sense of propriety stops him from acknowledging Clare as he passes her.

That's that. The spice of May Foage has been cleansed from his flesh and his spirit. The child looks miserable today. I wonder what's wrong? Better not ask her. It'll be some quarrel that's blown up between her and Hannah. And now she's exaggerated it into sin in her own mind, no doubt. He smiles fondly at the thought of his daughter's innocent conscience. But he'd felt sorry for her, kneeling there, looking small and young and extinguished. She isn't pretty at all at the moment. Slate shadows round slate eyes, her face narrow and pinched, with spots of colour on the cheek-bones. It takes him back to the sight of her when she was ten or eleven, with all that fierce hair strained back into tight plaits. She used to kneel beside him during Mass and hold up her fingers in front of her eyes to make patterns of light through them. She didn't have her mother to make the church a proper home to her, that was the root of it. Even if she'd lived, Susannah wouldn't have known how to do it. She was stiff and not a quick learner. She would never have called in easily with Clare on her way back from the shops, to light a candle, pray for an anniversary or remember a small local saint. Besides, this church wasn't built then, and Susannah would have been even more uneasy in the over-intimate atmosphere of the Mission. And he too had failed. Perhaps it was because he was a man. Somehow he did not have the gift of making her faith both immediate and mysterious to her, in the way it had been to his sisters. He had spent too long explaining her faith to her. Clare fidgeted, he became impatient. If she wanted familiarity, she went down to Nan's.

Now there's this business of the Red Cross concert. I suppose she's going because John William's home on leave. They've always got on well. The two of them talking, talking, thin clever faces across the kitchen-table. But that was a long time ago now. Ah, well, she'll be safe enough with Hannah and Harry and John William, listening to the warblings of some lachrymose Belgian. All the cousins are going, apparently.

Clare hears the church door thud shut behind her father. She presses her face deeper into her warm hands and gabbles through her prayers of preparation: 'I desire now to confess sincerely all my sins to you and your priest, and for this purpose I wish to know myself and call myself to account by a diligent examination of my conscience . . .'

Her mind scutters through prayer after prayer. The worn phrases click and whirr. But it isn't true. I don't desire it. I don't want to know all my sins and call myself to account. So what am I doing here? John William's grin. John William's warm arm around her waist, his hand on her stomach, the spreading tingle in her breasts, the sweet heaviness in her groin. That's why I'm here. Because all that is sinful.

'Grant me, Father, this change of heart . . .' But a song is hurdy-gurdying round inside her all the while.

> We're here because we're here because we're here
> because we're here because . . .

There's no beginning or ending to this song. It goes on for ever, picked up by one voice as soon as it's dropped by another, just as the army lives on while the individual men die, one by one. It's a song for marching. It goes with the lift and crash of thousands of boots, and with the weary stumble of men who can scarcely put one foot in front of another any more. The army goes on for ever to the noise of boots and trench songs:

> Send out the boys of the Old Brigade
> Who made Old England free,
> Send out my mother, my sister and my brother,
> But for Gawd's sake don't send me.

Sam sang the song to Hannah and Clare. At first they were shocked, though they wouldn't show it to Sam. Later, talking in Clare's bedroom, Hannah said, 'But you have to look at it their way. When you think of it, all the time they're singing they're getting closer to the Front.'

Sam has got a girl up in London. They'll go to the music-hall together. The last number is always a throbbing romantic song, and there'll be swaying rows of soldiers up on the balcony with their best girls, the girls they're treating tonight. Then it's over and the lights go up and they'll spill out into the dusk, art silk rubbing against khaki, pressed close together and not giggling any more but solemn, drifting away down the streets, away from lights and music and the smell of wine and beer on warm breath. They'll go into the parks where there's a smell of jasmine and rank laurel and the night policeman turns a blind eye to movements in the shadows.

She sighs and shifts her weight to her left knee.

'I wish Hannah was there for Sam.'

She is being stupid anyway. Sam will not dare to go to a public place for fear of the military police. John William must have been joking when he said Sam was going to a show.

'But what will it avail to know my sins if you do not also give me the grace of sorrow and repentance?'

Sam is sinning: Hannah is sinning: I am sinning. Clare presses down a bubbling giggle. She's reminded irresistibly of the conjugation of French verbs. The perfect, the pluperfect, the imperfect. I shall have sinned, he will have sinned, we shall all have sinned . . .

Mrs Hore sighs enormously and creaks off her knees and into a box. She is so heavily in mourning she seems to drip black behind her. You look for a slow stain of black spreading out on the floor where she's been kneeling. Muttering begins again from the confessional. There's no one before me now. She glances sideways. It's the Driscoll girl who works as a maid up at Middleton House. Bouncy, red-faced Driscoll girl, not bouncy any more. Things have gone badly for her. Her brother, Caddie Driscoll – what was it they said about him? Poor soul, he was not right in his mind any more, not since he came home from the war. And the Driscolls had been going about boasting that they'd got him back without even a Blighty one, before they realized what it meant and that they'd got him back without the spirit in him any more. He'd never have been sent back unless he was fit for nothing but to be spat out by the war. Shell-shock was what he had. Clare had seen him bobbing and trembling in the back pew at Benediction. But he had to go out of the church because he could not bear the noise, and the smoke from the censer frightened him. His face was as white as a wax candle.

She turns and whispers to Annie Driscoll: 'Should you like to go before me?'

'Are you not ready?'

'Not yet.'

No, I'm not ready. More prayers. Can't leave now when there's six behind me, all murmuring, knowing, watching. And a quizzical face with a blazing beard questioning in front of my eyes.

> O purify me, then I shall be clean
> O wash me, I shall be whiter than snow . . .

She's loved those words so much, but today they don't work. She doesn't want them to: she'd rather cling to the sweetness of John William. The Driscoll girl ducks her head as she comes out, flushed, with her curls bobbing against her cheeks. A pause while the queue waits to see if Clare's piety will lead her into a yet more scrupulously lengthy examination of conscience. The pressure of their waiting defeats her and she goes in.

She drops to her knees, rubs her fingers against the splintery wood of the ledge below the grille, and speaks. In the close, dark silence her panic dissolves. The statue of Our Lady floats in her niche above Clare's head. The cool syllables of the priest's listening voice fall across her restless conscience as they have always fallen, quietening it. She accuses herself of impurity of thought and deed and thanks God for the phrases which shawl her meaning even from herself as her words leave her lips. It will not happen again. In the dark she detests her sins. For the first time that day she can think of John William without a prickle in her conscience or her breasts. Now, with the cool web of the Church embracing her, it seems impossible that she has burned all day long, her heart thudding suddenly each time she realizes that she's one hour nearer to night, to seeing him again. It seems impossible that she, Clare Coyne, has spent her whole day planning, intending, longing to commit the sin of fornication with her cousin John William. How easy it is to resist sins once they are put into ugly words. It is all so much easier than she'd thought it was going to be.

The mild implacability of the priest's voice warms after absolution, as he blesses her. Here she kneels in the confessional's wooden heart as she's done from the age of seven, confessing to greed over sweets, to disobedience, to anger, to stealing a red hair-ribbon which belonged to her cousin Hannah and which she never wore but hid away in her underclothes drawer. It wouldn't have suited her anyway, she knows that now. Gorgeous on dark-haired Hannah, infinitely desirable, but a flat glare of colour against her own complexion. Here she kneels, empty and grateful. She is still Clare Coyne, the same Clare Coyne, brushing dust off her skirts as she stands, her cheeks pale now that the rare high colour which has flared in them all day has gone. Her hips sway composedly as she taps her way across the floor and into a pew to say her penance, which is going to take her some considerable time.

Clare threads her way quickly down Tregenna Hill, up Gabriel Street and through Wesley Place. On and up she goes, up Windsor Hill with her quick, elastic, virtuous step, on and up to crest the hill above Barnoon Cemetery. Her head is down. She is not so much praying as telling over her prayers like beads.

A shrill whistle. She looks up.

'Clarey.'

She looks wildly left and right, and there's Kitchie sitting on the cemetery wall, his head framed by a bent Scotch pine. He lounges, looking at her satirically. He knows the Coyne religious routines, and has his own Treveal reservations about them.

'Been to get it all off your chest?' he inquires.

How long his legs are now. He's nearly a man. Kitchie's cap's always been too big for him – that's just Kitchie. But now it fits him. And his hair springs less wildly than it did. He is like her mother, they say, but she can't remember her mother as a distinct face. Only the shape and smell of her. Kitchie puts oil on his hair now, she supposes.

She grins back. It is always good to see Kitchie.

'Don't you wish you might do as much, you cheeky monkey. I'm glad I haven't got your conscience. What are you doing here, anyway?'

'Waiting for you. Knew you'd come up this way.'

'Did you! Then next time I'll go round by the beach, just to spite you.'

'Then you'll spite yourself with a longer walk.'

Yes, he's nearly a man. He has thickened up this past year. He is still the noisiest of them all, and he never seems to know what he's going to say until he's said it, but he's a good worker up at the farm with his cousins. He has the kind of hands which can repair anything. Quick and instinctive, they feel for the right place to slot a newly oiled bolt, or a strip of leather he's cut and stitched to repair the harness. But however good he is, however valuable he is to Uncle John and Aunt Annie, they won't keep him on the farm once he reaches call-up age, not with Albert and George and Jo, their own sons, precariously holding on to their exemptions. One more application might be the straw that breaks the camel's back, and all the Treveal boys would whirl together into the mouth of the war. That must never happen. It's agreed. Kitchie's mother knows the war's got to be over by the time Kitchie's eighteen. How can they take her Kitchie from her, when he's the only one left to her out of the four children born to her? Dead Florrie, dead Rebecca, dead little William. Clare remembers their blue wizened faces in their small rough coffins which Aunt Mabel lined each time with the shawl she crocheted for each baby as she waited for it to be born. A waste, Nan muttered. There were plenty would be glad of the warmth of those shawls. But she helped Mabel to fold in the shawls around the small skulls with the deep dip of the fontanelle in them. Nobody would dare say anything to Mabel's white, frantic face.

They can't take Kitchie from Aunt Mabel. Why, it's impossible.

But Clare knows that they can, and that nothing is impossible any more. There is no language to describe the world she lives in now, where lists of thousands of dead are published in the newspapers each morning as routinely as the small advertisements. She reads the newspaper. Not in *The Times*, but in Grandad's *Daily Mail* there are stories of heroic mothers who give up eight sons, or ten sons, to conscription. Stories of families who have eighteen adult males fighting at the front – sons, cousins, husbands. And all we have is John William. Of course they'll take Kitchie. Her heart tightens as she looks at him in his best white shirt and a waistcoat she recognizes as an old one of John William's. He's brushed his hair down flat for the concert, and his Sunday boots are carefully cleaned and polished. He's ready and she's not. Quick, she must get changed – John William will be here at seven.

'Hannah sent this up for you,' says Kitchie. Messenger-boy Kitchie – now she sees that there's a flat brown paper parcel on the wall beside him, beautifully tied with string. A draper's parcel. Kitchie's grin widens as he hands it to her.

'Go on, then – open it. I know you want to.'

'Don't be silly, Kitchie, not out here. But thank Hannah for me and tell her I'll see her down at the hall with the rest of you. She is coming, isn't she?'

'She wasn't going to, but John William brought her round. She's thinking of that bugger Sam.'

'Kitchie,' Clare murmurs, automatically reproving. But he has never minded his language in front of her. And she doesn't mind either. It's part of their shared escape from Nan and Grandad.

'Aren't you going to ask me in?' he reminds her.

She starts. How stupid of her. She should have remembered how much Kitchie likes coming to the Coyne house.

'You'll come in and have a cup of tea with us? Then I'll have to get dressed.'

'I don't mind,' he says, and swings himself off the wall and into step beside her as they cross the road up from Porthmeor Beach and into Clare's row of villas.

Kitchie scans the sea to their right. 'They say those U-boats come skulking in round Zennor Head Wednesday night. I heard tell yesterday they've got a cache in under Tregerthen cliff. Fuel and food. The coast-watchers've been up and around there, Jim Bossinney told me.'

'They're always up and down there. It doesn't mean anything,' says Clare.

'How can you say that when they've sunk so many good ships?' says Kitchie in passionate reproof of her automatic coolness and good sense.

And Kitchie doesn't speak alone. As their footsteps clip along the pavement to Clare's door, he is joined by innumerable, swelling voices. The air is thick with them. The war is not going well. After three years it is bloated and invalidish. And each month it grows trickier to handle. Generals shift and scramble and make stratagems and bury their mistakes. U-boats nose impudently all along the Western Approaches, drowning men, sinking ships full of supplies while bread queues lengthen. Rusty, split tins of food are washed up on the beaches. Three ships sunk between Land's End and St Ives a couple of months ago. And in January farmers had to watch from the cliffs above Zennor as a Norwegian vessel wallowed and her crew drowned in front of their eyes. Lords and politicians quietly panic inside the fastnesses of the War Office.

And now we need more enemies. Even the Germans are not enough any more. So many men are gone, so many are wounded. So many have their minds and spirits destroyed, and the news of this leaks from family to neighbour to acquaintance and spills into newsprint. Look at this group photograph of wounded veterans. Seven of them. Count the limbs. Between the seven of them they have one leg, and even that one leg lacks a foot. Their faces stare unreadably at the camera. Their hair is mostly parted to the side, but one has an exquisite, knife-sharp central parting. Two are moustached, five clean-shaven. Their round collars are white and immaculate. Behind them dense, heavy summer foliage stirs a little in a breeze which also ruffles the hair of the one man who looks upward, away from the camera. He is perhaps the oldest of them, with a bony, vivid face. He must be thirty at least. He looks like a man standing on a cliff in the face of a sea-breeze, wondering if the weather is about to change. He cannot bear to look into the camera. On his far right there are two handsome legless boys, one with his hands folded in his lap, the other with his trunk perched on a high stool between wheelchairs, balancing himself with an arm round the shoulders of the men on his right hand and on his left hand.

Up and down, even and then uneven, runs the row of heads.

The faces are young, fully moulded and perfect. There are no lines on them but for the tight line of each mouth holding back what it is never going to say, not now, not here. The youngest of them is only three or four years older than Kitchie. No wonder he cries out.

In the dull anger of late May 1917 Kitchie's not alone. Shops open and close, newspapers are printed, girls make their summer dresses and make themselves beautiful even though they have more best boys among the dead than among the living. An animal anger growls and murmurs. The war is full grown, lolling over its attendants, sprawled like a giant child which still won't fend for itself. The War Office scuttles to shovel it full of living food, for who knows what will happen if it gets hungry? And we've got Lloyd George now, not Squiffy Asquith. Lloyd George knows how to talk to people. He understands from deep inside himself the sway of public passions, and how to point them out and away from himself. He is the master of the jabbing finger, the whipped-up passion, the sweet permission to hate. Revenge is good and revenge is justified. As for enemies, let us also look within.

'Come on in, Kitchie,' says Clare, holding the front door open as she counts over the contents of her larder in her mind and wonders what she can offer him. She's prepared a cold supper for Father and herself. Hard-boiled eggs from the farm, lettuce, new potatoes, a bit of gooseberry tart Nan sent up. That'll do. She wouldn't have time to eat hers anyway.

'Will you have a bit of supper here, Kitchie?'

He will. He can always eat.

She leaves him breaking open white, fresh potatoes, like little eggs themselves, and picks up Hannah's parcel as she goes through the hall and up to her bedroom to change. Her room is warm with trapped heat, even though she's left the window open at the top. She drops the parcel on to her bed and tears it open. A blue and white striped fold of cloth ripples out. Hannah's new summer skirt. And a note: 'You can wear this to the concert if you like. Wear your white Sunday blouse with it, and your white belt.'

Hannah can't be going to the concert, if she's lending me her skirt. Clare strokes the material. It still smells of newness to her, although Hannah has worn it and washed it. It's a heavy French cotton, pre-war. If Sam had come home, Hannah would be wearing it and they'd be out, strolling along the beach or down to the harbour, having a quiet hour together after tea at Nan's.

But, in spite of her scruples, Clare can't bear not to wear it. She strips off her grey dress and washes quickly. Her white petticoat is clean, and her white cotton stockings. She steps into the skirt and shakes it out around her. It hangs beautifully, but the waist is too big – she'll have to thread the loops through her belt and pull it in evenly all the way round. There. She glances back at the brown paper and string on the bed and sees something small and round tucked into the corner of the parcel. She picks it up and examines it. Rouge-papers. She rubs her cheeks carefully, over the bone, then damps her lips and rubs the paper over them too. In the glass her eyes are big and hectic. The rouge changes her face into a narrow, inviting muzzle. She runs her hands carefully back through her hair to loosen it, so that it will cloud a little around her temples. The blouse is dull, but it will do. The skirt says everything. She turns, making it switch at her hips, then she kicks her grey dress under the chair and goes out, running lightly down the stairs to show Kitchie.

'My eye!' he exclaims gratifyingly; then, 'That's Hannah's skirt you've got on.'

'I know. She's lent it to me for the concert. Do you like it?'

She can't resist twirling, even for Kitchie. If only she could cut out patterns like Hannah! – or pay to have someone like Hannah cut out for her.

'Where's Uncle Francis?' asks Kitchie through a mouthful of gooseberry tart. 'This tart Nan's?'

'Mine's as good and you know it. Father was in church – I don't know where he went. He's not coming to the concert.'

'Well, he never does, does he?'

Sensing criticism, Clare says quickly, 'He always sends in money to the Red Cross. He doesn't like the crowds.'

'Oh, no, it wouldn't suit Uncle Francis,' agrees Kitchie tolerantly. 'You got any more of this tart, Clarey?'

She goes over to cut him another slice, but at that moment Francis Coyne's clock strikes the three quarters. Clare snatches Kitchie's plate from under him, makes a dive to brush off his crumbs with the tea-cloth, and chivvies him out of his chair.

'Come *on*, Kitchie! There's no time for that now. Here, I'll wrap it in a bit of paper and you can put it in your pocket.'

But he's aggrieved. He's a young man in his best, off to a concert, not a kid with his pockets full of sweet-stuff.

'And I never had my tea,' he grumbles, moving towards the door reluctantly. 'What's the rush? It's only a concert.'

'I know, I know! Never mind the plate, Kitchie – I've just got to – ' and she flurries to the back door. She'll pick a flower. But which? Not a marigold. Hannah'd never forgive her.

'You ought to of asked Nan for one of her roses.'

He's watching her fly about, noticing the colour rise in her cheeks again.

'Go *on*, Kitchie!'

The door slams.

Ten

The woman is bent over, sobbing, shaking out sparks of tears and rage. The solidly beautiful golden flesh of her shoulders is chased over by cloud shadows through the bedroom window. Her face is broad, wet and furious. Her hair spills down in a rough bright rope, over her collar-bone and her breasts.

'And as for you, Lorenzo – ha! I spit on you, you and your dirty little games, your fools of farmers. Just because they will listen to you and think you are God Almighty you run to them every day and leave me here alone. I am nothing! I am the Hunwife! Leave her, she is stupid, she will not understand. Go to Gurnard's Head to your Heseltines, your Grays, go down to the farm to talk with your William Henrys. I am only your wife! See if I will weep for you!'

Tears splatter across her face as she feels with a sure hand for a painted Italian plate on her dressing-table, swipes it up and sends it singing through the air at her husband's head. He steps sideways and the plate thuds against the wall and breaks. But for once he won't take up the challenge. They are both so tired, and he is beginning to realize how much confidence it takes to fight as they have fought.

'*Nu*, Frieda,' he begins quietly, watchfully.

'They are all spying on me!' she screams out. 'This hateful spying everywhere. Because I am a German they must hide in ditches and under our windows to hear what I am saying. Fools, nothing but fools. We should laugh in their faces.'

'We should do no such thing. You know that. We should lie as still as hares in the field, and let them forget us.'

'Ha! That is fine from you, you who go around telling the farm-people the war is evil and that they are going down the slope to Hell. Tell me you don't talk to William Henry and Stanley about the war! I have heard you. And you dare to tell me that I must be silent.'

He frowns. She is right, and yet not right. Things are shifting so fast now, and so dangerously. The immense apparatus of censorship and surveillance is not new-born and timid any more; it flexes its muscles and looks about it for new opportunities. Three years ago we had freedom, such freedom that we did not even know we had it, and now it is gone.

He has seen which way the wind is blowing now, how hard it is and how cold. He no longer hopes to sway, to convince, to stand in the shallows and hold back the tide of the war. He is holding tightly, light-footedly now, clinging on to the rocks while the war lashes at his feet, hungry to tear him away and smash him to pulp. The militarism he has spoken against and written against for three years is now as powerful as he foresaw it would become. It can swat him, humiliate him, destroy him. It can force him on to a train to the barracks at Bodmin, it can strip him naked and part his buttocks to stare up his anus as part of a 'medical examination'. It can jeer at him. It can open his letters and question his friends. It can treat his wife as a creature less than human, to be watched and judged. It can talk over his head, civilly, smoothly, so that his writing is stoppered and even his friends feel entitled to juggle opinions about him.

He is extreme. He is half mad. He is doing himself no good, and he makes enemies everywhere. If only he would keep quiet. Who is he to preach and lecture to us? Can't he understand how people take it? You

*would think he'd be more careful; after all, he has a German wife.
That's the root of it. Frieda has changed him. She is ruining him. All
that brilliance – do you remember? Now she has crammed him full of
her German ideas, this semi-mystical philosophical rubbish which no one
wants to read. And how charming he used to be. It is the fault of that
German woman . . .*

'We must keep ourselves apart, in our souls,' he says, frowning,
disliking the words even as they come out of his mouth. There are
too many words. He has spoken too many, written too many. Just
now, just this summer, he has had enough of words. He prefers to
walk down to the farm and help with the hay harvest, and collect
eggs, and eat fried potatoes with the Hockings in the farm
kitchen, and teach Stanley French. It reminds him of his days up at
The Haggs, years ago when he was a boy, teaching Jessie French,
peeling a basketful of pickling onions for Mrs Chambers and
going up with the men to work in the hay-fields at Greasley.

The war wants to crush him, he knows that. And he knows
now that he can be crushed as easily as a snail is battered to bits
by a thrush which does not even want to eat it. He is no good
to the war. Any military doctor can tell it at a glance. He is
white, and thin, and when they listen to his lungs they can hear
the harsh noise of his breathing. He has had pleurisy twice, and
double pneumonia, but he can manage his body if he is left
alone. It is serviceable to him. He cannot bear the way they
look him up and down, these doctors, sneering and dismissing
him. They would like to play with him like cats with a mouse.
They would like to pass him 'Fit for Non-military Duties', so
that they would have him to play with until he was broken.
They want to force him to clean out latrines. He must be
cleverer then they are, he must be still and watchful and keep
out of their snares. He will be as wise as a serpent, as silent as

an adder. He will write careful letters to his friends. And he will cry out against Frieda if she dances in the wind with her scarf flying above her like a banner. She dances for pure joy, but the war does not recognize that kind of dancing. It knows that she's twirling her scarf in a prearranged signal to the U-boats lying out offshore, waiting. And how shocked she is when he shouts at her for a fool, because, for all her passionate antagonism to the coldly watchful times in which she finds herself, Frieda does not yet realize how much she is hated. They would be glad to knock her over the cliff, and him too, if they could get away with it. But they do not quite dare; not yet.

He has a quick, bright vision of his vegetable patch. His onions are already swelling on the surface of the soil, strongly fattening themselves, half secret and half exposed. Water drains away quickly here, and the ground is dry. His hoe scratches between the onion rows and lettuces. Perhaps they'll have rain soon. The bare, blowing slopes between Higher Tregerthen and the sea are enough for him now. He will go no farther. Besides, the return fare to London is three pounds, ten shillings – money they haven't got. They have their cottage, where they can live cheaply. They have even bought a cottage piano, as well as their rosewood table and the chairs he has mended and painted.

Why isn't it enough for Frieda? A year ago he would have chased her around the kitchen-table and given as good as he had got for the throwing of that plate, but now he hasn't the heart for it. Besides, she is very strong. A powerful woman, Frieda von Richthofen, he thinks, looking at her admiringly, ruefully. A woman who would crack a plate across your head when your back was turned. And indeed has done so.

She is not crying any more. She gets up wearily, pads to the window, stares down.

'Why can't they leave us alone here?' she asks. 'We need so little. Just this house. Why can't they let us have our home in peace?'

But it's not enough any more to have few wants and try to hide away from the war in the hollow of an empty landscape. There aren't any empty landscapes, though you think there are when you first arrive, full of pure naïvety and hope. It won't work. Ordinary things are dangerous. They must not show a light, they must not tar their chimney, they must not have curtains of different colours hanging in the same window, they must not sing German folk songs on Christmas Eve in the tower with the Hockings. They must not try out Hebridean lullabies in case the outlandish sounds are taken for coded German. A block of salt in a bag may be a spy's camera. Oh, it's not the civil police – they are decent enough men. They don't like what they are doing. They aren't yet in the habit of believing that a man's life is not his own affair. It is the military police, tumbling over themselves to produce reports, to magnify gossip, to lurk shamelessly under windows and garden walls. They are ridiculous, really, but they don't care that they are ridiculous. They are only doing their job, and their job has to be done.

Yes, it's the military police, thinks Frieda. Never would she have believed it possible, but now she has seen it with her own eyes. She should laugh in their faces with derision, but by now even Lorenzo has realized that this is dangerous. But her anger comes up – she cannot help herself. They are opening letters from her mother in Germany, she knows it, and letters from Nusch. And there's the way even the decent people look at you now, so that she scarcely ever goes into the town any more. The Cornish people are still human, still individuals, but the war is winning. People don't meet her eyes, or they go past with an embarrassed, regretful half-nod. They have read about Hunwives in the newspapers, and how they must be on their guard.

Shame it has to be like this.

We didn't want it, you know.

But still. While there's the war on . . .

This isn't the right place for you.

And the others, the ones who hate nakedly. Poison seeps out of their eyes as they watch Frieda lugging her shopping up the long, lonely road to the cottage.

Big bag she's got there.

Makes you wonder what she's got in it.

It does.

They ought to do something about it. It's not right.

They are foreigners twice over, he with his red beard, she with her red stockings. There she goes with her loud voice, unashamedly German, with her big scandalous body vivid with life when so many good men have died.

Letters, she gets.

And sends them.

We know.

Who is not for me, is against me. Who does not love the war, will lose it.

He sighs. He cannot fight with Frieda now. The vigour of it's gone, and they are unsafe and exposed enough as it is.

'Put your shawl on, Frieda, and come out for a walk.'

'I suppose you have hidden away my white scarf,' she says bitterly.

He watches her as she twists up her hair again. She never looks in the mirror save for one confident narrowing of the eyes when she is finished. Her hands seem incapable of making a wrong move. Her body cannot be awkward. Now she ducks her head round and looks at him, her face bathed in sudden radiance. 'It looks nice, I think, my new blouse?'

They walk up the lane side by side. They will walk into Zennor, proudly, her blouse glowing. Frieda walks quickly because, although she is not angry any more, there is still anger in her body. They link arms and he feels the pace and heat of her movements, and knows why she is walking so fast. No matter how furious she makes him, he loves her perfect physical honesty. If she is angry she spits and throws things. If she is happy she runs and dances. If she is sad her whole body is heavy with it. She does not lie or cover things up. He has never met another woman like her.

The lane turns and they see William Henry sauntering down from the high road, bare-headed, the collie bitch at his heels. He walks slowly towards them, nods to Frieda. The bitch growls but a sharp word silences her.

'Good afternoon, Mrs Lawrence. Shall you come down to see us tonight?' he asks, turning to Lawrence, who hesitates before he answers,

'I have some new music from London – you know, Frieda, the songs Dollie Radford sent. Perhaps Stanley would like to learn them? I'll bring them down and show them to you after supper.'

'Will you come, Mrs Lawrence?' asks William Henry.

His eyes are so dark that they are quite unreadable. Lawrence is right, there is something uncanny about him, as if he scarcely belongs to this century at all. Once, in a rare moment of expansiveness with Frieda, he told her that his fields were still the same shape as they had been in Celtic times, when the Celtic farmers had cleared the ground and made granite hedges of the boulders. He spoke as if those farmers were as close to him as his own grandparents, as if he could turn and see the shadows of them working his fields.

'Thank you, not tonight,' she replies.

No, he did not want her to come. He nods quickly at her refusal.

'You been walking over to St Ives by the coast,' he remarks to Lawrence. It is not a question.

'Yesterday, you mean? No, not all the way. But I walked along the cliff-path.'

'That's what I heard. They say you met Miss Coyne – the Treveals' Clare.'

Lawrence's nostrils tighten. Frieda knows how such gossip annoys him, as much the sly satisfaction with which it is brought out as what is actually said.

'I did. We spoke about painting. We hope she will come here and meet Frieda.'

'Oh. Yess,' says William Henry, drawing out the long soft Cornish *s*. 'That'ud be the way of it. I made sure it'ud be something like that. But you know how folks are here in Zennor. They'd say she didn't belong to be roaming off by herself, since she's half a lady.'

'Can't a girl do something as harmless as go for a walk without people watching and tattling about her?' bursts out Frieda in disgust and quick sympathy with Clare.

'Oh, she *can*,' says William Henry, watching Frieda. 'She *can* do what she like. But folks'll talk, for she's Francis Coyne's daughter.'

Frieda shrugs. 'Well, I'm sure *we* shall take no notice of what they say,' she remarks with an hauteur which goes straight back to the court of Kaiser Wilhelm.

'It's getting late,' says Lawrence. 'If we want our walk, we must go on now.'

They say goodbye to William Henry, and he lounges off down the lane towards the farm, the dog pattering behind him.

'What foul gossip,' says Frieda.

'William Henry is my friend,' remarks Lawrence. 'So you can imagine what the rest of 'em are saying. It was good of him to warn us.'

Frieda gives a slight, impatient toss of her head, and walks on. After a while she asks, 'Is your Clare like the Hockings?' He glances sideways at the word 'your', but there is no weight behind it. She is offended by William Henry and the whole population of Zennor and St Ives, not by Clare or Lawrence.

'Why, she's not my Clare! You know that. I hope she'll be yours, really. She's so quick and bright, yet I'm sure she's never met a woman who thinks for herself. She knows scarcely any educated people. You could show her so much.'

A breath of Frieda's pioneer spirit stirs in her at the thought of a girl who is gifted and eager and new to everything. But a breath of suspicion counters it. Is he offering her Clare so that he can have William Henry? She brushes the thought away. I am tired, she thinks, and I am letting myself grow weak and afraid. I must not be afraid. We started from nothing and look, here we are, in this place which can be more beautiful than anywhere in the world when it wants. We have our little house, and I am not ill any more. And Lorenzo says the sea-air is making him stronger. We will not have another winter such as we had last year. Let this Clare come and see what we have.

Eleven

Clare sees John William coming along on the other side of the road from where she stands tucked right in at one side of her window, with her hand on the curtain to twitch it over if he looks up. How strangely he walks. This is not John William, who walks with easy grace and never seems to hurry. This is someone holding himself painfully upright against a storm. Yet the evening is perfectly still. He comes closer, and she sees him glance up at the house. Suddenly her blouse feels dreary and everyday. But there's no time to do anything about it, so she hoists in her belt another notch, ducks down to the mirror which plays back leaping lozenges of light and tells her nothing, then skims across her room, across the landing, and down the worn stair-carpet to wait by the newel-post, her heart thumping. She isn't going to be caught just inside the front door, where he can see her through the stained glass. But what if he goes round the back? No, he won't. Even when he was the grocer's errand boy, bringing up her pound and a half of lentils and yellow soap, he was too proud ever to go round the back entry. And here he is, fine and soft and clean in his uniform. She's flustered at the suddenness of him and the way he fills up the hall.

'Come in – come in and have something, John William. Will you have a glass of Father's sherry?'

'We'd much better get down along,' he says easily. 'Concert starts in ten minutes.'

And it does, she knows that, for hasn't she been watching each quivering touch of the long hand on to the minute all day long? But now she looks behind her and dismisses the face of the clock airily. 'Oh, is it so late? I hadn't realized.'

'Not that they ever start on time. You got your wrap – or something?'

She shakes her head.

'It's warm enough. I don't need anything.'

'You might be needing it later. It gets cool.' He's smiling.

She darts into her father's room and snatches up the Indian shawl he keeps draped over a chair. It is dark and gorgeous, though it smells of her father and his tobacco and his closed room.

'That's pretty,' says John William. 'Silk.'

He rubs the fine shawl between his fingers approvingly. He has always liked the things about her which are different from Hannah and the cousins. They stand in the empty, dim hall with evening sunlight filtering on to them through coloured panes of glass. The house is luxurious, suddenly, as she sees it through his senses, with its space and smell of polish. The polish has been rubbed in by Clare herself, but if he liked he could imagine that she has sat in a room playing the piano and asking some Annie or Edith to do the banisters again, because they are smeared. Behind them the clock which came from Coyne ticks, measuring out time. John William glances at it, watches the second hand go round at the top of the dial. It never stops; Francis Coyne says that it has been going since before Clare was born. She watches John William watching it. Time sweeping away, time which will sweep him away from her. She touches his arm, and he turns away from the clock and looks at her. Here is Clare with an Indian shawl gliding over her arms. Her workaday blouse is hidden, and the broad flirtatious stripes of Hannah's skirt. She moves slightly, reservedly, feeling herself to be desirable. This time John William doesn't try to touch her. He points at the undulating stained-glass maiden with her heavy knot of red hair and her rapt expression which Clare once loved and now mocks.

'She looks like you, Clarey,' he says.

She thinks he is teasing her, but no. He is serious as he traces the outline of hair, cheek-bone, neck on the stained glass. She knows how the glass feels under his finger.

'She looks like you look sometimes. Always in a dream. Maybe that's a good way to be.' He turns round to her and smiles.

Clare stills her lips and looks down. This is important. This is what John William wants, so it can't be ridiculous.

They open the door, and he folds her arm through his as they meet the flood of evening light and step out past the little staring row of tiptoe houses.

But unlike the Pre-Raphaelite beauty on her front door, Clare can't keep her mouth shut. She starts by making conversation, but soon she's accelerating through the void of his lack of response. And she can't be silent, as she has always been able to be with John William. Even though she hears herself gabbling and wants to stop herself, she can't. Words fall out, and they are all the wrong words.

'How is Sam *really*? Will you see him at the end of your leave? What will you say to him? Don't you think someone ought to say something – after all, there's Hannah . . .'

When? Why? What has come over him, how can he, how can he do this to Hannah? I don't understand.

John William's arm stiffens to wood. Clare ceases to be his

133

young woman and becomes a canary clinging desperately to its perch as they reach the steepest part of the hill. She nags on, her voice high and shrill. Sam and Hannah. His own sister. What's changed Sam so much?

And then, unforgivably at last, what she really wants to know. She burns at her own words, driven on by a curiosity which feels more shameful than the curiosity which led them to lift skirts and unbutton knickerbockers when they were all young together and knew nothing but this town and one another. She asks about the war. About being *out there*. What is it like? What it is *really* like. The war. Your friends around you, dying. Billy. No one tells us anything. But you know. Tell me, John William . . .

Tell me. Let me sympathize. Let me be the one.

You can talk to me.

You can spill yourself on me.

She doesn't even need to say it. He knows it. She is warm and sticky and eager. But he wants none of it. He cannot expose his exhaustion to Clare. It is all right for her to try to draw his soul out of him, but he has got to go back into the world of the war. He cannot look to the left of him or to the right of him.

She looks up and sees the tight skin around his eyes and the set of his mouth. It is only his heavy tan that makes him look healthy, she realizes. Under it his colour is bad. How they used to swing along together, arm in arm, she and Hannah and John William. They could walk for miles. But it hurts her to walk with him now. They hurt each other.

And here's the Drill Hall and so he doesn't have to say anything. And here's Pretty Peggy, free for the evening, dancing up to them. Little Georgie's in bed, and her employers were only too pleased to let her go to a Red Cross concert.

Peggy's eyes dart over Clare and John William as they barge forward together, out of step with one another. Clare bangs the back of her hand against the rough wall. She reddens slightly with the effort of suppressing pain. Peggy's little, off-centre face glows at John William. She is really lovely tonight, dressed in something he doesn't notice – white, perhaps. Cool. She teases him.

'I wouldn't have known you in that uniform, John William. He's grown so handsome, hasn't he, Clare?'

Now, appealing to Clare, she becomes the privileged friend, licensed to flirtatious sisterliness with John William.

Clare says nothing. Somehow she and John William have dropped arms. Her own arm feels numb where he held it, and she'd like to rub it. Instead she pulls the shawl round her more closely, because he's right, it is getting colder already.

Peggy puts up a little, light hand to marvel at the shortness of John William's hair. She caresses the bristle at the back of his neck. And he just stands there like a prize bull, thinks Clare. Her offended body recoils farther from his.

'Such a shame there's no dancing tonight,' says Peggy. 'I love dancing, Clare can tell you. But we haven't had any for ages, with all you boys gone.'

'You *should* dance, in that dress,' says John William. The breeze stirs a wisp of it and the skirts flatten against Peggy's slender legs.

'Oh, well,' she says. She looks down, then up again, under lasholened eyelids.

'We ought to get our tickets,' says Clare. Her voice feels clumsy in her mouth. If only Hannah were here. She always knew how to deal with Peggy. When they were children, it was Clare who snapped at Peggy's provocations, and raged and pulled hair and got a whipping from Nan for treating poor little Peggy like that. Hannah sized up situations and then deflated them.

'In a minute,' says John William. The crowd bulges around the entrance, under the bunting, the home-made red, white and blue decorations and the skewed portrait of the King. There are farmers, shop-people, fishermen and swarms of kids without tickets getting their caps knocked off as they dive under people's elbows to see through the door. Not many in khaki. They'd all make way for John William. The Belgian singer has arrived. She's in the back, resting her voice. She's been sucking glycerine lozenges since noon, they say, because this is the last leg of a tour which has taken her from Exeter all down Cornwall. Travelling through all that dust, no wonder she's hoarse. But she's good. Oh, yes, there's no doubt about that. Your Uncle Arthur spoke to someone at Penzance market who heard her up at Plymouth and he did say . . .

Uncle Arthur and Aunt Sarah. Even Aunt Mabel who never comes to things and looks as washed out and wobbly as ever, with her fingers tense on Uncle William's sleeve. Kitchie ducks through the crowd towards Clare, lighting up at the sight of John William. Two gulls swing over the crowd, louder than the milling voices below. They poise on a current of air and then dive-bomb Mrs Cocking's feathered Sunday hat. There are shrieks of laughter, and she too decides she'd better make light of it in spite of her annoyance at the damned thing and the sight of her mangled, claw-struck best straw. Besides, one of the gulls has shat on it in fright. There's the black shape of Mrs Hore. The crowd makes space for her, respecting her inky trail of grief.

'Hello, John William,' says Kitchie. 'Hello, Peggy.'

For they stand together. They are a couple, suddenly, her white dress hazing his uniform, her laughter drawing in Kitchie too. Her eyes flit over Clare without looking at her. But tomorrow they'll be friends again.

'You looked *lovely* in that skirt of Hannah's last night, Clarey,' she'll say tomorrow, widening her eyes. Because Peggy will never let herself know anything. What is there to know? If you said anything, she'd answer, 'But what's the matter with you? We were only having a bit of fun.' All she's doing is having a bit of fun and a lovely time. Everybody's having a lovely time. The sky's clear blue, striped with mackerel, the gulls are raving over fish-heads, Peggy's got the evening off and everybody loves her. Even little Georgie wouldn't go to sleep tonight without a kiss from his Peggy.

Peggy's flittering eyes have spotted the skirt Clare's wearing and identified it instantly, but she won't say anything about it now, because she's not that sort of a girl.

'He's so *brown*, isn't he, Clare?' she coos. 'Even the back of his neck!' And she just touches it.

'It goes down farther'n that,' says John William, with his straight, unreadable look, and Peggy flushes deliciously and shrinks towards him.

'I expect you'd like to take a look, wouldn't you, Peg?' a voice remarks. 'I'm sure we could arrange it for you, couldn't we, Clare?' It's Hannah, slipping in suddenly beside Kitchie, wearing just her plain navy skirt and white blouse. Peggy frowns. Her native prudishness peeks out as she says, 'Really, Hannah, what a thing to suggest.'

But everyone is looking at Hannah now, not at Peggy. You can't keep a good story hidden. Everyone knows Sam's got leave but he hasn't come home. How will Hannah take it? Shame on him. You've got to feel sorry for the girl.

But you don't and you can't feel sorry for her, not when Hannah is there before you. Her eyes are steady, and after a few moments the furtive glances die down like a breeze-eddy on the bay.

She smiles warmly at Clare. 'You look lovely, Clare,' she says. 'Doesn't she, Johnnie?' Only Hannah calls him that, and hardly ever. But she does so now, asserting that *she's* John William's sister as she moves in close to him, leaving no space for Peggy's insinuating sisterliness. As Hannah moves forward, she seems to draw Clare closer too.

'You and Clarey better be going on in,' she tells her brother. 'You don't want to be stuck in those nasty seats at the back, not with our Clarey, do you?'

She winks at the couple. They have all heard Grandad fulminating against 'those nasty seats at the back of the cinema', and the evils they hold for the young girls of Penzance when the boys are on leave. There's a ripple of laughter. Kitchie guffaws, then glances quickly at John William. Only Peggy does not see the joke.

Clare's breathing steadies. She is *their* Clarey.

'All right, let's get our tickets, shall we?' says John William. 'Three, is it, Hannah?'

'I've got mine. I'm over there with Nan. Come on, Peggy, Nan was wanting to have a word with you. Come and sit with us.' And she tows off the reluctant Peggy, who is by now rather chilly in her white dress, and glad enough to be in with the press of warm, breathing people.

Some instinct keeps Clare very still. She draws her shawl close, and looks down.

'There's such a crowd,' she demurs. Hannah would be proud of her. John William takes her arm, and thrusts forward with the other shoulder. As she's expected, the people around them make way. All the farmers struggling for exemptions for their sons want to be seen here tonight at the Red Cross concert. They make way for John William and murmur approving nothings to him as he goes by. Clare and John William are drawn through the narrow central doorway and into the hall.

It is true enough about the glycerine lozenges. In the small side room Eliane leans into a mirror which has been propped ready for her. Her practised fingers twist up the last scraps of her reddish hair over her false hairpiece and jab in the pins. She hennas her hair and she had better do it again soon, because a narrow strip of grey is worming its way to the surface at her parting. However, no one will see it on stage. She damps her index finger with spit and combs the hair a little looser, clouding, hiding. Once she's back in London she'll go to Emile to have her hair cleaned, then she'll henna it again. But her costume is perfect. Dove-grey, demure but piquant, trimmed with black velvet. Eliane despises singers who trail about in flowing white with patriotic sashes, particularly those who continue to do so once they are over thirty. Who do they imagine they are deceiving? Besides, they have no elegance. Do they wish to pretend they are still at their First Communion? Then they should put a veil over their heads and have done with it.

Exeter, Plymouth, Bodmin, Liskeard, Truro, Redruth. St Ives tonight, Penzance tomorrow, and there's an end of it, for this tour at least. Back to London on what passes for a fast train these days, crowded with soldiers who will give up two seats if she asks them, so that she can keep her hatboxes beside her. Then she can draw her veil over her face and turn to the window and sleep. There is a place for veils, certainly: Eliane knows that no woman is at her most charming when she is sleeping. No woman over thirty, that is sure, when her unguarded jaw sags a little and a bubble of spittle comes out at the corner of her mouth. It's necessary to give thought to such things.

She finishes putting kohl around her eyes. The art lies in wiping nearly all of it away again, so that there is only a suggestion of shadowiness around the pure violet which is her best feature – really, she knows, her only feature. Her nose is little but poorly shaped; her mouth elegant, nothing more. And another week of these train-smuts will ruin her complexion for good. But her eyes are unassailable. She turns, opening them slowly to their most direct, most shadowy regard. Her face vanishes and there is a garden at dusk, a bowl of hyacinths, the sea at Naxos. Everything has been said already and sometimes she wonders if she will ever hear it again, when she wakes up in the train and for the hundredth time adjusts the tired, crumpled flesh of her face into a vase for her eyes.

They are terrible, these little towns. Smells of sweat and dust, great red faces lolling on the other side of the stage, greedy for her but always holding themselves back, never really enthralled. She knows quite well that even as her husky, hesitant voice casts out its spell and trawls among them a good third are still thinking of their dinner, or whether the position of their seat adequately reflects their social position, or how much money they need to put into the collection. If they are women, they are wondering about Eliane. Is she married or not married, is she – you know – people on the stage . . . They sit there preening themselves a little beside the bulwark of their Sunday-best husbands, who are bolt upright, hands on thighs, straining the cloth of their good Sunday suits. What they are thinking glides under the surface of their eyes as they devour her body and her clothes, and are satisfied that after all, there's nothing so special about her. But they can never quite satisfy themselves. Afterwards, if there is a reception and she must talk to the mayor or the freemen of the town or the local vicar, she will feel the prickle of eyes upon her still. What is it about her? Her dress is quite ordinary. The eyes cost it. Plain fine grey wool. Velvet trimmings, one and six-three the yard. No jewels. You would think she would be more – well, dressed up.

And yet the mayor and the curate kindle in spite of themselves. Warmth rises; one, more daring or simply more human than the others, presses her hand as he assures her again that it was magnificent, deeply moving. It's there again, that curious ethereal element which is called her success. It glows around her as she smiles faintly at the joke of one, or acknowledges the bow of another. And the more it grows, the more the faces smile and the crowd thickens around her, the more she longs to be in the next dirty train, with the window open and the cold night air coming in, on her way to her next engagement.

She isn't sleeping here tonight; she will go on to Penzance after the concert and spend the next morning resting her face and her voice in her hotel. There have been too many concerts and that faint, attractive huskiness is becoming too pronounced.

She has rubbed off most of the rouge too. Time to go on. She puts down her handkerchief.

Clare and John William are in the middle of their row and near the front. They both sit stiffly upright, conscious of their position among Chellews and Stephens and isn't that the Canon there, on the right? But then John William turns and gives Clare a lightning wink and suddenly this is their own concert, their night out together, and no one has more right here than they have. Clare glows and relaxes for the first time since morning.

Eliane steps out on to the stage, and stands there in front of them, 'quite simply', in a way which is so accomplished that it looks perfectly natural, her hands clasped at her waist. Her hands are extraordinarily white and fine, but that may be the light on them, thinks Clare. Eliane gives a little smile and lets her blue gaze cross the audience.

'I am going to sing for you first – a little song of my country – where some of you may have been,' and she gives a small, acknowledging nod towards the nearest man in khaki, who happens to be John William.

Clare's French is just about up to the song.

> Little pigeon on my sweetheart's roof
> Little pigeon with grey feathers
> Fly to my sweetheart's soft breast
> And tell him of my love . . .

John William does not understand, thinks Clare, glancing at him. But from the look on his face she wonders if he might have learned some French over there. And everyone knows the word for love.

The songs follow one another tenderly, hesitantly, humorously. Little villages sleep in the sun, girls are married, lovers run away, old mothers long for their sons to come home. Eliane sketches out the meaning of each song to them before she sings it. A red cockerel is deceived by a sly brown hen. A young girl sings in the early morning as she tills her vegetable garden. Then there's a funny one with a chorus about a little sailor who runs back home to his mother. Eliane translates for them and coaches them in the French chorus, and they sing along, first shyly and then with gusto as she draws them in with her white fingers. One last time, the little sailor runs away to sea and does not like the look of the dark green waves. His little boat shakes and makes him afraid. He wants to be home by the fireside, does he, drinking his soup? But he has to go, there's no way out of it. The contingent from downalong roars its approval. They know the feeling.

Then there is a change of tone. The piano accompanist drops his hands to his lap. Eliane steps forward almost to the edge of the stage. She closes her eyes and her eye-sockets became huge and shadowy but remain violet, as if the colour is still shining through her closed lids. She cannot sing this one with her eyes open. The audience leans forward. She says, 'This is a song I wrote myself, about my country. I am going to sing it to you now in English.'

> In my country there grows an apple tree
> Full of white blossom
> The blossom is blowing
>
> In my country there grows an apple tree
> Full of green apples
> The apples are ripening
>
> In my country there grows an apple tree
> Full of red apples
> The apples are falling
>
> In my country there grows an apple tree
> Black and empty
> The wind is blowing . . .

It works. It always works. The slender, intimate thread of Eliane's voice swells and dies down. The tree is empty, the orchard has been broken open, and the fields are ploughed up by guns and shells. There will never be any apples any more.

Eliane stands very still, her hands folded. She opens her eyes and looks along the rows. Each man thinks she is scanning the row to find his face. Clare sits back in her seat. Father should have come – this wasn't at all the usual Belgian thing. Not a mention of priests, churchbells, atrocities, flags, vengeance or valorous resistance. And people are standing up in their seats, applauding Eliane. Waves of sound beat around her grey dress and her small bowed head. Clare looks around at the audience, because for some reason she does not want to look at Eliane any more. Their faces glisten as they clap and cheer; only a few matrons sit it out, with reserved, sceptical looks on their faces. One or two are already striding purposefully towards the collecting boxes, ready to position themselves at the exit. Eliane remains still, and it is obvious that she's not going to sing again. She bows once and leaves the stage, and the steady clapping dissolves at once into hubbub as each person turns to a neighbour to say the same things about the singer. They are quickly said, and then it's time to scan the audience. Who's here, who's unaccountably absent, who is with whom, what is she wearing, *she* looks very bad poor soul, is that John William Treveal, I wouldn't have known him.

John William doesn't say anything. He is still looking at the stage, though Eliane is no longer on it. He is grey with fatigue, and he is unnaturally still, leaning forward slightly, as if he hears something Clare cannot hear. There is a light film of sweat on his forehead. He does not look well, but perhaps that is the heat of the hall and the noise of the people? Clare touches his arm, and he turns towards her like someone waking up.

'That apple song,' says Clare. 'It reminds me of the orchard where you caught the hen.'

'The orchard she was singing about,' he says. 'You want to find it every day when you wake up. You would give the rest of your life to wake up in that orchard, with one blackbird singing. All grey and cool with wet grass, Clarey, and so quiet you can hear the leaves moving. Only you never get there. You start hearing the guns.'

'Do you want to stay on?' she asks, feeling her own generosity. 'Do you want to speak to her? After all *you've* been over there . . .'

'Me and how many more? No. She's got nothing more to say to me than she's said already, and anyone who thinks otherwise is fooling himself.' But he speaks harshly, as if he's crushing down the person who might think otherwise and fool himself.

'We'll go, then, will we?' says Clare, and they stand and he takes her arm and they wait while the press of people thins. Then she sees something at the other side of the room. Red, flaming, jutting. A beard. Well, she would have never thought to see him here. This would have been the very last place. But the crowd is sweeping her closer to him. If he doesn't move, they're going to pass right by him. Will he speak? Should she? Will other people know who he is?

He turns and sees her and his face dissolves into a smile of such warmth that she smiles back at once, openly, the way a baby does to its mother, without even thinking about it. He reaches and takes her hand and pulls her out of the stream of people. She catches a curious look from Aunt Mabel. She's going to hear about this later, for sure. John William still has hold of her arm and suddenly there they are, the three of them forming an island among the people.

Lawrence speaks only to Clare, quickly and intimately: 'What did you think? Did you like her?'

She hesitates, then tells the truth.

'Not really. I felt as if I were *meant* to be feeling something, but I couldn't feel it.'

He laughs. 'It's true, she hasn't a good voice. But *can't* she put it over!'

Clare smiles back at him, delighted. 'You didn't like her either!'

'Nevertheless she knows her stuff. Look at 'em!' He gestures at the buoyant, glistening, departing crowd, fumbling in its pockets, smiling gratefully at the collectors as if glad to be given the chance to express its feelings in coin.

Beside them, John William darkens so perceptibly that Clare remembers him with a start.

'This is my cousin, John William Treveal. John William, this is Mr Lawrence. He's staying up at Higher Tregerthen.'

The men acknowledge one another. John William's eyes make the rapid, automatic scan of the conscripted soldier. A man of military age. Civilian clothes. He notes the oddness of the clothes, but doesn't bother to think about it yet. Not called up. Why not? Health, probably. Rejected. Look at his colour. And his thinness.

'You are on leave, I think, Mr Treveal?' inquires Lawrence, and in spite of himself John William finds himself responding.

'I'm due at the training camp tomorrow night,' he says.

'And you liked Eliane?'

'I did.'

Clare looks from one face to the other. John William's is alive now, and intelligent. He has lost the small-headed animal look he had on him in the morning, down by the sea. He looks like what he is, her cousin with his books and his night-school and his carefully guarded plans, and his wild fights under the hedges.

'I'm glad. Your time is so short, you should enjoy it.'

John William says, 'There's a woman who knows what it's like over there. No one here does.'

He is unanswerable. He has played his card and the two of them are silenced.

'And if I'd a wanted *that* sort of enjoyment I'd a stayed in London,' continues John William, who is clearly responding to some argument which has been going on inside himself, rather than to what is actually being said.

What sort of enjoyment does he mean, thinks Clare? Oh. He thinks Lawrence is telling him to have a good time, the way soldiers are supposed to. He's offended. He imagines Lawrence thinks he is not clever, that he is just a common soldier. But I'm sure he is mistaken. Lawrence is watching John William attentively. The words between them have been prickly, but the two men don't now feel unsympathetic to one another. Suddenly Clare can imagine them walking together, talking. But now there are people jostling at their backs – they are in the way here.

'I must go,' says Lawrence. 'Frieda doesn't like to be alone late at night. She's expecting you on Tuesday, Miss Coyne.'

'How will you get back – you won't walk, surely?' For it's late, and dark, and six and a half miles to Higher Tregerthen.

'I shall walk. I shall like to walk. There'll be a moon.'

He must be stronger than he looks, thinks John William.

He'll walk through the moonlight, on the high road up to Zennor. The coolness and freshness of that walk through the night sweeps over him suddenly like the most desirable thing in the world. He must go too – but there's Clarey, holding on to his arm. But Clare won't mind. She will know how he feels.

'If you like,' he says to Lawrence, 'I'll walk my cousin home, then give you company up to Zennor.'

Lawrence must have caught the shock of disappointment that went through Clare, or the look in her eyes before she drops her lids. He says quickly, 'I don't want to take you out of your way. I s'll enjoy the walk.'

'I may as well walk,' says John William. 'I walked all last night. I don't sleep here.'

'You slept this afternoon, Kitchie said,' Clare reminds him.

He hitches his shoulders. 'That was easy. Nan was talking.'

'John William!'

'I don't mean it like that, though. She was talking to Aunt Mag, not to me. Only, it felt good to sleep while she was in the room.'

'Yes, you sleep best in the presence of someone who loves you,' says Lawrence. 'But walking may do it too. You can fall asleep on your feet. *I* shan't stop you.'

'I've seen columns of men marching, all of them asleep,' says John William. 'And you should hear the sound of their boots when they go out of step. It's like waves breaking on Treen Cove in a south-westerly. D'you know Treen Cove?'

Lawrence nods.

'We walk all along – all around the country,' he says.

'Ah, then you're a real Zennor goat!' says John William.

Clare says nothing as they laugh. She is very tired suddenly and knows that she looks pale and shrunken. Now she has swallowed her first disappointment, she wants to be rid of them both. She hasn't got close to John William at all the whole evening. First Peggy, then Eliane, and now her own friend. And yet under it all there's some small, secret part of her which is relieved. What might he want of her? They are not children any more. She begins to see how much John William might want of her now, and how much he could hurt her. If he asked something of her, she could never help giving it. If she could make herself into an orchard for him, she would be bound to do it.

They set out past the Wesley Chapel and turn up Wesley Place. As they come to Windsor Hill, the men each take one of Clare's arms, though she is supple and light and used to any hill. She has the red-bearded one on her left, moving quickly, though she hears the strain in his breathing, and her dark cousin on her right, drawing her arm close within his. The moon is up, just as Lawrence said, and there's honeysuckle in one of the gardens. She smells it briefly and tantalizingly as they go past its garden. In a few more minutes they are up on the top, with the cemetery beneath them. Clare looks along the row of houses and sees the light in her porch.

'Father will be waiting up for me,' she says. Let John William know that she never intended to do anything but accompany him to the concert and then home at perhaps just a slightly slower pace than the one they've taken. She is wanted, waited for, shielded by Father and this house and God's Holy Church and her own good sense. She is not like Hannah, she thinks betrayingly, then catches her hand on Hannah's skirt and flushes in the darkness, as if she's smirched Hannah's quick loyalty to her. How Hannah had spoken to Peggy – *that* was what Hannah was like. Hannah's brother stops in front of Clare's house.

'My train leaves at eleven,' he says. 'You'll be there, Clarey? You won't stay away this time?'

She nods. She'll come.

'I'll see you then.'

He leans over her and draws her shawl close over her shoulders, although the night's not cold and she's about to go indoors. His bare hand touches her neck and she shivers. He leaves his hand lying there, heavy and solid. He is not a ghost. He is real and present, but tomorrow he'll be gone. She tilts her head so that her cheek touches the back of his hand.

'You go on in now, Clarey. You don't want to catch cold.'

'Goodnight, John William.'

And she wants to cry out to Lawrence to be careful of him, not to let him roam back along the coast-path but to make him go home by the road. For it's night, and the moon'll set, and he's in the mood to think he hears singing from down in one of the coves. *Women's voices* . . . Don't leave him on his own up there, she wants to say, and what she sees is Eliane, gleaming on a black, salt-soaked rock with just enough moon to show her eyes and her small half-smile turned to the land, beckoning.

'Goodnight,' she says again and stretches up and brushes his cheek quickly, lightly, with her own. It's not really a kiss.

'Goodnight, Mr Lawrence,' she says into the dark where she can barely see his outline, and he answers, 'Be sure and come on Tuesday. Frieda expects you.'

She opens the house-door and there is the smell of her father's tobacco and a glint of Sheba disappearing down the passage.

Twelve

Father's study door opens as she crosses the hall, and he comes out, stooped and blinking. How old he looks. She's never noticed before that the space between his eyes is webbed with small lines. He'll have been straining his eyes, reading late in bad light, and tomorrow he'll have a headache.

'Ah! Clare. Did you enjoy the concert?'

'Yes, Father. It was very good. Have you had your Bengers? Shall I make some for us?'

He smiles gratefully. She is looking more like herself, he thinks. The concert has done her good. She ought to go out more. It's a pity there are so few people here for her to get to know. She should be going to dances, concerts, tea with friends, weekends in the country. Look at her now, all dressed up just to go out to a Red Cross concert with her cousins.

'I am glad you wore your grandmother's shawl,' he says.

'Oh!' She'd forgotten. She'd meant to slip the shawl back without his noticing. 'You don't mind?'

'Not at all, you wear it, you wear it. She would have liked you to have it. It was made to be wrapped around beautiful young ladies.'

She wishes he wouldn't talk like that. The role of creaking complimentary Papa doesn't suit him at all. She much prefers him bawling absent-mindedly for his cup of tea while she's in the middle of peeling potatoes. That's the way they've always lived together. He peers at Clare's skirt. That seems familiar too. Where has he seen it? He can't quite recall but it brings a disturbing association into his mind, one which doesn't belong with his Clare.

'I hope John William brought you home?' For these cousins can be careless. They forget that his Clare is not a child any more, to knock about the streets with them and find her own way home.

'Yes; he was going to go for a walk with a friend, so he brought me home first.'

A friend, thinks Francis Coyne. Clare is being discreet, or is she just innocent? John William is on leave, sandwiched between war and preparation for war. There's bound to be a woman somewhere who'll let him bury himself in her tonight. Someone he'll pay, or perhaps a girl who's always cared for him and won't wait now he may be going off again for ever. It happens all the time. Perhaps Clare even knows the girl. She was always closest to John William, out of all her boy cousins. Does he confide in her? Does he tell her things she ought not to know?

'How is your cousin?' he asks abruptly.

Clare moves off towards the kitchen, fidgeting with her shawl.

'Oh, well, you know John William. He hasn't said much. He looks well, though, doesn't he? Isn't he brown? Didn't you think so when you saw him?'

'He looks older. I'd never have thought the boy would grow up so fast.'

She rounds on him, blazing, her eyes dark in a white violent face.

'He isn't a boy any more, Father, he's a man.'

He is shocked. His Clare sounds as if she hates him.

'It was just a manner of speaking, Clare. Of course we are all proud of him. He's done great things, great things –'

'Or if he's a boy, then why don't the men go? The ones who are always telling us how much they'd like to go if they could? It makes me sick when Uncle John says he wishes he was twenty years younger. He knows it's a lie, and we know it's a lie. But we have to pretend to be grateful to him for what he'd never had done anyway.'

'But Clare – you know your Uncle John. He's not an educated man. He talks as he hears others talking.'

'Yes, why don't they all go,' she repeats bitterly. 'Why not Uncle Arthur and Uncle Stan and Uncle William and Uncle John, since they know so much about the war? They're always so proud of telling us what they've read in the *Daily Mail*.'

'I think you're being a little unfair. Look how hard Uncle John's worked to get the boys exempted.'

'He's tried for Albert, you mean. And Jo, and George. But not for Kitchie, has he? What about Kitchie when his time comes up? What about Harry? What's he going to do for Harry when they say that Harry's bad arm doesn't count any more, that's fine, he can still fight with it? Because they *will* say that, you know they will. And what about John William?' Her breath runs out, and her voice squeaks as she says John William's name. She stares at her father.

'Clare. Clare. Come now. I'm sure if you asked John William, he would tell you that he understands why we have to fight. And think how well John William's done. His commission will stand him in good stead after the war.'

He has to say it, and even six months ago he could just about have believed it. He could have believed in what they were fighting for, and in the evil of what they were fighting against.

But now he can't believe in it any more. He is reminded of the deadly frustration he used to feel when his mother called him into her bedroom because she had not seen him at the altar rails for months. She would talk to him of her own 'implicit faith', her God-given freedom from doubt or difficulty in matters of religion, and how she only longed to share this with him. He can see now her blind, ecstatic face as she told him she would pray night and day for God to grant him this same faith.

To cease to believe in the war feels like that loss of faith; it is something he has kept just as secret. All he can see is confusion, and newspaper columns full of deaths and explanations which mask still more confusion. We're frantic with fear of what we've already done, and what we're doing now, and what we're about to do, he thinks. But we have to go on pretending that we know what we are doing. Newspaper justifications. We are like children whose game has gone terribly wrong, all gathered round the one who's got hurt, begging him to say it's all right, it doesn't matter, the blood can be wiped off and we can all go home.

But we can't let out the truth, not now that so many have died. It would be like killing them again. We can't say how bloody and pointless it's become, and that we don't know what to do any more. These are our children who are dying, rows of them in uniform like the children they were a few years ago in their school photographs. Our sons, dying for us. It's the wrong way round. People die for their children, that's the way it has always been. Now we send them out fresh from school. Everything is confusion.

'Clare,' he goes on diffidently, 'has John William been talking to you about the war? Has it distressed you?'

She laughs, then her eyes fill with tears. Her face quivers and she hides it behind her hands, then sinks down on to the carpet, kneeling, obliterating herself, shaken with sobs.

Now he knows something must have happened. After the concert perhaps. How he dislikes these patriotic concerts. They send people out into the streets swollen with enjoyable sentimentalities which they confuse with feeling. This whole country is in love with the idea of death, as long as the death happens elsewhere.

He has a sudden vision of seven-year-old Clare, beside herself with rage, drumming the carpet with her heels. It's best for her if I let her cry, he tells himself, and the thought makes him easier. After a few moments, hovering, he says, 'I'll go and make our Bengers.'

A hot drink will do her good. He bustles gratefully to the kitchen, feels along the cupboard-top for the matches – isn't that where she keeps them? – and lights the stove. A soft blue bubble of flame comes up. He watches it, thinking of May. He tries to remember whether May has ever talked about the war. He doesn't think so – or if she has, it's only to say the same things everybody says. While he is with her, there is no world outside her cottage, her bed, the white, blue-hazed circle of her thighs.

He scrapes the bottom of the Bengers tin, stirs the powder into hot milk, fills two striped mugs and carries them back to Clare. Her hand slips out and takes one of the mugs. He sits down on the shabby carpet beside her and puts his arm around her. She is still shaking, but she seems calmer. She's over the worst of it. How she used to cry! He smiles, remembering. He'd think she would choke herself, or scream herself into a fit. He had nearly forgotten. When her grandmother used to scold her or Hannah wouldn't play or the others had gone off without her. And now she's grown up and he doesn't know what she cries about any more. Who does she talk to now?

'Clare,' he suggests, 'perhaps we should have the rosary tonight? With a special intention for John William?'

He braces himself for the sting of her refusal, but after a minute she nods. He was right not to talk about the war any more. They both need to recollect themselves. He goes and fetches their beads, and they kneel on the hall carpet together, with the cheap cord pressing into their flesh. He makes the sign of the Cross and leads the prayers, feeling his way forward through Clare's silence, until her voice responds in the third Hail Mary. He sighs in relief and plunges on through the decade of the Resurrection. This is putting things right! Somehow they've got out of the way of the evening rosary – he can't quite remember how it happened. He had always resolved to keep it going for Clare, no matter how he felt himself. Religion is more important to women. They are beautiful within it, he knows, thinking of his shy, plain sisters.

To Clare, the hall is as cold as the bottom of the sea, as cold as the current that tugs past the Island, taking dead things with it. She's stood there often in early spring and watched the mackerel luggers buck as they come out of the harbour and set sail south-west. From here you can look down on the men bending over their gear, with their backs to the land and their legs braced against the swing of the decks.

Prayers slip and drift behind her; her cold little beads trail through her fingers. She shuts her eyes. Now, she's leaning over the back of Uncle Arthur's rowing boat. The boys are rowing; Harry at the back because of his arm, John William pulling away strongly. The water is navy-blue and the sun blazes around the white circle of her cotton sun-bonnet. She is ten years old. She kneels in the stern and holds her beads down in the water, into the bubbling stream of the wake, and then slowly, slowly she uncurls her fingers and lets the sea slip the rosary right off her hand. There, it's gone. She looks over her shoulder at John William.

'An owl,' says John William. The two men look up and see its white spread wings ghost across the road in the moonlight.

'A little owl, isn't it?'

'Yes, that's what we get commonly round here. Sometimes you'll see a pair of short-eared owls hunting over the moor when we've a plague of voles. They'll raise two broods in a season then, and take hundreds of voles.'

They walk on in silence, as they have walked most of the last three miles, brushed by moths and night breezes. The moon is up, sheeted by a thin layer of cloud. Its light is grey and wan, like dawn. It has none of the glamour of unclouded moonlight and the two men's moon-shadows are vague splotches in front of them. Far off on their right the long Atlantic swell rolls in against the cliffs.

Their feet crunch loose stones. They are both wearing evening shoes, more suitable for the concert than for miles of country road. Lawrence had a lift into St Ives in the Hockings' trap earlier, and would have ridden home in it but for meeting Clare and John William. But it is good to walk. It feels like walking out of the world entirely, into a moonscape of sky and moorlands which were here long before the first people came to live in the hollows and valleys. Lawrence and John William walk on past streams rushing off the moor, through the smell of dung spread on fields, through knotty, complicated shadows of thorn-trees. Granite boulders loom, balancing on top of one another as they have done for more than two thousand years. They seem to pivot over the little fields like blind men. Surely they are moving? But when you stop, and blink, it is the effect of the moonlight. You walk on, and just out of the corner of your eye you see the loggans stir . . .

'Zennor witches,' says John William.

'This is a country for witches, isn't it? I've heard stories from the Hockings.'

'Oh, you'll hear stories from everyone here.'

Lawrence hears the other man's soft laugh. There is no humour in it. He glances at John William's face and sees that it is set hard. The moon draws out odd resemblances. John William's bulky shoulders and blunt, cropped head make him seem like a cousin of those standing stones. But how ill he looks, suddenly. The wash of moonlight shows a sheen of sweat on his face.

'So, you are going to study medicine after the war?' Lawrence prompts him, wanting to resume the conversation they'd started as they left behind the last few houses of St Ives.

John William lowers his head, draws in a deep breath of exhaustion. 'Yes,' he says vaguely.

'You are tired. I should not have brought you so far,' says Lawrence with quick, warm sympathy. 'Should you like to stay at the cottage with us? We have only two rooms, but we can make up a comfortable bed for you. It is very quiet – only Frieda and myself. You could walk back to St Ives in the morning.'

John William shakes his head slowly, as if to clear it. His footsteps drag. His shoe scuffs against gravel, then he stands stock-still.

'Listen,' he whispers.

The soughing of the wind, the sea's slow suck and heave, the thousand sounds of the countryside stirring at night. A small agonized squeak, cut off as soon as it forms. Around the moon the clouds thin and race north.

'Listen,' whispers John William, 'listen. Can't you hear them?'

'No, I hear nothing,' says Lawrence.

John William sinks with a slow staggering motion to his knees. His fists clench, his face turns up to the moon, he scans the thorn-bushes. *There it is.* He freezes, staring, then, 'Get down, Hawker! Get down! Get your fucking head down!'

A pause. The breeze lifts Lawrence's hair as John William slowly lowers his own head and knuckles his fists against his eyes, hiding what they have seen. In the quiet Lawrence hears his short, harsh breathing. He waits, not daring to touch or speak to the kneeling man. Slowly the shoulders relax and sag. Lawrence reaches out and puts his hand on John William's arm. He shudders, but does not strike out at the other man.

'Come on,' says Lawrence. 'Best come to the cottage. You can rest there.'

John William takes his hands from his face, shivers slightly, and looks up. His face is blank for a moment or two, then it relaxes. He says in the same easy tones in which he discussed his career in medicine, 'I ought to get back now.'

'Ought you?' asks Lawrence carefully.

'There's not much time,' explains John William.

'No, you are going back to camp tomorrow, of course. You will want to be with your family tonight.'

'You know Clarey's my cousin?'

'Yes. Yes, I did know.'

'Cousin Clarey,' repeats John William thoughtfully. His smile is real now, and he gets up lithely, sweeping the dirt off his knees as if it's an immense joke to find himself kneeling in the road.

'But you should not go back so soon. You aren't well.'

'Me?' asks John William. He sounds astonished. 'Why, I'm well enough. Fit for an officer.' He laughs again, looks around, says, 'We used to walk up here, you know. All the way to Zennor we'd walk, Clare and Hannah and me. The whole day up on the moor with our dinner basket Nan gave us. When we were tired, Hannah made house for us under a thorn-tree. Clare always wanted to go and see the little mermaid.'

'And did she?'

'Oh, yes. We got as far as the church one time. Then we had milk at one of the farms, warm out of the cow. The farm-people knew Nan. They wanted Clare to drink buttermilk because she was so pale, but she pressed her mouth shut. She didn't like it.'

His smile is pure reminiscent affection. Lawrence sees that he remembers nothing of Hawker now. John William has gone back to where Clare is a stubborn child in a grass-stained petticoat, lips pinched to a thin line, and Hawker is an unknown boy of seven somewhere in England, wandering out with his pail to pick blackberries or blubbing in a corner because he has had the strap.

'So you'll turn here?'

'I shall,' says John William. The two men are very close. Far off, a chained dog barks, but they feel themselves to be the only living creatures in the landscape. The cloud is dissolving now, blowing into flakes over the moon, and the light is strong. They shake hands, feeling the living flesh behind the transfer of warmth. They move apart.

'Come and visit us when you are next on leave,' says Lawrence.

'I shall,' says John William. He smiles, turns and walks swiftly back along the road to St Ives while Lawrence watches. John William doesn't hesitate or look back; he looks neither to the right of him nor to the left of him.

Thirteen

He comes whistling into her dreams. The sea tosses; she stirs uneasily. Don't go so close in to the rocks, she begs him, in small desperate whispers. But he pulls harder, hauling at the sweat-worn oars. They are toiling out into the bay – she can see Clodgy Point with white foam smothering the rocks, then the waves roll back and the rock streams black and clear. The sea heaves as it roughens, but there is no sound of wind or water, only thin whistling, on and on.

And she wakes. The whistling goes on like bad luck. What had Nan told her? 'It's ill-luck to whistle, for you never know what you're calling to come to you. Don't let the men hear you.' The boys knew they must never whistle at night. The seven whistlers mean death when you hear them. But the night is still and there's someone out in it, whistling for Clare.

She slithers out of her bed. Her night-gown sticks to her, damp with nightmare. She lifts aside an inch of the curtain, and looks down. Dark shadows and a skim of moonlight show on the sea, and she still hears that thin whistling, insistent, on one note, then fluking up, then down to its home note again. Ah, but she knows that whistle, the one he was whipped for. And there's his dark shape too, and she's looking down on a strange new map of him in the moonlight, all face and dwindling legs. He is staring whitely up at her window. Cautiously, she pushes up the sash, and the whistling stops. They look at one another, neither knowing how much the other can see. Clare scrapes the window up a little farther and leans out and whispers, pointing down the road.

'Go round the back! Go round the entry. I'll come down.'

He nods, and disappears.

No time for anything. She throws on her dressing-gown and shakes her hair back, and runs on her bare feet down the stairs, through kitchen and scullery, to fumble with the bolts. The top one's rusty – everything rusts if you don't keep oiling it. And there he is already, close and sudden, making her catch her breath and shrink back. Even now, knowing who it is, she's afraid of him. It is blind dark in the kitchen, and she feels for the matches, but: 'Don't light the candle, Clarey! Come on out.'

'But I'm only in my night-dress. I can't.'

'You'll be warm enough. It's still as still out here. The sea's flat as a plate but for the swell. Come on, Clarey, come down and see it with me. There's no one about to look at you. All the tabbies have been in their beds for hours.'

He sounds as young and eager as Kitchie. She thrusts out a bare white foot and says, 'Wait a moment.'

Her old boots are in the cupboard under the stairs. She knows them well enough to lace them in the dark. There. She draws her dressing-gown sash tight and runs back to him. They listen, but the house is quite silent.

'Father never wakes,' says Clare. But he sleeps at the back of the house, and they are right under him.

They slip through the door and the little moonlit garden with white shells glowing at the path edge. Clare knocks her foot at the gate, then they are down the alley, over the ash and clinker, past the grumble of sleepy Kaiser at the Lees' ('I call him Kaiser so I can say "Down, Kaiser", see'), and then out on to the flat whitish top road.

'We'll go down through the cemetery,' says John William.

'Where are we going?'

'To the sea,' he says, as if there's no other answer.

They take the diagonal path across the steepness of the cemetery where she's so often played and hidden. For a moment she can feel all the sleepers moan and turn over beneath her. All their poor bones, some of them scarcely laid down, she thinks, and now here we are disturbing them. Our footprints are too light. We ought to be sad and heavy, carrying water and flowers. They'll know we're not thinking of them. But John William catches her waist and she laughs aloud. If anyone hears it, they'll only stop their ears and pray to God to deliver them from seeing a ghost that night. Her dressing-gown sash is loose and her white night-dress billows and glimmers as they flit down the slopes between the stones. And down they go out of the cemetery, past St Ia's holy well and along the top of the beach, towards the rocks. He is heading for the coast-path, and she'll come with him, no matter where. Tonight her feet are light and sure and she cannot lose her footing. The grass is tussocky and cold around the tops of her boots and dew wipes against her calves. They used to go out like this just as it got light, mushrooming. Hannah, John William, little Kitchie, Clare. Albert would meet them up at the leys. The air smells sweetly of salt and gorse, and though it is so still they begin to feel the thud and shock of the swell coming against the rocks, coming in under the rocks to its secret caverns.

Now they must climb. John William goes first, takes her hand, and swings her. She makes a long sure step and she's beside him. They are up on the rocks, with black sea in front and to their sides, and the land behind. There, on the left, the swell comes in under a jumble of rocks. They hear the surface noise of the water, and under it something deeper and darker, like a kept caged lion waiting for food which comes too late and never enough.

Here they are. There is always wind here, enough to flap her white skirts and strew her hair over her face. He is fully dressed and they have cut his hair so close that the wind can do nothing but comb through it. They stand side by side on the rock, facing out to sea. They are hidden from land here. Even spies would see nothing of them. Clare's heard how people used to spy on lovers on the Island, in their private places where they thought they were alone. Some of the watchers even took a telescope and claimed they were watching the boats go out. Then there would be scandal, hot and delicious, licking up narrow streets until it reached the watched girl's home in a thunderous explosion. The wind blows John William and Clare. It feels strong and warm, even though she knows it cannot be warm, for this is only May and long past midnight.

Her dressing-gown peels back, catching on her arms. They are side by side and then John William turns to her and suddenly, quickly, he ducks and with one movement sweeps his bare hands up under the night-dress from her calves to her thighs to her buttocks and round to her stomach and her breasts, sweeping so firmly that it is hardly a caress, rucking up her night-dress so that her bare white legs and stomach are exposed and she stands there and laughs at him, feeling the wind blowing all over her and his hands all over her. He pulls her close to him, his hands under her armpits, and all sensation goes as she rubs against his buttons and rough cloth and his stubbled cheeks. They buckle together and lie down. They are on the black, glistening edge of the rock, but they are safely wedged. Now, with her head on the rock, she hears the underground lion's cough and then the pause and shock of the wave beneath her. John William is pulling off his clothes. He bites his lip as he unbuttons his trousers, the way he always does when he's concentrating. He looks up and gives her his sudden, intimate, white-toothed, cousinly smile.

'Lay down your dressing-gown,' he says. 'It'll be better'n lying on the rock.'

She kneels up and her night-dress drops down, covering her body while she spreads out the dressing-gown. It's like laying out the rugs to air on the back lawn, after she's beaten them. The thought makes her pause. But already he's lying down, and he pulls his cousin on top of him. What kind of game is this? Is this how you play it? She's always thought –

He draws her night-dress up to her neck again, and she lies white and spread on top of him, her back to the moon.

'Open your legs, Clarey!' he says, and because he has always known how to do things she opens them and he runs his hands up the inside of her thighs and along the cleft of her buttocks and up to the moist surface of her vulva. And again. And again. He makes velvet of her. So this is what you do. She jolts and laughs and rubs her face against his.

'You touch me, Clarey. You touch me.' His voice sounds as if she is hurting him.

But she doesn't know how, or where to touch him, and when he guides her fingers she is astonished, for where can such a thing have come from or grown in the few years since she's seen John William naked, swimming around the boat? And it's hard. Is this what is supposed to go inside her? How can it? But all the same she touches him, first tentatively, then boldly exploring, caressing him as he has caressed. He groans and twists his face into the angle of her neck. She feels his tongue lick her skin, and she relaxes. Now she feels older than him and sure of herself. She is doing it right.

He raises himself and twists them both over so that she is underneath. He rests on his elbows, his face above hers so she can't see it in the shadow.

'You never done it, have you, Clarey?'

'No.'

'I knew you wouldn't've. Here. Lie like this. Put your legs up. I won't hurt you.'

And he doesn't. She's wet and ready for him. Maybe all that swimming and running and those pretend weddings with Hannah have made her ready. He is too big, she thinks, and for a desperate minute it won't work, it's all impossible and he strains while she tries to arch back from him and hits solid rock. Then with a sharp burn he's in her and it's done and they fit as she widens and has him. He's so heavy, but she has the rhythm now and then she's leading them. There's a rise in the rock under her back, just where it needs to be. Her body knows what to do now – she spreads herself wider and wider and then just like a sea-anemone when the tide goes out she folds in and laces her legs across his back and now they are one rocking thing, sweating and crying out with the thump of the sea and their own blood equal in their ears.

The wind sifts against Clare's naked left side. She lies triumphant, taking John William's weight. There is cold air blowing around the soles of her feet. She doesn't care. She lies still for as long as she can, then the pressure of rock under her wins and she shifts minutely.

'Mind out,' says John William. 'We're near the edge.' The words echo.

'Not too near,' she says.

'No, not too near.'

She moves another quarter-inch and her lips brush his shoulder.

'Here, keep still,' he says, easing himself off her. 'I've made you messy.'

He reaches for his cotton singlet and wipes down her stomach and the inside of her thighs. She wriggles to free her night-dress, and he smooths it down over her legs.

'There. That's it. You're fine,' he says. 'I didn't hurt you, did I?'

'No,' she says. 'It didn't hurt at all.'

Does he remember that she never used to cry at falls and fights? Only at words. He picked her up once, after she'd fallen running down Smeaton's Pier and cut her knee open so blood splashed on the cobbles, and he rode her home to Nan's on his back. There should be blood, she knows, since she's a virgin. But now she's like Hannah, not a virgin any more.

'There'll be rain tomorrow,' he says, looking at the little clouds shadowing the moon.

'Is it tomorrow now – or today?'

'Today, I reckon.'

She says nothing more. If it's today, then it's already the morning when John William leaves on the eleven o'clock train.

'Hours to go,' she says. 'The moon's not even set.'

She sits up on the rock and looks out to sea. It winks and glitters – maybe there's a shoal of mackerel running. Like a shoal-place in a moonlit field.

'Take off your things,' says John William. 'You don't know how nice you are without your clothes.'

'Do you remember,' she starts, then trails off. She feels herself blushing through the dark.

'What?'

'You know. When we were little. That game we used to play. You and me and Hannah.'

Silence for a moment, then he laughs softly. 'I'd a thought you'd forgotten all about that, Clarey.'

Does he see what she sees?

Two solid, bare little girls caper in the cove. They are Hannah and Clare, prancing in warm, shallow water. John William has his back to them, because he is digging the deepest hole in the world. His skin is dark brown all over but for the shallower tan over his buttocks. He is slicing through cold, hard, water-seeping sand towards Australia.

'Let's play our game,' says Hannah.

They sidle up to John William. Now he's standing aside from his hole. He is very busy, mending gear. Bits of driftwood criss-cross importantly on the sand.

'Please, sir,' says Hannah. 'I found a mermaid.'

'Oh a mermaid,' says John William in a deep, growling voice. 'S'pose I better take a look at her.'

'Here she is, sir,' says Hannah, leading up Clare.

'You lay her down on the rock and I'll take a look and tell you if she's a true mermaid. Hide your eyes and stand over there till I tell you.'

Hannah arranges Clare on a flat rock, legs together, arms straight by her sides.

'Shut your eyes. Remember you can't talk cos you're a mermaid.'

Then she leaves Clare and stands in the cold shadows at the back of the cove, digging her feet into wet sand, knuckling her eyes until red spots come.

John William walks over to Clare with his hands folded

behind his back. He marches up and down beside the rock on which she lies. Her legs are in the shape of a tail, and her eyes are screwed tight shut. After a minute she peeps at him through the slit of her eyelid. His face is solemn as he parts her knees with a smooth bit of driftwood and looks at her bare little vulva. Now she pretends to wake up. She sighs and opens her eyes.

'Are you a human boy?' and her blind, straying hand touches his little coiled penis. She shuts her eyes.

He turns and calls to Hannah, 'This is a true mermaid you found! Now take her back to the sea before she dies.'

He bends down, digging, while Hannah leads Clare into the water. But suddenly they see a jellyfish and Clare shrieks and the game is forgotten. It goes down and down to the bottom of their minds and they never even think of it until next time.

How many times did they play it? She can't remember. All these years she's never once thought of it. The next summer Hannah and Clare wore their bathing-dresses and screeched if anyone even caught a glimpse of them changing. John William swam with the boys then.

Now Clare sits naked on the rock for John William. They're quiet for a long while and they don't touch. It's getting darker, and the moon is going down. There's not much time – soon dawn will start to streak in the sky behind them, and there'll be people about, and voices, and the milk-cart moving, and the boats ready to go out, and the coal that's lying heaped in the sidings will be stoked into the train John William will catch. But she'll keep her back to all of it – she'll only look at the sea. Or she'll shut her eyes and when she opens them it'll be blazing July and they'll be six years old again, sent out for the day by Nan with their pasties and a bottle of cold tea and a handful of cherries. 'And don't come in till you hear five o'clock on the church bell, for I've all my washing to do. And you, Hannah, you're the eldest, you watch out for our Clarey. Mind she don't run too much and start up her coughing.' For Hannah is seven, and responsible for them.

'I'll watch Clare,' says John William.

She opens her eyes and it's dark. The waves shoot in under the rock with a sound like gunfire. They say in the south of England you can hear the guns from France.

'Come here,' says John William. 'S'pose I better make sure if I found a true mermaid, before I take you home.'

Fourteen

John William was right about the rain. By ten to eleven on Grandad's watch big drops of rain are falling, pocking the sand of Porthminster Beach below the railway station. The wind has whipped up coldly, and everyone's clothes are quickly spattered. They stand in a tight family bunch, smelling of damp cloth and hair. Nan is in her best black, standing with Aunt Annie and Aunt Mag. Aunt Mabel isn't here yet — perhaps she's not coming. The women surround Aunt Sarah, who is struggling to keep back tears the way she managed to do last autumn, when John William went out first time. She held them back until the train was past the platform then. Heroic, uncharacteristic effort; but it's plain she won't equal it today. Uncle Arthur stands aside, talking to Uncle John. They've heard this morning that Harry has been called up for re-examination. Clare watches Uncle Arthur fumble the letter out of his pocket and show it to his brother.

The station is full of family and well-wishers, for three other young men are going out. One has come in on a farm trap from Zennor. He has a basket of eggs with him, hard-boiled, and his mother is fussing over two which have cracked, for fear the dirt will get into them.

Nobody fusses John William. He has his greaseproof packet of ham sandwiches in his pocket, and his cigarettes, and his kitbag. He stands with Hannah and Clare. The train is in already, hissing in the wet, but nobody gets on to it. They stand still, and the rain begins to fall more heavily, in long vertical streaks. Clare looks right through the train windows and sees a mist of rain settling on the sea.

'I better say goodbye to Mother now,' John William says to Hannah.

'She looks very bad. Do it as quick as you can.'

He pushes his way through the aunts to Aunt Sarah. She turns and sees him, and she can't hold back any more: she clings to his arms and his shoulders, terrible jerking sobs come out of her, her hat falls off, and she would fall herself if he wasn't holding her.

'There now, Sarey, come away now, come away,' says Nan, gripping her daughter-in-law's arm. Sarah shudders all over, and peels herself off from her son. They grip her, Uncle Arthur on one side, Nan on the other. The aunts flurry their goodbyes. If only the train'll go now, and it'll be over and they can get Sarah home. She'd've been all right, if it hadn't been for that letter about Harry coming this morning.

'Johnnie,' says Hannah. She hugs him, but she does not cling. She is giving him her strength, thinks Clare, not draining his courage out of him. And I shall do the same.

'There's my girl,' says John William.

'Write, mind.'

Now it's Clare. And it's really time to go now – people are bundling on to the train. Some of them are going on ordinary errands, Sunday visits from which they'll come back safe tonight with eggs or butter in their baskets. Back home, back safe. Shielded from the rest of his family by Hannah, John William takes Clare fully into his arms. It feels strange. They have no public history together. They know each other naked, not clothed. They've never held each other like this with their clothes on. Everything has been the wrong way round. Pudding before meat, Nan would say. His cheeks are smooth – he must have shaved. She feels the shape of him through the clothes – his arms tight, his chest flat and hard, her breast bruising against him. She breathes in the smell of him.

'Look out for me now,' he says, then there's nothing against her and he's gone. He pulls down the window strap and the window is full of him, looking out over her head at Aunt Sarah, who cannot look at him because she has turned faint and they are forcing her head down. The guard walks swiftly past with his two flags in his hand, then waves down the green one and steps on to the train. It's moving. Steam hisses and the engine pours down a rain of smuts on them. Kitchie begins to run along the platform, waving his cap in his hand. The rain slashes.

'Get in, get in!' shouts Hannah, seeing her brother take the rain full in his face. And he's gone.

Clare sees her father on the edge of the family group, looking down the line after the train. She hadn't noticed him there. The rest are still gathered around Sarah, who is smelling Nan's salts and coughing.

'I'll walk up along with you,' says Hannah to Clare.

'No, let's go by the harbour.'

'All right, if you don't mind the rain.'

Clare doesn't.

'No Peggy this morning,' remarks Hannah dryly.

'She'll be at chapel with little Georgie, I daresay.'

'I thought they were church?'

'Yes, I suppose they are,' says Clare dully. She hasn't the heart for malice just yet. She yawns hugely.

'Johnnie was late home last night, after the concert,' remarks Hannah.

'Yes,' says Clare.

'I was glad of it.'

No need to say anything. Hannah knows. It has made her glad to think of John William being with Clare, on his last night. The last night of his leave, that is, she corrects herself quickly.

But what about Sam? She hasn't asked Hannah – she hasn't helped Hannah. She's only thought of herself. And yet Hannah looks happier than she did the day before. Has she heard something? Has she had a letter too?

'Hannah. Have you heard from Sam?'

'I got another letter.' Her voice is low; she glances around. Nothing but seagulls and a thicket of masts and sails humping up and down in the choppy harbour water. The cobbles gleam with rain.

'What's it say?' asks Clare.

'He's going to stop in London for a while.'

So she knows. How much does she know? I must pretend it is new to me.

'What do you mean – stop in London? He can't. He's in the army.'

'London's a big place, isn't it? You've been there, Clarey. You should know. People can lose themselves there, easy.'

'But not if you're in the army. They'll come looking for him. There's the military police, you know. Then he'll be court-martialled.'

'There's a girl,' says Hannah with difficulty. 'He'll be staying with her. He won't need to go out. Nobody'll know.'

Clare is silent.

'But Hannah –'

'Why should I mind?' says Hannah fiercely. 'She'll keep him

175

alive, won't she? If he can get through this war alive, what've I got to mind for? When it's over, he'll come home.'

'Do you think he'll be able to?'

'He'll have to,' says Hannah simply. 'I know Sam. He won't be able to keep himself from coming home. He'll be lonely for it.'

'And you don't mind – if he's a deserter?'

'Once the war's over, they won't shoot them for it any more, John William says. He might have to go to prison, but he'll come back. It won't be for ever. Not like it'd be for ever, if he's killed.'

'A deserter,' says Clare, trying the word over in her mind.

'And I wish they *would* desert, all of them, every last one,' says Hannah. 'But they won't. Our Johnnie won't, so there's no use ever thinking of it. But now he's to get his commission, maybe that'll keep him safe.'

There's a couple of kids playing out, barefoot, their hair streaking down over their faces. Hannah knows the mother, who drinks. She'll be snoring without so much as a fire lit in the house. The kids play out forlornly in the rain, with no one to shout at them or to chivvy them back home.

We'll talk about it later, thinks Clare. She is so tired now that she cannot help Hannah. And Hannah is braver than she is. Clare's missed first Mass now, and second Mass. Anyway, she isn't going to go. She'll be no worse off committing two mortal sins than one.

'I'm going home to sleep,' says Clare. 'My head aches.'

'You might as well. A day like this, there's nothing to stay awake for.'

Better to sleep. She might dream. His touch. The smell of him is still on her. The inner muscles of her thighs ache from gripping his back, and she's sore, bruised, tender. She'll tell Father she's ill, and climb the stairs to her bed and lie in her cool sheets and go back in time, holding on to the night before. The wind's rising – she'll hear the noise of it roaming over the bay from her bedroom, and the noise of the waves around the rocks where she lay with John William.

But the sheets are cold, and her room is not a refuge. Rain skitters down the window. The wind is veering west, and rough gusts blow up off the sea. Her window always bangs when the wind is in this direction. She ought to get up and wedge it with newspaper, but she's too tired and cold and sore to bother. In the time it takes thinking about it, and being irritated by the irregular banging of window against frame, she could have been up and mended it six times.

Downstairs her father clatters about. It's not so much that he wants to wake Clare, as that he finds himself doing the things which will stop her from sleeping. He goes to open the front door – she can't think why. Then he must have gone back into the kitchen without shutting the door properly because she hears wind sucking and whining down the hall, gathering force until the door leaps open and crashes against the porch wall. She nearly springs out of bed, thinking of the glass panels, but stops herself. Then he leaves the kitchen door open so she can hear him banging about with the saucepans, until he finds one in which he can boil his solitary, pathetic Sunday egg. What a meal for a man. No wonder he has to clash her careful nest of saucepans until the enamel chips. He is angry with Clare in the way children are angry with mothers who suddenly stop their perpetual motion in kitchen and backyard and shops, and take off their aprons and say in flat voices which the children have never heard before: *I can't be doing with it any more. Go on out with this (she hands out doorsteps of bread with no butter or jam) and stay out till your father comes home.*

Clare knows all about this. She knows how she ought to be downstairs, slapping slices of cold pork on to plates; it's the least she can do when there's no Sunday dinner made, and he has come back from church cold and wet and out of temper. And she has not gone with him. And he has had no sponge-cake for his Sunday tea for weeks. He likes it dredged with sugar, but they can't get enough sugar to whiten the surface the way she used to, or to make patterns by shaking the sugar through a paper cut-out. How quickly her father would brighten if she went down now. He would flap about, making her a cup of tea while she sliced bread and butter with a small martyrish smile.

She twists in the bed, fighting off thoughts which elbow their way through. Hannah has gone home to cook and keep house; she will not slummock in bed indulging herself like Clare. Besides, there's no room for it. The house will echo like a drum to Aunt Sarah's weeping. Nan will be helping with her, and no doubt Aunt Mabel and Aunt Annie and Aunt Mag too, gathered round the steaming broth of Aunt Sarah's emotions. Oh, yes, they'll be comforting her all right, thinks Clare, and Aunt Sarah won't know about the avidity in their faces when they talk about her in the kitchen as they bolt down the meal which decorum insists they don't eat in front of grieving Sarah. Then Grandad'll lead them all in prayer. Clare shudders.

They will pray to God for John William's safe homecoming, their faces red and relieved because they're doing something for him. Even Aunt Sarah will feel the better for it as she whimpers over the best tea-cups. Poor Aunt Sarah with her red eyes and her red worn hands. And everyone telling her they'll never take Harry, it won't be allowed.

Her bed is as uncomfortable as the bottom of a boat in an uneasy sea. Sam has deserted. Does anyone know but John William and Hannah and me? Hannah thinks I'm safe with a secret. She doesn't know how I feel about Sam rolling up his big body like a hedgehog in a hole in London, to crouch there behind some girl for the duration. Why should he? Why should it be easy for him?

I don't think that John William would desert like Sam, even if the idea had occurred to him. Not because he's braver than Sam. Sam's brave enough, when it's wanted, but he'd say he won't be brave for nothing.

'Where's the sense of it?' that's what Sam would say. 'All of us getting killed like rabbits.'

Perhaps it's that Sam doesn't care what people think of him. He doesn't mind if he loses his place among 'all the fine young men we've sent over there'. He would rather that people looked sidelong at him for the rest of his life than go back to fight – that is if Hannah's right and they won't shoot him for desertion once the war's over.

'I'm not having any more of it. Let the rest of em make fools of theirselves. Not me.'

No. That's not Sam either. What the rest of them think and do has always been important to Sam. He was proud to swing Hannah on his arm because all the boys were after her and she could sew so fine and earn her own living. He'd got what the rest of them wanted.

Clare turns her face into the pillow and grips it. Hannah hinted at something in Sam's letter; something which had happened to Sam, and changed him. There must be things I don't know and can't begin to imagine. Experiences which no one in England can share. But now I know how Hannah feels after Sam has gone.

John William won't ever desert. I know that – I am sure he won't. He will never give people that chance to scorn him. He'll call himself a fool, but he'll rather die than give anyone else the right to name him one. He might mock them for making him an officer, but he's glad that it forces fools to respect him. And Sam will survive in his burrow in London, doing what any creature in its senses does when it hears the guns. Doing what you get shot for doing now. But John William's on the train, laughing maybe and talking to men whom I don't know and who will never hear of me – not from him. They'll ask if he had a good time at home and he'll smile and say something which will satisfy them but give away nothing. John William is good at smiling and giving nothing away. He never got into rages. If you lose your temper, you lose yourself. Other people learn what you want. Now I must hold myself still, like him, thinks Clare.

'My cousin Clarey.' He'll hold a letter from her, creased and rumpled from being reread as the guns boom and the men wait, tense, to go over the top. Or he'll tuck a bit of her hair under his tunic.

You fool, you fool, she tells herself, thumping the pillow.

'Men don't want spoiled goods,' says Nan. 'A man'll say anything on God's earth to get you to go with him, and then you'll never see his face again – you'll see nothing but the back of his britches when he sees you coming.'

It was advice given to Hannah and meant for her and Clare. Clare might be half a lady but all girls need watching, in Nan's experience. There's nothing worse than a fool who's a fool to herself.

Clare turns and lies on her back. Runnels of rain run down straight now, breaking their channels, sluicing the window.

What did Mr Lawrence say to John William, all that time they were walking together? What did John William tell him, that he couldn't tell me?

Fifteen

I was on Tom Stevens's croft.

And that's where you saw em?

That's it. Brazen as you like, sat there on the cliff-top. He didn't give tuppence who saw em, nor by the look of it did she neither.

That's one in the eye for the Treveals.

It is.

Well, now, who'd a thought it. Clare Coyne. Go on. What did you see?

I'd stopped by with Tom. He was cutting furze with the two lads and I stopped to inquire after Ettie. He was telling me that brendy cow of his isn't doing. Well, we were standing there like I said; you know how Tom Stevens's croft run down to the cliff-path?

I do.

And we see em there, the two of em at it in God's good daylight.

And Tom Stevens being strong Chapel too. Must a bin a shock for him.

He is. A powerful voice for the Lord, Tom Stevens.

Course the Coyne girl's a Roman.

That's so. Not that I've anything against the Romans . . .

No.

They have their ways and we have ours.

That's just so. You hit it. And coddling and kissing with foreigners in brazen daylight isn't our way.

Mind, I'm not saying there was anything in it.

Oh, no!

But a young girl and a married man.

That's just it. No hiding theirselves either. You can see that red beard of his six miles off.

You can.

And the girl with her red hair too.

Hot

   blood

   wonder if it's the same red down below

   like a couple of foxes getting together

   stink

   smell of my Susan when she's got her visitor

So what did you do then?

Went back. Tom had a couple of pigs to alter.

She wants to get him *altered, that wife of his does. Keep him and his red beard safe at home.*

Then after he left her he went on over to the Hockings.

Teaching Stanley Hocking French, it is now. And piano. I heard William Henry tell it at Penzance market.

Piano. I wonder the Hockings don't throw him out of their house. Sits there in the kitchen like he belongs there, talking against the war.

What's Tom getting for his pigs now?

Ten and eleven-three a score, last I heard.

Is he now?

Selling em up to Redruth bacon factory. Ask him yourself at St Ives Saturday market.

And then the girl went home?

Back along the cliff-path.

And he don't know nothing, her father?

Too busy going over Newlyn himself, I reckon. But that's an old story.

Same as May Foage's an old story.

Ah, well that's just the beauty of it for the Romans. It don't matter what they do all week just so long as they go along into the box and tell the priest all about it on a Saturday. Then there they are, ready to start up again on Saturday night. Just like magic.

But he's not a Roman, is he? Red-beard?

He's purely Godforsaken. Said as bold as brass to Rector he didn't hold with Church nor Chapel. Said a man should take care of his soul for hisself.

That'll've pleased Rector.

It did. He called Red-beard a snake in the grass, outside church Sunday before last. Tom had it from Jo Quick. Said we should remember how the serpent spoke smooth to tempt Eve.

The Rector sits at his desk. A blob of ink wavers on the end of his nib, but the flat creamy sheets of paper on which he writes his sermon are still blank. Words run through his mind:

The serpent was more subtil than any beast of the field which the Lord God had made. Dear people, my dear people, consider what these words mean. None of us, alas, can hope to see the Garden of Eden with our earthly eyes. With the hope given to us by God's infinite mercy we may trust that one day our eyes will be opened. Our eyes are clouded by sin. Our minds are dark and wretched, but even in our darkness we struggle to turn towards the glorious light of our Redeemer. But there are some who love the darkness. When they see the light of God they hide their faces and hate it. They love their own sins and abominations more than the light. They cling to them. Their Prince is the Prince of Darkness. They will come to you with words like honey; they will speak to you with as smooth a tongue as the serpent's when he spoke to Eve in the Garden of Eden, and drove the children of this world to damnation. They will speak with the tongue of the Great Deceiver who is their Lord and Master and if you listen they will tempt you.

He imagines the upturned faces of his parishioners, shrewd, subtle, earthly. 'Rector give it us hot this mornin.'

And then there's his insolence. The way he looks at me. One day I met him in the churchyard. What was he doing? Looking at the sundial, he said. That beard of his. It ought to be shaved off. His clothes. He's a figure of fun. And his wife's a madwoman or worse. Consider a serpent with the head of a man. Here I am holding back darkness. My people are never far from it. They speak of witches and loggans and mermaids and when I come by they fall silent. Once I thought I would write down the old stories and kill off their magic, but the stories still slip from mouth to ear, born in darkness and told by lamplight. There was a witch up here who worked her magic in the shape of a hare, and even when four strong men carried her up to God's holy churchyard in her coffin they couldn't hold her. The coffin shivered and turned over like an eel in their arms and there she went fleeting across the grass.

He dips his pen and begins to write. The first few words stick as his pen digs into the paper, then his fingers relax and lines of black firm writing fly down the page.

Evil goes fleeting across the earth, making a mock of all that good men hold dear. It will mock your wives and your daughters. It will mock your country and all we are fighting for. All those fine young men who have answered the call of King and Country, soberly, advisedly, knowing what is asked of them – are they to be made a mockery? Evil will mock at them and make a bonfire of their sacrifices. It will hiss and whisper in your ears. There is evil everywhere, prowling our countryside, waiting for the breach through which it can enter. It will settle here and make a home for itself. It will work through our land like a snake, and make rotten where it touches.

He stops writing and chews his pen. He knows that he will never say these words aloud; not as they stand. They are to be dropped, one by one, a word here and a murmur there.

He blots the paper and folds it over, stamping the crease with the side of his fist. These are notes to himself. They will keep his purpose firm.

Lawrence isn't writing. He has his flower and vegetable gardens to keep up, both the little plot which goes with the cottage at a shilling a year, and the two plots he has rented from the Hock-ings. The land is full of granite stones, standing upright or leaning over so that you think in a year or two they'll fall. But they don't fall. In a hundred years they might add a fraction of an inch to their angle. Here and there shoal-places break the surface of the fields. The stones are thick as fish under thin soil. He has learned to cultivate around the stones without driving his spade or hoe against them. The stones have been here longer than anyone knows. Long ago the first Celtic farmers shaped their small fields around granite boulders, and their granite hedges remain. Druids left the stones, as thick a crop of them as you get anywhere in this world. The work of the farms goes on around them so that you might think no one thinks of them or looks at them. But how can these stones fail to enter you somewhere? There are the shadows of them falling on your back as you earth up potatoes, or spray soapy water on blackfly-ridden runner beans. Or they stand at the base of the hedge in a froth of montbretia and wild fuchsia, their grey sides licked by purple and scarlet and flame. As you go down the little deep lane to the Hockings, tall stones stand in the field on your right, peering over the hedge at you. You might believe that at night when there's no one to watch them, they walk.

Walking stones. Lawrence thinks of the moon-blank loggans the night before, and the sweat on John William's face. Hawker. Who was Hawker? What was it that John William saw when he dropped to his knees on the road to Zennor?

The night-owl was flying. If a man believed in souls, how many of them would be flying now, looking for home? Thousands of them released every evening into the low grey skies above the Flanders plains, hungry for the lives they had been torn from, wanting to tell someone. Like souls in the Inferno they would press forward, naked and shivering, drifting like brown leaves on the banks of the Styx, squeaking. Behind them there crowd the next battalions, more and more until they are beyond counting. He thinks of the sigh that would go up from them.

He finds he is standing still, holding his hoe, too tired to grub up the weeds between another row of beans. He has some rare things planted. There are scorzonera and salsify, vegetables new to William Henry, who touches them with curious fingers and asks what they are good for. But where is Frieda? She left a note that she had gone out walking. She is so careless. She

never says where she is going, though there are cliffs and dangerous places all around. She might stumble and turn her ankle,
then call for hours. He smiles. He cannot really imagine Frieda
calling for hours, and nobody coming. All her life people have
come. She is as irresistible as wind or sun. Besides, she is not
really careless. She knows that there are risks but she still takes
them, just as she did when she gave up house and husband and
children and threw in her life with Lawrence after knowing him
for six weeks.

How quiet the cottage is without her. He potters through the
kitchen, washing pearly scarlet and white radishes, tapping the
bottom of the loaves he made earlier. They are perfectly baked.
He lays out china on the little table, and sets their black-
bottomed kettle on the fire. Soon she will be home, bursting
open the cottage door, dropping a bunch of bluebells on a chair,
unpinning her hat. The room will flare with life and vigour.

'Ah, Lorenzo!' she will exclaim, shedding gloves as she claps
her hands for joy at the sight of the tea laid ready. 'Such a walk!
You cannot imagine . . .'

And she will sit down opposite him and make a festival of
the meal.

But it is late and she is not home. He cannot get the sound of
John William's voice out of his head. For once, briefly, he
allows himself to think how much he needs his wife.

Sixteen

'Father.'

Francis flails his *Times* open and hits the dish of rhubarb jam. There is no marmalade; there never seems to be any these days. Every day starts wrong for him as he bites through a greasy layer of margarine and then tastes this jam which leaves a metallic coating on his teeth for the rest of the morning. Why hasn't Clare got any butter? Surely to God, she ought to be able to manage it, with all her family slipping each other parcels of this and that the whole day long. And the damned paper won't fold in the middle either.

Clare pokes a spoon critically into the jam dish. Yes, she thought as much. There wasn't enough sugar when she made it and now the jam is beginning to ferment. There'll be mould frilling the jars in a few more days. Perhaps if she boils up the jam again with a bit more of next week's sugar which she's hidden in a blue canister marked 'salt'? But it takes a lot of fuel to boil jam. Nothing on the table is as it should be. The bread is grey. The margarine tastes like axle-grease, Father says, though how he knows what axle-grease tastes like she can't imagine.

Francis Coyne thrashes the newspaper. Pinkish brown streaks of rhubarb fibre cling to the corner of the front page.

'Father,' says Clare.

'Mmm? What?'

'I'm going up to Zennor today, to get some eggs and butter.'

'Zennor! Why would you go all the way up there for eggs and butter? Haven't you asked your uncle?'

'I can't keep asking Uncle John, Father. He can get much more for butter at the market than we pay him.'

It's true, but it's a slander to Uncle John all the same. He takes pride in himself as provider for the Treveals. She knows that if she asked him Albert or Jo would be sent down that same evening with a plump pound of butter wrapped in a damp muslin cloth. 'The sweetest butter in all Cornwall,' Uncle John called it, when he was feeling sentimental, and, 'It's all due to the hand at the churn,' looking at Aunt Annie, who bridled at that because she had a girl to help her now, and it was the girl's hand at the churn.

'But really,' Clare goes on quickly, 'I want to take my sketching things. I want to draw the white Himalayan balsam in the churchtown. We haven't an illustration of it yet.'

But he frowns and twitches another piece of toast on to his plate.

'Don't be ridiculous, Clare, it won't be in flower for a good two months. Sometimes I think I've taught you nothing.'

'And I'm going to visit Mr Lawrence and his wife. They have asked me to tea with them.'

'Mr Lawrence? Mr Lawrence? Who is he? I seem to know the name, but I can't place him. What sort of people are they?'

'He's a writer, Father. They've taken a cottage at Higher Tregerthen.'

'And how did you meet them?'

'At the concert, with my cousins.'

It sounds all right. She is margarining a slice of bread, rubbing the grease carefully into the crumb. There's something tricky here which he can't put his finger on. Something's been up with the child since – when? Last Friday? Saturday? And then her cousin leaving on Sunday will have upset her, though she's said nothing. He hopes they aren't going to have any more upsets like the one they had after the concert. This is where a girl misses her mother. The trouble is that Clare reads the newspapers and she knows what is going on. It would be easier for her if she were stupid. And now these new people – surely he's heard that name somewhere? Lawrence. Of course. The writer-fellow there's been all the trouble about. A German wife or something. And they won't like that round here. It's quite bad enough to be a Catholic from London; Francis Coyne is well aware that he is a foreigner and will remain a foreigner long after he has been buried in Coyne Chapel. Let her go. It will do her good to see new people, and a different way of life. A writer ought to have something to talk about beyond the price of pork and pilchards. And if his wife is German, perhaps she is a Catholic? He remembers Bavaria, and his walking tour there during the Long. People walked miles over the mountains to Mass, women in their costumes, men in black hats. And that greeting of theirs: '*Grüss Gott, Grüss Gott.*' God's greeting. A true Catholic country; it had touched him more than he expected. He could open any church door and find himself at home. All the beautiful churches were still ours. And now we're fighting them. What a country it was. Those lakes we bathed in – as cold as death in the height of summer, cold like iron bracelets around wrists and ankles when we swam, weighing us down. We must have walked fifteen miles a day through the forests. The smell of resin, and the silence of the birds. White-haired children herding goats who made the sign of the evil eye as we went past. Those children will be old enough to fight now, I daresay.

'How will you get there? Is somebody going up in a trap?'

'I shall walk. It will do me good,' she says firmly.

'Higher Tregerthen; that's this side of the churchtown. Still, it must be six miles.'

'Oh, Father, you know six miles is nothing. And look what a perfect day it is! And it'll be downhill coming home. I'll take my sketchbook in case I see anything interesting.'

She will too. You need a salting of truth in the broth of a lie. She wants to sketch Frieda. Frieda will be beautiful, she is sure of it, even though Mr Lawrence is not beautiful at all. But he is a person whose wife would not be like anybody else's. You would find yourself looking longest at Mr Lawrence in any crowded room. He'd seem insignificant at a first glance, but your eye would be drawn back to him. He looks so alive.

The day is alive too, and glorious, even the golden slice of it which is all they can see through their window as they breakfast. Francis looks at his daughter affectionately, reaches over and pats her hand. His strong girl.

'Will you be going over to Newlyn?' she asks, collecting teacups. Her face is averted, her voice casual.

'Why, no – you know I only went there last Thursday. I have no business there today. Why do you ask?'

'I only just wondered – I wasn't sure.'

A very slight tremor in the hand which holds the cups, then she's gone, whisking up from the table with a pile of crockery. Could she have been laughing? Could she have been teasing him? Does she know – has she guessed? Could someone have spoken to her? One of her uncles, letting something slip, trusting the words not to mean anything to her. They don't know his Clare's intelligence.

But no. If she is intelligent, she is also innocent. It's impossible that she should think or suspect any such thing of her own father.

'I shall go to my study now, Clare.'

'I'm going down to Nan's to help with her ironing. Then we'll have lunch early, at twelve. Pickled herring,' she adds, knowing that her father likes to know but hates to appear greedy. 'And I have some spring onions.'

'Have you!' he brightens. 'Do you know, Clare, I think I shan't work on my classifications today.'

'Shan't you?'

'No. I have something else in mind.' He pauses, shyly, importantly.

'What is it, Father?'

'I thought I'd like to attempt a little sketch of my Oxford days. Nothing significant. I don't pretend to be in the same league as your Mr Lawrence,' he disclaims, wondering what Mr Lawrence *does* write. He must try to find out. He could ask the Rector of Zennor when he next meets him in town. The Rector is an educated man, and must know these Lawrences. It would be interesting to have his opinion of them. And the Rector might be interested in Francis's memories of Oxford too?

'A small volume, Clare. It could be printed privately, for circulation among friends.' Francis Coyne looks at his daughter expectantly.

'Oh, yes, Father, that does sound interesting.'

'When we were all young together.' He puts irony into his voice but there's something else there too, something which she hears far more rarely from him. Eagerness.

'Stacey – Montfort – all of them. They were wonderful fellows. I made sure Montfort would make his name as a poet – we all did.'

He sees dripping sun; tall glasses of hock and seltzer. Montfort has just finished reading his new poem. They sprawl in a circle and he stands, his back to the chimney-piece. One of his arms lies easily along the stone shelf, but his left hand grips the paper tight, with the words on it which he's worked at from tipsy midnight through to morning. He stares round at his friends. For all his nervousness he can't help knowing, *knowing*, that they must find it good, as he does. Stacey, Coyne, Chatterne. What will they say?

'Well, what do you say?' He trusts them enough to ask, to risk it. Tender, humorous, mockingly affectionate, their words swarm in the sunlit room.

'You've really done it this time, old fellow!'

'Stupendous.'

'That line about the lily.'

'Let's hear it again – I thought I detected a false quantity in line 47.'

They all laugh.

'God, I feel – I can't tell you!'

'Sit on that man, someone.'

A cushion is hurled, a wine-glass topples, a bubbling pool of wine and water runs over the carpet.

His Clare is looking at him. If only he could show her – make her see – but all that comes out is a repeated 'They were wonderful fellows'.

Clare smiles, and straightens the table-cloth.

Stacey. Montfort. Chatterne. And Eliot, and Stillington too, and all of them. Their sons ought to be at Oxford now, drinking wine and feeling as if it were the morning of the world. Getting drunk and writing poetry and travelling to Prague in the Long. Stacey went to Rome and wrote back, 'It is all just as we imagined it.' He fell in love there – we talked of it all Michaelmas term.

But Oxford's empty now. All the young men are in France, buried or still breathing, turning up their faces to the sun to feel its warmth. Ranks of schoolboys come up behind to replace them. We have not been able to give our sons anything. Not even one golden year. Gashed and splattered . . .

He fumbles *The Times* in his hands. But he has his Clare, and here she is beside him, solid and warm.

'It was just a thought,' he apologizes. 'I don't suppose I shall do it.'

She is not interested, he thinks, shutting the study door. He does not guess that she will think of him all the way up the long steep pull of hill out of St Ives, and keep on thinking of him as the road bends and rises and she walks at a good easy pace the six miles to Higher Tregerthen. She thinks of his loneliness. She has always known about it, all her life, because it is half hers. If it weren't for Nan, and Grandad, and Hannah and Aunt Mag and all of them, and John William and Kitchie and the boys, she would live in the same globe of loneliness as he does. Her mother's family have a family liking for her father and they respect him, but she knows that they cannot really include him in their lives. None of them can be themselves while he is there. When he comes stooping through Nan's low doorway the atmosphere changes. Clare and Hannah are chivvied up from the table where they have been sprawling over the trimming of Hannah's new petticoat, threading ribbons at bodice and hem. Nan talks differently. Grandad leaves off bellowing hymns. Nobody can be himself or herself, even though Francis Coyne must have spent hundreds of hours with them over the years.

He spends less time now. Now she comes to think of it, she realizes that he hardly ever goes down to Nan's. He seems to think that now Clare is grown up, and there is no obvious reason for him to call to fetch her or to ask Nan's advice over a cough or a bad tooth, he has no place there. He has done his duty. That particular tangle of family doesn't require his presence any more. Nan likes him, but either he doesn't know it or it wouldn't mean anything to him. Nan says to Clare: 'Your father has beautiful teeth.' That's so like Nan. She fancies the idea of a son-in-law with beautiful teeth, instead of her broad, lummocking sons. Oh, yes, she likes his teeth and his way of eating and his fineness, but what good's that if you can't be happy in the same room together?

And he's not at ease with new people. It's just the same in the Church. He hates meetings, shrinks from comfortable intimacy with 'Father'. He couldn't do a good work to save his life, thinks Clare, though he gives enough to charity to stop mouths against him.

Yes, he's lonely. Better not think about it. It's like a bruise, and the day is magnificent. You could sing aloud, glorying in it. You could understand that the Magnificat was once a wild and unstoppable song of triumph, not a delicate lacework of church voices. Little complicated fields glitter. The sun is high and hot, but a breeze keeps the temperature perfect. She's walking up into wildness, up the little road with rising land on her left. The bracken's uncurling, white and hooked over at the top of each frond. Rough boulders glitter and the larks' song melts into the flare of gorse. On her right the sea shines like a shield. She shades her eyes and picks out farms, set in where a hollow will protect them from sea-gales, reached by thick-tunnelled lanes full of hart's tongue ferns, foxgloves, yarrow. She has been walking for two hours, and soon she should come to the lane for Higher Tregerthen and the farm.

And there it is, sandy and open at first, and then it turns and is coolly shaded by the high bank on the left.

'Just a little way down,' he'd said, and soon she sees it. But not one cottage – there are two or three, with the long front of the second one facing the track, just before another turn in the lane. This must be the place. Her boots and stockings and her skirt hem are thick with dust. She stops, and bangs some of it off.

The door's open. A snatch of voice – a woman's voice, quite deep and rich. Then a burst of song without recognizable words. Is it German? No, surely not. It sounds wilder than German. Someone begins to play the piano, not very well. About as well as Clare plays herself.

Clare walks quietly to the deep-set open door, which is slightly below the level of the lane. She's looking straight into the one room – and straight through it, for there's the window through on the other side, looking out over fields and down to the sea. It's like looking straight through the train John William left on. The room is dark. There she is, a big yellow-haired woman in a white blouse at a cottage piano.

'Hello,' says Clare.

The hands drop from the keys and snatch up a Paisley shawl. The woman looks round at her. A broad face, tense and watchful. She does not want anybody here.

'Who are you? What do you want?'

'I'm Clare Coyne. I've come for tea – have I got the day right? It *was* Tuesday, wasn't it?'

The face changes completely. The woman jumps up and comes to the doorway and holds out her hands, both hands. Direct, warm, impulsive. This is her real face, thinks Clare, the other one was what she has learned to put on. Why?

Frieda takes Clare's hand and holds it between hers.

'Of course, I know now. You will think I am so stupid but I am playing the piano and dreaming and did not know the time. And Lorenzo is not here to tell me.'

'Oh. Isn't he at home?'

'He is only in his garden. His everlasting garden I call it, but I should not complain for he grows us many good things to eat. Radishes and lettuce and carrots and so. You will see. I will call him.'

She goes to the back and sings out in a full-throated way which reminds Clare more of the women downalong than any lady: 'Lor-enzo-o! Come!' Then she turns to Clare and announces confidently, 'He will come. And he will make tea for us and we have some little cakes too, I think.'

Gracious, how peculiar, thinks Clare. Isn't she going to make the tea herself?

'I am lazy, I know,' confides Frieda. 'But I have been ill – very ill. Neuritis so bad I could not walk.'

'I'm sorry. Is it better now?'

'Oh, it's nothing now,' shrugs Frieda, losing interest in the topic. 'Illness is boring, eh? Especially the illnesses of other people. It was so cold, so long a winter here. So much wind and rain – did you not think so?'

'I like the wind – or perhaps I'm used to it. And I think it is wilder up here than in St Ives. You are more exposed.'

'Oh, yes, it's wild. Why, at night, when Lorenzo was out' – she breaks off, glances out the back to see if he is coming, then continues – 'when he was out, I would be sitting here and the door would bang open – so – just of itself – and all the wind would fly around our house and the curtains would flap and these cups would shake so I think they would fall off. It would be like a wild animal in the house. A wolf perhaps.'

'Have you ever seen a wolf?' asks Clare eagerly. Germany, after all . . .

'No – oo, no wolves! When I was a girl we would hear of wolves coming down off the mountains, in the winter, when it had frozen hard for weeks. But I never saw it. We did not live in those parts. But such frosts! – you cannot imagine them. My sister and I would wrap ourselves up in furs, right to our noses.'

Clare looks around the room. The walls are washed pink – it is not so very dark, after all. The little boxed staircase goes straight up on the right-hand side, opposite the deep black fireplace. And the floor-stones are reddish too, scrubbed very clean. It is a queer, definite little room, quite unlike any she has seen before. No farm-worker's wife would think of making her cottage like this.

'I like your furniture,' she says, looking at the round rosewood table. 'Did it come with the cottage?'

She has said the right thing. Frieda glows, and reaches out to stroke the lovely, responsive wood.

'No, no, we bought it in St Ives for sixpence!' cries Frieda. 'They are so stupid there that nobody wants it. They must have new things. Everything must be new and ugly. What fools! So we buy all this, and bring it up on a cart and make our home. Even the piano.'

'You didn't get that for sixpence!' says Clare, laughing.

'No, that is quite true, it was very extravagant, it cost us five pounds. We only bought it this spring, but now we play it all the time, and sing.'

'And your china too – it's so pretty.' For Frieda has arranged it, none of it matching, bright, curious, delicate. One vase is stuffed with bluebells. They keel over lightly, beautifully, dipping their heads, bringing their smoky hyacinthine scent into the room.

'Ah! Now he comes!'

He is at the back, taking off his soil-clodded boots. He nods at Clare as he comes in and goes straight to the stone sink to wash his hands, which he does carefully, turning one hand over the other to examine his nails. All his movements are neat and exact. Unlike Frieda, he looks as if he belongs in a place like this. And yet he's a gentleman, isn't he? A writer? Or perhaps he's a half-and-half, like her.

'I'll put the kettle on,' he says. 'She's given you nothing to eat or drink, I'll be bound.'

'Why should I, when I know you will come and do it so *beautifully*,' mocks Frieda. 'You see, Clare, I am nothing here – just a useless wife.'

'She's like one of those lambs out there, frisking about in the sunshine, looking as if butter wouldn't melt in her mouth. "Oh, aren't they *perfect*, aren't they *heaven*?" Yes, but they've eaten my broad beans, for all that.'

Frieda laughs. Clare thinks she relishes the imitation – it is of some other woman, affectedly ladylike. He is a good mimic. And Frieda appears not to resent the comparison of herself with the lambs.

Clare has never heard husband and wife talk to one another like this. In fact she is not used to hearing husband and wife talk to each other very much at all. Nan and the aunts talk together; Grandad with the uncles. An intimate, personal conversation between a married couple is something she is not used to and she finds it both exciting and embarrassing.

The house is spotless – as clean as Nan's. Lawrence builds up the fire with turves, and sets the kettle to boil.

'We'll have a proper tea, Clare,' he announces. 'Should you like that? I've some eggs, laid this morning, and bread and butter, and lettuce.'

'Such good things!' says Frieda.

Clare is hungry after the walk, and says so. They both approve.

'Clare's no lady, you see,' remarks Lawrence. 'She walks from St Ives to have tea with us. Now that is what I call friendship.'

Clare beams. His snub, ugly face charms her. Someone like this to talk to all the time! How lucky Frieda is.

Frieda looks carefully sidelong at Clare. No. This one is all right. She is no moth sucked to the flame of Lorenzo's vitality, convinced that she and only she can make a life worth living for him; once Frieda is out of the way. There have been several of them, and there will be more, Frieda knows. It's inevitable. But this girl, though friendly and eager, is shielded by something. Her eyes are not hungry, even though she responds to his jokes and his quick, warm way of looking round over his shoulder to answer her, as he sets out the tea-things and puts the eggs to boil. He likes her. Probably she is already in love, thinks Frieda, to whom such a solution will always be the first and most natural. And she is intelligent. Not the kind of girl you would expect to find down here. 'Half a peasant and half a lady,' Lorenzo had described her. 'And she can draw too. She has the energy to do something, but she doesn't yet know what it is.'

'I liked your drawing of Lorenzo very much,' says Frieda now. 'See, there it is, on the wall.' And there it is, not badly framed, although the frame is a little too heavy for a pencil drawing.

'Lorenzo found the frame, at the market. There was only rubbish in it. The wife of a farmer – oh so miserable, she was!

So we took her out, and Lorenzo cleaned the frame, and made a new back for it. See! Doesn't your drawing look nice in it!'

'I'm glad you like it.' The girl flushes a little with pleasure, then frowns. 'But it wasn't quite right. It would have been better if I had drawn him here, in this room. The light's right – and the shape of things around him. I ought to draw him now, just as he is. But I wanted to draw *you* today, if you'd let me. I brought my sketchbook. But perhaps there won't be time.'

Frieda lies back in her armchair. She is fully herself: supple, radiant, beautiful in a way Clare has not thought of women being beautiful before. She is pleased, but not surprised, that someone should wish to draw her. It must have happened many times before, thinks Clare, when she was young. Her confidence fills the room like sunlight. Lawrence and Clare lean forward looking at her. Clare measures the curves of flesh over strong bone, the spring of hair, the white swell of the forearm, the vitality of the pose. Lawrence looks at his wife.

'I should like that,' he says quietly.

The tea is fresh and fragrant, the eggs well cooked, the bread and butter good. Clare praises the bread and is told it is home-made.

'And the butter's from the farm – Lower Tregerthen. Do you know it?' asks Lawrence.

'I haven't been there, but I know the people – the Hockings. They come into market. And my cousins know William Henry.'

'I work down there sometimes,' says Lawrence.

'Do you?' She's surprised. What would the Hockings be doing with a man like Lawrence on their land? All this gardening he does too. And yet he doesn't look strong. He has that look on him, indefinable but familiar. It's the look of a sick man, for all his vitality.

'Yes. I like it.'

'It's heavy work, though, this time of the year,' goes on Clare, thinking of what Uncle John and the boys say. 'Leasing stones and cutting the furze.'

'I was hoeing mangels with Stanley this morning,' he says. 'But the work goes like steam, you know, when you are talking. We only stopped for croust. And I used to work on a farm when I was a boy. I know the way of it.'

Clearly this is important to him. How extraordinary. You would think a *writer* . . . but then I don't know much about writers. Frieda doesn't look too pleased about it. I wonder why? Doesn't she like them at the farm? Perhaps she thinks he ought not to waste his time there.

'Has your cousin gone back?' Lawrence asks abruptly.

The small neat room darkens. Clare puts down her bread and butter. There are too many faces.

'Yes,' she says. 'He went on the eleven o'clock train on Sunday morning.'

Her heart beats hard, right up in her throat, so that her voice is forced to squeak past the pressure of it.

'He walked back with me all the way after the concert – did he tell you?'

'Yes. At least – he said he was going to. There wasn't much time to talk at the station, not with all the family there.'

And we would have had much better things to talk about anyway, she thinks. Things about ourselves. But they hadn't talked about themselves. They hadn't said any of those things.

'He talked about medicine,' says Lawrence. 'But I wish he had talked about the war. I think he needed to talk. There was something he said . . .'

'What?'

'About a man called Hawker. I think he was shot. Do you know who he means? Was he a friend of your cousin? Did he talk to you about it?'

'No.'

Clare feels as if he has hit her. Six miles; two hours of talking. Telling Lawrence things he would not tell her. Sharing the life she has not shared. But she won't ask questions; she won't hear any of it second-hand.

Lawrence passes her cup to her. He looks into her pale face, closed in on its distress. He's seen that look before. Clare and John William are more like one another than he had realized.

'It can't go on like this. Things must be different by the time your cousin has finished his training,' exclaims Frieda, her sympathy quickened towards Clare.

'Now the French have got rid of Nivelle,' says Lawrence, 'their army's in a queer state. Pétain'll have to handle 'em with kid gloves if he wants to avoid a mutiny. Everything will fall on our army this summer. And Haig won't mind that, because it'll give him a free hand.'

Tactics. Clare's used to that. The maps, and pins, and names of little woods and hills suddenly on everybody's lips. And at first nobody knows how to pronounce the names, then the more that are killed there, the more we get used to saying the names of the places where they died. You think they are huge places, but the men say, no, they are just little woods and orchards, like those we have here.

'And what do you think?' she asks. 'Will it succeed – will they advance?'

She's never seen anyone's face change so fast. A bitter, jeering black look comes down on it.

'Oh – they'll advance. Have you ever heard men singing – a

mass of men swaying together? They sing ragtime, your cousin says. Can't you hear it? Death in the air, everything dark, nobody daring to show a light. Can't you feel that there's murder in the air, even here? It is not just death but hatred of life, a desire that life *should not be*. And they sing ragtime on the troop trains.'

'Lorenzo,' says Frieda, her voice uninflected, warning.

'I can't write any more,' he says. His voice is thin and exhausted. 'How is it possible to write in the middle of this? The only way is simply *not to think*, to work in the fields and in the gardens and slip back and forget it all. Let your soul go into abeyance and think of nothing. After all, there are living things . . .' His hands sketch softly, subtly in the air. She seems to see something growing there.

'So I plant my potatoes and my broad beans.'

'And the lambs eat them,' remarks Frieda.

'You are quite right. But at least the lambs have no evil intentions. They are just following their nature. I can curse them and chase them out of my field plot, and in a minute they'll whisk up their tails and forget it. They don't bear a grudge against me – they just look for another occasion to eat my broad beans.'

'But John William isn't like that,' insists Clare, brushing aside this talk of lambs and beans.

'How can you say that? On his own, he is not. Here, he's single and separate. Even aloof. But once they are there, they are not men, they are machines. They belong to the military, and it can do as it likes with them. And they are glad of it, somewhere in them. They let go of their wills, and lapse, and accept the will of the military.'

'All the same, you're wrong. I know him. He's my cousin, I've known him all my life.'

And besides – but she doesn't say it. She holds it back.

And besides, he came to me. Where were you when we were lying on the rocks? *That* was John William, not the man you talked to. He'd let you say anything you wanted to. He wouldn't argue with you – that's not his way. John William keeps quiet for a long time, and then he turns . . .

. . . to fighting with teeth and fists and nails under the schoolyard wall, or to making love.

She is proud. She has her secret. She's got something of John William and let no one dare take it away from her – not even this man.

Frieda watches the taut, vixenish face. They must be careful. Lorenzo has promised her that he will not talk to the Cornish about the war any more. He will not tell them that what is in the newspapers is a pack of lies, and that Lloyd George is a little trickster, slippery as butter, a corner-shop grocer who will say anything. But Lorenzo likes this girl, and so he will talk to her. Doesn't he realize that what he is telling her is that the young man she loves has gone off to a war which is nothing but pointless destruction? That he will die for nothing? How can she accept that? She must deny it. And then he wonders that the people here don't love him. In some part of himself he is always quite simply surprised when people don't love him. Because so often they do, and then they turn against him, and they hate him more than if they had never loved him. He is always telling people things they don't want to hear. And for all his cleverness, he doesn't understand soldiers, as she does. When she was a girl, living near the barracks at Metz, she knew soldiers. And he should keep quiet now, in front of this girl.

'Will you draw me now?' she asks Clare. 'And Lorenzo will make us some more tea.'

'No, first she must see my garden,' he cries. The dark cloud slips away. Clare is swept out along with him to look at his vegetable and flower plots, stone-walled, high above farmland and sea. The Hockings have let him cultivate a corner of one of their fields, as well as his own cottage garden. The gardens are warm and well kept, the vegetables free of pests or mildew. Better than her own. He has manure from the farm, he tells her, and the soil is good – see –

'There are lapwings round here,' he says. 'And a goldcrest, once.' She smiles at his funny, possessive way of speaking of the land. But she has to admit that he seems to understand it. He is getting good crops out of it, and he knows the flowers and the birds better than she does. But she is sick of knowing about flowers. How restful it is just to notice vaguely that they are white, or yellow, or that they smell sweet. The small noise of bees makes the garden intimate.

'Do they keep stocks, down at the farm?' she asks. He looks puzzled, and she realizes he doesn't understand her.

'I mean, beehives.'

'They do, I believe. We shall have honey later on. Frieda will like that.'

'I must go in. I should like to draw her now.' She touches the sun-heated stone wall.

'I like this,' she says, noting valerian and foxglove. 'It's a good wall. Our house is new – we have nothing like this.'

'Folk seem to find it convenient,' he replies, dryly.

'Why? How do you mean?'

'The Cornish seem to think nothing of lying under a wall to spy on their neighbours.'

'Spy? On you?'

'Or of lying in a ditch either,' he goes on, his eyes amused but hard, fixed on her face. 'They seem to find our conversation interesting.'

She turns her head away. She is angry, not ashamed. What is he suggesting?

'I'm very sure they do not!' she flashes back at him. Then she remembers the click of insinuations she has heard in Nan's front-room. And where has that information come from?

'You have to understand people,' she says. 'They've always lived here. You're very strange to them.'

'I feel as if the whole of England's a stranger to me now,' he says harshly. 'And those who are destroying it are the first to claim that they are defending it.'

'They *do* say things . . .' she begins, and then hesitates.

'What?'

'It is too stupid. I can't say it. The colour of your wife's stockings – they think they are a signal.'

He barks with laughter.

'And our curtains. You'll have heard of that. And the way we tar our chimney. They are fools enough to think anything – or to pretend that they think it. Poor Frieda is terrified of showing a light. She would rather sit in the dark some evenings than risk lighting a chill.'

'Is she afraid? She doesn't seem so.'

'I think it's harder for a woman. She should have friends – woman friends. She needs other women about her. Someone to talk to. But here there is no one. I thought, perhaps you might come up here sometimes?'

'Let's go in now,' she says.

The drawing doesn't go well. The sunlight has gone out of the room, and Frieda changes so quickly. An hour ago Clare could have drawn a sure line around that contained energy and form, but now Frieda is restless. Her restlessness reminds Clare of Sheba padding from room to room with a kitten in her mouth, looking for a new nest after Hat stupidly tipped out the safe home she had made for her litter in the boot-box. One of the kittens died. Sheba could not look after them properly any more. Why is Frieda so uneasy? Once Clare sees her eyes fill with tears, but, rather than let them fall, she tips her head slightly back so that they are absorbed again, swallowed without acknowledgement. How hard it is when people won't tell you what is wrong with them. Was it because they talked about the war? It is difficult to keep on remembering that Frieda is German.

Frieda sits there with her hands in her lap. Now she is the grand lady, abrupt and distant. The daughter of a baron, Lawrence has told Clare. She quite defeats Clare, who pencils on laboriously, knowing that there is no rhythm in the drawing. The portrait is a disappointment, and Frieda does not hide it. Yet she has resisted being drawn as hard as she could. Now she turns over the pages of Clare's sketchbook. Once again she is eager and appreciative, praising drawings of Kitchie and Hannah. She looks for a long while at an old sketch of Nan.

'Have it,' cries Clare, tearing out the page and giving it to Frieda. There. How odd – she never does things like that.

'It reminds me a little of my mother,' says Frieda. 'It is a long time since I have seen her.'

'Where is she?'

'She is in Germany. Things are terrible for her there. They have nothing. I am so worried about her. She cannot get food and firewood, and old people must keep warm. It is much worse than here.'

Clare snaps a band round her sketchbook, and stands up. She

does not know what to say to Frieda. It was so lovely earlier on, and now the war is here too. It seeps everywhere, like dark-brown London fog. It's time to go – besides, it's getting late. Well past six o'clock, and although Clare has left a cold supper ready, her father will worry if she is not back by nine. Now she looks forward to the walk home, in the long, light, sweet May evening.

Frieda comes to the door with her. Lawrence will see her to the lane-end. She must often stay there alone, thinks Clare, remembering the conversation, watching the light drain out over the fields towards evening. She looks sad. Behind her there is the little, bravely washed room, the five-pound cottage piano, the quiet fields. The air smells of turned soil, cattle and salt. Where does a woman like Frieda belong? Not here, surely. And the war has caught her. Suddenly she is no longer interestingly exotic. She is the enemy.

'Goodbye, Clare. Come again and see us. We had no singing – or playing. I meant us to have singing. And we have some new songs – Hebridean lullabies. A friend has sent them to us. They are beautiful, are they not, Lorenzo?'

But he hums another tune:

Schatz, mein Schatz, reite nicht so weit . . .

Frieda smiles.

'I shall think of your cousin,' she says. 'You know I have cousins of my own at the war. And you must come again. It is so good to have friends near us.'

How magnificent she is in the dark doorway. That lovely, sure outline as she stands with her arms folded in the quickly changing May light. Irresolutely, Clare takes half a step towards her. Their cheeks brush softly. For a moment Clare is in the world of Frieda's skin and scent and rough golden hair, as if a wave has lifted her there.

'Goodbye.'

'Goodbye.'

It will be dusk, and big moths will be flying across the white road, by the time she gets home.

'Come again.'

'Come on, Clare,' says Lawrence, touching her elbow.

Seventeen

He says very little as they walk up the lane side by side. The silence is cool spring water after so much talk. And such talk! – she can't absorb it all at once. She'll have to take it in slowly, while she wipes the plates and sets the table for tomorrow's breakfast and talks to her father of spring onions and Sheba. Lawrence points to a clump of white foxgloves, like the ones she drew. They are flowering early this year, forced on by the heat of May. The bracken has unfurled to fresh silvery points. She catches one between her fingers, and it breaks off with a dull, tender snap. Puffs of dust kick up under their boots. Clare is tired: the day's been so long, and she's swung far out of the orbit of home and Nan. Yet she's excited too. Suddenly it seems much too tame just to turn left and walk down the quiet high road home, towards her father and the smells of polish and pickled herring. They are nearly at the top of the lane, and the sweet evening wind is blowing from the sea. The light's golden here, glowing, almost incandescent. If she were to paint someone in this light . . . Lawrence, say . . . to paint him out of pure light and show the way his solid form makes the light jump and dance . . . And yet she's got to go home, just when she feels so alive. She could stay up all night, walk all night, paint as she's never painted in her life.

'Why do we live in houses?' she demands and stands still, reaching up into the warm sky, bathing her hands in the breeze, laughing at the feel of it, laughing back at Lawrence.

'What do you want to do – pull down the sky?' asks Lawrence, but she looks at his face and knows that the same restless energy is licking through him, filling his limbs, his hands, his voice. She stares out at the big sun as it drops quickly westward.

'I don't want to go home,' she says.

'No. Why should you?' he responds. But he's waiting for her to take the lead. She's in charge.

'Let's go the other way,' she says.

'What, towards the churchtown? Do you still want to go there?'

'How do you mean – still?'

'Something your cousin said. That you always wanted to go to the church, to see the mermaid.'

'Did he say that? Why, I'd forgotten. I haven't thought of that for years. How strange . . .'

It's certainly strange. She doesn't forget much to do with John William. She fumbles for the memory but it won't come; there's a blur of sensation, nothing more. Never mind, it'll come back if she doesn't force it. Everything to do with John William comes back in the end.

'We'll go there now,' she announces. Lawrence will come. He's bound to do what she wants. Just at this moment she knows that everything is with her; the warm expectant evening, the long *hush* of the sea, the constant secret presence of John William. 'Are you coming?' she challenges.

'Look, there's the moon,' he answers. There it hangs, pale and insignificant. Daylight takes a long time to die here.

'Frieda will be all right, won't she?' asks Clare.

'Oh, she's used to it. I often go out in the evenings. I can't stay cooped in one place, thinking. She knows that, really.'

'You go down to the farm, don't you?'

'Yes, or I go walking with William Henry. Like us, now. It's the best time. You feel you can do anything: run over the fields to the sea, turn round and find the farm gone and nothing there but little dark Cornish farmers from a thousand years ago, looking at you . . . have you ever noticed the way the Cornish look at you? No, of course you haven't. This is your place, isn't it, Clare Coyne? But you haven't got those Cornish eyes – soft and dark and a bit inscrutable. Your cousin Hannah has those eyes. Do you know William Henry?'

'Yes, he comes into market, doesn't he – and my uncle knows him. My Uncle John, who has the farm.'

'Everyone knows everyone here. I'm a fool to forget it. But William Henry – he's not like a common farmer. Those eyes of his – they draw all your thoughts out of you. Yet there's something else there – something a bit sceptical – even jeering – as if he'd like to do you down for getting close to him.'

Where's she heard that tone before? Wistful, puzzling, eager? Why, in herself. That's what she hears when she turns over and over the secret of John William, like turning a coin in her pocket at full moon, and the secret quickens into life, flames up, dies down. When you love someone, you just want to say his name. That's what Nan told her years ago, when Clare asked how it was that she always knew when a girl liked a boy long before anything was ever said. No courtship, no marriage, no pregnancy had ever surprised Nan.

'It's from watching, Clarey. Most folk walk around with their eyes shut. And there's other sure signs: say, if a girl always brings a man's name into her conversation where it doesn't belong, then you know she's saying it for the pure pleasure of having his name in her mouth. Names are magical things, Clarey, never forget that.'

But how can Lawrence feel anything like that about another man? She must have misunderstood, that's all.

He's walking with her and the last bees swing past them, heavily laden, down to the farm stocks. They fly close to the earth now, late in the evening, going home. Frieda will be waiting. No she won't, thinks Clare quickly. She's not like the women of the town, pulling the potatoes off the fire before they boil to rags, keeping her man's plate covered and warm at the bottom of the range for fear of feeling the back of his hand when he comes home late and truculent to a spoiled dinner. Frieda does not cook or sweep or spin. Frieda sits in her chair like a queen. Clare smiles, making it up, but her powers of invention falter as the road opens to the right and reveals the long, changeful, violet-shadowed slope to the sea.

The graveyard is full of people Clare has known. She kneels, examining names, tracing family trees, stories, allegiances, old hates and likings, while Lawrence sits back on his heels and urges her on. She matches each name to its own patch of earth: to the one it tilled before it came here, or to the restless acres of the sea. There are Celtic crosses, trefoils and rough, potent granite stones too hard for a name to be worn into them. They rise like a wave towards the sweep of the moor. She stops, exhausted and looks up at him.

'That's a funny way of sitting,' she says.

'It's very comfortable. You ought to try it. It's the way all the miners sit at home, squatting against the walls after the shift. I used to pass them on my way home from school. My father'ud be there too, making them all laugh.'

'Did he?'

'Oh, yes. He was famous through the whole pit. He could mimic anyone: the men loved him.'

The bitterness in his voice is so much at odds with his words that she searches his face, puzzled.

'Didn't you like that?'

There's a pause. Carefully Lawrence selects a blade of grass from a long tangled clump, breaks it off, raises it to his lips and blows. There's a feeble fluttering squeak, then he blows again and a keen whistle parts the air. She smiles: it's ages since she thought of doing that. He grins back at her.

'My father taught me,' he says. 'He taught me lots of things like that. Trouble was, I never thought they were worth anything. Not compared to real learning, the kind of thing they taught us at school. And my mother agreed with me.'

'That was sad.'

'Yes,' he agrees. 'It was, though at the time I though it was just what I wanted. Once I went back home, and an old man who'd known my father stopped me in the street. I can see him now, in his clean Sunday clothes, a bit bent and having to walk carefully. He'd danced with my father when they were young . . . but now he was old and tired and angry. He said that I'd shamed a finer man than I'd ever be, writing of him in my books. He stood there telling me this, and I couldn't even remember his name. My father knew every man in the pit, and they all knew him. But my father's friends never came to our house. He would meet them in the pub. When I was little I'd think what a place it must be, that all the men wanted to go there so badly. But my mother said it was a nasty place where men went to drink away the money that might have made decent-looking women of their wives and chances for their children. He used to run a dancing-class . . .'

'Your father?'

'The best dancer for miles around, they said he was, before

216

he married. But he'd long stopped dancing by the time I knew him. And my mother never danced with him once she was married. He was the best dancer, and the handsomest – so quick and always the kind of man you warmed to – you couldn't help yourself. Unless you'd grown to hate him . . .'

There he goes, brooding over his father just like he brooded over William Henry, with the same helpless regret and longing. Why can't he stop thinking of them both and sit in the last bit of sun and whistle with the grass? He ought to have seen Francis Coyne and Susannah Treveal together. That would have given him something to think about.

'They were as different as cream from herring,' said Nan, when Clare asked for stories of her parents. But Nan would never say that cream was better than herring; each was good in its kind. And you would sicken of the one in time, and want the other.

Lawrence smiles suddenly, unfolds himself and stands over her. He reaches out his hand.

'Come on. We'll go and look inside the church.'

She takes his hand, smiling back, and yields to let him pull her up.

Neither of them sees that they are seen. At that moment the Rector goes down the path from the church door, head down. He catches a movement to his right and turns and there they are: two figures balanced like figures in a dance, one lifting, one lifted, both smiling, the warm evening sun catching and lighting them. Unmistakably they flame in consecrated ground: the daughter of his friend with her rare flag of red hair, and his outlandish red-bearded enemy. There they are. They have not seen him. He steps forward as if to speak, then moves back. He will watch. He will let them betray themselves. Even from here he can see that the girl is flushed, and her hair has come loose around her face. There she is lolling on a gravestone, on the bones of Christ's chosen. He moves back further, into the shadows, and watches. They stand, and after a long interval their parted hands separate. The girl brushes herself down, then turns as if to display herself. The man leans forward and brushes grass from her back, her skirt. They pick their way through the gravestones, faces animated and bent together, noticing nothing. They turn towards the church porch, and the Rector wants to cry out against sacrilege, but he holds back the cry. Let them eat and drink to their own damnation. They melt into the porch and he hears the click and groan of the church door, then they are gone. Out of their own mouths they have condemned themselves. What I have seen I have seen, he mutters quoting wildly from his own scriptures as he backs out and confronts the Tinner's Arms, glaring.

'Is it this way?'

They blunder down the aisle. The church is dark and cool, a vessel of stone-chilled air. It feels so cold that Clare shivers. She begins to remember something – some dim recollection of stumbling out of the blaze of a summer day, the church air washing over a prickle of sunburn, the sudden silence.

'It's down here.'

Lawrence's voice sounds frighteningly loud, but he is only talking as he usually does.

'Do you always whisper in churches?' he mocks. 'Who do you think is listening?'

No one at all. There's no steady red glow and dip of the sanctuary lamp, no candles flickering with the prayers of those who have already walked out into the sunlight, no murmur of voices from the confessionals. Only this ancient, untenanted silence. You couldn't say a prayer here. It would be soaked up at once by these granite walls, and blotted out.

'It's cold in here,' she whispers.

But he's not listening. 'Here she is,' he says, and kneels. The little mermaid, carved into dark wood. And Clare knows her. Her fingers reach out for the familiar curves of that body which drew her again and again in her childhood. How could she have forgotten.

'Little mermaid,' Clare greets her.

She has got no more wounds since Clare last touched her. Those gashes are polished with age now, and if she is lucky no one will add to them. Will they throw her out of the church again, as they have done before? She smiles and raises her arms, and will not answer. Does she even know what she can stir in those who crouch beside her to pray or to draw out a knife? 'Virgin most pure, star of the sea,' Clare mutters. That was it. That was what she used to sing, blurring this beautiful thing in her heart with the Virgin she was taught to love. And Hannah laughed once and they fought blindly and silently, scuffling on the cold floor for fear of waking the echoes. And John William traced the mermaid's scales and her round breasts and said nothing.

'She doesn't belong here,' says Lawrence.

'Why, of course she does!' says Clare, far more loudly than she intended, surprised by the force of her own anger. 'It's only bigots who say she doesn't, and try to drive her out.'

'No,' says Lawrence slowly. 'She doesn't belong. She's half and half. They laugh at her on land, and hate her. And when she's in the sea, she can't breathe. So what's left for her? She can only sit on her rock, neither on land nor in the sea, and wait, and drive men mad. So they hate her all the more, all the time they're pretending to love her and want her –'

'But why? Why do they have to hate her? I don't under-stand.'

'Because she makes people think that there's something more – something they haven't been told about. And they'll never have it. Look at her face.'

'It's worn to nothing,' says Clare.

'Only because so many people have touched it. It makes her more beautiful.'

Clare does not want to hear any more. His words are taking the little mermaid away from her.

'There's another way of looking at it,' she says. 'She can swim and she can breathe – and she loves both. She has both. Why should there be anything sad about it?'

He turns to her and smiles. It's a smile fully for herself, acknowledging, appreciative.

'Long may you believe that, Clare Coyne,' he answers.

Eighteen

Two weeks later, out in her backyard in the morning sun, Clare thinks she would like to go and see Frieda again. Lugging the heavy wash-basket of wet clothes into the garden has made her think of Frieda. What does she do on washing-day? No doubt she laughs and says Lorenzo must do it, he does it so beautifully. Once in her life, Frieda scrubbed a floor, or so Lawrence said. But it was only once. She wasn't brought up to do such work – not like us.

Not like us, indeed, thinks Clare grimly, as she hauls out the first twisted sheet from her pile, ready to put it through the mangle. Prices are going up all the time, but their income has dipped again. She's decided that they'll have to stop sending the sheets to the laundry. She has always done the clothes-washing at home, but it was her luxury not to wash the sheets and to get them back from the laundry in a brown-paper parcel, starched so stiff so that they creaked when she unfolded them. It is heavy work to fold over the wet sheets and feed them little by little through the mangle, and into the zinc bucket on the other side. The mangle-rollers ride roughly over four thicknesses of sheet. Her hands are red and raw from washing-soda, and her hair sticks to her forehead in tight curls from the steam. She's sweating so much that her overall sticks to her. She wriggles inside it. The sun beats on the back of the house, and bounces against the whitewashed garden wall. They have even mentioned *this unusual spell of fine weather* in the newspaper. But other news is crowding for space. There was a bad air-raid in London yesterday, one of the worst of the war. Here the sky stays empty and blue. What must it be like to live in London and see bombs falling out of the skies? But here the talk is of U-boats, not aeroplanes. Everyone is asking what Jellicoe's going to do about the latest sinkings. It can't go on like this, with the Germans stealing in under our very noses. Those U-boats do just as they like. They pick off our supply-ships one by one.

Oh, there's good news too. There's always good news. The country has been on the point of a decisive victory for three years now. Now the papers are full of General Plumer's triumph at the Messines Ridge. It's better to write about the million tons of TNT it took to blow up the ridge than of the 600,000 tons of shipping lost to the U-boats every month.

'Haig's chance has come,' said her father that morning. 'Now they'll have to give him a free hand.'

He sounds eager, as if the news has refreshed him. He has started to order the *Morning Post*, as well as *The Times*, to find out what Gwynne's got to say.

'He's after Lloyd George to "take charge" in France. Thinks the French would move aside for our Welsh Wizard. Mark you, Clare, Gwynne's got no more time for Lloyd George than he has for any other politician. What he wants is for the generals to get a free hand.'

Clare thinks that the cost of two newspapers a day would go a long way to paying her laundry bills.

How they long for a final onslaught, no matter what it costs. If only it could all be over, no matter what. Last night, slicing a pair of raw kidneys, she was dizzy, seeing how the newly sharpened knife parted the caul and exposed a delicate tracery of ducts. All so exquisitely made, and so easy to spoil. Those kidneys would begin to stink within the hour in this hot weather if she left the meat-dish out in the sun. Then the blowflies would come. She shuddered, covered the kidneys with a plate and put them in the meat-safe until supper-time. The third sheet. Only this one, and one more. Then the table-cloths, and her boiled glass-cloths and dish-rags. She'd rest for a minute before pegging up the sheets. She dreads doing it today; the line is so heavy once all the clothes are on it and it has to be hoisted up into the sunshine by the pulley. She shivers. She must have got over-heated. Just this one sheet now.

And there's Hannah, a blur of light at the back-entry gate. Good. That means I'll have to stop for a bit. Hannah wavers on, indistinct in the blinding light, fumbling with the gate-latch. It always sticks, but Hannah knows the way of it — why is she taking so long?

'Lift the gate — it's got stuck,' Clare calls. Hannah's face is averted under the brim of her straw hat. Then she pushes the gate open, and comes on down the path.

The path is twenty feet long, no more. Hannah takes two steps, and Clare lets the sheet fall. It will get grass stains on it, it will all have to be done again, she thinks with one part of her mind. She sees her own hand gripping the handle of the mangle.

'Hannah,' she cries out. 'Go away.'

But Hannah comes on. Her face is a colour Clare has never seen it. Her yellow skin sticks to her bones. Her eyes are startled, wide-open and staring. She doesn't say anything. She comes up and lays both her hands on top of the mangle, and looks at Clare.

'Mind your fingers,' says Clare in a quick, frightened voice.

'Clare,' says Hannah.

'I know what you're going to say. Don't say it.'

'You got to come downalong to Nan's, Clarey.'

'No, I can't, I'm in the middle of my washing.'

'Bugger your washing,' says Hannah. Now she is round the other side of the mangle, with Clare. She puts her arm around Clare's waist. Clare is sweating. Hannah can smell her frightened sweat.

The two girls go into the scullery, and Hannah pours two glasses of water from the big jug Clare keeps on a stone slab behind the door, covered.

'But it can't be,' says Clare. 'He was safe. He was in camp. He was training to be an officer.'

'It was an accident,' says Hannah, her mouth shaking. 'It was an accident in training. He was killed instantly, it said.'

The two girls look at each other. They both know that is what telegrams always say.

'But it can't be true,' says Clare. 'He'd got out of it. He was safe. He can't have been killed in an officers' training camp. Not after all that long time in France.'

Surely this is some awful joke. Perhaps it's a test. Perhaps it's a test to see if they're fit to be an officer's family. But then she looks at Hannah's face and sees that John William is already dead there.

'Do you know when it was?'

'Saturday.'

'When we were digging up the end of the vegetable plot, then.'

For Clare had thought she would plant cauliflower, and winter cabbage, and Hannah had come up to help her after work. They had dibbed in the young plants, and watered them in the early evening –

'And then we walked over to meet Peggy – didn't we?'

Hannah nods. That's what they did, and some time in between their planting the winter cabbages and hustling Peggy out for an hour's evening walk, John William had died. But the cabbages would live, because Clare had been watering them every day, carrying the water carefully across to the plot.

'I shall stop watering them,' she says aloud.

'What?'

'The cabbages. I shall stop watering them. It's not right that they should keep growing when he's dead.'

She has said it now. When he's dead. The words go down through her like stones falling through deep water. It feels as if those words have opened up some new place in her, which has never been touched before. But she will have to say them again, and again, because it will never not be true now.

They finish drinking the water, and Clare says she will go upstairs to take off her overall.

'But Hannah! What can I do? I've no mourning.'

'Bring down your silk. Nan'll dye it. She's dyeing our dresses tonight.'

'When did the telegram come?'

'An hour ago. I was at work. Kitchie was round at Nan's, and he fetched me home. He wanted to come up here with me, but I didn't let him.'

Yes, Hannah has her black work dress on. What had she been doing when Kitchie came into the shop? Trying to get rid of a tiresome customer who came in for a packet of needles and stayed to talk for twenty minutes? Pulling down the blinds because the sun was threatening to fade a roll of cretonne at 1/9d a yard? Hannah moving. The way she would reach up with the blind-pole and hook the blind down. Supple and full of life. Drat the thing, it always catches. Wants oiling. John William's smell of carbolic and, under it, almonds. They could never kill the smell of his skin.

Those kidneys. Don't think of them.

'Hannah, I'm going to be sick.'

She gets to the privy in time and vomits, while Hannah holds her head and strokes her forehead.

'It's all right now, Clarey. It's all right.' Now Hannah is crying.

The privy stinks of vomit and sweat as Clare struggles up. She is dizzy, and there are red sparks coming and going in front of her eyes.

You have to keep on doing things; you can't stop, even when this happens. Now I have to rinse out my mouth or else it will smell. I must wash, and comb my hair, and put on different clothes. I have to do that, but I can leave the washing. I needn't think about that now, but I shall have to think of it later, for there's no one else who will.

Hannah is crying. Hannah must sit down at the table, and I'll make us both tea. It won't matter if we don't go straight down to Nan's. Hannah cries. She has forgotten Clare now. She sits at the kitchen table with her head on her arms, her back shaking, curled in on herself and private. She can't cry at home, thinks Clare, because of Aunt Sarah. Everybody will be round Aunt Sarah, the way they were at the railway station. They will expect Hannah to be strong.

For a moment Clare hates Aunt Sarah – weak, greedy Aunt Sarah, who will feebly gulp down a macaroon in the middle of a fit of hysterics. Licensed mourner, chief in suffering. And I am just his cousin.

Clare puts on her grey dress and packs her Sunday dress into a brown-paper parcel. How strange: for once she is the competent one, the one who does things, while Hannah sits at the table. She looks out of the window and the sun is just the same, falling on the white tangle of sheet on the grass, and the loaded line with the other sheets nearly touching the worn grass. I shall go out and peg up the rest of it, and raise the line. But not yet. Hannah will think it isn't seemly, even though it doesn't make any difference if I do it now or tonight. John William is dead. He will always be dead.

They go out of the house and creep down the hill close together, dark, dull blotches on the brilliant morning. The cemetery looks beautiful, warm in the sun, curled up asleep on the curve of the hill. When they were children and they went out mackerel fishing, they would look back and see the cemetery, bigger than the town itself from the sea. Only John William wouldn't look up. He frowned with concentration as he baited the lines.

'Isn't that a shoal of mackerel there?' she cries.

'No,' says Hannah. 'Just a bit of wind getting up.'

As they come into Nan's, they're engulfed by a close, suffocating smell of black dye. Nan's decided not to wait; she has begun on her vat of mourning. Curtains are drawn, rooms are in shadow. There's steam in the kitchen, snaking up from the vat of dye where deep bubbles pock and the clothes writhe slowly to the surface to be poked down again by Nan's long wooden spoon. The kettle steams too, and the biggest tea-pot is drawing at the side of the range. Nan slices bread, and one of Uncle John's hams sits at her right hand. The flesh of it is dark and rosy, exquisitely marbled with white fat. A basin of brown eggs waits to be hard-boiled.

'That poor useless Ellen-creature brought them. She had them from her sister. Not that I would wish to eat out of Ellen's kitchen, but there's little enough she can do to an egg.'

Nan taps the eggs and tells Clare to get them hard-boiled. Her face is tired and severe, but there are no marks of tears on it. Like Clare, she hasn't cried yet. Sarah is lying down in the back-bedroom. She took on terribly, but she's fallen into a drowse now. Hannah must go and sit with her mother.

'But where's Uncle Arthur?' asks Clare.

Nan shrimps up her lips.

'Your Uncle Arthur's gone out cursing God and all Creation – that's the way it took him.'

How can Nan be like this? Her hands slice ham unerringly.

'Fetch the mustard, Clarey, and there's a last big jar of those pickled onions I put up in the winter. He's better that way,' says Nan. 'Sometimes a man's better on his own.'

'Nan,' says Clare. 'Why don't you sit down? I can do this.'

'There's plenty for all of us to do,' says Nan. 'Better to be doing than thinking. You might just turn those clothes, case they scorch on the bottom.'

The clothes smell ugly. The fume of the dye catches at the back of Clare's throat and brings tears to her eyes.

'I'll have to see about the cards,' continues Nan, running down her thoughts aloud.

The cards. They will have to be in all the shop windows by tomorrow morning.

WILL FRIENDS PLEASE ACCEPT THIS THE ONLY INTIMATION

How often she had seen a new card in a window as she went by, stopped to read it and thought vaguely of the gone dead one, Stevens or Rosewall or Date. And deep down in the impulse of sympathy there had been guilty gladness, as if to read of another's death left her twice as alive. When they were children they used to play in the cemetery. They didn't mind the dead. They would pick daisies and yarrow and make tiny wreaths for the graves. Those dead ones were another race. They had never really been alive. Caught, weak and silent: they could not run in the sunshine, scream with laughter, nibble the fat juicy ends of summer grasses. Death was something that was never going to happen to us.

Clare can picture the people stopping by the shop windows to read the cards. The cards will have John William's name on them. How strange and impossible that seems, when only a little over a fortnight before he had been walking in these streets, buying Grandad a present of tobacco in the very shop that will bear his name in its window now. One person will stop, then two, then a little bunch. If they haven't heard already, they will catch in their breath and say how terrible it must be for the Treveals, just when they were so proud of their John William going for an officer. If they already know, they will find their knowledge stamped there in black, black-bordered letters. They will linger, tracing over each letter. Then they will walk on in the sunshine, twice as rich as before. The boys John William fought with, the ones who would have liked to jeer at his ambitions but did not dare. For he was going to do it, she thinks hotly. He would have shown them all.

'Don't put the cards in, Nan,' begs Clare.

'Why, Clarey, what can you be thinking of? Don't you know what's right?'

Silence in the kitchen. They'll all be here soon, snatched out of their daily lives, wreathed in shawls. Aunt Mag's come already, and she is padding about upstairs, tending to Aunt

Sarah. And your father, Clare? He doesn't know. He was out when Hannah came.

Ah, yes. Out. That secret place that men go to and women don't know about.

'He'll be back soon, Clarey. He'll be down, soon as he hears.'

Nan is trying to comfort her, and Clare can't say that her father will be no help to her now.

The door bangs hard. Clare jumps and gives a small ridiculous shriek. Now there is a blundering of boots at the door, quickly stilled by Nan. For a terrible moment she thinks they are bringing in John William's coffin. But no – it can't be. And at the door there are three lads, grown huge in the crowded space. A Harte and two Lees. Jack, Sammie and Esau. There they stand in their boots, with a white, mauled-looking Harry, barely on his feet between them.

'There's bin an accident,' blurts Jack Harte. 'It's is arm. Is bad arm's smashed up.'

They will not come into the house out of respect for the dead, for they are in their working clothes. So they know about John William already, thinks Clare. So quick: the cards not in the windows yet. They stand at the cottage doorway nervously, gaping with respect for its time of sorrow.

'When did this happen?' asks Nan, whisking over to white-faced Harry. She bends and examines his arm without touching it.

'Help him in, then. Don't just let him stand there,' she orders, and they tramp over the threshold and deposit Harry with clumsy gentleness on the kitchen settle, then stand around uneasily, sniffing the dye and meat-smells that mean death in the house. A thread of spittle comes out of Harry's mouth as he sags down and shuts his eyes. Esau Lee wipes his hands against his trousers.

'When did this happen?' asks Nan again.

'Not long after your Kitchie come up and told us about John William. Bit a gear we got wanted fixing – it went an caught Harry's arm.' The Harte boy looks beyond Nan, at the wall.

'Don't let our Sarah hear em,' says Nan sharply to Clare. 'Now, Kitchie, run for Dr Kernack.'

'It's bad,' says Jack Harte. What's that in his voice? Something queer that ought not be there. You might almost say . . . satisfaction? Nan nods. She looks Jack straight in the eye and she nods slowly, acknowledging that same strange *something*. It's bad enough. It'll do. Clare has the feeling they are speaking another language, one which she is not quick enough to catch. But they've scarcely said anything, so how can that be?

'I'll tell Mother,' says Hannah, who has been drawn downstairs by the noise of boots and voices.

'You will not,' says Nan. 'They say one sorrow drives out another, but Sarah needs rest.'

'She's not resting,' says Hannah.

Nan thinks for a minute. Sarah's a poor thing, but she's sharp enough. She'll cotton on.

'Maybe you're right. Maybe it's best she thinks of Harry rather than our Johnnie. Now wait there, Jack, Esau, Samuel.'

Sweat and tears are gathering on Harry's face, but Nan takes no notice of them yet. She goes upstairs, and they hear her feet creak across the bedroom boards, and then the lock of her trunk snick, and the lid squeaking back. When she comes down, she has in her hand a screw of paper with something hidden in it. She closes Jack Harte's fingers around it and pats his hand. But he pulls back. He won't take it from her. She will need it – specially at a time like this.

'You take it,' she says. 'Take it and don't add to my troubles. You're good boys, all of you.'

'How much did you give em?' asks Hannah, in quite her usual voice, the minute they are out of the house and clumping off up the street, back to work.

'That's for you to ask and me to know,' says Nan, as if Hannah were six years old again.

'Well, they can't call him up now!' exclaims Clare, suddenly realizing.

Nan and Hannah exchange slow, ironic glances. 'Quick, isn't she,' remarks Hannah.

'Get a bucket for Harry,' says Nan, watching his colour.

'Don't let the doctor put his hands on me, Nan, don't let the doctor touch me,' he begs, his courage all drained now the lads have gone. 'You do it, you can set a bone, Nan, you do it.'

'I can't handle an injury like this one, my boy,' she says. 'You should of thought a that before you did it.'

'Don't mind, Harry, Dr Kernack will give you chloroform,' says Clare.

'Dear God, how's all this to be paid for,' fusses Nan.

And there's Sarah in the doorway, her face white as a halibut's belly, gaping at them.

'Our Harry's hurt his arm, Mother,' says Hannah distinctly. 'So bad they won't be able to send him to the war.'

Nothing from Sarah.

'Did you hear me, Mother? Harry'll be all right. They won't be able to send Harry.'

Sarah's face crumbles. She totters towards Harry and crouches by his feet, stroking his leg. Then she gets hold of his whole, living hand and kisses it over and over, covering it with tears. Clare looks away. In spite of herself, she is disgusted by Aunt Sarah, greedily crouching over Harry. Hannah shrugs imperceptibly.

'There now,' says Nan. 'She'll be all right. Mind, Hannah, your mother's to be the one that looks after Harry. Don't you go doing nothing. Leave her to do it.'

Kitchie comes flying through the door.

'Doctor's coming soon as he can!' he announces.

I've got to get out of here, thinks Clare. Blood and chloroform and bits of bone. And Nan too; I know it's her way to turn to what's living and what needs to be done, but I can't bear it.

'Clare. Open your legs.'

'Please, sir, I found a mermaid.'

'Are you a human boy?'

'Are you a true mermaid?'

Nan, I'm going out. But she doesn't say it. She is ensnared by Aunt Sarah's snorting sobs of relief over her Harry, by the rolling boil of the black clothes, by the click of Nan's knife over the meat.

At tea-time they are all still there, all gathered: John William's flesh and blood. Clare's father has arrived, and he is in the front-room with Uncle Arthur. Both of them smell of brandy. Uncle Arthur doesn't like Francis Coyne, but now he is spilling out his life to him in raw gobbets of bewilderment and sorrow. Father says nothing. He has a hip-flask which he offers to Uncle Arthur from time to time. Occasionally he murmurs that John William was a fine boy, a fine boy.

For one hour the story of Uncle Arthur and his boy rambles, takes shape and becomes beautiful. He makes Francis see the boy standing in front of him, outfacing him, dark and insolent. Any father would chastise him – wouldn't you? Speak the truth, now. I tell you, Francis, I wanted to knock it out of him. It was my duty as his father. I thought he was a fool to himself, always after what he could never have.

'But then they wanted him for an officer,' says Uncle Arthur, in the voice of someone slapping down his full hand on the table. He counts them off on his fingers: 'He'd been Lance-Corporal. Corporal. Sergeant. And then he'd a had his commission, not a doubt of it. Learning was nothing to John William.'

No one can take that away from him: not now. Harry may be Sarah's boy, but, dead, John William is his father's.

In the kitchen there is still a pile of ham sandwiches by the tea-pot. Nan has been cutting and replenishing all afternoon. Uncle John reaches out and weighs his sandwich in his hand before biting into it. He smells the meat. It is moist and succulent, just as it ought to be. He bred the pig, and the sow which farrowed it. He looks around, holding the sandwich ostentatiously. Sure enough, Nan says, 'If you hadn't a made us a present of that ham, John, I don't know what we should a done, not with all these that've been in here today.'

'Well, I don't know,' he says consideringly, turning the sandwich. 'Good enough. Good enough, eh, Kitchie.'

Kitchie, scarlet, bolts his sandwich. That was rough of Uncle John. Kitchie can't help being greedy, not even today. But at least he doesn't pretend about it. He doesn't say in a faint voice that he couldn't eat a morsel, like Aunt Sarah, then gnaw her way through three sandwiches. If John William was here, he'd spot that. And maybe he'd give Clare a smile so quick nobody else would see it, and one of his split-second winks. How she envied him for that when she was little – he could wink, and whistle through his teeth, and imitate a dog barking. He tried to teach her, but she never learned. Once she thought she'd got it, but he made her look in the glass and she saw that all she was doing was to screw up both eyes and look foolish.

The men are talking about the funeral. Will John William's

body be brought home for burial here? Uncle John is blustering, sounding important but knowing nothing. Her father says quietly, 'I don't think that they will release his body for burial here.'

Clare looks at him, startled. She has hardly ever heard such finality in her father's voice. She cannot think why he says it, for surely he knows nothing more than any of them? But the family defers to him. He is a gentleman, and he knows the way of the world and the ways of officers.

'They'll give him a military funeral, with full honours,' says Father.

'I don't know about that,' begins Aunt Mag, eyes darting around for support. 'Surely he did ought to be brought home? It's only right – '

Unexpectedly Nan quells her. 'He's a soldier, Mag. He got to have what soldiers have.'

Surely Nan would want John William brought home, so he could rest here in his coffin and the neighbours could come in and pay their respects, and look at him before the coffin was closed. If he'd been killed in France, we would know that couldn't happen. But he's here, in England. Why doesn't Nan want it? Why is she agreeing with Father?

'There will be a letter, from the camp commander, to notify us,' says Father.

Nan nods. A look passes between the two of them: Nan in her black, for she always wears black and needs to dye nothing; Father with his fine, thin face turned to her. Something is between the two of them, as if they are alone in the room. Now Nan's face is slack and heavy with sorrow. She looks old, and afraid. But Nan isn't afraid of death, Clare knows. Clare cries out silently to the two of them, 'Don't let them bring him here. Take it away from me.'

She sees a day of blazing sun, and the coffin bobbing down the steep path through Barnoon Cemetery, and the people of the town following it with faces like hungry gulls.

'Nan, take it away from me. Make it not happen.'

Nan sighs. She is very tired, but she will not give way yet. There are things to be taken care of first, and this is something they are taking care of between the two of them, she and Francis Coyne.

Nineteen

At first light the next day Clare hears her father creak past on the landing. Thank God, it's morning, even though the room's still shadowy because of its heavy curtains. Last night she went to bed thinking that she'd never be able to get to sleep, but she slept heavily, scarcely moving in the bed, plummeting so far into solid waveless sleep that she was beyond dreaming until the last minutes of the night. Then, in her dream, the church of the Sacred Heart and St Ia was being built again, this time with a smooth forest of slender marble columns supporting a roof so fragile that Clare could not tell if it were made of glass or air. The old altar had vanished, and a new altar was being built into the side of the church. It was made of marble, the colour of sweet butter and scrolled with carving.

In her dream Clare advanced down the quiet church, stepping on sheets spattered with white and gold, past stepladders and chisels and fine brushes for applying gold-leaf. All the tools looked as if they had just been put down a moment before. One drop of gold paint hung on the end of a brush, a globe ready to topple. There was no one to be seen, but she must find the builders and tell them they were making the altar in the wrong place. The altar must be in the front of the church. But just as she reached the altar someone took her right hand. The grip was no more than a band of warmth around her little finger. She did not see the person who touched her, because in the dream she knew she was not allowed to look sideways. She had to look ahead of her. Suddenly she wasn't worried about anything any more. Let them build the altar where they liked. It was beautiful. She laughed as she touched a coil of marble, not caring about the sound of laughter in the empty church. Then the building was suddenly full of people, talking and laughing and making more noise than she had ever heard in a church before. They were hanging branches of cherry and bunches of grapes around the altar, so that leaves, tendrils and fruit curved over the swell of the marble. Now its marble hollows were flushed with crimson from the colour of the cherry-flesh. Slowly Clare felt the grip on her finger thin away like mist. She was released. She turned and saw that it was John William walking swiftly away towards the door. He did not look at her. She knew when he opened the door that he would walk out into the sunlight.

Clare could not be sad to see him go. He had to leave. She could tell that from the set of his back as he turned, and the way he looked as if he were hurrying towards something she could not see. At that same moment she saw that someone had planted a naked baby in one of the hollows of marble. It lay there cupped, on its back, looking up through leaves and fruit. Then, as Clare watched, a big man with a battered face knelt on the step of the altar and reached up to the child in its stone cradle. Clare knew his face: he was a herring fisherman. He held out his finger, calloused from handling the nets, and the child grasped it. There they remained. Now there was no one else in the church, and Clare woke.

'Clare. Clare.'

'Yes, I'm awake.'

He pushes open her door. His voice is tired. Has he slept?

He never gets up this early. Clare hoists herself up on her elbows and says, 'Draw the curtains, Father, I can't see you.'

But he stays in the doorway.

'Clare, I'm taking the half past seven train. I am going to make arrangements at the officers' training camp. I have been thinking about it, and I must go. I won't be home tonight, so you must get Hannah to come up and sleep with you, if your Aunt Sarah can spare her.'

'But why are you going, Father? What about Uncle Arthur?'

'Arthur is in no fit state. It's better that I go. And Arthur would get nothing out of the people in charge. They would know they could get away with telling him anything, and he would take it gratefully, no matter what the truth of it.'

The truth? Why is he talking like this? There's no truth except that John William is dead. Or does he think – can he possibly think –

'Father! Could it have been a mistake? Do you think it's possible? Is that why you're going?'

'No, no, Clare, not that. There can be no mistake, not here in England. If it had happened in France, perhaps: though the communications are excellent, I believe. But we ought to know what kind of accident it was.'

'I see,' she says. She had not really thought it could be a mistake. She could not wake up and believe John William was alive. She could not be like Mrs Hore who still said that she would hark as she sat by her fire in the evening and think she heard her William's footstep. There was not a trace of John William left in the world. Only his body; an unthinkable thing, slumped, never moving any more. Even in her dream he was walking away; but he had touched her before he left her, and that dream-touch was still as real as anything that had happened between her and John William.

'Wait, Father, I'll get up and make your breakfast. You mustn't go without eating anything. You know what the trains are like: it will take hours.'

'Go back to sleep. You need to sleep. I only put my head round the door to tell you I was going.'

'I don't mind. I shan't sleep now.'

She throws on her dressing-gown and stumbles downstairs to boil an egg and cut bread and butter for her father. At least there is butter today. For once her father wants to talk to her. He wants to share this with her – his fears, whatever they are. Is she going to let him? Or will she cook for him and tidy up after him and let him go without asking questions?

The way I always do.

Francis Coyne sits there, grey and old with a shaving cut on his right cheek and a rusty bubble of blood oozing over the lint he has put on it. He chips off the top of his egg and the kitchen fills with the murky smell of it. Yet he lifts his spoon absently. He's going to eat it. She sweeps the plate away from him.

'That egg is bad. Can't you smell it, Father? Eat your bread and wait five minutes while I cook you another. You have twenty minutes yet.' Reckless of their bare larder, she takes another egg off the shelf and boils it. Fresh tea for them both. Her head is thick and aching. She has just these few minutes before it boils. Heart thumping, she sits down opposite him, elbows on the table, and asks, 'Tell me why are you going. Truly.'

He sighs. 'It would be wrong to say anything before I am sure.'

'But you can say it to me. You can tell me what it is you are afraid of.'

'I want to find out more about the accident. How it happened.

240

Clare, John William has been two years in France. How many came safe through that? But he did. I know they used to say he was wild, but I always thought he was a careful enough boy, when it mattered. He knew his job, or they would never have thought of making him an officer. He was used to taking charge of men. He had his platoon. They will not tell your Uncle Arthur. Probably they will not tell me the truth either, but I shall be able to piece it out from what they don't tell me.'

Yes, her father is right. He knew John William better than she thought. Her father goes on, 'They said it was a miracle he came through two years in France, but John William knew it wasn't. You weren't there when he was talking down at your grandmother's. We were all in the parlour – the men. Your Aunt Sarah had gone to bed, so I suppose he felt freer to talk.

'No, it wasn't a miracle. There was luck in it, perhaps nine tenths of it was luck, but without the tenth part all the luck in the world wouldn't have got him through it. And I am sure that the tenth part was his carefulness, Clare. He never let up on himself. He said he always had to think ahead, even when the noise of shells made them all stupid, and the starlights bursting over their heads knocked their senses out of them. What were those other things he spoke of? Whizz-bangs. We can't imagine it. Now I see that I have never let myself imagine it. Barbed-wire entanglements, and shell-craters everywhere, and smoke so thick that you can't see the man next to you. And always the fear that it would be gas next time, not smoke. You can tell gas by its colour, but by the time it is near enough for you to tell, it is too late. The men cough until they cough their own lungs up. He told us in some sections of the Front there wasn't a blade of grass left, though it had all been farmland and woodland. There were only a few trees left sticking up out of the mud with all their branches splintered, and rags hanging down from them where a man's clothes had been blown off him in a shell explosion. Or his flesh. Everywhere there were pieces of equipment the men had abandoned in retreat, or when they'd been killed. You didn't always know if the stuff was British or German, for the line swayed back and forth over the same land like a tug-of-war. Tin hats. Bully-beef tins. They had to walk on duck-boards over the shell-holes. The holes filled up with water, you see. Men drowned in them – can you imagine it, Clare? Wounded men, unable to get their mouths out of the mud, drowning. But even in the middle of all this your cousin was careful of himself. And he was careful of his men once they gave him men to look after. He would have made a good officer, Clare. I'm sure he was a damned fine sergeant.'

Her cool father swallows.

'He was just as careful over the men. He knew which ones had given up already long before they knew that they had. They had a look on them, he said. He forced all his men to take care of their feet. Even when they were too tired to stand, he'd have them take off their boots and dry their feet when they could. They'd curse him for it, but they didn't get trench-foot. On hot days when they were behind the lines he'd tell them to strip off their shirts and hang them over their rifle butts – bayonets fixed and the whole thing stuck into the ground – and then the sun would draw out the lice from the seams of their shirts. Clever notion, whoever thought of it. You could kill the lice with a lighted match once they came out. Lice weaken a man, you see, Clare, quite apart from the disease they might bring. And a lice-ridden man takes less care of himself than a clean one.'

He talks of lice as he might talk of stamens, or pollination. He says, 'It made me feel ashamed, because I didn't know what he was talking about. He had to explain it all.'

But you asked, thinks Clare, and he answered. Mr Lawrence was right. He did need to talk. He could have talked to me too, but perhaps I did not ask the right questions. But Father is right about his carefulness. John William was always careful when it mattered. If we were fishing with maggots, he would hook them on just right, through the loose skin at the top, so that none of their inner juices would spurt out. And he could bring in a rowing-boat through thickets of masts and hulls when the herring-fleet was in, and never once graze another boat. But the thing she sees most vividly is his hands pouring an exact pound of pearl barley into a blue paper bag, then sealing the top. Not a grain spilt.

'You will lose your train,' she says. 'And you haven't had your egg.'

'Leave it now. You eat it later,' says Francis Coyne. 'All those young men, learning all those things we never knew. And then he's thrown away in an accident after two years of the war.'

They will tell Father, Clare thinks, because he is one of them. A gentleman – like John William would have been. And because he is angry. They won't know why, but there's a force in him she has scarcely ever sensed before.

Francis Coyne picks up hat and overcoat and his polished London walking-stick and kisses her. He has sixteen minutes before his train, and he will do it easily. There'll be nobody about, he says.

'What shall I tell Hannah?'

'Just that I've gone to make the funeral arrangements.'

She smells the sharp, new morning as she lets him out, and he raises his stick and walks swiftly away. He looks purposeful: not like Father at all.

Inside, she sets the kettle on again. The kitchen looks cluttered and dismal. She shovels her father's crusts into the compost bin, and, as she does so, she sees the sheets still in the bucket and on the grass. The smell of the bad egg is sickening, and her father smelled old this morning. She had had to turn her face aside when he kissed her. Then he said, 'Make sure you pray for your cousin.'

Now I'm alone, with the washing, and some dried cod to soak for tomorrow, and a message to send down to Hat to tell her not to come today, for I can't bear to have her clattering around the house, sympathizing with those big greedy eyes. I shall scrub the floor myself. I shall wash those sheets again, and water my vegetables, for we're going to need them. What will Father's train fare be? I ought to have asked him. But he will find it from somewhere, I suppose. Perhaps he will sell more books, although last time he told me it was not worth the journey to Truro to sell them. He ought to have sold them in London, but we cannot go there.

Kitchie will come up. Another day of everyone crowding together. And I cannot bear any of it. I would like the day to be over already, and the night here. And then tomorrow to be over, and another night.

Hannah sleeps, worn out after a day with her mother and Harry. Harry's arm had kept them awake the whole of the previous night, fetching drinks and wiping sweat from him and easing pillows under his shoulder to keep pressure off his arm. It is a bad break, and now he is feverish. And Harry is a terrible patient. He will not keep still. He tosses to rid himself of pain, and then the tossing jars his arm, and he cries out. He was confused after the chloroform Dr Kernack gave him when he set the bone.

'I don't know where I am! I don't know where I am!' he cried, clinging on to Hannah, his eyes wide and black and horror-struck.

'And who's to pay the doctor's bill, I don't know,' said Hannah, as she drank the cocoa Clare made for her. 'Nan had to fetch him out again today, Harry was so bad.'

'What about your mother? Can't she nurse him?'

Hannah made a quick, dismissive motion of her hand. She was tired, and she didn't want to talk.

'Mother can't. But I have to be back at work tomorrow. Father can't manage the shop on his own. But Nan'll be there, and Aunt Mag. You have to mind him. If he sets up an inflammation . . .'

'You should let your mother nurse him. You should *make* her do it, Hannah. You're too soft on her.'

'It's not in her nature, Clare, and that's all there is to it. Besides, she's thinking of Johnnie – '

Or you want to believe she is, thought Clare. No. Aunt Sarah's shallow whirlpool of feeling was something Clare refused to enter.

The house makes settling night noises around the two girls, one sleeping, one wide awake. Hannah has the best half of Clare's bed and her warmth fills it. She lies round and peaceful and still, drinking up sleep, snuffling against the pillow, her dark night-plait coiled against her spine. But Clare lies on the cold edge of the bed, so that her body will not touch Hannah's. She does not want to touch anybody. She lies on her back, her arms behind her head like a declaration of wakefulness, and she stares into the dark. It is not so very late: it is somewhere between quarter to twelve and midnight. Soon the clock in the hall will strike, because her father is not here to muffle it for the night. It will go on striking each quarter until morning. But Clare prefers not to tamper with it. That clock is one of the few things in the house which her father takes care of, and Clare was told too often as a child that its delicate coilings could be wrecked for ever by one interfering finger.

If I could hear him calling out in the street, and lift the window, and go down through the graves again. This time I wouldn't be frightened. I would know what it all meant. Afterwards I would make him sit on the rock and I would draw him and talk to him and I would have him for ever.

'For ever? A man who didn't want you enough to spend more than an hour with you before he went?'

'He did. It was the war. He had to get away from people.'

'People? If you love someone, they're not "people".'

'He needed to be on his own. He needed to walk it out of himself.'

'Oh, yes? And the way he looked at Peggy? But he knew he wouldn't get up Peggy's skirt without marrying her, because Peggy's a good girl. So, since it wasn't worth wasting time on Peggy, he had a quick look round and there was Cousin Clare to hand.'

'It wasn't like that.'

'It never is, is it? But all the same, he's just like any other man, your precious John William. As soon as he's got what he wants, he'll show you the back of his britches.'

'You're wrong. He didn't turn his back on me. When we were at the station saying goodbye, he kissed me in front of all of the family.'

'In front of all of them. Are you so sure about that? The way

246

I remember it, Hannah was standing in front of you, blocking the sight of the pair of you. Anyway, he could afford to kiss you. He was going off to the war, wasn't he? Anyone can kiss a girl then, especially if she's his cousin. And any sensible girl would forget about it right away.'

'No. You've got it all wrong. He was going off to the training camp. He was going to get his commission. He would have been safe for three months, at least. That's what he told me. He'd have written to me. He might even have had leave again.'

'But it wasn't safe, was it. He's dead.'

'He didn't know he was going to die! He didn't know it when he did those things with me out on the rocks. He thought he was going to live. That's why he felt so bad, because he was going to live and all his friends were dying. They'd picked him out to be an officer and a gentleman.'

'Gentleman! Very much the gentleman he looked that night, to be sure. I wish the pair of you could have seen yourselves.'

'It wasn't like that. You can't tell what love feels like from the outside. And he would have come back to me, I know he would. He would have come back and married me. Cousins can marry.'

'They can; yes, they can. *If* they want to. But it's not going to happen, is it? He went and died, didn't he?'

'He didn't know he was going to die.'

'Didn't he?'

'No, he didn't. He didn't. How could he? How can anybody know he's going to die? That's all rubbish and superstition and I'm not going to listen to another word of it.'

'Ah. You're not listening anyway, are you? You don't want to, in case it spoils your pretty pictures. But you will. You'll have to. You don't believe it now, but you'll want to.'

Twenty

The train creaks into Lelant Saltings, and lets off steam. Let it stay here, thinks Francis Coyne, looking out of the window at the wet spits of the saltings lying ready for the next tide. The window is open at the top, and a smell of salt and rain blows in. Let it stay here and never move again. It is grey today and the wind is blowing, so that when we come round to the sea there won't be that shockingly beautiful vision of dark blue water and purple water and white sands. Porth Kidney Sands and Carbis Bay. Coming home. Susannah showed them to me first. Could I have loved them if they hadn't belonged to her? She would not share them. She kept this landscape locked tight inside herself and never said whether she found it beautiful or not. It was just there – hers. No doubt she couldn't have lived without it, after so many hungry years in London, but then she didn't live long with it either. She fussed with plant-stands and lace mats on polished tables and frilled pinafores for Clare. Only once I came into the bedroom and saw her by the open window, with the cold air streaming over her, look-ing out at the sea. I heard the thud of waves hitting rock. She did not seem to hear it, or feel the wind. I told her to shut her window, for the cold would hurt her, and then she turned to me but she still said nothing. She put up her hand to her mouth to stifle the cough that was bubbling there. She had no shawl. Her face was white and red in patches, the skin stretched over her cheek-bones. She could not stop coughing. I took hold of her and felt her vibrate with the cough, as if there were something alive there tearing its way out of her. I held her while she coughed, and I closed the window, and drew the curtains across so that she might sleep in the darkened room.

She's left me nothing to love here, only my Clare. I can see the beauty everywhere, and it pierces me, but I am never at home. It is a beauty which disturbs me without ever offering the comfort of familiarity or possession. I live with my back turned to everything I know, and no matter how long I live here it will be the same. I would find it easier if the place were less beautiful.

The glass in the train window rattles. Cold for June, they'll say, just as they said before that it was hot for May. There is strangeness in the weather these days. It is as if the days have misplaced themselves. Sometimes the wind tastes as if it has blown here across a desert. Heat swells until it seems as if the spirits-of-wine will burst through the top of the thermometer. The sky is brassy and frighteningly indifferent. Why shouldn't it roast us if it wants? We believe it will not do so, because it has never done so before. This is our world, and it will not turn on us and rend us. But it's the same sun that glitters over the trenches on perfect June mornings before the obliteration of thousands in a couple of hours. Men who shave themselves in the morning, and put tissue-paper over a shaving cut are blown to rags by noon. Phoebus Apollo, flame-crowned. What are those lines?

> Stand in the trench, Achilles,
> flame-capped, and shout for me . . .

Yes. It sounds glorious. It does not sound like a man trying to scrabble his way up the greased yellow walls of a flooded shell-hole. It does not sound like a man trying to force his wet, squirming, glistening bowels back into the hole in his stomach. Dying in a lather of blood and excrement, yapping like a puppy. No words, no tears, no prayers. *You wouldn't think the insides of a man would a been such a colour.* We sat in our seats, and we listened as the women made the food in the kitchen. We could not relish our ham and gooseberry tart after that. John William broke the compact: soldiers are not supposed to tell us about such things.

How does the poem begin? Now I have it:

> I saw a man this morning
> Who did not wish to die
> I ask but cannot answer
> If otherwise wish I . . .

I see them. Young men like we were when we travelled through Europe. Young men in an *estaminet*, drunk on fear and cheap wine and exhaustion. Young men in orchards which won't fruit this year, because they'll be blown to bits before the blossom is off the branches. Rags of flesh the colour of cherries before they brown and harden.

> . . . who did not wish to die . . .

The train jerks forward. The fat guard hangs dreamily from the window, looking over the estuary to Hayle Towans. He lifts his hand – who can he be waving to? Francis Coyne can see no one. That's where Clare bathes. Not too near the estuary, I hope. Dangerous water.

... who did not wish ...

And the wheels go rumptitump, rumptitump, *wish to die, wish to die*.

They said he should not see John William's body and he had not insisted. Coward. It would serve no purpose they said. There was no question of identification.

The Colonel who had come in from somewhere was confidential in the smoky small room. From time to time a young man entered, saluted, took away a file.

'If I am not disturbing you, sir.'

Perfect manners. What were they – adjutants?

'It's the calibre of a man which matters to us now. Not his background. That's all old hat,' said the Colonel.

You mean you are desperate for new men, thought Francis Coyne, watching the young officer's small, perfect salute as he withdrew.

'John William Treveal. Terrible business. A moment's careless-ness,' he told Francis Coyne. His fire bubbled in the corner. 'Splendid report came with him from his platoon officer.' He twitched another file over the desk. 'Yes. Here.' He read it through, but did not offer to show it across the desk.

'You can be proud of him. Be sure of that. A terrible thing, but it's happened before and it'll happen again. The best man can get careless cleaning his rifle. Why, at home – ' But he broke off without relating his anecdote of a safe, domestic shooting accident.

He got careless. No, there is no purpose to be served by your seeing the body. A drink? No? As you wish. The funeral arrange-ments. Yes.

Francis Coyne walked through the camp on his way back to

the world. He was offered an escort, but no, he preferred to be alone. They understood. Of course. The Colonel stood, and Francis stood, and there were handshakes. They trusted him to be stupid and to ask no questions. He was given a packet containing ten pounds in cash, which he signed for, and John William's watch. The other effects would be sent on.

He paused to watch a group of soldiers playing football. They were not officers yet – or were they? They leapt and yelled and there was a little mild horseplay of the kind that is only to be expected of young men filled with adrenalin and bully-beef. They had all been out there. Some of them would have known John William. The ball shot past him – he kicked at it too late, ineffectually civilian, but the man who pounded after it didn't mind. His boots thumped the dry turf. He was big, muscled and tanned, panting with the exercise. He stopped by Francis Coyne.

'Looking for someone?' he asked.

'No. No. I am here to see after something. Someone. My nephew. John William Treveal.'

The man's face changed. He turned and threw the ball back into the field and shouted, 'Get Simcox in. I'm wanted here a minute.'

The pair of them walked away from the field.

'Who have you seen?' asked the man.

'Colonel Lacey.'

'What did he tell you?'

'About the accident. He said John William was cleaning his rifle. But . . .' He looked carefully into the soldier's face. 'Did you know my nephew? Did you know John William?'

'Yes, I knew him. We were over from Boulogne on the same boat. Right away to Blighty! I still couldn't believe it, and I don't think he could either. I can't yet. I had a twenty-franc note in my pocket and the sun was shining and we were out of the war. We were leaning on the rails, looking down on the men throwing the ropes off down on the quayside, making a lot of racket. Just like the French.'

'Did you see him? Before the accident?'

The man paused and glanced round. He was very close, so close that Francis Coyne could smell his sweat. He spoke quietly.

'When he came back, he wasn't the same.'

'After his leave.'

'Yes. Course it takes a man all ways, seeing his home again. I'd allow for that. But with John William it was different. He got into a wild rage the first night here. Something was said – I thought he should a killed a chap. But we all got hold of him, asked him did he want to get himself RTU.'

'What do you mean?'

'Returned To Unit. That's the penalty – worst thing that can happen.'

'What did he say?'

The man frowned. 'Seemed like he didn't care any more. The others thought he had drink taken, but I knew he hadn't. He wasn't one for making a beast of himself.'

'So what was it?'

'Later, when I was asleep, I woke up cos I heard him moving about. He was feeling for something under his bed, it looked like. Sort of groping. Somehow I didn't care for it. I called to him, soft-like. I don't know why but he didn't look right to me. Not like a man should.'

'I suppose you get used to spotting that, out in the trenches.'

'You do. You have to. So I motion him to come outside the

hut and he does, quite meek he was. Not like himself. And I said to him, "What's up?" and then I saw he was trembling. Well, I felt it, really.'

'What did you do?'

'I put my arm around him.' He flashed a look at Francis Coyne. 'And he didn't shake me off neither.'

'No.'

'He was crying. I asked what was up with him, and he said he had done wrong.'

'What was it? Did he say?'

'I thought it might a been a girl, seeing as he had been home. I didn't get it clear, sir, but it was that he thought he had left someone. He thought he had abandoned them. He ought to be out in France still, that's what it was. He thought he had let the men down, coming here to be an officer when they were over there in Hell still. Course it was rubbish, and I told him so, and he must a known it. I was surprised at him. He struck me as level-headed enough most of the time, John William, for all there was a wild streak in him.'

'And was he better?'

'I thought he was. Then, as we were going in again, he freezes up and he says, *"Hammond!"* (that's my name, sir) and then *"Can't you hear them?"* and I say, what, there's nothing to hear, trying to calm him down, like, and he says again just like this, *"Can't you hear them? Those 5.9s? Don't tell me you can't hear them?"* '

'So what did you do?'

'Well, I knew of other men it had taken that way. I thought I had better go along with it, to humour him. But it was a queer thing – I could feel gooseflesh creeping out all along my arms, though it wasn't a cold night. And as I listened I was half

254

thinking I would hear them too, and maybe voices singing out the way they do in the trenches. So I was humouring him, and not humouring him, if you see what I mean.'

'Yes, I do. Go on.'

'And so then I said, *"Come on. Come along out of it and get some kip,"* like I was relieving him from duty, and he came with me. He was stiff under my hands, and he still had a listening look on him. He wasn't right. So I thought I would go and have a word with the medical orderly the next day, not naming his name, just to find out what might be helpful to him. For I know men who've been taken like that. I've seen it. It's in any man, if he's tired enough, or if he's just seen his pal killed in front of him. But in the morning he was fine again, shaving hisself with a steady hand, for I took note of it, and eating his breakfast. One moment, he was laughing at something Simcox said. I can see him now – soap all over his face, laughing. So I wasn't worried. When I got a quiet minute I said to him, "Everything all right now?" He looked at me as if he didn't know what I was talking about. So I said no more, for it felt awkward. Strange things happen at night, and a man'ull say things he wouldn't want remembered in cold daylight. And that was on the Saturday. We went on parade, then there was drill, and map-work, and then he wasn't with us. I wondered for a minute, then it went out of my mind. The next we heard was Lucas howling out from the huts.'

'Howling?'

'Well, he'd seen dead men before; lived with them, you might say. But he didn't expect to find one back in Blighty; not in the officers' training camp.'

'Hammond, I am going to ask you a question. You needn't say a word if you prefer not: just signify to me, yes or no.

Would it be in order for a man to clean his rifle where they say that John William was cleaning his when it went off?'

'I can answer that,' said Hammond readily. 'It would not.'

'Let me ask you something more. Did you or any of the other men see John William's body – apart from Lucas?'

Slowly, Hammond shook his head. 'We did not. Our hut was put out of bounds to us, except for the detail which took away his body and cleaned the place.'

'You didn't happen – did you? – to speak to any of that detail?'

'I did,' said Hammond. His eyes were pleading. 'I made it my business to speak to them. I had to satisfy myself of what had happened to him.'

'You did right. And that is why I am here too. What did they say?'

'They said that he had shot hisself.'

The two men had stopped, but now they walked on, close together, taking pace after pace, heads down. Francis Coyne said, 'Thank you. Don't be afraid – you are not telling me anything I hadn't feared.'

'It's a mortal sin, they say,' ventured Hammond, turning over the words.

'Are you a Catholic?'

'I was brought up to it. But out there – it changes you. If there is damnation, you don't have to look far for it. And I can't believe any God would damn a man for not being able to get those guns out of his head – can you?'

'No. No, I can't believe that.'

'Or if He does, then I want none of Him,' said Hammond.

'I shall tell no one of what you have told me. Only my daughter. It's best his family doesn't know.'

'They'd stop being so proud of him then, would they?' said Hammond. How they must despise us, thought Francis Coyne, safe at home, judging their courage. He would like to give this man something. Would he take it?

'They have given me John William's watch. Will you have it?' he asked. 'As a friend?'

'There'll be plenty closer who should have it, surely. He'd no son, a course, but maybe there was a girl?'

'Not many close when he needed us,' said Francis, putting the watch into Hammond's hand.

Now he is coming home with ten pounds, and a story no one is going to hear. He thinks of May's eyes glazing over briefly, masking her irritation that he should try to harrow her with it. Isn't there enough to think of in life without wallowing in other people's troubles?

Old Mrs Treveal knows. He's sure of it. He doesn't think that she will ever allude to it, or ask questions of him, but he has seen that she knows. And perhaps she won't ever need to tell or to talk about it. That's strength, he supposes. She also knows what people are made of, and that Sarah and Arthur won't be able to stand knowing what has happened to their son. How quick she was to assure them that Francis must go to the camp, not them: they have fixed it up together, he and Nan, like a couple of conspirators. She will protect the family, even from its own child, even though there's no doubting that she loved John William purely, wanting nothing from him but that he should flourish and grow away from them. She'll forgo walking behind his coffin; she'll never be able to visit his grave; she'll silence the murmurs of townspeople who ask why the Treveals couldn't have brought home their John William.

And now for Clare. The weight of it: can she stand it? She

will have to stand it. He will tell Clare what has happened to her cousin. They will share the weight of it. They will share everything, and there will be no secrets between them any more. They have drifted so far apart; he had his own life, and thought that by having it he did not injure his daughter. But it is not so, he thinks now. The Church is right; our sins are small seeds which grow and flourish until they are great trees with shadowing branches and sucking roots, drawing the light and life out of the house. He will stop going to see May. It will be his sacrifice.

All that is over, he tells himself, exalted. He will never again see that closed look on his Clare's face. She will turn to him, her face cleft with grief, and he will hold her. There'll be an end to the two of them in the house, picking their way over silences. They have grown too far apart, and it is dangerous. He has let her smooth out his life for him and serve him, but he has not watched over her. He has let her go her own way, and the world is a wilder place than she knows. Even down here in St Ives we are blown by the desperate breath of those men struggling with their feet lodged in mud and foul water up to their lips.

Her cousin is dead. And he, her father, has been half asleep. He has let his Clare form an acquaintance with those Lawrences without bothering to find out if they were suitable people for her to know. Now he finds that they have roused the hatred of half the county. Now he hears that the Rector of Zennor fears the corruption of his parishioners.

God knows if there is any truth in what people say of them, but Francis Coyne knows the power of local voices. He knows the tentacle-grip of gossip. He ignores it, usually, and lets it flow past him without ever discerning the words. Gentlemen do not listen to gossip. It is less troublesome that way. But he came alive at the hint Sarah let drop, half fearful, half daring. Coupling the Red-beard's name with his Clare. The weak look of triumph on Sarah's face, as she taunted him with something she knew and he did not. He did not want to question her, for it would seem to give some credence to what she suggested. Anyway she had taken fright and hidden behind her easy tears, her fog of denials. He went home with sharp, prickling alarm in his breast. And then the Rector's curt, disgusted repudiation of Lawrence, and behind it a hint subtler than Sarah's, man to man, gentleman to gentleman.

But I did not know, Francis Coyne tells himself. How could I have stopped her meeting him?

You did not choose to know. You did not want to know. You left her unprotected, says the voice he is accustomed to calling his conscience.

It will end now. He will give up May. He'll give up hearing the cluck of water against the harbour wall at Newlyn, and the little intimate creak of May's door going backward and forward in the draught. He will not say her name softly any more, as he steps into her room. He will not trace the greeny branches of her veins, or lay his cheek against the mound of her belly and listen to the sea-like movement of food and blood. He will not run his tongue around the knobs of her nipples as they stiffen in the cold air of her bedroom. She lies on her back, eyes shut, mouth askew, breath quick.

John William lies on his hard wooden board, bandaged into shape. His mouth and nostrils are icy as the entrance to caves. A cold foul air sifts in and out of them. He is hard all over, his head cocked and propped so that it makes him look as if he is still listening.

Francis Coyne imagines, and blames himself. He ought to

have listened; he ought to have watched. He has abandoned John William just as he has neglected his Clare. No eye has looked on John William's body with love. No one has lit a candle at his head or at his foot, or twisted flowers into his hands, or kept watch over him through the night.

But he will tell Clare how her cousin died. She will understand the weight of it. She will cry out with her soft lips parted, and she will turn to him.

'Clare,' rehearses Francis Coyne. 'I am telling you this because . . .'

Twenty-one

Clare opens the door.

And there he is, Mr Lawrence in his worn green corduroy jacket, with a paper parcel under his arm which is neatly tied but which sifts out a thin stream of black soil from its corner.

'May I come in?'

She glances up the street and says, 'My father is away.'

'Surely you don't care for such things? And there is no one about.'

She laughs. 'At least six people will tell another six people each that you have been here. This is not London, you know.'

'And I am not a Londoner, tha knowst,' he says, teasing out the soft Midland dialect as he steps through her doorway.

In the hall both their smiles disappear.

'I heard in the town that your cousin was dead,' he says.

She waits for the conventional expressions of sympathy, but they do not come.

'I wrote once,' he says slowly. 'It was to another woman; very beautiful she was, in the English way, you know? With her little air of being somewhere else even while she was talking to you. Her brother was killed. I wrote to her that I would rather put out my eyes than stand as a witness to this deliberate horror. And I believed it. But now I would not put out my eyes. I need them to look on other things – flowers, and beasts, and a little hut in the mountains. So I set myself to *keep separate* – ' He breaks off.

'He was killed in an accident,' she says. 'When we thought he was home safe.'

'Yes, yes,' he says quickly, looking intently at her face as if willing her to follow his train of thought. 'You know that I was with your cousin after we left you? We walked up to Zennor that night after the concert.'

'Yes, when I came to your cottage for tea you told me you'd talked to John William that night.'

What did they say, she wonders? Did John William mention it? But she can't remember anything now, except, 'You don't know how nice you are without your clothes.' She feels her skin warming.

'He was sick to his soul too, though there wasn't any wound to see,' says Lawrence, looking at her out of his taut, white face. 'Perhaps that's what is coming – a time when men will go clean out of their minds. Except a man who can sit apart in his own soul and watch the foxgloves come out.'

'We can't all do that,' says Clare sharply.

'Why not? Why not, if it'll keep us living – *really* living, in the middle of all this madness?'

'John William wasn't mad,' says Clare. 'He knew what he was doing.'

'No one knows what he is doing any more. He is joined to a machine. He is not free to act as a man any longer. He is part of a machine of colossal stupidity. And I think your cousin knew it. He was a brave man, but he wasn't blessed with stupidity. It would have been easier for him if he had been able to sink into a state of mindlessness and forget that he was a man with a soul of his own for which he was responsible.'

'You talk of soldiers as if they were doing wrong – as if they were animals!'

'No; they are not animals. Perhaps it would be better for them if they were. An animal does only what is in its nature to do. It cannot kill its own instincts. Think of a fox when you come upon him suddenly. He looks straight at you, and knows you, and then he trots away, quite self-possessed. He knows whether you mean him harm or not. You can't fool him. But you can fool a man's soul out of him, if you set yourself to do it. The war has fooled England's soul out of her.'

He must have talked to you too, the way he talked to Father, thinks Clare. He showed you things about the war. But he wasn't like that with me. It was like when we were children. Why? Was it because he thought I wouldn't understand if he told me about men dying? Because he thought he had to protect me? Or perhaps he didn't choose at all. She remembers the lion roar of water under their bodies that night. John William's face, wiped clean and astonished back into the naked lines of childhood. He did not look like that the next day. The line of his body was stiff and burdened then.

She looks at Lawrence's face, clenched with marks of pain. There is no light in it any more. The vitality which would draw a friend to him across a crowded room has sunk down deep inside him. It is not a clear flame now, but something that smokes and smoulders and throws out long, frightening shadows. He talked to you, she thinks. And what did you say to him? What answer did you find?

'How did your cousin die?' asks Lawrence.

'It was an accident. We do not know any more yet. My father has gone to the camp, to talk to the commander.'

'An accident. Yet he was two years in France, I believe?'

He looks down, frowning. She hasn't offered him so much as a cup of tea, she thinks: and yet he and Frieda made her tea, and cake, and had flowers in the vases. Her boiled egg was set perfectly, its deep yellow yolk steaming as she cracked the top off it. Lawrence had kept cutting her more bread and butter, for he could not bear girls finicking at their food, and she had had a long walk. She had eaten five slices and he had wanted to wrap up a loaf for her to take home in greased paper, since she liked it so much. But today she stands in the hall with him, tense and fearful. She does not want to draw him deeper into her house. He makes sweat prickle on her palms and her breath come quickly. She is afraid he will tell her something about John William which she does not want to know.

'I brought you these new carrots, from my garden,' he says, unwrapping the parcel a little to show slender, clean roots. More soil falls from the paper.

'Come into the kitchen with them. I will make us tea.'

'Frieda eats them raw,' he says, following her and sitting down at the kitchen-table. 'She has fine teeth. I should leave them in the earth a little longer, to fatten, but they are so good like this.'

He unpacks the fronded bundle of carrots, and some spring onions.

'Thank you,' she says, thinking of Frieda's white teeth. She is alive, eating Cornish carrots with her white German teeth, looking out over our sea and exclaiming how beautiful it is, while John William is dead. There they live in their cottage, untouched, growing their vegetables, singing their songs. A pang of horror sweeps over her like sickness. John William has got to stay in the same place for ever. She won't ever see him swing round the corner towards her, frowning against the sun, lightening as he sees her.

'I am glad you like them,' says Lawrence. 'I shall send more down for you, on the farm trap. William Henry will bring them for you, when he comes into market. Shall you like that?'

'It is very good of you.'

'It's good for us to make a new friend. Frieda is lonely; I have the farm-people, but she has no one.'

He's told her this before – does he think she cares so much for his wife? He looks at her with simple pleasure in his face. He changes so quickly! – she cannot keep up with him. His face is warm again, because he has forgotten about the war for a moment. Let him forget it. It is all talk; all words. He did not know John William and John William's death is nothing to him.

He does not know me either. All I am is a girl who can draw, who might make a friend for his wife. She is lonely, is she? Let her get used to it. She likes me, does she? More's the pity. Why does he sit here looking like that, making me think?

'Perhaps you ought to go back to London,' she says lightly, pretending innocence, pretending that it scarcely matters if the Lawrences live in London or in Zennor. They think they are at home here. She hands him his cup. 'Perhaps you ought to think of leaving, if Frieda is so lonely. It is hard to make friends with Cornish people, they say.'

He looks at her, surprised, as if he is readjusting his ideas about her – as if she has proved less intelligent, or less perceptive, than he had thought. And she wants to cry out and reassure him. But he smiles, and explains:

'No, we are much better here. We have lived in so many places, and this cottage is ours, you know; we found it for ourselves. We pay the rent, and it is only five pounds a year. We can afford to stay here. And London is vile now; it makes me wretched to think of it. I should go mad if I had to live there now. But in Zennor we have a wild place of our own, where no one bothers us.'

'Don't they?' she asks.

'Oh – they try. They would like to. They would like to get their hands on the life we have and smear dirt all over it and make it vile too. But they do not quite dare. I am not speaking of the ordinary people, you understand; we have nothing to fear from them. It is the little officials of the war. Some of them are decent men, and they don't like what they are doing. But there are others who have wanted this war all their lives without knowing it. They have wanted the power it gives them. They would like to destroy us, but we don't let them. We lie low.'

She laughs, imagining Frieda lying low.

'Why do you laugh?'

'Because you are wrong. Because everyone sees everything here,' she says, meaning to disturb him, to hurt him. 'Just as they will be wondering why I should have you in my house, with your German wife, when my cousin has just been killed.'

But he does not take offence, as she expects.

'They *would* think that. It's only to be expected,' he says, his face hardening again with contempt. 'But you know better.'

You take too much for granted, she thinks from a cold hard space inside herself. You don't stop to think that I too might be wondering what I am doing.

The front door clicks, opens, closes gently.

'My father,' says Clare, jumping up as he calls her name from the hall.

'I had better leave you,' he says quickly. 'You will want to talk to him.'

But Francis Coyne is down the hall and into the kitchen. The two men will have to meet now, and as she realizes this Clare also realizes it would have been much better to keep them apart. Clare sees the scene as her father will see it: the cups of tea half drunk, carrots spilling across the table, her own hair pinned loosely and her sleeves rolled up, ready for housework. He hates other people to see her like this. Lawrence stands at one side of the table. His red beard flames and his deliberately self-possessed thin figure seems combative. Clare sees that her father is exhausted. His cheeks are sunk and white under his cheekbones, and there is a light film of sweat on his forehead. He knuckles his eyes for a moment, bewildered. He cannot take in what this man is doing here.

'Mr Lawrence,' he repeats.

'Mr Lawrence has taken a cottage at Zennor – Higher Tregerthen. You remember, Father, I visited them.'

'Ah, yes. I have heard about you,' says her father dryly. He straightens himself and scans Lawrence with cool, open dislike. Is it his clothes? Or his beard? What is it about Lawrence that her father dislikes so much? He did not react like this when she first told him she had met the Lawrences. And he is so polite, usually. Perhaps he is angry because Mr Lawrence has come to visit when she is alone in the house. Clare blunders on, 'Mr Lawrence came because he heard of John William's death. He came to offer his sympathy.'

'Very friendly of you,' says Francis Coyne. 'Now, Clare, if you will excuse me.'

He has not even offered Lawrence his hand. He mounts the stairs, thud, thud, thud, to his bedroom. The door shuts.

'I'm sorry,' says Clare. 'I'm so sorry. He is distressed – and the journey – '

But now she wants only to be rid of Lawrence. Something has happened – something terrible. Is it something her father has found out? What have they told him about John William, to drain the colour out of her father's face and make him look as if he does not know where he is? She must go to him. She gives her hand to Lawrence to hurry him out of the house. He bows, a small bow. His hand is warm and hard and he does not let go of hers; he looks into her face. He wants something more from her, some warmth to heal her father's coldness. But she has nothing to give, and he is too quick not to spot this at once. He looks at her consideringly for a minute, holding her hand in his, then he says, 'Goodbye, Clare. Remember Frieda – won't you?'

She cannot answer him. She feels an absurd desire to raise his warm hand to her cheek, and pillow her face against it, and sleep. To be in the darkness where none of this is happening. Then he smiles and he's gone.

He's gone. She flies up the stairs and knocks at her father's door. He is sitting on his bed, taking off his boots.

'I don't want that man in my house ever again,' he says. 'What were you thinking of to ask him here, Clare?'

'But, Father – you knew I had met him. You knew I had been to their house. And I didn't ask him; he heard of John William's death in the town, and called in.'

'I hadn't realized. I hadn't thought. I have been remiss towards you, Clare. Your Mr Lawrence is a dangerous man. There's talk in the town, and it isn't just the usual gossip, I believe. You may not have heard it, or understood what it means. You can't understand what it might mean to have your name coupled with a man like that. He has a reputation. And his wife's a German. They are not fit people for you to know.'

He sounds like one of her uncles. What can have happened? Father never talks like this. Dull red mottles his neck as he struggles with his left boot.

'Let me.'

'No, I have it. There.'

'Father, what happened?'

She is terrified by the bitterness in his voice. The flat ungiving-ness of it. Everyone is changing – even her father is no longer the same.

'Tell me.'

'You must give me your word that what I tell you will never be repeated.'

'Aren't you going to tell Aunt Sarah – or Nan?'

'It must never be repeated.'

'All right. I promise.'

And he tells her. The day is dark already, so it does not darken. The grey sky stays just as grey, and the swiftly moving clouds do not stop, or turn backward in their course. The noise of the sea goes on and on. The war continues at Passchendaele in the Ypres sector. The noise of guns.

'Can't you hear it? Can't you hear it?'

Francis Coyne can hear it now, and the voices singing out, and the cry of wounded men as they hold their entrails together and beg for water which cannot come until dark when a stretcher-party will try to reach them. The faces of the stretcher-bearers are no longer appalled by anything, but their hands are still gentle as they refuse to put in the bullet the wounded man screams for. They are men, not beasts.

John William had a revolver. He put it into his mouth, pointed it upwards, and squeezed the trigger. He was used to shooting. He did not make any stupid mistake like trying to shoot himself through the heart, and he made no error in the angle of the barrel. All the same it was lucky he could not foresee the heart-stopping spray of his brains and bone over the whitewashed walls of the hut, or the way he spoiled the clean laundry for eight men. And someone had to pick it all up, and clean it away. One of the detail said, 'Yer'd a thought the bugger could've done it out in the woods.' For that was the way they talked, to make it all bearable. And perhaps the bugger could have, or perhaps he'd had enough of men dying in mud and dirt holes where no one had to clear up after them. Maybe he thought he would spoil one white room in Blighty, and make them clean it, and know that a man had died there.

There is Clare with her white, white face, his own daughter shrinking back from him.

'Did you see him?' she whispers at last.

He shakes his head.

She raises both her clenched fists and bangs them against the side of her head, at the temples.

'Why did you tell me!' she screams. 'I shall never get it out of my mind.'

And she bangs and batters, as if she will fight her way into her own skull and beat out the knowledge which he has put in there. He seizes her hands, and holds them down. He is just stronger than her.

'Clare. Clare. Clare, listen to me . . .'

And she collapses against him, burrowing her head into his chest. It is frightful, he thinks. He would never have thought she'd take it like this. Could there have been something between them – some understanding he didn't know about? No, it couldn't be. The rest of the family would have known about it. Nan would have told him. And Clare is half a child still. It is the shock.

'Clare, Clare,' he remonstrates, rocking her. But he is fiercely glad. She is his, his own daughter, his own Clare. His little red-haired one. Let Nan and Hannah and Mag and all the rest of them know it. They are outside, and he is inside. He will be the one who comforts her.

'Nan,' she hiccups. 'Nan.'

'What, my darling?'

'Don't tell her.'

'I won't tell her. I won't tell anyone. We shall be the only ones who know.'

'Don't light the candle, Clarey! Come on out.'

'But I'm only in my night-dress. I can't.'

'You'll be warm enough.'

We shall be the only ones who know.

'Stop that whistling, John William! You'll whistle up ill-luck for yourself.'

We shall be the only ones who know.

'Where are we going?'

'Down to the sea.'

'Which way are we going?'

'Down through the cemetery.'

'Are you a mermaid?'

'Are you a human boy?'

'Come here and let me hold you.'

We shall be the only ones who know.

Twenty-two

Little Clarey in her black dress, a smudge on the front steps, in high-walled steep alleys. The houses are white cliffs to Clare, and the women who lean out of their windows to screech across at one another and hang out their washing are seagulls roosting fiercely in the cliff crevices. They are big women with brawny arms and hard hands who will slap Clare if she goes near their washing baskets and meddles. Nan has put her out for the morning. All the others are at school, and Clare isn't to have her lessons today because Miss Purse's mother has had one of her turns. (Gagging, reeling Mrs Purse with her face like a white and red crumpled cloth at the door of the poky parlour where Clare is taught.) But Nan and Aunt Mag have got the morning-room curtains to finish for Carrack House, and if they are not delivered on time a shilling must be deducted from the charge.

Clare rumples up her petticoat and sits on the thickness of it, because the stone is cold. Her black bonnet drags at the back of her neck by the strings which she has nearly chewed through. Her red hair straggles over her shoulders. A grey day. No Nan and no cousins. Grandad is not there for her to smell his tobacco and play round his feet. Clare has a thick piece of bread with lardy bacon in it for her dinner. She must mind and play and be a good girl and not run off.

She stands up and pats the warm nibbled lump of bread in

her pocket. And down the cobbles she goes, stepping from one to another, pretending that she is crossing a river, pretending to herself that she does not notice that she is getting farther and farther from the cottage door. Now she is out of Nan's hearing. Now she is under the arch, and she skips across the deep launder, hopscotch, back and forth, draggling her skirt in the dirty running water. A big seagull voice cawks at her, and she dodges off, farther again, slipping along by the high steps on one side of the houses. And down, and down, until the sheer white light of the harbour bursts all over her and she blinks and screws up her eyes. She will watch the carts and horses drawing off the pilchards.

Everyone's working. No one notices Clare except to shout her out of the way once, when she comes close to the hoofs of a straining horse and an arm reaches out and half lifts, half knocks her out of its path. For a second the horse's huge, hairy hoof is by her temples. It strikes out, struggling for a grip on the fish-slimed cobbles. She tumbles out of its way and makes off up the harbour wall with a curse after her. The sails are the colour of blood setting on a scab, she thinks, and remembers her knee, and picks at it slowly, deliciously, easing the big brown crust off the shiny pink surface of new skin underneath. Half off. She will eat it. Already she can taste its dense chewiness. But the middle of the scab won't come. She pulls again and there it is, with blood on it, and a new dent of blood where the scab was, slowly filling up. She eats the scab and tastes fresh salty blood on it. The air wheels with screaming seagulls, plummeting and rising high into the air again, maddened by the dense silver mountains of pilchards. She looks down and is giddy with pilchards. Are they alive still? Oh, the man with his hands plunged into them, his hands all scaled and rich with silver pilchards, and then he lets them fall as if he were lifting them like silver money for the pure joy of having and letting go.

Clare shies her way back up the alley, face bland, eyes watchful. How long has she been gone? She is not properly sure if she's been asleep or not. It was warm by the bollard, and she ate her bread and bacon in mouse-bites, hiding it inside her hand against seagulls and bad boys who hadn't gone to school. She made herself small and put her apron over her head to dull the horses and carts and men and women and screaming gulls. Beat after beat of voice and noises. Dark. Sharp. Dark. Sharp. Clouds going over the sun when Clare's eyes are shut.

I'm dawdling, she thinks now, tasting the word as she comes up the cobbles, battering her stout little boots the way she's been told never to do, for it wastes shoe-leather. Nan's always telling her to run and not dawdle. The bread and bacon is not solid inside her any more. It must be a long, long time since she ate it, and perhaps it's nearly night now. She looks up at the sky and can't tell. Night has a way of slamming down on her, pouring out stars when she is playing out wildly, ready to play for ever.

A hand snatches her from behind.

'You young divil!'

It's Grandad.

'Don't yer know yer Nan 'n' Aunt Mag've had to run all over the town looking for you stead a getting their work done? Where've you been to?'

But she stands brazenly looking up at him, straight at him without a tear or a blush. He sees she has the devil in her today. Five years old and fit to lie her head off like a woman of fifty. Satan has got half his work done for him here. Grandad roars out, and Nan and Aunt Mag come to the door. A flock of seagulls from the opposite cottages leans out of the windows and caws to the Treveals.

'Thank the Lord you've found her!' cries Nan.

'Found her! She's found herself! Run off for pure devilment, that's all it was!'

'You bad girl,' says Nan, but the relief in her voice is stronger than the anger. Clare smiles, and makes to run and snuggle against her, but this is more than Grandad can bear. He catches her back, switches up her dress and petticoats and pulls down her drawers. Clare struggles to run, but with her drawers round her ankles she cannot. Instead she screeches shrilly, 'Bog! Bog!' which is all she dares to say of the word 'bugger'.

However, it is enough for Grandad, and for the amusement of the watching women. In a second he has hauled her over his knee. In a second she has twisted round and bitten the side of his left hand, which is holding her down across the back and shoulders. She tastes the familiar smell of blood, spits and shrieks again.

'Bog! Bog! Bog, Grandad!'

'Tell she's got red hair without lookin at er,' remarks one woman to another in the next doorway.

Grandad smacks Clare so hard that Nan darts forward to catch hold of his arm. But before she can do so, he shoves the child off his knee and stamps into the house, leaving Clare up-ended on the cobbles, still screeching. But she stops at once as Nan picks her up.

'Pull yer drawers up, Clarey. What a sight! And everyone looking at yer.'

Clare is silent at once. She settles her own clothes as coolly as if she were getting dressed in the morning in her own bedroom. She will not let Nan help her. Then she takes Nan's hand and tucks her thumb inside Nan's in their 'special' way, and walks into the cottage, her head well up. Mute, and stubborn, she is put to bed until her father should fetch her. Rumblings downstairs. Nan's voice, then Grandad's.

Clare sleeps again. When she wakes, her father has come for her, but Nan and Aunt Mag are still working. Nan gets up from her chair, blinking as she looks up from the fine stuff she's sewing, putting one hand to her tired back. She kisses Clare just as she always does, and says, 'Go and kiss Grandad.'

But Clare will not. She pretends to be sleepy, and clings to her father's hand, and stumbles out past Grandad without looking at him. When she has gone, he laughs. He is tickled by her small fierce face, her deliberate aloofness.

'Did you see that, Alice? Er won't come to me! Er won't come to me!'

'She'll come,' murmurs Nan, frowning over the gathers.

'Just because I tan her backside for her, our Clarey won't as much as look at me!' he marvels, almost appreciatively. Nan smiles. Thank the Lord the child's devilment's caught his fancy.

Mag's lips narrow. She's heard enough from Stan of thrashings handed out to the boys when they were young. Lucky Stan's not here now. Nothing makes him angrier than Grandad's softness to Hannah and Clare.

Nan sews. Her thoughts are like stitches, each one tiny and precise and not much in itself, but making up the strong seam. She thinks about Clare, and her responsibility for Clare. She weighs over Francis Coyne in her mind, and what can be expected from him. But she cannot judge the weight of him. Is he going to be able to rear that child as she should be reared? In her mind she feels around the edges of what Francis Coyne lacks. It is hard to put into words, and she does not need to try.

These thoughts are for herself alone. Clare's red hair and her white, wild face. Say what you like, but some things are born, not bred, and you can't change them. A good child seven days out of the seven, but she's good because she wants to be, not because it's in her nature. Nan sighs and smiles, thinking of the turn of Clare's thumb under her own, the secret sign of love. How she watches us all. Well, we can do nothing but pray to the Lord and watch her. Keep her with her cousins. She's safe enough along with them. Better than with Miss Purse. Nan's face wrinkles in distaste for the Purse family's fits and vapours.

Fifteen years later Nan sews and thinks of Clare. She treadles the Singer in its placid, slightly irregular rhythm, and yards of plain seaming spill down over her sewing-table. Her eyes are not good tonight. It has strained them to make Sarah's mourning. Sarah would not have her Sunday dress dyed like the rest of them, and Arthur was weak and gave in to her. You would never think how black would grow to dazzle your eyes as you sat sewing it. Still, these sheets are white. Good, seemly white sheets. Nan feels the quality of the cotton twill. Not like the rubbish we get now, since the war.

Well, Sarah and Harry are back in their own place now. Nan doesn't like the look of Harry's arm. It wasn't more than a week before she knew it was going to take bad ways. And she'd been right. Dr Kernack had gone quiet the last time he looked at it, then he had spoken to her privately in the kitchen and told her that Harry would lose the use of it entirely. The nerve had been severed. But there was no use troubling Sarah. Let her come to that when she must. She was a poor thing at the best of times and what sense she had was driven out of her by John William's death. It was as well she had a daughter like Hannah.

Clare. Paler than ever, and she never had but a pinch of

colour at the best of times. Now she's like whey. No one'd look at her.

Nan treadles, and pushes the cloth smoothly under the machine-foot. Thoughts of Susannah. Push them away, don't let them form. They do nothing but harm. Besides, Susannah had a good colour right up to the day the doctor told them there was no hope for her. Clare is a Coyne through and through to look at her. There's not a red hair among all the Treveals, nor one face the colour of Clare's.

Nan treadles on. The things they think they hide from us, these girls. Take Hannah now. Hannah tearing out her heart over Sam and saying nothing. But I could tell her, he'll be back, you can be sure of it. Because he needs you, Hannah, because your Sam is a poor thing for all he's so handsome and six foot in his stockings. But there's no telling you that. There's trouble between you now, I know, but your trouble will pass. Or you will think it's passed, though to my mind it will be only just beginning.

But Clare. My Clarey. Hovering in the doorway, with her shawl wrapped around her like a smudge on a ghost.

'I think I won't stop, Nan. I ought to get Father's supper. And I'm colouring a drawing for him.'

Your father's supper has never been started at four o'clock since this world began. I want to tell you to come on in, girl, and get your things off and sit down with your Nan, but I don't say anything. For fear of scaring you. You don't want to be with us, do you, my lovey? You don't want us to share your grieving. You don't want your Nan.

Oh, if I could just look up now and see the pair of you laughing over your nonsense. But Hannah's taken up entirely with Harry, because that's the way she wants to be. To stop her thinking. And what's my Clarey taken up with?

Nan treadles on. A quiet house for once, with Sarah back in her own kitchen, and Hannah hanging over her brother, and Mag visiting John and Annie purely for the sake of coming back snappish and discontented. There's nothing worse in God's creation than a discontented woman. But there's no Clarey coming in through the doorway on a swirl of wind, and John bellowing out to the girls to keep the door shut. Or maybe I should go up there and see her? But it'll seem strange to her. Better let her think she's able to hide her troubles.

Clare crouches on the middle of the kitchen-table in her stocking-feet. She shifts her weight cautiously to the edge of the table. It creaks, but does not tip. A bit farther. Then she braces her calf and thigh muscles, and springs out towards the hard stone floor. Her heels strike with a sickening jar which goes right up through her spine, making her gag. Again. If only the kitchen ceiling was higher and she could stand up and jump properly. That would be sure to work better. She crouches again, shuts her eyes and springs. But this time she misjudges it so badly that she falls backwards, striking the knob of her spine against the table-leg and biting her tongue. Once more. I must do it once more, then I'll let myself go and lie down. Her next jump is soft and useless. She despises herself, but she can't bring herself to scramble back on to that table. She limps upstairs and lies down on her bed.

It's not easy to say why suspicion and fear and curiosity and excitement and disbelief should suddenly vanish, leaving nothing but hard certainty. But it's very easy to say when it happened. It was at quarter to five last Friday evening, between peeling the potatoes and dropping them into a panful of cold salted water. Before, when she fetched the potatoes out of the cellar, she was not pregnant. Her *visitor* was late: but then it had been late before. Eight days; well, perhaps not quite as late before. Fourteen days. It is the shock of John William. I'm quite well and not any fatter. Peer in the mirror: my face is thinner, if anything. Look at my eyes. Seventeen days. A hot, insistent beat of panic behind everything, all day long. Twenty-one days. A surge of confidence. I am stupid to worry. It's perfectly all right. It is simply that I'm going to miss out one month, and then everything will go on as usual.

And then, suddenly, twenty-two days late and I'm peeling the potatoes and I know I'm pregnant. There's no need to think and guess any more. My breasts haven't ever felt like this before, so sore that I wince when I put my clothes on in the mornings. I don't want to eat anything until I've drunk cup after cup of boiling hot weak tea. And the sight of Father's egg makes me leave the table, pretending I've got to fetch something from the scullery or the larder. And most of all the way nothing feels close or real any more. Not Nan, not Father, not Hannah. Even John William is behind me, outside the circle, tapping on my shoulder but I don't turn round to him.

I'm surprised by how cold and practical I feel inside. No one would think it who has seen me jumping off that table, but I know exactly what I am doing. I know it can't work that easily. I have to do it, but I don't have to hope that it will work. If it was so easy to shake a baby out of the womb, there wouldn't be a single girl brought to shame anywhere. They say the Baptists put a black hood on a girl who has fallen, and make her stand before the deacons to be banished from the congregation. But no one is going to touch me. And when I've finished jumping off the table, I'll go up and lie on my bed and curl my arms around myself and shut out all the light, and hold myself so tight that I feel the blood bumping in the big vein in my arm.

Bump, bump, bump, bump. The sound of it is fast and perfect, as if my blood knows exactly what it is doing.

I know what I am going to tell them. I will not let them send me away, though Father will want to. He will want to pretend that I am married, one of those hasty war marriages, and send me up to Coyne. My aunt and uncle might even believe him, because they think we have such strange ways down here that it would be quite possible for me to get married with no announcement, no presents and no ceremony.

But I will not go there. I will not creep off with John William's baby like an ant rolling a crumb which is too big for it into its hole. The baby belongs here. It is more Treveal than I am. It is nearly pure Treveal. Nan will see that as soon as she looks at it. She will see and she'll say nothing, just as I'll say nothing. I won't have to explain anything to Nan. She loved John William.

I will tell Hannah, and she will say to Aunt Sarah and Uncle Arthur that John William and I were secretly engaged, and we meant to marry. It happens. Even in the newspaper you can read about war babies now. There are so many they can't hush it up any more. I will say that we were going to marry. Aunt Sarah will scream and snivel, and the uncles will bluster, and Father will look white and thin and appalled, and I will not care for any of them. I will not let them upset me, for now I have to think of my baby. Mine and John William's. It is more important than any of them.

If I have to, I can do anything. Mr Lawrence pays five pounds a year for his cottage. And what do they spend beside that? He earns everything they live on by his writing. Frieda told me she has not a penny of her own. They don't get their money from investments which are always going down. They don't need to keep up appearances: they scrub their own floors, and the doorstep too. It doesn't matter what people see. And they have friends who live the same way: writers and painters. They get little cottages and they do their own work and they get their furniture from places like Benny's Sale Rooms. And they have children too, some of them. One of their friends is going to have a child, and she's writing a book too.

And in the end Father will say nothing. He will want something of John William to live. He will outface them all by not even seeming to notice what they think, just as he must have done over marrying Mother; or if he doesn't, I shall make him. He will never turn me out of this house. 'All those young men dead, leaving nothing behind them.' That is what he said, when he came back from the camp where they killed John William. And let no one dare say to me that they did not kill him; let no one dare say to me that he wanted to die. They made it impossible for him to want to live any more. It may have been his hand that pointed the gun, but who forced it there? They owe John William his child.

I don't think about that night when we were together now. I think about when we were little, before any of this happened, when people meant something different if they said the word 'war'. I think about John William and Hannah and me, and our games, and the way the tide came in and we ran and screamed and kicked down our own sandcastles rather than let the water break them. I think about the way we would cling on to one another when the waves were rough and we swam in the breakers, and then how we'd huddle together when we got out and the wind was cold and we would hop about drying ourselves on my flannel petticoat. We all had to share it, because I was the only one who had flannel petticoats. Nan thought my chest might be weak, like my mother's. And we would giggle when John William's penis went stiff as we dried it, and he would look proud. I wonder if people ever saw us? If they did, they left us alone. We were always hungry. What did Nan give us? Jam sandwiches, and sometimes it was meat-paste for a treat. We would share them out, every bit, then John William would run and get water for us to drink from the well, because he had his tin water-bottle.

So I am not going to Coyne, and I am not going to disappear up to London so that no one will know me, and I will not bring shame on the Coynes and the Treveals. I am staying here. Later, I shall go to Zennor again, to talk to Frieda and Mr Lawrence. I shall write and tell them first. They do what no one approves of, but they survive. They have made a life for themselves. And it is not their fault that John William died. I shall talk to Hannah in the morning, and then I shall tell Father. Let him ask what questions he wants: I know the answers I shall give. And some of the questions I shall never answer.

Twenty-three

Francis Coyne wakes to the drum of rain out on the roof. His room is dark, with only a trace of grey light leaking over the top of the blind. The gutter rushes with water. He remembers that it needs repairing, and that he had put it off early in spring because he had not enough money to pay the bill. The water will run down the side of the house and damp will spread across the inside wall. He sighs, turns over in bed and swims down into a drowse again. No sound of Clare moving yet. She is getting up late these mornings. She yawns, and rubs bleary eyes, and drinks tea endlessly, and eats nothing. He asks her what is the matter, is she ill, and she says there is nothing wrong. She is just tired. His heart tightens briefly in fear: for years he has watched over her for signs of the consumption which ate away her mother's lungs and turned her into a dry skeleton with red-splashed cheeks who put up her arms to him at the last and asked him to hold her. 'I can't feel myself, Francis. I don't know where I am.'

But Clare is not getting thinner. There are splotches of shadow under her eyes, but her cheeks are rounder if anything, and there is a new fullness under her jaw. Francis Coyne humps the bedclothes tight round him and pulls the counterpane over his ears to block out the scream of the gulls.

He is back at Coyne. He is thirteen, a tall, gangling boy with a tutor who is too old for him. He is growing so fast that his wrists bulge from his cuffs and his knuckles are always skinned and he hunches himself awkwardly when he sits down. He never seems quite to know how much of him there is to be folded away. His features have grown too big for his face and they are topped incongruously by a cloud of fine, soft, downy hair, child's hair still, which will not lie down over his collar no matter how much he stabs at it with his sponge in the mornings. He looks down when he is spoken to and people say he is growing sullen. As soon as his lessons are over, he is off across the fields to shoot in Pesthouse Wood. He shoots rabbits, mostly. His brother Benedict, who inclines towards the Franciscan, shudders when he sees his own Francis come home mud-clotted and blood-streaked, with a couple of bundles of limp fur dangling from a belt the keeper has given him. He skins his rabbits too, quickly and skilfully, but the family will not eat them. The scullery-maid tucks them under her cloak and runs with them down to her mother's cottage in the village. He looks down so he will not have to meet her timid, grateful eyes.

The water-supply at Coyne is erratic: the well does not give enough water for the house, and washing-day is becoming a nightmare. A new well is to be sunk. A man is coming from far away, down in Cornwall, to find the site. There have been arguments about it, and Father McLennan has been consulted in case water-divining should be against the teachings of the Church. But Father McLennan is a practical man, who has to live at Coyne and bath in an inch of muddy water. He will bless the new well: God wishes us to use all His gifts.

The diviner comes from a family of diviners. It has been their everyday job for generations. They travel around Cornwall and Devon, up to Dorset and Somerset, around the outlying farms and homesteads where the well has dried or the spring is tainted.

The family's reputation goes before them, and in remote parts their coming is as good as a festival. They marry among themselves, it's said, or else they pick a girl who carries the gift.

Francis does not go to the woods with his gun on the day the diviner is due to arrive. He is more curious than he wants to admit, so he fiddles with cleaning a gun-barrel, then lounges around the paddocks with his bitch Maisie fawning before him. There is a little crowd gathered by the time the diviner's cart arrives. It has a broad blue stripe painted on it, and the pony is a tough little cob which drops its head and starts to tear at the rich grass with its yellow teeth as soon as the cart comes to a halt. Francis does not go forward with the others. He hangs back, watching the diviner. He is not going to gape like Adie there with her mouth open. The diviner is a strongly built man with a tanned, outdoor face. He does not look at all magical. Before he starts his work he has to come into the house and eat and drink: it is part of the ritual. He must eat the food of the house. It's the custom, though very likely it has only grown into a custom because any man is naturally hungry and thirsty after a dawn start and a cross-country journey from the last farm. And he has come a long way, he says. Since June he has been in three counties. The scullery-maid and the garden-boy marvel: they have never been more than eight miles from Coyne.

When the diviner comes out of the kitchen, wiping his mouth after his bread and cheese and pickles and his pint of cider, Francis is still waiting. Maisie whines at his heel, shivering, for she is afraid of the diviner's dog. The little group walks down the drive to the soft, spongy grass at the side of the first paddock, where the washing-lines are hung on Mondays. It is quite hidden from the house. The grass is bright green and succulent here, and in winter it keeps its colour and quakes under your boots. The diviner stops. He walks around, quartering the area of grass, stops again. Seems to listen, to smell the air. He touches the grass briefly, and stands up again, hitching his trousers. He nods to Francis, to the servants, to Benedict, who is watching with his face pursed in disapproval. The girls are there too, fluttering, excited and half afraid. The diviner stumps off to his cart.

Francis thought he would have a wand, a light, flexible twig which would yield to each tiny twitch of the finger so that it could be said to be moving with the flow of the water. He frowns in surprise when he sees the diviner returning with a strong, forked, polished-looking branch. It looks used and ancient. Black sweat from generations of hands has put that sheen on it. It is not the only fork he has, the scullery-maid whispers. He has three others, but he has set his dog to watch over them. And the teeth on the animal – you durst never go near the cart. That band of blue paint is magic too, to watch over his wands.

The diviner shoves his hat farther back on his head, rolls up his sleeves and steps lightly over the grass as if he were walking over the body of some huge animal – a whale, perhaps, cast up and sleeping. He treads his path back over the way he walked before. Then without any show he stops and holds out the rod of hazel, a fork in each fist. Nothing. He steps on. Francis watches, eyes narrowed now, waiting for the trickery. As if an arm has reached up from the ground and grabbed it, the hazel rod jolts down. The muscles in the man's forearms bulge.

'Iss strong here,' he comments.

He is workman-like. It might be the weight of any common thing he is judging. Yet he moves as if he is aware of something infinitely stronger than himself, just under the ground. He moves again, tests. The rod jerks less powerfully. He steps back, presenting the little patch of bright green grass to them all.

'This yer's the place,' he remarks.

Francis finds he has moved to the front of the little crowd. The diviner catches his eye as he straightens with the rod in his hand.

'Like ter feel it?' he asks.

Francis is astonished. He was sure the diviner would keep his magic to himself, but he goes forward.

'Will I be able?'

The diviner ignores the question. He places Francis's hands on the forks of the hazel branch, and turns his body round a little. There is force in the diviner's hands. I wouldn't want to have to fight him, thinks Francis. He angles the boy so that he is standing by the place where the water was strongest. Francis balances the hazel branch nervously.

'Not like that. Yer got ter get a grip on im. The water's strong when it comes. It'll tear that wand out a yer ands.'

For a moment it feels to Francis as if he is trying to turn a key in a lock which doesn't fit. Nothing happens but the grate and click of a false turn. The door remains blank, immovable. Then he grips the rod more tightly and moves forward a little. There is a pulse through the length of it. It twists violently and is nearly pulled out of his hands. He is breathless. He finds he has jumped back in fear and in wonder. He had thought it would be a little twitch, something gossamer, something you could fool yourself about and pretend you had felt when you had not felt anything. Not this real thing, as dangerous as the kick of a horse.

The diviner's weather-seamed face has creaked into a smile.

'Yer felt it, then?'

Francis nods.

'Iss not the water yer feeling – iss what the water's carryin.'

'How far down is it?'

The diviner shrugs. 'Thirty foot. An there's enough water down there ter wash an army clean.'

Francis turns in his bed again. He remembers how the new water tasted, once they had bored the well. It was full of iron, and you could not leave white clothes to soak in it or they would be stained with orange. The taste of metal in it made your mouth pucker, if it was the first thing you drank in the morning. Next day the cart with its blue stripe had gone. The dog looked over the side of it, still showing his teeth.

But still no sound of Clare. What can ail her? Suddenly anxious, he hauls himself out of the bed's warm frowst and ties on his dressing-gown. The house is much too quiet, apart from the lick and spatter of rain. He will make her a cup of tea and take it into her.

He treads lightly along the landing, not wanting to disturb her. But by her door he pauses. A tiny sound. Is it a moan? Is she crying? Or ill, hurt? Her thick door is firmly closed, and he can hear nothing more. But he lingers. Should he leave her be? No, he will just look in and see that she is all right. She has not been herself since her cousin's death.

He opens the door to a pale flood of rainy light. He blinks. The curtains are pulled back, the window is open, and chill air sucks out the curtains as the draught from the door reaches them. Clare turns at the sound of the door opening. She is standing naked by her wash-stand, with the ewer in her hand, pouring a thin stream of water into her bowl. The window squeaks as the wind blows it. That is the moaning sound he heard.

He has not seen his daughter naked since she was a child. Why does he not back out, babble apologies and shut the door? She stands quite still, her level grey eyes finding his. She has ceased to pour out the water. Surely she must be cold, standing there? She is a blur, blue-veined, branched, a spreading map of flesh. Her head looks small because she has twisted up her hair and knotted it tight. Or else it looks small because her body is so vast. It seems to fill the room with its own light. The sight of it goes through him like electricity, like the jolt of the hazel branch in his hand. His daughter's white body is alive with something deep inside it. The heaviness under her jaw, the startling blueness of veins over her breasts, the swelling knot of them around her dark-tipped nipples, the blurring lines of her stomach: his daughter is pregnant.

She continues to meet his eyes without shielding her body. She puts down the ewer.

'Shut the window, Clare, you will get cold,' he says, and goes out of her room.

I will not think. I will not think. I will not try to understand it. There is water underneath us wherever we walk. We walk on the crust of it. We jump and balance. How old she looked. She is older than I ever imagined. My daughter.

Does she know? Does she understand what is happening to her? Is she afraid?

I left her unprotected. We have left all our children unprotected, to scramble their way out of shell-holes, or crawl across no-man's-land with blood in their mouths.

When I looked at her naked body, I was afraid that she would arouse me. But she did not. I felt something immense for her, something deep inside me, alive. I could not move for pity of her.

Her cousin killed himself. He blew his head off because this world had become a place of horror to him. That must never happen to Clare.

Twenty-four

Three girls walk gently on the cliff-path. There is not room for them all to walk abreast, so two walk ahead and one a little behind. They are going so slowly that they can still talk quite comfortably between the three of them. Sometimes the red-haired and the fair-haired girls form a couple, sometimes the red-head and the dark girl. They talk over their shoulders to the one behind, but their talk is quiet, as if they do not want to disturb the peace they are walking through. At the moment Peggy is ahead, scuffing up dry earth into dust with her light canvas boots. For the whole summer has been hot, and even now in early September the sun is low but warm. There are vipers on these hills. More have been seen this summer than ever before, and they have been brought into the St Ives pubs hanging crushed and limp from the end of sticks. Clare walks on the inside, carefully, for here the path narrows and the cliff falls away sheer only a foot or so from their feet. She has seen no adders, but there are butterflies everywhere. She has never seen so many butterflies sunning themselves on this path. Their wings flirt up at the vibration of the girls' boots. They tilt off into the hazy sunshine, over a drop of a hundred feet to the water, or brushing among yellow-tipped bracken. Far below, bladder wrack and oar-weed stir with the tide in water which is so clear you cannot tell its depth.

Peggy calls back, 'Are you all right, Clare? Are we walking too fast for you?'

'No, I'm fine,' says Clare. It is too much to hope that Peggy's rather greedy sympathy can be satisfied without constant references to Clare's pregnancy. She wants every detail. Sickness, tightness of clothes, names for the child. Above all Peggy wants to ask the unanswerable question: 'But what does it feel like, Clare? What is it really like?' Clare can only shrug and say that she doesn't feel so very different, not yet. The baby hasn't quickened, but Clare is beginning to show now, even though Nan has altered her waistbands cleverly, letting in a panel of matching fabric and taking out tucks. This skirt will do her for another couple of months.

'Where are we going, anyway?' asks Hannah, but no one knows. Just as far as they can, and then perhaps they'll pick blackberries on their way back, on the open slope of rough land which catches the sun most of the day and always ripens the sweetest blackberries. But the blackberries are small this year because there has been so little rain.

In Flanders the struggle for the Passchendaele Ridge continues. The poppy-blowing fields are ploughed by German and English guns, and sown with a litter of lost equipment, a seeding of blood and bone. Soon it will be autumn there too, and heavy northern rains will fall. Men will be listed *missing, presumed drowned* – a new classification for the lists in the newspaper. They are presumed drowned in the mud in which they live and often die. The men who came 'right away to Blighty' with John William will return to Flanders with their new commissions soon. Their training lasts only three months, and then they are wanted back at the Front. Hammond will die on a mission described to him by a senior officer as 'rather a tricky bit of patrol-work'. His body will not be found. Simcox, a dozen feet to the left of him, will survive.

'Clare, I really think you ought to rest for a while. Let's all sit down here.'

Peggy's sharp blue eyes never seem to leave Clare. The girls sit on hummocks of grass and look out to sea, idly at first, and then they watch another patrol-boat coming close in below them. Patrols have been stepped up again.

'U-boats about,' says Peggy knowledgeably.

Hannah sighs in exasperation. Peggy is always the same. If she tells you that the sun's shining, she manages to make it sound like a piece of privileged information.

'Aren't they always?'

Hannah is a little thinner, but nothing can diminish her, thinks Clare, looking at her cousin's profile. Hannah's broad brow is exposed by her new way of dressing her hair, without a parting and drawn back. Her lower lip is caught in by two of her bottom teeth. These days Hannah looks puzzled when her face is in repose. The slight line she has always had between her eyebrows has deepened. She has not heard from Sam, but then she couldn't expect to, Clare reassures her. It would be danger- ous for him. Sam. They are looking for him: they have even visited Hannah's house, to ask questions, thinking perhaps that she was concealing him in the wash-house, says Hannah scorn- fully. For where is there to hide in a place like St Ives, where everybody knows everyone else's business? How would they feed him, even, without the shop-people noting the extra quarter of a pound of sago, the extra quarter pound of butter?

'You got a visitor, then, Hannah?'

'No one need know. After all, you might get food from your uncle's farm. You Treveals could be feeding an army,' suggests Peggy helpfully.

But there are no more secrets. Hannah is not hiding Sam

romantically in wash-house or sea-cove. Sam remains in London; in Wapping to be exact, where he has melted into a shadowy city-life which accepts what comes and asks no questions. They know; maybe. People in cities are as quick-guessing and inquisitive as people anywhere, but Sam's girl is the daughter and sister of prize-fighters, and Sam is her best boy, and as such he is to be left alone. So what if he lounges in the courtyard's one scrap of dirty sunlight, yawning and scratching himself, never doing a stroke of work while his girl pounds clothes at the laundry where she works a ten-hour day for 2/7d? She would be better off in munitions, but her father has sworn no girl of his will ever get a yellow face as a munitionette, no matter what. And she goes along with it all, placidly. She likes the laundry: there is a bit of life there with the other girls, and one day, after the war, when Sam can work, things will be different . . . For she is not a prostitute, as John William supposed, and as Clare and Hannah now believe. She is not a girl who has picked up Sam lightly out of the whirlpool of war-time London, when girls have money and men have leave and desperation. She is not one of the girls the Bishop of London thundered against; she is not even particularly pretty. But she has a room, and in that room she has Sam.

Clare's body is rounding daily, but it does not matter now. Everyone knows. Gossip is like a furze fire: it burns hard, then the wind changes and it flares off elsewhere, racing and crackling. The story of Red-beard and Clare Coyne has died down, though it is not quite dead yet. Some red embers sleep in the white ash, but the flame and the fire are on another hillside now, eagerly consuming the story of Clare Coyne and her dead cousin.

Nan has a way of putting things which is almost magically

effective in silencing vicious tongues before they can begin to cut. Nan knows exactly what gossip she wants to seed. She must have thought hard and well in the long night after Francis Coyne came down to her cottage and talked to her alone. She must have known that Treveal secrecy would not serve the family now. The Treveals must bend if Clare was not to be broken; or they must appear to bend. Nan knew in whose ear to drop her flattering confidences, in the sure knowledge that they would be passed on with an insider's pride in her source of information. Soon everyone in St Ives would know that Clare Coyne had had an understanding with her dead cousin, and that the two would have married on his next leave if he had not died for his country. The Treveals had kept it close, but didn't they always? But now secrecy was beyond them. They have broken the habit of generations and made the town privy to their family secrets.

'They do keep themselves to themselves, the Treveals, but Mrs Treveal said to me that at times like this you have to go outside the family – and since we're old neighbours she came to me . . .'

Clare is drawn into the curious embrace of the town as her story passes like a delicious spice from lip to lip. She is one of their own again, shared among them. And wasn't John William a soldier, going for an officer? The mothers and fathers of exempted sons know better than to open their mouths against John William and Clare Coyne: And it has to be admitted that these things do happen. How many young people of the town anticipate their weddings, and then draw a quick veil of respectability over a too-short pregnancy? And are we to blame Clare more than all those girls, just because her young man died before he could marry her? And he would have married her.

Everyone knows the Treveal closeness. They would never bring shame on one of their own. Whatever you may think of first cousins marrying, there is no doubt that a wedding would have taken place.

Nan watches, bird-sharp and apparently indifferent. Nan listens with satisfaction to the coupling of her grandchildren's names. The breath of open scandal has licked at Clare, and receded. She is safe for now.

Even the Church has hesitated to condemn Clare. That first Sunday after her pregnancy became talked of in the town, she came up with her father to first Mass. She had been seen going to confession the evening before. Her father gave her his arm, his face impassive as the two of them walked into the church. Now his long-cultivated distance and indifference worked in his favour. There had never been such a show of style in St Ives. The daughter did not blush or look aside from the devouring stares; the father bowed slightly to one or two acquaintances, and showed no consciousness of any change in his own position. Almost against their will, his fellow-parishioners have found themselves treating Clare more as a young widow to be commiserated with, than as a fornicatress who is likely to burn in Hell if she should happen not to survive childbirth. And fortunately the priest who heard Clare's confession is likely to remain silent upon the subject. A little of her father's indifference has rubbed off on Clare. Shielded by the child, she does not care so very much what people think of her now. As long as they believe that John William loved her, she does not care how sinful they think she is. And since she does not care, they find themselves chatting to her for a few moments in the porch, on ordinary topics, quite as usual. And then the chance to scorn Clare Coyne has gone, if they ever wanted it. Everywhere there is news of death, and more death. Perhaps that is why the news of a birth does not seem so terrible.

'It just goes to show,' says the less charitable Methodists of the town. 'How those Romans do think nothing of their sins.'

But they do not say it very loud, for Nan has vanquished them. One or two strong Chapel women are even to be seen knitting for the little Coyne baby. Their fingers, hypnotized by Nan, click over their white-woolled needles.

Peggy looks down at the sea nostalgically.

'No more swimming this year,' she says. 'Remember that swim we had at Hayle, Clarey? May, wasn't it? Ooh! I could've died of the cold!' The other two exchange glances and smile.

'I made sure I'd catch pneumonia and die,' continues Peggy, then stops abruptly, for it is not right to talk about death with Clare in her present condition. 'But I didn't,' she adds lamely.

'Scarcely surprising, Peg, considering you were never in the water,' remarks Hannah.

'Yes; I remember it,' says Clare, answering not Hannah but some train of thought of her own. And next year, she thinks, the baby will be three months old. Old enough to have his toes dipped in the water.

'How old were we when we started to swim?' she asks Hannah, who shrugs.

'I don't know. We were always swimming. Johnnie – ' She's said his name. She doesn't often. 'Johnnie was the one for swimming.'

'Yes.'

A beach. Cold footprints in cold incoming sea. Bare skin tingling with sunburn, but beginning to chill.

'Quick, get your clothes on.'

'I can't find my drawers!'

'Why, there they are, Clarey. You weren't looking.'

'Where's John William?'

'He's still out there. Can't you see him? Look. Out past the rocks. He's gone too far out again. Johnnie! Johnnie! You shout too, Clarey. Nan'll kill me if we're not back in time.'

'John Will-i-am! John Will-i-am!'

He turns, his black head sleek with water. He turns and dives to tease them. The water grows smooth over his head. He's gone.

Francis Coyne watches from the window of Clare's bedroom as the girls set off on their walk. He has the afternoon sun in his eyes, but he can still see the three figures distinctly: Hannah, Peggy and his Clare between them. The slight breeze blows back their skirts over their legs. Three young girls against the softly glowing sea. They look mysterious now, the way people you love look when they walk away from you and disappear into a landscape, their colours melting into pleats of light and shadow.

He sighs, and turns his back to the window, and cracks his finger-joints in the way he is trying not to do when Clare is with him. It's a new habit, and one which maddens her. He goes down to his study, which is dim and cool. There is no work on his desk. He has not touched his book for weeks; he has had other things to think of. Money. They must have more money. He knows now that prices will never come down, not even after the war is over, and his investments will never right themselves. He cracks his knuckles and thinks of money and how he can get it. Clare is quite sure. Her confidence astonishes him. Sometimes she frightens him, for she seems so changed.

She goes here and there and she makes inquiries and she comes home and tells him what she has done. She is going to take up her portrait-sketching seriously, and sell sketches of summer visitors. She is sure they will pay a good price, especially for sketches of their children. She has been to talk to a lady at the St Ives Arts Club who liked Clare's drawings and thought her plans perfectly possible. She is going to give Clare some introductions. She has heard Clare's story, though she does not tell her this, and thinks it is romantic. Very Cornish, she thinks. And she finds it quite moving, she tells her friends from London, the way the people of the town accept Clare and look after her. She is one of their own really. You would not find *that* spirit in Lewisham, she laughs.

Francis will continue to sell whatever he has of value, though there is not much left. He will swallow his pride – or that's what he'll call it, though he will neither feel nor seem in the least humble – and he will ask his brother for money. He has never asked for himself, but he will ask for Clare. He will give Benedict and Marie-Thérèse to understand that she had actually married her cousin, and it will suit them very well to accept what he tells them.

And no one will ever know the truth. He is amazed at Clare's silence and how she has kept it up. She has never so much as hinted at where the real blame lies. She sticks to her story, and it is a good one since the only man who might have contradicted it is dead. She astonishes him. He had thought a girl in her position would melt with shame and grief and sob out her accusations against the man who had seduced and then betrayed her. For she has been betrayed. What story can that man have told her? He must have taken her by surprise, in her innocence. She will not tell anyone, and it seems she is too proud even to tell her father, who would defend her against the whole world, he feels now with a rush of emotion he has not known since he took her away from the Treveals after her mother's funeral. She is his Clare, his daughter, part of him. And they are so alike that she cannot keep the truth from him. He knows that her cousin's part in this baby is nothing but a convenient fiction, but he does not blame her for using it. It is not such a slur on John William's memory. There's a sense of gladness in the Treveals, even, now that they are used to the idea.

He had gone to the cottage that night in desperation, ready to confide all his fears in Nan, but he did not need to. When he met her blue gaze, even he could believe for a moment that the baby could only be John William's. Her eyes presented no other possibility. Yet in the depths of their directness secrets swam. He could never fathom Clare's grandmother, but they could work together. He has watched with admiration the skill with which Nan has handled the gossips of St Ives and has helped Francis Coyne to protect his child.

Clare's cousin is buried now and can never deny the child she is fathering on him. Surely John William would want to help Clare? They were always close. It cannot really harm him to be thought the father of her child. Clare has put her child first, not her own sense of betrayal or her desire for revenge. She must desire it. She is his daughter after all. But however bitter it feels he must not punish his daughter's seducer, if by doing so he exposes Clare. There'd be no place for her in the town once the truth was known.

There was gossip in the town and he heard it. It flared up and he saw the danger, but with Nan's help it has died down. He has seen idle malice in street-corner faces as he passed them, but he thinks Clare never knew of it. She never knew that she had been seen with that man on the cliffs. That she had been seen talking alone with him in his cottage garden. That he had called her across the concert room to him, and she had gone, dragging her cousin with her. That they were watched as they laughed and lolled on gravestones in Zennor churchyard. All this people saw, and her father knows. They say Lawrence visited her in her father's house, in her father's absence.

The voices have been silenced and the ash of gossip looks cool. But can Lawrence be trusted to keep quiet? A man who writes about the most sacred and intimate aspects of life as if he were a dog in the gutter, the Rector told Francis. What if Lawrence should take it into his head to notice the gossip and speak of Clare? What if the Rector were to say what he saw and what he knows? So far the rumours have done nothing but deepen local hatred of the Lawrences, but fire can spurt up and run with the wind again, Francis knows.

Francis knows the truth. He has seen Lawrence with his own eyes, elbows on the table in the Coyne kitchen, familiar. The man must have known her father was away and Clare was without protection. He had seized the opportunity of John William's death. In Francis Coyne's house he sat alone with Clare. God knows how long he had been there, or what he had done to her. And then he got up and went out with his red beard jutting in front of him. Now everything is clear. Clare's weeping, her anger, her wild ideas. Everything that had puzzled her father. All of it had come from that man. He would have made her hate her own father if he could, and her home, and those who loved her.

The gossip has only died down because a better rumour killed it: Clare Coyne carrying her cousin's child. No one couples Red-beard's name with his daughter's now. Perhaps they think there was nothing in it.

Thank God, thinks Francis Coyne, that my daughter has red hair. There will be nothing remarkable in her having a red-haired child. There will be no link with him.

He is a little in awe of Clare's silence. Sometimes he wishes he could go to her and tell her that he knows, he understands, he will punish the guilty. She was too innocent. She had never been anywhere, and she knew nothing. For a man of that type she must have been easy prey. Anger against Lawrence swells in him again.

Anger against Lawrence and his German wife swells like a tide through the countryside, filling hungry lips. Now, with the third battle of Ypres floundering into mud, the couple is an offence in its very existence. The Lawrences must be watched. It is an honourable duty to spy upon them. They are not people like us. They have no place here. Young military police visit them in groups of three or four to keep each other from bamboozlement and contamination. Reports are gathered and sent to Southern Command in Salisbury. Military men, official men, take a serious interest in this case. It is swelling like a boil upon the body of this suffering country, on the fragile and exposed flank of England.

Hundreds of thousands of men have died, thinks Francis Coyne. They've died hearing the sound of the guns, like John William.

'Can't you hear em? Those 5.9s? Don't tell me you can't hear em?'

He would have died hearing that surf-noise of guns, wilder than any storm we have here and more pitiless. Surely he shot himself because he could not get the noise of the guns out of his head.

Francis Coyne thinks of the football field and strong boots battering the turf. Men who had come through two years of the war, like John William. And this man, with his beard waggling and his eyes staring at you so that you felt you could not bear to look at him, sat talking to his daughter in the kitchen while John William lay in the mortuary with half his head blown off.

Such men are dangerous. They are injurious to our peace. They do not belong here. Whatever wind blew those two to Zennor, let it blow them away again.

Once they are gone, thinks Francis, we shall be safe. Red-beard will be forgotten and no one will measure his features against the child's.

Francis Coyne picks up his pen. He cannot go to this man and tell him he has injured his daughter, but the war has given him another way. She will be walking by the sea now. She mustn't tire herself. But Hannah is a sensible girl, and she will make Clare rest. They will not be back for an hour at least.

He has a sheet of his best cream-laid paper in front of him. Nearly the last of the stock, and he won't be able to buy any more. No more cream-laid paper; no more May Foage. He puts the paper up to his lips and tastes its cool smoothness. But he has Clare, and he will have her child. It will be Clare's child only, like its mother with its red hair. That other will be blotted out. He is going to disappear and it will be as if he had never been. For the first time in all these years Francis Coyne feels a tremor of Cornishness in him as he thinks of the landscape around Zennor empty of Red-beard and his German wife. A Prussian, they say she is. Poor brute, one might even feel sorry for him.

He dips his pen, and begins to write.

Dear Sir,
As a resident of St Ives, and a patriotic subject of his Majesty

the King, I feel it is my unpleasant duty to inform you in strictest confidence . . .

He grimaces fastidiously. The language is distressingly crude. It curdles as he writes it. But he continues, and the long elegant lines of his black writing unreel across the surface of the paper to the luxurious scratching of his nib. He scarcely has to think. He signs the letter, blots it, folds it into an envelope. He leans his fist on the envelope, presses down with all his weight. Yes, the thing is abominable. But he believes it may work.

Twenty-five

A cool, still October morning in Zennor. It is early, not quite yet eight o'clock. Four men turn off the high road which leads from St Ives to Zennor, and tramp down the farm lane towards Higher Tregerthen. Pods of Himalayan balsam burst with sudden explosions as the men brush past them. They know their way; they have been here before. They know every inch of the Lawrences' bare little cottage with its bits of fabric draped over furniture and its pink-washed walls. They have flipped over Frieda's embroideries and left them lying skew-whiffed. They would not be caught dead living in a place like this themselves. They are contemptuous of the Lawrences' meagre possessions. And yet this Lawrence is an educated man – surely it only confirms the suspicion that he must have some hidden motive for living in such an out-of-the-way place, high above the coast where a light can be seen for miles out to sea? They have rifled the cottage once, and it will open its doors to them easily this time. The man is as frail as a dandelion puff, so there is no fear of a fight there. And if need be they can put the fear of God into the German woman. A few words about the risk of internment should silence her.

If the cottage ever had that virginity of lostness and secrecy which Lawrence once thought it possessed, it is gone now. The red floor is printed over with clumsy bootmarks from yesterday's search. The searchers did not care what traces they left. They wanted the Lawrences to know that their lives had been stripped bare and pawed over. Drawers have been pulled open, small belongings tipped out and searched. Letters and manuscripts have been taken.

The Lawrences were not at home when the men came yesterday. The first search is over, and nothing that follows it can shock them as sharply. Frieda came home humming to herself, pushed her door open absently, thinking of something else, and found her home broken open like an egg.

But this morning they are in their cottage when the army officer, the two detectives, and the police sergeant from St Ives knock on their door. Frieda has got up first, and she is drinking her tea standing up by the fireplace. She does not want to sit down in any of the chairs, or touch her own things. She shrinks from them as if they have been contaminated. Even her clothes smell wrong, as her children do now on the rare occasions when she is able to see them and take them into her arms. They smell of the other people who have taken possession of them. Last night she could scarcely sleep in her bed for the knowledge that her sheets and blankets had been switched back by the searchers as they made their way quietly and methodically through the cottage. There was a small stain of blood on her undersheet. They would have seen it. But she will not feel humiliated: she *will not*. It is for them to feel shame, after what they have done. Let them tell her the cause for what they have done, if they dare.

By eleven o'clock the second search is over and the men have gone. They have left behind the smear of the oldest message in the world: 'We can do what we like to you, and you cannot stop us, for we have the power and you are powerless.' She has writhed and wept under the weight of it, and her own helplessness, but now she is silent. In the solicitor's office she learned the cost of leaving her husband for Lawrence. Now she learns that the cost of living with him still has to be paid, over and over. She will pay it.

Lawrence fingers the official notice they have left, as if he would like to tear it up. It orders them to leave Cornwall by Monday, to live subsequently within an unprohibited area, and to report to the police. Its curt, chopped words bristle off the page at him. He smiles slightly, involuntarily, as the style of it reaches him. He could write it so much better himself.

Yet he is white with shock. For two hours the four men have thrashed through the cottage, touching everything, emptying pails and buckets, opening cupboards, feeling in jacket pockets. They have found nothing new – the cottage is so small that they can have missed nothing during their first search yesterday. But they needed to hunt and paw again in front of the Lawrences. They needed to make the couple watch while they read letters, combed through address books, opened underclothes-drawers. For where is the point of a demonstration of power if there is no one there to be crushed by it?

Well, they have had their satisfaction. Frieda's face is snail-tracked with tears. He wishes she had not wept in front of them. He will not let his own rage rise in him yet. If he does, it will shake him apart.

He looks down at the pile of papers smashed into a heap on the rosewood table. These are the ones the officials discarded as not worth bothering about. They had found so little to take, really, for all their frowning and leafing – a few letters from Frieda's mother, some notes.

'Shameless little article, wasn't he – the ferrety one?' he remarks.

She smiles faintly. 'Lorenzo, you know he was not at all like a ferret. A bit more like . . .' She thinks. 'A bit more like a warthog!'

'Blessed if I'd know one of 'em if I saw 'em. But let him be one, if it pleases you.'

She bends down to pick up a piece of red and gentian embroidery which has slithered off the back of the table. He riffles through the notes and letters.

There is another knock at the door. Frieda jumps, looks at Lawrence with suddenly darkened eyes, then goes to open it in response to his almost imperceptible nod. There stands one of the little boys Frieda knows to smile to, a farm-worker's child. He is out of breath, puffing with excitement and importance. But, on seeing Frieda, he suddenly turns shy, and thrusts out his hand with a bit of paper in it.

'Why, what's that?' asks Lawrence.

Frieda looks at it. In pencil, on the outside of the letter, someone has written in neat, ticked-off letters: 'Am returning this as a private communication.'

'Must be one of our letters,' says Lawrence. 'What's he up to, sending it back?' And he frowns, suspecting another trap. 'Did an army man give this to you?' he asks the child, but the boy backs out of the doorway, giving only a sudden, violent nod before he pelts off down the lane.

'What can he mean, a "private communication"?' puzzles Frieda. 'He has only just taken it from my drawer. He must know that it is private! He did not let that stop him before. They have taken all my mother's letters.'

Lawrence takes the letter from her and unfolds the paper. The large, strongly curved, slightly childish lines are instantly familiar. They have read over this letter many times, and discussed it late into the night. But they have not yet answered it, for they are waiting for replies from friends in London who may be interested in Clare's work. The letter is from Clare, and it is addressed to Lawrence:

There is something I must tell you which you may have heard already in Zennor or in St Ives. We both know how news travels here. And how lies travel too. So I thought I would write to you and tell you that this time it is not lies, or gossip, but the truth. I am expecting a child. I shall continue to live with my father, and I am hoping to make my living as you do, by my own work. Already I have met a woman in a gallery who thinks she can sell my things. I draw every day – I should like to show you. My own drawings, not flowers any more. I enclose a sketch so that you can see. Perhaps, if you have any friends who would like to have their portraits drawn, you might mention me to them? I believe you liked my work.

Perhaps I should not write to you and tell you this. But I had never met anyone like you before. And you knew John William.

Tell Frieda I would like to see her, if she still wants to see me. I want to draw her properly: she is beautiful.

Yours truly
Clare Coyne

He pinches the stilted little letter along its crease. Stilted, but with a rush of confidence in the middle of it: 'My own drawings, not flowers any more.'

'Did they take the sketch?' he asks.

'No, I have it. I put it into the frame, behind the one she drew of you, so that it would not crease. You had not fastened the back of the frame.'

Lawrence lifts the picture off the wall, removes the back of the frame, eases out the two drawings.

'Be careful! They are stuck together – they will tear,' says Frieda.

'It's the damp,' says Lawrence, unpeeling the top sketch with skilful fingers. 'There's no damage. Lucky it's not charcoal.'

He spreads the two portraits on the table, side by side. The two faces look at one another. 'David Herbert Lawrence, by Clare Coyne.' 'Francis Coyne, by Clare Coyne.'

'The portrait of her father is very good,' observes Frieda.

High forehead, finely moulded temples, dark receding hair. The eyes are deeply set and the eyelids curve down, half hiding the eyes. Shy, or remote? But this face has its own fierceness. It would not be entirely out of place in the von Richthofen album, thinks Frieda. The hooded eyes stare at the portrait of her husband, but they seem not to see it or to take note of it.

The portrait of Lawrence is less confident. It is only a few months since Clare drew it, but how much she has improved since then, to judge by the recent sketch of her father. Frieda bends over her husband's pencilled face. The eyes meet hers. Their startling directness is a promise which can surely never quite be fulfilled? But he is not really looking at her. This is how he looked at Clare as she drew him. The rest of the face is not quite as good, though she has caught a likeness. Who could ever capture that vitality? As soon as you think you have grasped it, it moves on. Frieda looks up from the drawing to the living man.

'We have not answered her letter,' says Lawrence.

'No,' laments Frieda, as if this is the last, unbearable disappointment of these bitter two days. 'And now we shall not see her. We shall never see her again.'

But Lawrence rereads Clare's letter, his face alight with amused sympathy.

'She will be all right,' he says. 'See, even now she thinks ahead. She thinks that we may be useful to her. And we can write to her from London. She might come to see us there – you know she told me she had visited London before. I am sure I shall hear something from Lady Cynthia. She has so many rich friends – some of 'em *must* want their portraits done. Or their children's – such women always "adore" their children.'

Frieda pulls a quick face at Lady Cynthia's name.

'Let her help *you* first!' she exclaims. 'You have so many friends, yet you cannot get your own books published!'

It is too true. He will have to pack up thick wads of the novel which he may never publish. And yet it is good: he knows it. But they will stop this new novel too. They will put their censor's boot down on it, just as they did on *The Rainbow*. He looks around the room. It is empty for him now. They have two days to pack up their things and get out of Cornwall. But he has not the heart for preserving this small temporary home so that they can start again and re-create it in yet another cheap cottage found for them by friends. Perhaps one day they will come back to the only home they've found and paid for themselves. The war cannot go on for ever. Let the piano and the rosewood table stay here, and Frieda's bits and pieces. There are onions and leeks left in the soil, and winter cabbages. Let them stand there until the salt or the frost rots them. Or the Hockings will come up from the farm and harvest them. They will be sorry to lose his company, the stories in the kitchen, Stanley's French lessons and piano lessons, the jokes, the political discussions while they picked over the peas or skinned pickling onions. But regret will not stop William Henry from eating the vegetables Lawrence has planted. His dark, wary face is the face of a survivor whose family has held on to their land through centuries of storms. And why not? So much waste, everywhere. Why shouldn't something be saved?

The marigolds will seed themselves and the white foxglove will come out again at the bottom of the wall, like a ghost in the summer light, and there will be fine flowers on the hydrangea. He has been feeding the soil around it with spent tea-leaves all year. How many times he's stepped out into the earth-scented, pearl-coloured evenings and tipped the tea-pot out around its roots. It takes time to build up the soil. Stanley carted up five loads of manure from the farm midden, for the vegetable gardens.

But he will not think of that – not now. It would drive him mad. This is the place where he once thought he would build his ideal community: his Rananim. There will never be Rananim at Zennor now. He thinks of the Murrys, leaving a few weeks after they arrived. He had such blazing hopes for life together here, the four of them. And yet – he smiles without meaning to, without knowing he was going to smile. How funny they had looked, Jack and Katherine packing up their cart with their things, Katherine so meticulous, so dark and neat, with her face set mute and purposeful towards the south, away from the Lawrences. There was no changing her mind. And now he and Frieda are to be kicked out of Cornwall. He would like to shake off this country entirely and go westward to America, but the authorities will not let him. They will not endorse his passport. Again, they give the excuse of war.

Now he and Frieda must go. Another cart full of furniture, another couple of bedraggled wanderers balancing perilously on top of their possessions. Back up the spine of Cornwall towards the seething madness of London with its newsboys in the streets, its Zeppelin raids, its crowds of feverish soldiers on leave spilling out of the pubs and theatres. If only they would all kneel down on the London pavements as John William had knelt on the white Zennor road, and cry out for the dead men who were walking at their shoulders.

'Perhaps Clare will bring her baby here, when we are gone,' says Frieda suddenly. 'We have paid the rent until next summer. It is good for babies to sunbathe. She could put him in the garden to kick in the sun on a blanket. The air is so pure here. I have never tasted air like it.'

She has gone into the scullery and is wrapping cups in newspaper. He glances at her face quickly, suspiciously. Is she thinking of her own children again? But no, that look of mingled grief and inwardness is absent.

'Not she,' says Lawrence. 'What would there be for Clare in Zennor? She has her own life.'

'And her own place,' says Frieda. She has moved back to the main room and is folding up the table-cloth. And he, usually so deft and handy, does nothing to help her. He just stands there.

'I used to think, when we got here,' continues Frieda. 'When we looked out of our window on a clear night, it was like a door into heaven. So many stars! Nothing but stars between us and the sea.'

'Stars!' he exclaims. 'I'm glad you think so well of 'em, for they're all we've got, or likely to have.'

He will not think now. His skin prickles, receiving the impression of the tumbled room, his tear-streaked wife packing away their linen, the cold smell of autumn air seeping in through the door neither of them has bothered to close, for there's no safety or privacy left here to guard. Soon the Hockings will come up from the farm, wondering, knowing, guessing. Stanley will help to pile their books into boxes with his big clumsy hands. And William Henry will want to talk. He will want to tease out what has happened in his slow, taunting Cornish voice.

He must not think, he must keep still and let it all happen to him without resisting it. Clare is going to have a child. He thinks of her, ruffled and sweaty with wind and sun, drawing his portrait on the edge of the cliff. How she frowned as she concentrated. Her tense little fox-face was not pretty at all, and she did not care. She thought of nothing but her drawing. He smiles.

'It is good that he left a child,' says Frieda, kneeling to roll up a rug.

'What?'

'That young man. Her cousin. It is good that he left something behind him that she will love.'

'Oh – love,' he says, tasting the word as if it comes from a foreign language. 'Yes, I daresay she'll do that.'

They look at one another, then she stoops and packs on, indefatigable. Her crown of rich rough hair glistens, though the day is sunless. She has rolled up her sleeves for work and there are shadows in the creamy hollows inside her elbows. She has stripped off her rings, and her bare fingers move confidently, filling up space in the boxes. He watches her for a while, his face smoothing, relaxing. Suddenly it sharpens, attentive as the muzzle of a fox scenting down the wind. The scent blows sharp, then thins to nothing, leaving an itch against his senses. The packing-cases vanish; Frieda blurs to gold. He goes to the table, shoves the muddle of their things aside, pulls paper and pen towards him, and begins to write.

He just wanted a decent book to read ...

Not too much to ask, is it? It was in 1935 when Allen Lane, Managing Director of Bodley Head Publishers, stood on a platform at Exeter railway station looking for something good to read on his journey back to London. His choice was limited to popular magazines and poor-quality paperbacks – the same choice faced every day by the vast majority of readers, few of whom could afford hardbacks. Lane's disappointment and subsequent anger at the range of books generally available led him to found a company – and change the world.

'We believed in the existence in this country of a vast reading public for intelligent books at a low price, and staked everything on it'
Sir Allen Lane, 1902–1970, founder of Penguin Books

The quality paperback had arrived – and not just in bookshops. Lane was adamant that his Penguins should appear in chain stores and tobacconists, and should cost no more than a packet of cigarettes.

Reading habits (and cigarette prices) have changed since 1935, but Penguin still believes in publishing the best books for everybody to enjoy. We still believe that good design costs no more than bad design, and we still believe that quality books published passionately and responsibly make the world a better place.

So wherever you see the little bird – whether it's on a piece of prize-winning literary fiction or a celebrity autobiography, political tour de force or historical masterpiece, a serial-killer thriller, reference book, world classic or a piece of pure escapism – you can bet that it represents the very best that the genre has to offer.

Whatever you like to read – trust Penguin.